PRAISE FOR *A WOM*

'Tania Blanchard is back with a fresh, exciting and inspiring tale of the women who fought for their right to vote – women who quite literally changed the world. Main character, Hannah, is a true woman of courage, brought to life by elegant prose, meticulous research and a stunning narrative. This is a story bursting with charm, heart and hope' **Natasha Lester,** *New York Times*-**bestselling author of** *The Three Lives of Alix St Pierre*

'A timely reminder of how small acts of courage can change the world. Hannah's journey to self-discovery and her unwavering belief in the power and strength of women's independence made this a pleasure to read. A beautiful tale of courage and resilience from a born storyteller' **Lauren Chater, bestselling author of** *The Winter Dress*

PRAISE FOR TANIA BLANCHARD

'Richly imagined, heartbreaking and utterly captivating ... yet another outstanding piece of historical fiction from Blanchard, cementing her place at the top of this genre' *Better Reading*

'Blanchard at her breathtaking best. Rich in every sight, taste and smell' *Australian Women's Weekly*

'Packs an emotional punch that will reverberate far and wide' *Weekly Times*

Tania Blanchard writes historical fiction inspired by the true stories and the rich cultural heritage of her family's history. Her acclaimed stories of love, loss and hope and the challenges facing women in defining moments in modern history span world wars and pivotal moments in time during great social and political upheaval, and are beloved by readers everywhere. Her books *The Girl from Munich*, *Suitcase of Dreams*, *Letters from Berlin* and *Daughter of Calabria* are bestsellers. She lives in Sydney with her husband and three children. Visit www.taniablanchard.com.au.

A
WOMAN
OF
COURAGE

TANIA BLANCHARD

HarperCollins*Publishers*

HarperCollins*Publishers*

Australia • Brazil • Canada • France • Germany • Holland • India
Italy • Japan • Mexico • New Zealand • Poland • Spain • Sweden
Switzerland • United Kingdom • United States of America

HarperCollins acknowledges the Traditional Custodians
of the land upon which we live and work, and pays respect
to Elders past and present.

First published on Gadigal Country in Australia in 2023
by HarperCollins*Publishers* Australia Pty Limited
ABN 36 009 913 517
harpercollins.com.au

A catalogue record for this book is available from the National Library of Australia

ISBN 978 1 4607 6409 1 (paperback)
ISBN 978 1 4607 1624 3 (ebook)
ISBN 978 1 4607 3456 8 (audiobook)

Cover design by Louisa Maggio, HarperCollins Design Studio
Cover image: Woman © Ildiko Neer / Trevillion Images; decorative elements
by shutterstock.com
Author photograph by Kate Buechner
Typeset in Sabon LT Std by Kirby Jones
Printed and bound in Australia by McPherson's Printing Group

*To Eleanor Blanchard – the woman who
inspired this story.
And to her descendants:
Trish, one of the strongest women I know;
Chris, Hollie, Nathan and Benjamin – who live with
heart and soul.
Each changing the world in their own way.*

Courage calls to courage everywhere,
and its voice cannot be denied.

– Millicent Fawcett

PROLOGUE

My time at teachers' college has opened my mind to equal
education across the sexes, voting rights for women and
the welfare of children. I'll leave marriage to my sisters ... I
must be a part of the change that is coming.
From the journal of Hannah Todd

EBBERFIELD, NORTHERN ENGLAND
DECEMBER 1890

'Welcome to your new home!' Papa grinned from ear to ear,
flushed with excitement at showing me the public house he
was now the proud owner of.

I gazed down the street. My heart sank. There wasn't much
to see; the trees were stark and bare and chickens wandered
loose, scratching at the ground. A jumble of buildings led down
the hill towards the centre of the village, and on the other side, I
saw green pastures and rolling farmland all the way to the sea.
Ebberfield was tiny compared to the bustling port city of West
Hartlepool, where I'd lived for the first eighteen years of my
life, and Durham, where I'd spent the last two years at college.

Stiff limbed after the five-mile ride from the nearest
railway station, I forced a smile onto my face. The public
house was a whitewashed, two-storey building, and the sign
over its doorway read '*The Ox and Plough – William Todd –
Licensed Victualler*'. Despite my disappointment, a burst of
warmth spread from my chest.

'That's you, Papa!' I said. 'Your very own business.'

'It's not just a business,' he said. 'It's a way of life, a vocation.'

I nodded. 'I'm happy for you, Papa. I know you'll be a wonderful publican.'

'Come on inside,' he said. 'Your mother can't wait to see you.' He opened the door and ushered me through. 'Ellen! She's home!'

The pub was quiet, almost peaceful; the fire crackled, and pretty curtains on the front window and the golden tones of the furniture made the room cosy. But the rich timber counter that ran the length of the room left no doubt about the life I was about to step into.

'Hannah! You're finally here!'

I could hear the joy in Mama's voice even before I saw her. She appeared from a doorway behind the counter, wiping her hands on her apron and smiling, her curly hair, now more silver than gold, escaping its tight bun to float free around her face like an angel's halo.

She held me tight. 'I'm so happy you've come,' she said softly. 'Let's go to the cottage and get you settled. Papa can take over here until I bring him his dinner.'

Papa was beaming. His beard, an inch or so long, was completely white now. 'It's good to finally have you home again,' he said. He hugged me to his side, like he had when I was young, and I still tucked under his chin even though I'd just turned twenty. 'I've missed your smiling face and our conversations.' He blinked furiously, his hazel eyes, just like mine, suddenly moist. 'I know it's very different from Hartlepool but I think you'll like it here. It's a lovely village and I hope you enjoy living here as much as we do.'

I smiled tentatively, though my stomach was in knots. 'I'll do my best, Papa,' I said, kissing him on the cheek.

I followed Mama out onto the street to the adjoining cottage but stopped at the sight of men bearing a coffin on their shoulders in the graveyard opposite, a procession of mourners dressed in black behind them. A small boy was sobbing as though his heart would break and a young man scooped him up, trying to console him. The man held the boy tight, his other arm around an older woman as if to keep her upright as they followed the coffin. The man glanced across the road and for a brief second our eyes met. Even from here, I could see the raw grief on his face. Then they were gone, disappearing into the graveyard.

Mama led me into my new home. 'It's much bigger than our place in Hartlepool. Your room is upstairs but I'll show you around after we've had a cup of tea,' she said, taking my coat and hanging it on a hook in the hallway. 'Come and help me in the kitchen.'

I laid my hat and gloves on the hall table, smoothed back the strands of brown hair that had escaped the simple knot at the back of my head, and followed her to the back of the house, feeling a little dazed.

'How has it been?' I asked when we sat in the parlour with our tea and cake. The room was comfortable, the walls lined with pale green wallpaper decorated with tiny birds and climbing roses, the wooden floors covered by soft, colourful rugs. The lounges were clustered around the fireplace and under the windows to make the most of the light. A large bookcase half-filled with books lined one wall, and Mama's sewing basket sat beside one of the lounges, along with several lush green pot plants. It was lovely and I was glad Mama had her own space, rather than the cramped kitchen table in Hartlepool.

Mama sipped her sweet black tea. 'Your father is doing well.'

I smiled. As usual, Mama had known what I was really asking and had got to the heart of the matter immediately. Papa was the talker, the one everyone was drawn to, but Mama was the strength.

'The brewery sent a man to teach him the ropes when we first came and we have an experienced barman here on busy days. Now he's familiar with the process of running a public house, your father's more relaxed. It's been three months, and I've noticed the difference in him already. His mood and headaches are better, and he's had no chesty colds so far this winter. He loves the village – people are so friendly. It's as if he's back to his old self.'

While I was away at teacher's college, Papa had been diagnosed with a condition called manganism, developed from years of breathing fumes while welding steel as an engine fitter in the shipyards. The doctor had recommended rest, fresh air and a break from his job. Papa's answer was to buy a public house in the country.

I sagged with relief and she reached across the table and squeezed my hand in reassurance. My parents had asked me to come with them to Ebberfield and I couldn't abandon them after everything they'd done for me.

'I know this is a big change from Hartlepool but you'll find your feet once you begin work at the elementary school. I'm glad you wrote to them and secured a position. Won't be long before you feel part of this place too.'

I squeezed Mama's hand back. I hoped she was right, but my purpose hadn't changed. Teachers' college had only strengthened my resolve to make this world a better place. I would stay until Papa recovered and my parents no longer needed me. Then I could begin the life I'd envisioned for myself in London.

1

I am surprised to learn that Ebberfield had been an important administrative centre in days gone by, with a large poor union workhouse situated at the eastern end of the village. The workhouse should be a refuge but it's an inescapable sentence for many, forced to endure harsh conditions and hard labour, stripped of any dignity or control of their own circumstances.

Ebberfield was just as I had feared. Surrounded almost completely by mining towns and villages to the west, and the sea only two miles to the east, the village was a small, quaint, agricultural community, lost somewhere in the last century. On the western outskirts stood an old mill, now transformed into the local isolation hospital. The oldest and largest pub, The Rose and Crown Inn, was run by the publican, Mr Franks. He was a short and stocky man who made up for his lack of height by thrusting his barrel-shaped chest out and walking with an arrogant swagger that I found almost amusing, demanding to see Papa as soon as he set foot inside The Ox and Plough.

'I'm invitin' you to the committee meetin', about Plough Monday,' he said to Papa quite magnanimously, ignoring Mama and me.

'Ah, yes,' said Papa. 'Reverend Mason has already invited me, and I've put in my extra order with the brewery.'

Mr Franks' face went a blotchy red. 'But we talk about each pub's contribution to the celebrations at the meetin',' he blustered.

'I thought we all contribute equally,' said Papa, frowning.

'No, no, no,' said Mr Franks, shaking his head emphatically 'The Rose and Crown leads the celebrations and this year ain't any different. It'd be a shame if you have leftover beer that spoils.' He sighed and thumped Papa on the back. 'But you're new at this. Follow my lead and I'll see you right,' he conceded, puffing out his chest once more. He nodded curtly and strode from the bar like a dark storm cloud.

Clearly, we should be feeling grateful he invited Papa himself, but all the same, Papa declined Mr Franks' offer to take him under his wing.

Plough Monday, I learnt from our farming customers, marked the beginning of the agricultural year when the fields were ploughed, ready to receive seed, and also the end of the Christmas holiday. On the day, a plough decorated with sheaths of wheat and hay was pulled by a man dressed as a fool wearing animal skins and a fox tail as part of a small procession of dancers through the village. A boy pretending to be an old woman rattled a tin cup, looking for donations from the villagers and children who had gathered to watch, along with the tenant farmers, who owned small holds, and even the wealthy landowners of the district. Then the celebrations turned to the entertainment in the inns, taverns and pubs, where Mr Franks' pub, The Rose and Crown, held a monopoly on the best music, singing, games – and the cheapest beer of the day.

If Papa was going to make a decent living, he had to raise the profile of The Ox and Plough.

January, 1891

My dearest Hannah,

It breaks my heart to read that you're feeling so unhappy in Ebberfield. I wish it was different, but my responsibilities lie with my own family. You know that Mary and George would have had you in Hartlepool if they could, but they just don't have the room, and Jane and Bert aren't any better off. Let me tell you, you'd grow tired of the sound of whingeing children and crying babies before too long!

Mama and Papa need you, Hannah. Mama told us that getting out of the city, owning a business and being at the heart of a community is something Papa has always dreamed of. Ebberfield might be small but with four other pubs Papa will have his work cut out for him making a success of his business. Why don't you put your considerable talents and efforts into helping Papa build up the pub? You're just like him; warm, charming and kind. People are drawn to you.

I hope you find some happiness in Ebberfield, Hannah. Surely between your teaching and helping at the pub you can find fulfilment until you decide to marry.

Chin up. Keep busy. It will get better soon.

Your loving sister,

Sarah

January heralded the return to school, my first day with my class and the first heavy snow of the winter, which left a glittering layer of white across the bare trees and shrubs. It made the village seem far prettier than the industrial city I'd grown up in.

The walk to the parish school took me no more than five minutes. I passed the graveyard and the centuries-old stone church across the road from The Ox and Plough, which stood on the hill, the highest point of the village, like a silent guardian. From here farmland surrounded the village as far as the eye could see, encroaching on the moors to the west and to the coast in the east and the North Sea. The medieval rectory opposite the church was still inhabited by the rector and curate of the parish. The walk through the wooded school grounds opened up to the schoolyard and school building. The school was bigger than I'd expected, until I realised that all the children of the township attended, including the farms and small hamlets of the surrounding district.

I had a class of seven- and eight-year-olds who were only just beginning to grasp the basics of reading, writing and arithmetic. Many had lots of questions and needed frequent reassurance that they were doing the right thing, especially the younger ones like Anthony and Rory.

'Yes, Anthony?' I said a couple of weeks later, the little boy's hand shooting up into the air.

His best friend, Rory, who usually sat behind him, was absent again. The day before he'd had to mind his younger siblings, and the day before that, he didn't have any boots to wear to school. The week before it had been because he'd had to help his father on the farm. There were some days he'd had only a shrivelled apple and a few crusts of bread for his lunch, which I'd seen his older sister, Kitty, give him from her own pockets. She was in my fellow teacher Clementine Foster's class for eleven- and twelve-year-olds, and I made a mental note to go and see her after class.

'Is this right, miss?' Anthony asked, holding up his slate.

'You're almost there. Show me how you would work out this sum,' I said, moving the abacus towards him. Thankfully the girl next to him, Jemima, had already finished her work and didn't need the abacus they shared. I'd have to find something harder for her, or perhaps, as her reading was already quite advanced, begin her on one of my favourite children's books, *Black Beauty*, or *Alice's Adventures in Wonderland*.

The headmaster Benjamin Burnett and his young family lived a few doors down from The Ox and Plough. His wife, Laura, had told me proudly that since their arrival a year earlier from Sussex, he had managed to acquire chalkboards and slates for each classroom, funded by local ratepayers and the church parish. I was relieved to know he was open to improving the school, and I'd already made a mental note to ask for more resources: slate boards, books, abacuses, simple readers; more ink and paper. I'd been so spoilt by the facilities in West Hartlepool and Durham University, where reading rooms and libraries were heaving with books and journals. In Ebberfield there was only one reading room, at the Recreation Club, which held newspapers and the odd periodical, but nowhere was there a collection of books that could be accessed by the schoolchildren or the public. Literacy was key to understanding subjects in the higher educational levels – and in understanding the world around us. It had been a shock to realise that some of the parents or grandparents of my students couldn't read the handwritten notes I'd sent home to them. Evening classes at different clubs and associations were available in the city and I wondered if people would come if classes were available here.

Anthony glanced at the chalkboard and then his slate, before slowly moving the beads across the abacus, deep in concentration, his tongue between his teeth. He looked up at me expectantly when he was finished and I nodded and smiled, relieved that he'd got it. He was a little younger than the other children and it sometimes took him longer to pick up a concept.

'Very good,' I said proudly. 'That's right. Just finish the rest of the sums now.'

It was lunchtime and I was musing over my small sense of satisfaction at the work I'd achieved with the children that morning when I heard screaming across the playground. I rushed towards the noise, pushing through the group of stunned children to find a little girl on the ground.

'What's the matter?' I asked gently, kneeling next to her. 'Did you fall over?' She shook her head and only cried harder. 'Has someone pushed you?' She said nothing, just curling into a tighter ball on the ground. 'What happened here?' I demanded, looking at the faces of the children gathered around her. The children remained silent. I glared at them, and at last one of the boys stepped forward.

'I didn't push her, Miss. I only wanted her to play hide and seek with us. I tried to grab her arm, but she fell to the ground screaming.'

Another boy stepped forward. 'It's true Miss. We wanted her to be "it".'

I glanced around the group, pale faces staring wide-eyed at the little girl on the ground. 'Are you hurt?' I asked her. I reached for her arm, but she clutched it to her chest, whimpering. 'All right, off you go,' I said to the crowd gathered around us. 'Go and play.' As the children dispersed, my attention turned to the girl. Her hair was unkempt and her dress was rumpled, dirt and grease smeared across the front of it. 'Let me see your arm,' I said gently, slowly lifting her sleeve. She flinched and I stifled a gasp at the mottled purple and green bruises on her skin. I wondered what other injuries were hidden under her clothes. I felt heat behind my eyes and my heart began to race. 'Who did this to you?' I whispered, pushing my shock and anger down. The eyes that gazed back at me were world weary and no longer those of a child.

'I thought the boys wanted to play with me like my new papa does,' she said, beginning to shake.

My heart dropped to my stomach like a lead weight. I'd expected to see hardship and deprivation up close but this ... the abuse of a tiny, vulnerable girl was despicable.

'Nobody will hurt you here,' I said soothingly. I helped her carefully from the ground, then drew her scrawny body to me and held her until the shaking subsided.

After school, I knocked on the door of Clementine's classroom before poking my head into the room, empty of children.

'Hello, Hannah,' said Clementine, rising from her desk. She was a few years older than me, tall, slim and dressed neatly in a simple woollen skirt, bodice and jacket, with bright auburn hair pulled into a plain bun at the back of her head.

'Am I disturbing you?' I asked.

'Not at all,' she said warmly. I only hoped she'd be able to help. 'How are you managing?' she asked, gesturing to her chair while she perched on the edge of one of the desks.

I grimaced wryly and told her about my progress with the children and then about the girl in the playground who had eventually been whisked away by her class teacher.

Clementine nodded thoughtfully. 'It's a shock to see the underbelly of a conservative community like this, and so quickly too. The children can't hide what happens behind closed doors, but the abuse is usually difficult to prove. It's a harsh side of teaching, and we're never warned about it or told how to manage it.'

'Teachers' college didn't prepare me for this,' I said softly, shaking my head. I had trained as a pupil teacher in Hartlepool before I was awarded the Queen's Scholarship to the Diocesan Training College for Schoolmistresses in Durham and there had been barely any references to this troubling reality. 'But they need protection. Surely we have a responsibility to keep them safe?'

'We do have the law on our side in serious cases, but it's not enough. Most people turn a blind eye to violence against women and children and so nothing changes.'

I nodded. It was sobering. Social problems took so much longer to solve. 'But what can we do at school to help? Because it's not just physical abuse, it's also the neglect.'

Clementine sighed. 'I know. I'm having the same problems with Kitty. I think she must give Rory whatever she has because she often has nothing to eat. Usually I give her half of my sandwich because I can't bear to see her hungry. I've asked Mrs Burrows, the president of the church aid society, to find some warm clothes and shoes for both children too. It's no wonder they don't come to school when they're cold and hungry.' I liked Clementine already. She was somebody who saw things the way I did and took action.

'Children like them are missing so much school. There must be something else we can do,' I said.

'I've spoken to Kitty and her parents but ... nothing. Many of the children only come to school when work on the farms allows. Benjamin is a progressive headmaster but he's still trying to convince parents and the rest of the village of the importance of regular schooling.'

'What do you mean?' I asked, leaning forward in my chair. 'It's compulsory until they're eleven!'

Clementine threw her hands in the air. 'You try telling them that. I feel like I'm hitting my head against a wall. I've been here three years now and each summer class numbers drop during harvest time. And then there's market day once a month with the local cattle and livestock sale. Many children of farming families help prepare for that too. Most teachers agree that something has to change but they're too overwhelmed with problems in the classroom to really do anything. But we have to, for the sake of the children.'

'What are you thinking about?' I asked, excited. Clementine was energetic and passionate – someone I could work with.

'Well, two heads are better than one,' she said, her eyes sparkling. 'Perhaps together we can find some solutions we can take to Benjamin?'

'When can we start?' I asked with a grin.

*

Later that week, I was on duty for the first time, waiting for the youngest children to be picked up at the end of the day. Anthony was the last student and I was surprised to see him looking through the reader Jemima had finished, sounding out the more difficult words. But with the winter shadows growing long, darkness wasn't far away.

'Time for some light,' I said, reaching for the paraffin oil lamp. I'd been shocked to realise that these lamps were the main form of light in the village, along with candles and lanterns for outdoors. I was so used to the efficient gas lighting of the city that sometimes I felt like I'd been transported to the Middle Ages. Here, villagers still collected water from public water pumps and wells when places like Durham and Hartlepool had been supplied by piped water for decades. Some villagers even used ponds that livestock also drank from. My head spun at the public health implications of that. And, unlike in the city, there was no community transport or cab and omnibus service between the village and the closest railway station, five miles away; villagers had to walk or use a horse and cart, or buggy or sulky for those who could afford it.

I fumbled a little, lighting the lamp. It wasn't an automatic task yet, and I sighed as I adjusted the flame. I'd been here a month and I still didn't know how I was going to live without the bustle of a big city. I missed the mixing pot of intellectual and cultural influences found in the variety of clubs, shops and theatres, the exciting energy that felt progressive and modern. I felt stifled here.

The sound of boots in the corridor made me turn to the door. A young man dressed in workmen's clothes – jacket, trousers, soft cap and scuffed boots – stepped into the classroom. I noticed the small tool box he carried, which told me that he was a skilled artisan or tradesman of some kind.

Anthony was out of his seat, pulling on his coat and cap and collecting his satchel almost before I could blink. I had to hide my smile at his eagerness to be away.

'Hello, I'm Miss Todd,' I said to the man, looking at him properly for the first time. He was about my age, with startling blue eyes that seemed oddly familiar. 'I see you're here to pick up Anthony.'

He nodded, taking off his cap, his hair a riot of dark curls. 'I'm Roger Rainforth, Anthony's brother.' He greeted Anthony with a brief hug. He was tall, especially against the boy, and athletically built.

'She's my teacher,' whispered Anthony to his brother. Roger nodded solemnly. I realised then that I'd seen them both the very first day I'd arrived in the village, following the funeral procession. I wondered who'd they'd lost and made a mental note to ask Benjamin. I knew that loss could affect a child's learning.

'How are you finding our school?' asked Roger.

I smiled. 'I'm lucky to teach such an engaging group of children.'

'I hope Anthony's behaving and applying himself,' he said, tousling the boy's head. Anthony scowled.

I tried to keep a straight face. 'He always tries his hardest, which makes him an excellent student.'

'Well, that's good to hear. I suppose I'd better let you get home to your dinner. Good evening to you, Miss Todd.'

'Good evening, Miss Todd,' repeated Anthony, pulling on his brother's hand.

They were gone before I'd finished picking up the last of the chalk pieces lying on the bottom of the chalkboard. The sight of Anthony and his brother huddled together was a lovely way to end my day and I hoped that Roger would continue picking Anthony up through the dark winter afternoons.

I looked around the classroom, cosy and cheerful in the light of the lamp. Whatever I felt about being here in Ebberfield, I had to admit that I enjoyed teaching the children in my class and I looked forward to watching them learn and grow. It was my vocation, and my sisters might think that I'd be satisfied with that, but I still longed for more than I had here.

I loved my sisters but they didn't understand me. They were a different generation, already married with children when I was still at school. I'd seen how hard they worked but they hadn't lived the exciting life I had at college in Durham, where I learnt that a woman could be so much more than a wife and mother. Papa thought becoming a teacher meant I'd have some independence and wouldn't have to work as hard as Mama and my older sisters, but he didn't realise how much more I could do.

I would never settle in a small, restrictive village like this, waiting patiently until some man decided to whisk me off my feet and take ownership of me and my life. I still dreamed of the opportunities of working in a big city like London, where I could teach in one of the new higher schools for girls and maybe become headmistress one day. Some of the girls at teachers' college talked about living in lodging houses for women, where they could begin their new lives of independence. It was a thrilling prospect, and I so wanted to be part of the passionate drive for social and political reform – most urgently the vote for women – that I'd heard about in rousing speeches while at teachers' college.

Now those ideas and plans were on hold, but all was not lost. My purpose remained the same. I was part of a new generation who wanted to be at the forefront of change. I wouldn't be in Ebberfield forever and I'd make those dreams a reality. In the meantime, I'd do what I could to make a difference here, and then make my mark on the world.

2

I've seen the desperate conditions that the Great
Depression has left in its wake here. Cheap imported
grain from America and meat from the colonies have only
made it harder for local farmers to compete ... The friendly,
bright children that I teach are coming to school cold
and hungry.

THE OX AND PLOUGH
JANUARY, 1893

'It's finally happening,' I whispered to Mama. 'Our very first
suffrage meeting.'

It was the culmination of the two years I'd spent trying to
improve the lives of those who lived in the village. It had been
a slow and laborious process trying to change anything in
Ebberfield, so I'd decided to take matters into my own hands
and call for the local women to join me in raising our voices
for the betterment of the most disadvantaged in our district:
the women and children.

If I could be like Millicent Fawcett or the late Lydia Becker,
inspirational leaders of the suffrage movement, emulating the
rousing speeches I'd heard at the Durham rallies and showing
my own passion, I knew I could bring the women's suffrage
movement to conservative Ebberfield. The first societies for
women's suffrage had been formed in Manchester, Edinburgh
and London decades earlier, after the Second Reform Bill

failed to include enfranchisement – the parliamentary vote for women. I was inspired by the idea that only when women had voting rights the same as men could they have a say in what happened in their local communities, their schools, districts and even in the running of our country and supporting the issues that were important to us, our families and our communities. Our new suffrage society could bring about lasting change.

'Well, go on out there and tell the women who've come why they should join your society,' said Mama, preparing refreshments in the kitchen. 'You know what to say. You're just like your father.'

I took a deep breath to calm my nerves and nodded. Mama might not understand why I wanted to do this, but she supported me wholeheartedly. 'You're an idealist,' she'd said, kissing me on the head, when I'd told her of my plan. My sisters Jane and Sarah were like Mama, but Mary had shown an interest, perhaps because she had stayed at school longer and found employment before she married, working in the biggest draper's emporium in Hartlepool.

'The world needs more like you,' Papa had replied. 'How can the world change if we can't imagine a better vision of the future?' I wondered what his life might have been like if he'd had the opportunities I'd had. Perhaps he'd have been a teacher too, or maybe a vicar, although he was right at home now as a publican. He seemed to have found his calling late in life.

'Go on,' urged Mama. 'Your friends are waiting for you.' Clementine, Laura and Esther Burrows were chatting at the bottom of the stairs, ready to join me in the upstairs meeting room. Esther's mother, Mrs Burrows, was the head of the church aid society committee and the wife of a wealthy landowner in the district. My friendship with Esther since my early days with the group had helped make my life bearable here. The church aid society committee had recently transferred their monthly meeting to the new meeting rooms of The Ox and Plough as a result of the cordial relationship Papa had developed with the rector, Reverend Mason.

I couldn't believe I'd been here two years already. Between teaching, my community work and helping my parents, there had been so much to do. I'd been surprised to find how much time and energy working at The Ox and Plough had required of me even though I was only there in the evenings and on Saturday and Sunday – not in the cooking, cleaning and serving, but in helping Papa increase his clientele and to achieve his dream of making our public house the centre of the village. Besides wakes, and wedding and christening celebrations, The Ox and Plough had become the favourite venue for real estate auctions, coronial inquests and meetings of various groups. It had caused some tension with the publicans of the other pubs, especially Mr Franks, who had expected to keep most of the village's business at The Rose and Crown. It wouldn't be long until Papa's dream became reality. Although signs of Papa's illness had all but disappeared, I'd made a promise to myself to stay until he was established. And the village had grown on me a little.

I'd been giving extra lessons in one of the upstairs meeting rooms of the pub after school and in the holidays for any students who were struggling to learn in class, or who wanted a further challenge. When I noticed more children coming to school without lunch I began to take in extra food to share. But as the numbers grew, I had a small group come to The Ox and Plough for breakfast or lunch every school day. Soon, it became too much to manage without some recompense; the monthly payments to the brewery on the loan Papa took to purchase the pub meant that we operated on a tight budget.

Ever since Clementine had mentioned the work of the church aid society, I realised it was the best way to get what I needed to help the children. I joined the group led by the indomitable Mrs Burrows, and we raised funds for classroom resources: multiplication charts; weights and measures; geography and history readers; table books and copy books. But I felt a special sense of pride when after months of work, we were able to provide the school with a small but growing library, thanks to Edward Partridge, a local landowner and Justice of the Peace. He was a powerful and well-placed patron: on the Board of Guardians and the Rural Sanitary Authority, responsible for poor relief and public health of the district, along with Reverend Mason who oversaw the church aid society and another landowner, Mr James Duffield.

I'd had great hopes when I suggested that the church aid society might want to help provide meals to the students, but my excitement turned to dismay when Mrs Burrows reported back that the idea didn't have the full support of the senior churchmen. Apparently not everyone among the poor and destitute was deserving or worthy of assistance.

'How can anyone decide who's worthy and who's not?' I had whispered to Esther, outraged. Her mother was at the other end of the long table, in deep conversation with another woman.

Esther glanced quickly at her mother then turned back to me. 'It's the way things are done. We have to investigate each case, interview the members of the family, find the cause of their misfortune and how they contributed to it ... Most people don't want to end up in the workhouse and do their best to prove they're worthy of the charity. Then for the people who get help, we have to educate them on improving their circumstances and remind them of God's love and forgiveness through the scriptures.'

I nodded shortly, unable to trust myself to speak for a moment. This was a small community where everybody knew each other's business, but between my work at the pub and at the school, I'd seen the signs of families in real crisis. Men becoming violent the more they drank, women who cowered before their husbands, children who withdrew in the classroom and of course the physical injuries and bruises that were always explained away as accidents. Yet, as Clementine had told me when I'd first arrived, nobody spoke about these problems and women and children always seemed to be the victims, powerless to change their circumstances and doing whatever they could to survive. And in the worst cases, these vulnerable people ended up in workhouses, a fate I wouldn't wish upon anyone.

I glanced at Mrs Burrows. There was no doubt her heart was in the right place and she believed she was doing the right thing, even if she was as disappointed as I was. But how could she or the committee judge others when she could never know the true extent of the circumstances? 'And who decides which families are worthy?' I asked Esther.

'The county church committee. Our programs are approved by them, and the rural sanitary authorities,' she whispered, fiddling with the edge of a napkin.

'But how can they understand the causes of poverty when they have wealth and power?' These men were the administrators for the district, church and government, but many also worked to benefit themselves, and their political machinations were often at odds with the poor families who needed assistance or in fact for the rest of the township and surrounding district. 'Why is it that men make decisions that mainly affect women and children?' I asked, indignant. I couldn't believe the hoops we'd have to jump through to even get our meal club considered.

'It's not right, is it?' Esther replied. 'If we had more of a voice in these things, life would be very different here. My mother would like to do so much more but her hands are tied.'

I nodded. 'Maybe we should set up a suffrage society in the village,' I whispered. 'All we need is the right connections and we could support projects like this. Issues that concern women and their families are just as important as women's suffrage.'

Esther's grey eyes widened in surprise and I wondered if I'd gone too far. I'd already discussed my idea with Clementine and I was excited to find that she supported the suffrage movement.

'Mama wouldn't like that,' whispered Esther.

'You never know, she might change her mind if she sees what we're capable of achieving,' I said, smiling. 'What about you? Would you join me?'

'I'm up for the challenge. It's about time we had a society here.' Esther raised her chin in defiance. 'And I know I'm not the only woman who's tired of being told what I can and can't do.'

'Let's do it,' I said, my smile widening. 'It's the only way we'll really get things done around here.'

Now, I kissed Mama on the cheek and straightened my skirt as I made my way out to my friends. It was time to prove myself, to transform my passionate words into action.

Only once I was standing in front of the small group of about a dozen women seated in the meeting room did I feel a calm come over me. I gazed at their expectant faces, some excited, many curious and a few guarded. I knew what I wanted to say and I felt the energy build in me as I began to speak. 'One of the reasons I think we should begin a suffrage society is because women should have a say in what happens in this parish and district,' I said. 'Most men now have the right to vote; ratepayers and property owners, many tenants, and some agricultural workers. But nothing's changed for women.'

'What about women who own property?' asked Esther.

I shook my head. 'Married women and widows have the same rights as single women to own property and keep any income they make, but none of us has a voice. We need the vote.'

Esther's eyebrows rose, as did those of a few of the women, and I wondered if perhaps the first item on our agenda should be the education of girls and women about their rights.

'This inequality starts in the schoolroom. Girls deserve the same education as boys,' said Clementine, standing up beside me. She was strong, implacable and as passionate about creating a better world for girls as I was. She explained about the revolution in girls' education and about meeting the headmistresses of the few girls' schools that had been established around the country. 'There's no reason why girls can't study the same subjects as boys. Needlework is fine as an extra subject but girls' brains need challenging as much as boys' do. We'll never be taken seriously or given the same opportunities for university and jobs as doctors, lawyers and scientists if girls aren't allowed to take the same subjects.'

'I know that Benjamin allows the bright girls to join his extension classes for the older children,' said Laura, 'but perhaps girls and boys should learn from the same curriculum when they first start school.'

Esther nodded vigorously. 'I always wished I could have learnt science and mathematics as my brother did,' she said wistfully. 'I'm not that interested or skilled in needlework and I'd rather go to Papa's shed and tinker with his half-completed projects and his "inventions" as Mama calls them. But I'm told it's not ladylike.'

Clementine, Laura and I looked at each other in surprise. I hadn't guessed that Esther had secret yearnings to be a scientist or engineer. She was always so quiet, especially in her mother's presence.

Mama brought out a Victoria sandwich cake to have with our tea: a feather-light sponge filled with raspberry jam, and the group murmured with delight. I was touched by her gesture; she was determined to do what she could to make my meeting a success.

Clementine and I continued to share our thoughts and ideas. I told them about the society gatherings and rallies I'd attended at teachers' college which had lit a fire in me to create change.

'There are societies in villages like ours across the country,' said Clementine.

'So there are lots of women just like us who want change?' asked one of the women.

I nodded. 'Women who want to improve their lives and those of their daughters, friends and neighbours; women who want to have a say in the future of their communities.'

'But how can we do that?'

'We take our concerns and signed petitions to Parliament and explain our situation,' I said. 'We have to be accepted by the public as sensible citizens who deserve to vote the same as men.'

By the time our meeting concluded, we all agreed that we should formalise our small group of twelve members as the Ebberfield Society for Women's Suffrage and join the national society. I knew that we could be a part of the exciting change that was gaining ground across the country, something that would benefit us all.

3

Today I had an edifying discussion with Clementine about Darwin's theory of evolution and the controversy with the church. We agreed that the positivism movement that separated theology from the well-established scientific method of evidence, reason and logic made perfect sense.

Everyone looked forward to market day each month. It brought farmers, tenants, small and large landowners from all over the district to the cattle and livestock fair, often accompanied by their wives, who did their shopping. We'd not long since celebrated Plough Monday, and I was becoming familiar with the strange and arcane customs and agricultural festivals, and learning to welcome them because they brought people to the village – and to The Ox and Plough. Papa hoped that next year we'd be able to make the festival bigger and had some ideas of how we could sponsor some of the events.

'Could I order a pale ale and a brandy?' asked a woman in the downstairs lounge. She was there with Becky Johnston, the mother of one of my former students. 'And some bread and cheese.' She smiled. 'I don't know how long my husband is going to be.'

The room was almost full; wives, mothers and sisters sitting at the tables, children climbing over their mothers, playing on the floor and some running around the room. For many women on the outlying farms, market day was the only day they could visit friends and family in the village, and after all the shopping and chores had been done, they could relax in our pub's lounge.

Market day had been long for everyone and there would be a long night ahead. Our licence allowed us to stay open to one o'clock in the morning on these days instead of ten o'clock and we employed the local constable to remove anyone who was drunk or fighting. Already there was standing room only in the men-only main bar where we sold the cheapest beer and drinks. It wouldn't be long before the children were wilting, curled up in their mother's arms in the lounge as they waited for their menfolk.

'Hello, Miss Todd,' said Becky as I placed the pale ale and brandy on her table.

'Oh please, call me Hannah,' I said, smiling. 'Nice to see you, Becky. How's Jemima?' It was always tricky to stop and talk when the pub was so busy, but it was important to connect with our customers.

'She's doing well, still reading every day and always bringing home new books from the school library. She's never forgotten when you gave her *Black Beauty* and was so disappointed when she didn't get you as her teacher this year.'

I nodded, the satisfaction spreading over me like a warm blanket. 'She's such a bright spark. But Miss Foster is perfect to help her prepare for her Standard Five examinations this year. I have no doubt she'll end up in Mr Burnett's higher tops class in a year or two.'

I hesitated, glancing through the lace curtains onto the dark street. It was dinnertime and the sale was well and truly over. There were already a few more genteel men from around the district scattered through the lounge, drinking good whisky with their wives and families – wealthy landowners and professional men wearing broadcloth suits and holding

Homburg hats. I looked back at the woman who sat with Becky. They were alike: fair, with the same grey eyes; sisters, then, I thought, but Becky was clearly older, her face more weathered compared to her sister's milky complexion, and where Becky's bodice and woollen skirt showed signs of wear, her sister wore a well-tailored bodice with puffed shoulders in the latest fashion and a broad-striped skirt in expensive taffeta. Her husband must be someone of substance, perhaps one of the larger landowners in the district.

'Will your husband be joining you?' I asked Becky's sister. 'I can offer you something more substantial: mutton with potato and cabbage, cold beef or even a pie?'

The woman smiled. 'Thank you, but no. He went to a meeting of the Board of Guardians but he said he'd meet me here. If you see him, can you tell him where I am?'

'Have you met my sister?' asked Becky. I shook my head. 'This is Marjorie, Edward Partridge's wife.'

'Mrs Partridge, I'm glad to finally meet you,' I said warmly. 'I've been lucky enough to work with your husband on the library at the school. We have a lot to thank him for.'

'Please call me Marjorie,' she said, taking my hand. 'I've heard all about the library. Listening to Jemima read and watching the joy on her face has made me proud that Edward and I had a hand in it.' She frowned a moment. 'I recall him mentioning something about a lunch club at the school?'

'Ah, the lunch club,' I said, grimacing. 'It looks like it won't be going ahead, not through the church aid society anyway, too many rules and regulations to get it off the ground. But we've just begun a local suffrage society, and along with promoting the parliamentary vote for women, we want to do what we can to help women and families in need. We're hoping to begin the lunch program ourselves, but it's going to take time.'

'It sounds like a worthy cause,' Marjorie said, smiling. 'You should approach my husband. I'm sure he'd be happy to help out at the school again.'

'That sounds wonderful. Any assistance he could give would be much appreciated. Come to our next suffrage meeting if you can. You can explain what we do to your husband before I make an appointment to meet with him. You and Becky might even want to become members.'

'I like the idea of that,' said Marjorie.

'I could talk to you all night, but let me get your food. I hope to see you at the next meeting.'

I went to the kitchen where Mama was preparing the food. I couldn't wait to tell Clementine, Esther and Laura that we might have our very first project, and possibly even two new members. To see change happening here, the village slowly stepping out of the eighteenth century, was incredibly satisfying. Who knew what I could achieve in a bigger city once Papa had established his business?

The atmosphere in the pub was warm and cheerful, the noise of conversation peppered with laughter. The quartet had arrived and were preparing their fiddles in the lounge, ready to perform. Papa had done well to book them for the regular market day, as they were a favourite attraction that would draw more customers to us, rather than the other drinking establishments.

After directing Polly, our barmaid, to take the bread and cheese to Becky and Marjorie, I walked down the corridor to check on the main bar. I stopped for a moment, watching Papa work. Tall and wiry, his hands flew, moving automatically as he filled the glasses, his attention never wavering from the men in front of him. He could talk about anything, be friend and confidant alike, dispensing words of wisdom, humorous one-liners, gentle consolation like sweets. It was a joy to watch him in his element, every day a fresh delight to him as he welcomed people into his public house, listening as they shared their stories and taking great satisfaction in our place bringing people together. Papa adored being a publican and people came from miles around to enjoy his hospitality. He seemed to derive his energy from his connection with people, working from early in the morning until late at night. He was happy, well and back to his old self, oozing vitality and strength.

It was only at the end of the night, when Papa and I finally closed our doors behind the last of the staff, that I watched him sag.

'Another great night,' I said, as we checked that everything was clean and tidy in the main bar for the next day. 'It's the best market day we've had. You should be proud.'

'I am,' he said, smiling, dark smudges under his eyes. He'd be back in here again before dawn. Papa had never seemed to be getting old to me, but he *was* in his late sixties. I didn't know how he did it at his age. 'But I haven't done it alone. I have your mother and you.'

I moved the last of the bottles back into place on the shelf and turned to face him. 'But the success is because of you, Papa. Everybody loves you. Customers seem to tell you all sorts of things. Do you remember the party the shipyard had when I was little? It was in a beautiful garden ...'

Papa nodded, leaning against the counter, in no hurry to go. 'It was a fancy occasion. Mama sat at a garden table with the other wives, eating scones and sandwiches. But you, even in your best dress and bonnet, all you wanted was a ride on the pony.'

I laughed. 'You were surrounded by your crew, men who looked up to you and admired you. You left them to lead me around on that pony for what seemed like hours.'

'You were the apple of my eye. You still are.'

'Mama thought you were just spoiling me. But I'll never forget the looks on those men's faces as you told them a story. They were mesmerised. They'd have done anything for you. It wasn't until I was much older that I realised how you'd helped them.'

'Well, I was their foreman and they were like family. I was happy to help them however I could. I can't tell you how many weddings, christenings and funerals I've been to, the eulogies I've been asked to make. It was a privilege.'

'Nothing's changed here,' I said. Papa had seen and been through so much and still had much to give. I leant into him, our heads touching, and sighed. 'On a night like tonight it's hard to feel anything but part of the village.'

Papa kissed me on the forehead. 'I'm very proud of you.'

I blinked away the tears that sprang to my eyes, then put my arms around him and hugged him tight. 'I'm lucky. The apple doesn't fall far from the tree.'

*

Mama and I were walking through the village one Saturday afternoon in early February after visiting Mrs Pollock. Her bachelor son, a regular at The Ox and Plough, had passed away and now she lived alone.

'Miss Todd!'

Rory and Anthony, boys from my class, were coming towards us.

'Are you here to see the game?' asked Rory, excitement on his face.

'Are you playing cricket on the village green, dear?' asked Mama.

'No. Football. It's the local competition and we're playing Shotton. There's a big crowd today, but when we join the

Northern League, the green won't be big enough to hold the crowd.'

Football was rising in popularity in the north. West Hartlepool, the team Papa and I had followed for years, hadn't joined the recently formed Northern League yet either, but the boys talked of little on Monday mornings but the results of the games played on the weekend.

Anthony elbowed Rory in the ribs. 'What he's trying to say is will you come and watch the game?'

I glanced at Mama and she nodded. 'Go ahead, dear. I'll see you at home later.'

'I'd love to join you,' I said to the boys. 'Lead the way.'

'See that man dribbling the ball,' said Rory, pointing, his red hair glinting in the winter sun. 'That's Anthony's brother, David. He's only just joined the team. He's such a good player. We all want to be like him one day.'

I watched the young man duck and weave, moving closer to our goal. When it looked like Shotton was about to take the ball, he passed it to another player, who kicked it into the goal. I cheered as the crowd lining the field roared and David and the goalkicker hugged and slapped each other on the back.

'They play so well together,' said Rory. 'It's no wonder – they're brothers. But it's a shame they don't play every week.'

I squinted into the afternoon sun and realised that the goalkicker was Roger, Anthony's other brother. A thrill of excitement rushed through me. I'd seen him regularly in my first year here when he'd come to walk Anthony home from school in the winter darkness. Anthony had taken his father's death hard in those first months and as the oldest brother, Roger had stepped in as the protective male figure that Anthony had needed. We'd often talk a little about our day or any big news around the town and sometimes I'd join them on the walk home. We'd developed a friendship of sorts, but it was different from those childhood friendships I'd had with boys from my neighbourhood and school, and I'd been too busy at college to cultivate new friendships with anyone from the men's college. I was surprised to find myself disappointed that I hadn't seen Roger recently, even when I'd heard that he was working on a building project in another town.

'What do you mean?'

'David wants to play for a team in the Northern League and one day even in the FA Cup,' said Anthony. 'Roger just plays for fun and only makes it to the competition games when he's not working.'

'You boys play, don't you?' I asked. While watching the game, an idea had come to me. This year I had a class of nine- and ten-year-olds, the same children I'd taught in my first year at the school. Teaching them was a joy and I was excited to be able to foster a curiosity about the world and a love of learning. But managing their boisterous natures and balancing their need for physical activity with their class work was becoming difficult and their daily exercises just weren't enough. They needed something more.

'Of course!' said Rory.

'We play on the streets and on the green whenever we can,' said Anthony. 'I wish we could play properly, like my brothers.'

I took my idea to Benjamin when I returned to school and he agreed that it would be good to begin games at school for the older boys. 'We might even be able to get some local talent to help teach and inspire the boys. David Rainforth would be perfect,' he said.

'It'll be an excellent way to keep their attention on their schoolwork if they have something to look forward to,' I said. 'I could ask Anthony to talk to David, see if he's interested?'

I organised a fundraising concert that we held in the school hall for the equipment we needed for our new football program. The teachers, including myself, learnt all we could about the game from our local team, and how best to teach our boys to play. David and Roger Rainforth both gave generously of their time, first to explain the principles of the game with the teachers and then to help train the boys until the teachers gained more experience.

'Mr Burnett tells me that bringing football into the school was your idea,' said Roger one day as we packed up the balls and equipment following a skills session. 'Anthony talks of nothing else now.'

I shook my head and laughed as I picked up a basket of equipment and we began walking back to the school hall. 'He's thriving. He's so proud of you and David and he's suddenly seen as an expert by the other boys. It's wonderful to see him flourish, in fact, all the boys are much more settled in class, they're focusing better and learning more ... The days are more enjoyable for everyone.'

I was enjoying speaking with Roger again; he had such an easy manner and our conversation was always honest and uplifting. But I knew it was more than that. I liked being in his company. He made me smile and, I had to admit, my heart race.

'Thank you for looking out for Anthony. This football program seems like just the thing he needed,' said Roger softly, touching my arm briefly.

'I'm glad to see him so happy,' I murmured, butterflies filling my belly.

4

Parliamentary Member Henry Hunt presented a petition in support of women's suffrage in 1832 with the *First Reform Act*, which allowed a small number of men meeting the property qualifications to vote. One day it will be us.

The sun shone through the windows of the public bar, casting a golden gleam across the honey-coloured timber floors as we prepared for the May Day celebrations. Nevertheless, we had the fire stoked to keep the morning chill at bay. With a final flourish, I finished my letter to Mary and cast my gaze back over the page.

I cannot contain my excitement, so please forgive my rambling letter about the most recent developments! I received a letter from the Central Committee of the National Society for Women's Suffrage confirming that our local suffrage group is now a member society.

I'm thrilled to report that we have about twenty members now. Many are influential women in the town or district. With these women telling family and friends, we have more people coming to see what we're about with every meeting. But so far, no men. I hope that as we begin to achieve some of our aims in the community, we'll also have the support of prominent men in the district. I'm thinking about printing some pamphlets to hand out to the public, explaining our aims and projects.

There are so many matters to address: marital and parenting rights, the protection of children, literacy and adult education, public health and sanitation, equal elementary education and higher education access for all children, especially girls, and equitable property law between married and single women. I know we can't do it all and certainly not all at once – the question now is where to start!

With the glassy-eyed stare of the massive ox head on the wall overseeing my progress, its horns soon to be bedecked with wreaths of wildflowers, I'd already polished the windows and the timber counter, and made sure all the tables were wiped down. My next task after writing my letter was to check that the pewter mugs and glasses were clean and ready behind the counter for our barman, Bill Jackson, and Papa to serve beer and spirits in when we opened at lunchtime after the Sunday church service and before the festivities on the village green. The whole village was celebrating the end of the planting season and even the farmers would come into the village for the fete, the music and dancing, and the crowning of the May Queen. It was going to be a big night for all the pubs.

'I'm just going down to the cellar to check the barrels of beer,' said Papa, kissing the top of my head as he walked towards the scullery and the steps that led down to the underground cellar.

'But you were just down there.'

'Not this morning … not to check the barrels.'

I put down my nib pen. 'I swear you were checking the barrels when I was cleaning the floors.'

Papa shook his head and all I could do was nod, a spike of anxiety piercing my chest. I'd noticed a few occasions when he'd repeated things or had forgotten something he'd just done. And lately there were times when walking seemed more difficult, where he struggled to have fine control over his movements. I followed him into the scullery to check for more glasses and mugs. He was slow and stiff as he descended the stairs, brushing his hand against the brickwork as though to reassure himself that he had his balance. I prayed that whatever was happening was a temporary thing. He just needed more rest.

I poked my head into the kitchen where Mama was cooking pork pies and was hit by the rich aroma, my stomach clenching with hunger. The pies were always popular and would most likely sell out again today. 'Papa's not having a good morning,' I told Mama.

She nodded, wiping her hands on her apron and handing me a plate of pies. 'Try one and see if you like it. I've added nutmeg this time.'

'I thought you'd never ask,' I said with a sigh. I took a bite of the warm pie. The nutmeg certainly gave the pork a different flavour but it complemented it well, I thought. 'Delicious,' I said with my mouth still full.

'Do you think the customers will like it too?'

'Of course they will, but if not, there's more for me.' I winked and Mama laughed.

We turned to the sound of Papa coming back up the stairs. 'I have to order more barrels from the brewer,' he said, closing the scullery door.

'You did that yesterday,' said Mama, flashing a concerned glance in my direction.

Papa frowned with confusion. 'Did I?'

'Yes, don't you remember telling me yesterday morning before sending Reg to the brewery with a message?'

'Are you sure?'

Mama nodded. 'The barrels should be here soon.'

Papa stared at her, his brows knitted in concentration, and then nodded. 'That's right. I remember now.' He sighed. 'There's so much to do that sometimes I forget whether I've done something or not.'

'Not to worry, love,' said Mama. 'Make sure you write everything down, so you don't forget.'

'That's a good idea,' said Papa, brightening at the suggestion.

But I only felt the cold heaviness of dread swirl in my belly. This wasn't the first time Mama had reminded Papa to write things down.

'Sit down now for a few minutes,' said Mama. 'I want you to try my new pork pies and tell me what you think.'

'Your cooking's always wonderful, Ellen. It's brought more customers through our door and built up our regulars. If we keep going the way we are, we'll be able to pay off our loan sooner and then we'll be able to do what we like.'

Although Papa had contributed to the Society of Engineers for many years, as well as saving extra each month, he had only had enough for the deposit to buy the pub and cottage from his insurance. The rest he had to borrow from the biggest brewery in the district. The loan was attractive, but the catch was that he had to agree to exclusive supply of brewery products, such as their range of beers; mild, pale, porter and stout, some wine and spirits, and also ginger ale and lemonade. I wondered if the cause of Papa's relapse was his worry about the loan.

Papa reached for the plate, his hand trembling terribly as he picked up a pie. He put it down quickly and dropped his hand to his lap.

Mama glanced away for a moment. 'What about asking Bill to work the whole day?' she asked. 'I think it's going to be busier than we thought.'

A flash of anger darted across Papa's face, and my eyes widened in shock at the suddenness and ferocity of his emotion. Papa had always been a calm and kind father and husband. The expression faded quickly, then he nodded. 'I think that's a good idea. I'm feeling a little tired today.'

'Are you going to have your pie, Papa?' I asked, worried. 'Mama's used nutmeg and it's really very tasty.'

'In a moment, sweetheart.' He gazed out the window silently, lost in his own thoughts.

*

'I thought the aim of this suffrage society was to promote the vote for women?' asked Mrs Burrows, after I explained the national suffrage issues at our next monthly meeting. She was stony faced and belligerent, and although I was pleased that Esther had been able to persuade her mother to come to our meeting, I was worried she'd see what we did as a threat to her own aid society.

'It is, but we're fighting for social, legal *and* political equality,' I explained. 'And as much as I'd love to push immediately for full voting rights for women – it is our fundamental right after all – this is a process. Women are able to vote and be elected on school boards, but why shouldn't we be able to do more? The next step is to extend a woman's voting rights to local and district councils, where issues that are important to us and our community can be heard and acted upon. These are the same issues that are being fought for by the national society. If we can change things for the better in our own villages and districts, then we can show our mayors, chairmen and Members of Parliament that we're ready for the parliamentary vote.'

Mrs Burrows looked thoughtful. I scanned the crowd; most of the women seemed interested and curious, but there were some critical stares and impatient expressions. I needed to remember this wasn't one of my group meetings in Durham, where debate fuelled the passionate desire for change in most members. These women wanted to know how the national suffrage issues concerned them in their day-to-day lives.

'The main objective of our society is to support our local area in the best way we see fit,' I continued. 'How many of you know women who endure beatings or are trapped in marriages with the fear of losing their children and no income if they leave, because the law won't support them?'

More than one pair of eyes darted away. We all knew there were unsavoury things that happened behind closed doors, but it was our responsibility to bring these injustices to light. The image of the little girl screaming on the playground in my first week at the school came to mind. 'And what about our children? We want them safe whether they're at school or in the home. We've come a long way in protecting our children but we can do more to make sure vulnerable children and girls aren't exploited.'

Despite the rising tension in the room, I hammered my point home. 'We might not have children working half-days in the factories of the big cities or girls turning to prostitution because their parents have lost their jobs—' a few gasps went up from the women, '—but what about the children who don't attend school? I know farming families are struggling and children stay at home to help with harvests or with looking after younger children, but the law states that they should be at school. Sometimes they don't come because they have nothing to eat or they have no warm coats or boots to walk the long distances to and from school. These children need our help.'

I could feel the collective interest reach a crescendo. Good. 'So, our first proposal is a breakfast and lunch club for our students, and the provision of warm clothes to those who need them.'

Esther stood beside me. 'Do we agree that the first items we should discuss are how we can provide warm clothing and boots to children, and the possibility of feeding the children when the new school year begins?'

The women in the room nodded and I breathed a sigh of relief. Now it was time for me to reach out to Marjorie's husband.

*

Esther and I arranged to meet Edward and Marjorie in one of the meeting rooms at The Ox and Plough.

They cut a fine couple. They were certainly the darlings of the district. He was a bit older than Marjorie, closer to thirty and had the look of a man of the world, a man of experience. Mrs Scruton, who ran the tea rooms, knew most of what went on in the town and when she'd seen Marjorie at our suffrage meeting, she couldn't help but tell me how Edward had recently returned to the village after many years in London in banking and finance to take up his inheritance from his deceased uncle. The Partridges weren't landed aristocracy and Edward's mother still lived modestly in the village, but Edward's uncle, Philip Usher, had been a wealthy industrialist who had owned a coal mine before he bought his estate. Apparently, many mothers with single daughters had been perturbed when Edward had appeared with his new wife, Marjorie.

As Marjorie made the introductions, Esther nodded and smiled. 'Hello, Edward,' she said. 'It's been a long time. I was sorry to hear about your uncle. He and Papa were such good friends.'

'I remember,' said Edward, kissing Esther's hand and making her blush. 'Wandering Uncle Philip's farm was much more fun with company. We used to hide in his glasshouse when it was time for you to go home.'

Ah, so Esther and Edward had moved in the same circles, I thought.

'And when you came to visit us, we'd explore Papa's workshop and I'd explain his latest invention or project to you. You were the only one interested in what I had to say.'

Edward laughed. 'That's right. It seems like a lifetime ago.'

'Is the estate a working farm?' I asked.

Edward nodded. 'We raise sheep and cattle and grow crops, like most farms around here. My uncle made sure I learnt the basics when I was young, although the manager knows what to do. It allows me to continue with my own business and my work in the district.'

'How are you finding being back?' asked Esther, sitting at the table beside me.

Edward laughed, an infectious sound, and waved his hand in dismissal. 'I'm busier than ever. I've had enough of the high life in London, but my commitments see me travelling back and forth more often than I'd like. I hate being away from Marjorie.'

I would have thought that a good occupation in London was far superior to life in a small country town like Ebberfield, but Edward seemed to have the best of both worlds.

Marjorie smiled and shook her head. 'We've been married not even a year and already he's leaving me to go back to London. Luckily for me, I have plenty to do around the manor house and it gives me the chance to see Becky and her family. When Edward's home, we're never apart and he keeps me very occupied,' she said, grinning.

Edward shook his head, though he had a mischievous glint in his eye. 'Now, now, my love! The ladies don't want to hear about that.'

Marjorie only smiled more broadly.

'How did you meet?' I asked.

'My family is from Yorkshire but my aunt Milly and Edward's uncle were old friends, which is how Becky's husband was offered the position of overseeing the rectory lands here in Ebberfield. I first met Edward when I was visiting Aunt Milly in London a few years ago after my father died. I made sure I visited each year after and then last time …' Marjorie's face was radiant.

'She was just a slip of a girl when I first met her, but last time my heart was stolen by a vision of beauty and charm.'

'We were both smitten.' She gazed adoringly at Edward and I briefly wondered what it might be like to marry a man you were so passionate about. But it was silly to wonder, I was never going to marry. I'd seen how marriage had worn down my mother and sisters, the demands of children and husband taking every ounce of their identity, until they became only wives and mothers. I was too committed to my teaching and activism and valued my independence more than anything.

'I'm lucky to have such a wonderful husband,' Marjorie continued, 'one who takes an interest in helping the community.'

'Yes,' said Edward. 'Let's get to business. Tell me your proposal for the school lunch club and we can discuss some ways that I can help.'

I explained how school attendance and classroom performance had been affected by children having no food at school, and in an hour's time, Edward had agreed to cover the cost of building a new kitchenette at the school. Our suffrage society would raise funds for the initial set-up of pots, pans and crockery and the ongoing costs of food, and we'd canvass stores in the village, asking for donations and discounts on our standing orders.

'Again, the church may contribute to the cost of the food,' Edward said, 'but I think it would be prudent to have an extra kitty for those times when there's a shortfall in funds. Say we nominate an annual amount?' Edward rose an eyebrow in question.

I couldn't be happier. Edward had agreed to cover anything extra we required, and it was exciting to have support from such an influential man in the village.

All I needed to do was to set the wheels in motion.

5

I can't remember when my love of collecting began but
I do remember learning while browsing the wonderful
natural history collections in the university museum in
Durham that Darwin had begun as a self-taught naturalist,
before gaining high regard across the world with the
publication of his book *On The Origin of Species*.

School was over for another year and the summer holidays
had begun. Clementine and I were excited to cycle to the
beach and go sea bathing. Esther had never ridden a bicycle
before and had taken some persuading to learn to ride and
then needed plenty of practice before the three of us set off
for the seaside in our split skirts and wide-brimmed straw
hats, a ride of just over two miles.

We encountered some stares of disapproval as we rode
through the village and from farm workers harvesting barley
in the fields, but I didn't care, not on such a beautiful clear
and sunny day. It was exhilarating, riding through the verdant
countryside dotted with farm cottages, the air rushing against
my skin.

'They're such prudes,' I said. 'Women cycle everywhere in
Durham and even in Hartlepool, some in knickerbockers as
well.'

'At least we're still conservatively dressed,' Esther said.
'Reverend Mason would have an apoplexy if he saw a woman
in pantaloons!'

We all burst out laughing.

'Wait until we're in our bathing suits,' said Clementine, her eyebrows raised in mock horror. 'Absolutely scandalous!' We laughed so hard our bicycles wobbled on the path.

We rode through the gorse scrub to the top of the cliffs. The North Sea stretched out in front of us, deep blue and flat to the horizon, like shot silk. A small half-moon-shaped sand-and-pebble beach lay below us, protected by rugged limestone bluffs that jutted into the sea.

'Have you ever seen anything so lovely?' murmured Esther.

'How about we go down there?' asked Clementine, craning her head over the handlebars to look for the path, holding her hat down with one hand. The wind was much stronger here, pressing against us with force and whipping our voluminous skirts behind us.

'We can't swim here,' said Esther, shaking her head. 'There are no bathing machines for us to change in and retain our modesty. We have to cycle to the next beach.' I'd used bathing machines at the seaside near Hartlepool: small wooden huts on wheels in which you changed into your bathing suit, before it was dragged into the water by horse or hand, so you could emerge through the seaside door and submerge your body into the sea without being seen. All respectable women used them.

'All right,' I said. 'But while we're here, let's explore the beach. I want to see if this might be a good place to bring the girls for an outdoors excursion while the boys are training for football.'

Girls could do many things boys could. I knew that from teaching, as well as growing up with only sisters. But while I'd managed to set up football classes for the boys, girls weren't allowed to play. I'd had an idea to arrange activities for the girls – while gymnastics would be a good addition to our daily calisthenics, I wanted to extend them, and I thought a nature club might fit the bill.

We left our bicycles and found the sandy trail down to the shore.

'So, are you going to talk to Benjamin about your idea when school goes back?' Clementine asked as we climbed down, between the grassy knolls and sand dunes.

I nodded. We'd already received his approval for the meal club and the church was subsidising the program. I hoped he'd be just as receptive to my new idea. 'I want to get them outside. We can be amateur naturalists, studying the countryside and its changing environments.'

'That sounds like a wonderful idea,' said Esther. 'It makes me wish I was still at school.'

'Maybe you could join us as a local expert.'

Esther laughed. 'I'm no expert in anything.'

'That's not true,' said Clementine. 'Your knowledge of science far exceeds mine and we've seen your scrapbooks filled with drawings and descriptions of machines and inventions – and their inspiration from nature.'

'We could all learn a lot from you, Esther,' I said. Esther grinned, her cheeks pink.

We'd reached the beach and Esther began to walk along the shore, looking down at the sand. 'I've heard of fossils being found along this beach. It would be so exciting to find some.'

I nodded, a fizz of excitement rushing through me. 'They could be a perfect introduction to Darwin's theory of evolution.'

We wandered along the beach and I kept my eye out for any unusual rocks, shells or even feathers. Collecting fascinating objects reminded me that life was ever changing and nothing could ultimately resist the sweeping momentum of natural evolution. My favourite object was an ancient, fossilised acorn I'd found as a child. Papa and I had gone walking along the beach near West Hartlepool.

'What does it look like?' Papa had asked as I showed him a strange object I had picked up along the shore.

'It looks like an acorn,' I said. 'But it's shrivelled and black. What's it doing on the beach?'

He rose, took my hand and we continued walking along the shore. 'It's a fossilised acorn. A long time ago, this used to be a forest filled with oak and hazelnut trees.'

My eyes had been wide with amazement at the thought. 'Really?'

Papa smiled. 'Really. An archaeologist from the museum in London came and looked at some of the acorns and hazelnuts that people found here and said that they came from an ancient forest.'

I went home that day and wrote about what we'd found. It was my first journal entry, a habit I've continued ever since. Our discoveries had begun my interest in science and the natural world, another reason I wanted to go to teachers' college and study further. That fossilised acorn was a symbol of my determination to share the love of learning that my father had fostered in me with my own students.

'It's getting warm,' said Esther, shading her eyes with her hand. 'Let's cycle to the next beach before it's too hot.'

I gazed across the water, sparkling invitingly in the sunlight. 'Why don't we just swim here?'

Esther looked truly horrified and shook her head violently. 'No, we're not supposed to. What if someone sees us or a group of men come down here to swim?'

Clementine looked around her in an exaggerated manner. 'Where's your sense of adventure? Nobody's here. We're not going to be arrested.'

'Come on, Esther,' I said coaxingly. 'We can change behind the rocks, wrap ourselves in our towels, drop them on the sand and run very fast into the water.'

Esther looked unconvinced and Clementine and I shared a look of delicious wickedness.

'Race you!' I yelled, stripping down to my bloomers and chemise and discarding my corset, then ran to the water's edge.

Clementine and I both whooped in victory as the small waves splashed against our bare legs. We grinned at each other before moving deeper into the icy water. My undergarments were lighter than a bathing suit and much less restrictive as I floated on my back. Maybe I'd swim like this again. Then, anchoring my feet in the squelchy sand, I turned to Esther on the shore. 'Come on in,' I shouted. 'It's refreshing.'

'Live a little!' yelled Clementine.

Esther stood very still on the shore for a moment and then glanced furtively at the dunes and cliffs. Satisfied we were alone, she shed her clothing and, to the sound of our cheers of encouragement and congratulations, joined us in the sea.

*

I spent the rest of the summer break working at The Ox and Plough, but I didn't really mind. My friends were all away; Laura and Benjamin and Clementine had travelled home to visit their families in the south and Esther had gone with her family on their annual summer holiday to the seaside. But after the frenetic activity at the end of the school year, along with fundraising for the school meal club, a concert held in the school and a few fundraising nights at The Ox and Plough, I missed working with my friends. After a chance conversation at church, I began helping a small group of women to improve their reading in one of our meeting rooms. With the new school year, I'd ask the suffrage society to consider a program of adult education evening classes.

One July morning, as I was in the kitchen preparing a literacy class after placing the last pies in the oven, I heard Papa talking to Bill in the main bar. I popped my head out to see how the visit from the brewery agent had gone.

'I won't push drinks on my customers,' Papa was saying, slamming his hand down hard on the counter. 'I won't have the brewery tell me how to increase my sales. My regulars know what they like and anyone else should be able to buy what they want.'

The brewery sent a representative every few months to discuss our needs, promote certain products and ensure we were meeting our quotas. They were always encouraging Papa to find ways to increase our turnover. We'd more than met our quotas every month but because we were doing so well, increasing customers through the door and engaging in community events, the brewery had been pressuring Papa to take larger quantities of their products. He was irate, and rightly so.

'It's enough that we pay more for our beer than The Rose and Crown or The Hare's Foot but to have to keep our prices in line with theirs? The beer tax is going up again soon too and the brewery will pass that cost on to us.' He put his hands through his thinning hair and his eyes narrowed as another thought came to him. 'And how did he know what trade we did last market day?'

'I think they send spies,' said Bill.

'Spies?' I asked, incredulous.

Bill nodded. 'I've seen it before. When pubs tied to breweries aren't performing as well as the brewery would like they send in a man that nobody knows is working for the brewery to watch how the place is run, who their customers are, how they get patrons through the door, that sort of thing.'

'We're performing better than anyone imagined,' said Papa. 'We have more events than the previous owner did, more even than the other pubs except The Rose and Crown and The Hare's Foot, and if I have it my way, it won't be too long before we surpass them as well.' The Black Bull Tavern was the only other tied-house in the village and it wasn't doing anywhere near as well as we were.

'I know, and you're right,' said Bill with a sigh. 'The brewery can see what you've done. Customers love you but the brewery wants to push you to make even more money for them, it's as simple as that.'

Papa shook his head. 'Bloody bastards,' he growled.

Bill glanced at me, his eyebrows raised in surprise. Papa was usually a perfect gentleman, mild mannered, and he never cursed in front of women, not even his daughters. But I'd heard Papa use more colourful language in private of late when the frustration of his body refusing to respond became too much for him.

Mama and I did all we could to cover for Papa when he was having a bad day but I still hoped that this was a temporary relapse and he'd improve again soon. Otherwise, any hope of leaving for a city to pursue my dreams would become difficult. We tried to get him to rest more but he wouldn't hear of it. We had a loyal team who had been with us for years now, led by our experienced barman, Bill, our young potman, Reg Turner, who cleared the tables and collected empty mugs and glasses, and Polly Timms, the barmaid. We hadn't told them about Papa's condition but if he continued like this, we'd soon have to give them an explanation.

'Who do you think the spy is?' I asked.

Bill shrugged. 'It could be anyone: someone from the village, or an occasional customer.'

'How can we find out?'

'What does it matter?' replied Papa sharply. 'There's nothing we can do about it. We'll just have to get more customers through the door and find another way to drum up business.'

But I wondered. If we knew who the spy was, we could make him understand the terrible pressures the brewery was putting on us, the unfairness of it. Perhaps he'd have second thoughts about serving the brewery in such an underhanded way ... Anything to alleviate Papa's stress.

6

John Stuart Mill presented a petition with 1500 signatures in 1866 in the lead up to the *Second Reform Act*, where he proposed universal suffrage – a proposal that was denied. The *Second Reform Act* instead led to the vote for urban working-class men. I believe the parliamentary process is the only way.

August brought the local agricultural show. Farmers and families from all over the district and beyond would descend on a field on the outskirts of the village for a day of festivities. Papa had paid for the right to set up a refreshment booth at the show and we had a good central position with the animal exhibits on one side and the vegetable and art exhibits on the other. Papa and Bill had been at the field setting up our beer, lemonade and ginger ale long before the show opened.

'It's going to be a busy day,' said Mama, surveying the crowds that milled about the exhibits. She and I had arrived with pork pies and freshly made sandwiches.

Papa nodded. 'We've already sold some drinks, but your food should be the extra drawcard we need.' His burst of energy in preparing for the show over the past week had left Mama and me optimistic that his health was picking up again.

I saw Clementine approaching, weaving her way through the slow-moving groups of people. I grinned. Right on time. I was supposed to be helping Papa at the booth all day while Mama returned to the pub to help Bill. But Esther had begged for Clementine and me to come and see the new agricultural machine that her father was showcasing, which she'd helped invent. But if I was going to manage to get away at all, it had to be now, before the stall got too busy.

'Good morning, Clementine,' said Papa as she reached our booth. 'How is it out there?' My parents liked Clementine and Esther.

'It won't be long before people are queuing up to get in,' said Clementine, kissing Mama on the cheek.

'Have you seen the booths run by The Rose and Crown and The Hare's Foot?' asked Papa. There had been stiff competition to secure the only three refreshment stalls available for the show and Papa's community focus and his connections with the show committee had paid off.

Clementine nodded. 'They're the same size as yours but The Rose and Crown is near the judging tent and is offering food too. Though it didn't smell as good as here.'

Papa grunted, his lips pressed together in contained annoyance. 'Yes, I know. They always get the best position, no matter what the rest of us do. But what about the prices? Do you know what they're charging?'

Clementine thought for a moment and told Papa what she'd seen. Papa's face flushed red with anger. Both booths were charging substantially more than we were.

'That's highway robbery! How can they sleep at night?'

Clementine glanced at me uneasily, worried she'd done the wrong thing. I shook my head imperceptibly. I'd have to tell her what was going on.

'It's all right, William,' said Mama soothingly, rubbing his arm. 'Look on the bright side. Our reasonable prices will surely bring more people to us.'

'That may be so, but you know how popular The Rose and Crown and The Hare's Foot are. It upsets me to think of them taking advantage of people. They already get cheaper beer.' He shook his head. 'I just couldn't do something like that.'

'Do you need any help here?' Clementine asked, looking somewhat stricken.

Papa took a deep breath to steady his nerves. 'No, you girls go and enjoy the show. Ellen and I will hold the fort until you get back.'

I threw my arms around him in a big hug. 'Thank you, Papa. We won't be long and Clem and I'll tell you all about Esther's machine when we get back.' As an engine builder himself, he was intrigued to know more.

'I look forward to it,' he said, smiling now.

I turned to my mother. One eyebrow was raised, less than impressed.

'All right, Mama? Esther will be disappointed if I don't go to see her invention. I promise I'll be back before it gets busy.'

Mama nodded somewhat reluctantly.

I pecked her on the cheek and, taking Clementine's arm, stepped out into the crowd.

We had to push our way through the crush of people to the farm machinery pavilion where the invention Esther and her father had created was on display. It was a new type of engine that could be used to run farm machinery. Esther was on hand to answer any questions while her father was negotiating some business out the back of the stall.

I noticed that Esther had a stack of brochures about the suffrage society on the table, the same ones I'd put out at our refreshment booth. We'd had them printed in time for the show, hoping to boost interest in our society and in donating towards our school meal club. Men loitered by the stall, intrigued by the new engine, but few wanted to ask a woman about something that was clearly in the domain of not only men, but specifically men who understood the practicalities of farming. Some picked up the brochures but put them down quickly.

'Bloody ridiculous. What are women goin' to do with the vote?' muttered a farmer as he walked away. It seemed to be a common attitude and I wondered how Laura was faring with her pamphlets at the cake stall. It was next to the prize-winning cake display, where more women would visit. Even with our fundraising efforts so far, I was grateful for the variety of cakes made by society members and women of the community. We'd have no problem selling them all and would make a tidy sum towards funding our meal club. I knew we'd face some resistance to the idea of women's suffrage from the men in the town, but I hoped our community projects would show them we could make positive change in our village and should be given the chance to do more at a national level. Suffrage was about women lending their voices to issues that were important to them. The world outside of the town was changing and soon that change would be knocking on our own doors, whether people liked it or not.

'It's called an internal combustion engine, run by gasoline or petrol, which is a different type of fuel from coal,' she explained, her face flushed with excitement as she leant towards the engine. This was the moment she had been waiting for, someone to take an interest in their invention.

'Fascinating,' I said, suitably impressed. 'What can it do?' I knew that she and her father had been corresponding with the inventor Charles Parsons and his wife, Katharine, who worked alongside him. I remember Esther telling us that the Parsons' steam turbine was more efficient and smaller than the standard steam engine and was now being used in ships. But this gas engine seemed more advanced again.

'At the moment it's a single engine that can be moved around from place to place to power machinery, like the old steam engines used to do. But Papa and I have modified it and are doing some fine tuning to see how we can best incorporate one into a tractor. That will make the biggest difference to a farmer's life. It'll be less bulky and more economical and convenient to use.'

'You and your father are so innovative,' said Clementine. 'I'd love for you to show me how it works.'

Esther's face lit up. 'It would be my pleasure.'

'Miss Todd!'

I turned to find Anthony and Roger Rainforth walking towards us.

'Hello, Anthony,' I said smiling. 'How are you enjoying the show?'

'It's good. We've seen the prize-winning chickens and ducks.'

'We've yet to see the bulls and horses,' said Roger. His eyes met mine as he gave me a smile of greeting. I was surprised to see him in a suit and tie, and he cut an impressive figure, his hat at a jaunty angle. I was so used to seeing him in his workman's clothes that it took me a moment longer than it should have to look away. I hadn't seen Roger since the football season had ended, except for a few times at the pub, but I was always working and had little chance to talk to him.

'My father entered his best bull and breeding cow into the competition and Mama has her two-year-old filly,' said Esther. 'But we're up against Edward Partridge's bull and James Duffield's cows. They always have good livestock.'

Roger nodded. 'I saw John at the cattle pens waiting for the judging to start. He's hoping they'll win this year.'

'I haven't seen him in ages,' said Esther. 'I'll make sure I go and say hello later.' She turned to Clementine and me. 'John is James's son. He went to school with Roger and me. We were inseparable for a time, the Three Musketeers, until John went away to boarding school.'

Anthony pulled on Roger's sleeve. 'Rory's here and we're going to find Jemima and watch the plough racing competition.'

'All right. I'll meet you at the entrance at noon.'

Anthony raced away to catch Rory before he was gone.

'Are you all looking around?' Roger asked. 'It looks like my offsider has left me high and dry.'

'I'm waiting for Papa to come back before I can go,' said Esther.

'I'll wait with you and keep you company,' said Clementine. 'But you should go, Hannah.'

I stared at Clementine, my heart beating fast. I knew what she was trying to do. 'Are you sure?'

'Your parents are expecting you back and there's no point you missing out while I'm stuck here,' said Clementine.

'You're working?' Roger asked.

'At the refreshment booth and later at the pub.'

'Well, then, let me show you all the highlights,' said Roger, offering his arm.

I glanced at the girls.

'Go,' said Esther, shooing me away.

'I'll see you later,' I said, taking Roger's arm and feeling a little breathless.

'I'd better show you a good time so you have only nice things to say about me to your friends,' he said grinning.

I felt heat rise up my throat and into my cheeks. 'I don't know why I have to talk about you at all,' I said sharply, embarrassed by my reaction to his words, but he only grinned wider. I was twenty-two years old, not so young, and didn't know what to do with these feelings. I liked him but never expected to feel this way. It was only natural attraction to a handsome man, I reminded myself, and pushed it away. Instead, I pretended to be interested in the farm implements we were passing, but I still found it hard to focus on anything but his arm against mine.

As we wandered the animal exhibits, Roger pointed out the bulls, cows, sheep and horses of people I knew and why he thought certain animals would win the prizes. It was noisy, the deep lowing of the cattle set against the sound of agitated sheep and the honking of geese, just like an animal orchestra. I leant into Roger to better hear what he was saying, but his closeness was distracting and I barely noticed the animals at all.

'Gone are the days when Anthony wanted to do this with me,' said Roger ruefully as we made our way through the vegetable pavilion where prize-winning vegetables were on display, including some of the biggest pumpkins and marrows I'd ever seen. 'Thank you for keeping me company so I don't look like a total idiot on my own.'

'Ah, so now you only look slightly idiotic,' I retorted, trying not to smile.

Roger huffed a breath then smiled, changing the subject. 'Anthony's come a long way with his studies this year. He even likes school now because of you, and he brings books home from the library and actually reads them. My mother can't believe it. It's more than the rest of us ever did.'

'He's such a sweet boy, I'm happy to hear that he enjoys reading so much now. It helps children learn across all their subjects.'

'Maybe if we'd had a library when we were at school …'

The heady perfume of flowers assaulted my senses as we reached the flower displays, the riot of bright colours making me gasp in awe. 'We were so lucky to have Edward Partridge help us set up the library. We take reading for granted but I'm teaching literacy to women who didn't have the same opportunities that even you and I had. Now, he's helping our suffrage society with a breakfast and lunch club at school for children who are always hungry.'

'Like Rory?'

'Yes, exactly.' I nodded.

'Philip Usher was a generous benefactor in his day. It's good to see Edward follow suit, after everything his uncle did for him.'

'What do you mean?'

'Philip sent him to school in London and then to university in Oxford, before bringing him into his financial services business.'

'Well, he's been a wonderful help to our suffrage society.' I told him a little about how my concerns with the church aid society had motivated me to begin our own group.

'I'm just a tradesman, without the education you've had, but I understand your desire to change things. I belong to a trade society and read everything I can about my industry, and more general ideas too. We have monthly circulars and local trade council reports and it's a way for us to learn about what's happening in the world. Around the time I joined, our society began negotiations to improve wages and conditions, and now they're taking the next step to try to reform the law. We need more people, more groups, to show our district that things can be done differently. But Ebberfield is ...' He gestured at the villagers milling around the noisy livestock exhibits. 'Well, you've seen how hard it can be to change people's opinions and ideas when it's all they've ever known.'

I nodded. I did have my work cut out for me here. 'But there's always going to be opposition to change. Things remain as they are because it benefits powerful people or because others can't speak up. I'm determined to play my part.'

'Then the world had better watch out,' he said, teasing me gently, his eyes sparkling.

My chest fluttered as I watched his face. 'I know the society isn't enough, but I can't sit back and do nothing. If we can improve the lives of local women and children, then we must. Some of the women here have nowhere to turn but the workhouse, and they'd rather endure their circumstances than end up there.' I'd begun visiting families over the summer, who were suffering hardship, offering food parcels, letting them know I was there to listen with an unbiased ear and an offer of support at the suffrage society. The workhouse was a place they wanted to avoid at all costs. I'd heard the stories – separation of families, men, women and children in different wards, each wearing a uniform, adhering to the strict rules where deviations resulted in harsh discipline such as beatings, withholding of food and isolation. They were no better than prison inmates but they had committed no crime.

'My father and I used to build together, he was the joiner and I did the bricklaying. I lost some of the work we were doing after he died and there were times when I wondered if we'd end up in the workhouse.'

I took Roger's hand, solid and warm, and squeezed it in sympathy. 'It must have been such a difficult time for you all.'

Roger sighed, gazing at our joined hands. 'It was his heart ... but he was much too young, only forty-eight years old. After my mother came out of her shock, most of her attention went into working out how to survive and keep our family intact. She returned to dressmaking, but it's not always steady work when there are other more established dressmakers in the village. My two sisters were sent to work as servants at rectories near Durham and Chester-le-Street, where my mother's from. David and I were already working, bringing in an income, and Matthew was apprenticed.'

I nodded, touched by his revelation. Then I thought about

my own father, wondering what the future held for him, Mama and me, and shivered.

'Are you all right?'

I nodded. 'I'm sorry, it's just ...'

Roger frowned with concern and kept my hand in his. 'You know you can tell me anything.'

'My father hasn't been well,' I whispered. I told him about Papa's diagnosis. I took a deep breath, trying to swallow the sob that wanted to push its way up through my throat. 'Most days he's good, other days not so good. I have to believe that he'll get better again. My parents rely on that income and if something happened to Papa ...' I dropped my head in my hands, suddenly overwhelmed. The reality was too much to consider – the loss of the pub, the debt to the brewery. My teacher's salary wouldn't stretch far, and I shuddered at the thought of my darling mother in the workhouse. It would break us all.

When I felt Roger's arm around my shoulders, I lifted my head again in surprise, and then shook myself. Papa would be fine. He had to be. 'I'm all right,' I said embarrassed, quickly brushing tears away from my cheeks with my fingers.

'I know,' he said. 'You're a strong woman, anyone can see that. I pray that your father gets well, but just remember that you can talk to me any time.'

'Thank you. That means a lot.' I was glad to have someone who knew what I was going through, and I had some idea of the pain and loss he carried. But it was the support of his arm around me that truly made me realise I wasn't alone.

He withdrew his arm from my shoulders and offered his elbow as we began to walk again. He was a perfect gentleman but now I felt unsettled. Again, I shook myself, irritated at the feeling. He was offering me support and a safe and friendly ear, that was all. I was lucky to have such a good friend.

7

Disease is carried across the globe faster than ever as
more people travel by rail and steamer. I thought that
people understood that good hygiene and vaccination are
imperative to stop the spread. It has surprised me – many
here still believe the miasma theory, that disease is carried
in the air from bad odours and rotting matter.

'Where are they?' I muttered. I couldn't sit still as we waited
for the first children to arrive for our new breakfast and lunch
club – we'd resumed school in the autumn and everything was
finally in place. A small kitchenette had been installed in one of
the rooms attached to the school hall and we had a regular order
from the grocer and butcher. All we needed was the children.

I nervously checked that the tables were set with tablecloths,
serviettes and cutlery, stirred the porridge again and placed a
jug of milk on the bench.

'Relax,' said Clementine, opening the door to the school
hall. 'They'll be here.'

Of course, she was right.

'Come in, come in!' I called to the first children who
appeared at the door, waving them into the hall. Rory rushed
forward with his sister, Kitty, shyly behind him. She had
finished school two years earlier and Rory had told us that
she was working as a charwoman, cleaning shops and offices
in the village. We often saw her walking with Rory to school
in threadbare clothes, pitifully thin as ever.

'Are your hands washed?' asked Clementine, looking at the twelve children seated at the table. Some nodded enthusiastically but there were a few who looked sullenly to the floor. 'Off to the washroom and wash your hands with soap and water. Then you can have breakfast. The rest of you, Miss Todd and I will bring you your porridge.'

They all looked so excited. My heart gave a little squeeze that a bowl of oats could make a child so happy. I wondered what they usually had for breakfast, if anything at all. I noticed Kitty hanging back, perhaps to watch Rory eat his breakfast, and realised that her gaze was hungrily on the pot of porridge.

'Come on Kitty,' I said, calling her over. 'Miss Foster and I could use some help if you have time.'

She nodded eagerly and while she took the bowls to the table, I made sure there was some for her.

'We've made too much, but how about you take it as payment for your help this morning?' Perhaps we could make this a more permanent arrangement.

Her eyes went round and filled with tears. 'Thank you.'

Clementine followed behind, filling the cups with milk and depositing an apple in front of each child. Little faces gave up smiles of delight when they discovered the treacle drizzled across their bowls. It was a little treat and I was glad I'd insisted on it, despite the extra cost.

'Now, let's say grace,' I said. Each child dutifully bowed their head and recited the mealtime prayer then Clementine and I stepped back as the children ate.

'I think we can say that our first breakfast club was a success,' said Clementine.

'I have to agree,' I said, watching Kitty eat her breakfast swiftly. 'It's a very good start indeed.'

*

I'd come to realise that the new school year was the time for further projects that focused on the welfare of our community, especially the children, so it wasn't long before we learnt about a renewed vaccination program underway across the district.

'With the latest smallpox epidemic across Britain, concern has been raised over the increased number of deaths over the past couple of years compared to previous outbreaks. The health authorities believe it's linked to the decline in the rate of vaccination in recent years,' said Dr Richard Jenkins, addressing all the teachers in the school hall.

Dr Jenkins was new, a young doctor who had arrived in the village over summer, joining the general practice of the older and more experienced Dr Taylor. 'Vaccination to smallpox is compulsory and has been for the past forty years. The prescribed time for vaccination is before three months of age, but if we can raise the rate of vaccination, even in older children, we have a better chance of protecting the community, but especially our children.'

'We're happy enough to be involved in the program,' said Benjamin. 'But I'm not sure parents of unvaccinated children will be as there's a substantial fine for non-compliance.'

Dr Taylor shook his head. 'We've spoken to the vaccination officer. He's willing to waive the fine for any children between the ages of three months and fourteen years who is willingly vaccinated. With the Anti-Compulsory Vaccination League making noise we want to do all we can to reassure everyone that vaccination will protect their families.'

I nodded with approval. Before I was born, my parents had lost a baby girl, Beth, to smallpox and Mama's fear of the disease and the importance of vaccination had been ingrained in me. We were lucky to have someone so forward thinking and with such long experience as Dr Taylor, but with

Dr Jenkins' energy, enthusiasm and new ideas, the health of our village was in good hands. Change was coming to our small town and it was exciting to witness.

Later that afternoon, Clementine and I discussed the vaccination program while walking home. 'What if we promote the vaccination program through the suffrage society?' I suggested. 'If the members agree, we could speak with Dr Jenkins about printing an educational brochure to hand out to families. Perhaps he could talk at one of our meetings, too. We're lucky we haven't had any cases of smallpox here in Ebberfield but next time we might not be so lucky.'

'That's a good idea,' Clementine replied. 'How many children do you think are unvaccinated in your class?'

'I don't know. There must be a few at least. Maybe Michael, Henry and Frederick.'

'What about Anthony?'

I thought for a moment. 'I noticed Roger's vaccination scar when he was coaching football, so I suppose Anthony is vaccinated too.' I pushed my hands deep into my coat pockets, trying to ward off the cold. I was looking forward to a hot meal and a cup of tea.

'You're fond of him, aren't you?'

'Of course. He's a delightful boy, so bright—'

'I didn't mean Anthony.' She looked pointedly at me and I returned her gaze with a blank stare. She huffed. 'Roger,' she said softly.

'I don't know what you're talking about.'

'I've seen the way you smile when he comes to coach the boys and the way you look at him when you think nobody's watching. Then there was the agricultural show.'

'You and Esther were quick to suggest I go with him.'

'Well, I thought you might want to spend some time with him. Was I wrong?'

I sighed. 'I just feel as if I can talk to him. He understands me, that's all.'

'Mmm,' said Clementine, linking her arm with mine.

The truth was that I didn't know what to think or how to feel about Roger. He was my friend: easy to be around and I enjoyed his company, and although I'd found a place in village life and enjoyed the work I was doing, I still dreamed of taking my purpose bigger. I had decided not to marry a long time ago, so as not to interfere with my ambitions. With Papa not so well again, it might take longer than I'd hoped, but I was determined that one day I'd live in a big, bustling city, at the heart of it all, teaching at one of the high schools for girls, taking on a larger role in the suffrage movement and joining some of the many groups and committees to help women, children and the vulnerable. I'd make a difference where it really mattered.

*

Sarah surprised us with a visit for Papa's sixty-ninth birthday in September, bringing her oldest, Jenny, and three-month-old baby Arthur. His birth had been a temporary distraction from our worries about Papa, but when Mama went to Trimdon to help Sarah with her sixth child at the age of thirty-three, it had left me busier than ever, juggling school, the suffrage society and the pub, all while keeping an eye on my father. Papa's health had continued to fluctuate with the odd lapses of forgetfulness and outbursts of anger, and I'd noticed the tremors in his hands were worsening.

'I'm so very happy to have you here for my birthday, Beth,' said Papa from the head of the table, the birthday cake that Mama and I had baked in front of him.

Sarah shot me and Mama a worried glance. Beth had been dead for well over thirty years. Papa raised his glass with a shaky hand and we toasted his birthday. But the tremor didn't stop Papa slicing the cake and handing portions to each of us like he was presenting a precious gift.

Papa had always had a special way with babies and children and it was no different with baby Arthur. He held the baby, talking to him, and the baby stared back at him, mesmerised.

'When Mama came after Arthur was born, she told me Papa is getting worse again,' said Sarah as she paced my bedroom, trying to get the baby to sleep. 'I had to come. I knew how much he'd enjoy meeting Arthur before he gets much bigger.' I smiled at the sight of the baby sucking on his thumb. He really was very sweet.

'Some days he's his old self and we hope he's getting better but other days ...' I shrugged. 'I think the pressure the brewery is putting him under is making him worse.'

'It was the right thing, you coming here after teachers' college. They wouldn't have managed without you ... We're lucky he's been as good as he has been for this long. Perhaps if we can take some of the pressure off Papa, he'll get well. Jenny can stay to help. She's fifteen, finished her schooling and in need of regular work. It's the least she can do for her grandparents.'

'I'm sure that's all he needs,' I said, nodding.

Arthur's thumb popped out of his rosebud mouth as his eyes finally closed, looking like an angelic cherub in his slumber. Sarah stopped rocking and gazed through the closed door towards where Papa sat downstairs in the parlour. 'But it's probably time to take him back to the specialist in Durham.'

8

September, 1893

Dear Mary,

I had to write to tell you what's happened! I've received
a letter from the Central Committee of the National
Society for Women's Suffrage asking for our society to
sign a petition arguing for voting rights for women. It's to
be signed by women of all economic backgrounds and
political persuasions right across Britain.

The petition is organised by a Special Appeals
Committee headed by Mrs Millicent Fawcett. I'm not sure
if I've mentioned her to you, but I'm an avid admirer of her
and her advocacy of higher education for girls and the
parliamentary vote for women. I heard her speak when
I was at college and I'll never forget her saying that the
best protection a woman could have was the power to
protect herself. It really lit a fire in me – that was when I
became so passionate about the suffrage movement and
the fight for women's equality.

Mrs Fawcett has written the introduction for the
centenary edition of Mary Wollstonecraft's *A Vindication
of the Rights of Woman*, which I've read again. It talks
about the fundamental rights of women which are equal
to those of men, ground-breaking in its day, but when I
first read it at college, it opened my mind to the question
of what my generation could do for women's rights.

I digress! I just can't wait to tell everyone about the petition at our next meeting and begin the next stage of our work: our political fight.

Your loving sister,

Hannah

I picked up a small shell button from the floor of The Ox and Plough, and returned to the bar, deep in thought. I'd add it to my collection if nobody claimed it.

'It could be anyone,' I muttered to myself.

'Who could?' asked Bill, stacking the glasses that Jenny had washed. She was a great help in the kitchen and scullery, giving Mama a break from the preparation and cleaning especially when Papa was having a slow day.

'The brewery spy. If we could find out who it is,' I whispered, 'we can try to turn them to our way of thinking. The pressure the brewery is placing on Papa is making him sick. I don't know how much more he can deal with.' Papa had finally told Bill about his condition, after some gentle prodding from Mama.

Bill nodded and scanned the room. 'Probably a loner.'

My gaze fell on a man in a slightly worn yet good-quality suit. 'What about the travelling salesman?' I'd been searching for the odd person out, someone who wasn't with family or friends.

'No. It will be someone who can come at odd times whenever the brewery needs.'

'One of our regulars, then?' I looked around at the men at the bar and sitting in groups at the tables. They were salt of the earth, working men of all ages: farmers, tradesmen, shop owners or assistants, neighbours. These men were our bread and butter and friends to Papa. I couldn't imagine any of them spying on us.

Bill frowned. 'I don't think so. Your father has loyal customers. Maybe someone local who drinks at the other establishments or has no preference where he drinks.'

'Most locals have a preference, though. What about a man who comes to join friends or family who drink here?'

'Hmm, someone who tags along with our customers ... You might be onto something there.'

We scrutinised a group of men in the corner. There was a man who didn't seem to engage in conversation and kept looking around the room, watching the other drinkers. His eyes met ours and he looked away quickly to begin talking to his group.

'Did you see that?' I murmured. 'Could he be our spy?'

'Maybe,' Bill said slowly. 'We'll have to keep our eyes open, see what he does, watch for any patterns.'

'You agree we have to find him?'

'If we have any hope of helping your father, we do.'

'Good. Because I can't do this without you.'

*

Our first order of business at the next suffrage meeting was discussion about Mrs Fawcett's national petition. My eye caught the official picture of Queen Victoria that graced the wall of our meeting room: strong, powerful, a leader and a woman. Surely it was time for us to have the vote.

'Nobody pays attention to petitions,' scoffed Mrs Burrows, her arms already folded.

'You're right,' I said, looking her directly in the eye. Her opposition could hamper our efforts, making other women shy of spreading the word about the petition or even signing themselves. The society's work was generally accepted because it benefitted the village and hadn't challenged widely held attitudes and opinions, like the educational brochure on the vaccination program spearheaded by Dr Jenkins. But this petition was different. I'd been thinking long and hard, and if we were going to get the support we needed to make a decent contribution to the petition, we'd have to entice some serious influence to our ranks.

I had to hold my courage against Mrs Burrows' stony stare. I'd seen many quail in the face of it, but I refused to. 'Members of Parliament haven't taken notice in the past because there just weren't nearly enough signatures to make a difference, and there are too few MPs who champion our cause. The problem is that most think women simply aren't interested in the vote.'

'Like many of our menfolk,' called out Mrs Scruton, and a titter of laughter rippled through the audience.

I smiled. 'But this is our chance to prove *all* of them wrong by doing our bit to put as many signatures on this petition as possible, men included.' My first thought had been to approach Edward Partridge and possibly James Duffield as local Justices of the Peace. Reverend Mason was too conservative, but I wondered about Mrs Mason. There was Benjamin, our schoolmaster, Dr Jenkins and possibly Dr Taylor, Papa as publican, and the parish clerk and solicitor, Mr Sanderson, and maybe Mr Jones, the secretary of the Ebberfield Recreation Club, and some of the other publicans and their wives. I wondered if we could find a way to explain our cause to members of the rural sanitary board. Their support would certainly sway public opinion.

'But how will the petition help ordinary women like us?' asked a woman who hadn't been to one of our meetings before.

'If the petition does what we want it to, it will pave the way to the national vote, and that will affect all parts of our lives. We're the ones who really know what matters concern us, what needs to be reformed and what changes can be supported by law. But unless we can vote for the changes we want, nothing will improve.'

The woman nodded slowly, taking it all in.

'But why now?' asked Mrs Burrows.

'There's a new bill that includes women's representation in the national vote, which is likely to be added to the *Local Government Act*. Mrs Fawcett's committee will present the petition with the bill before the Parliament in the new year.'

Mrs Burrows suddenly looked more interested. The power of a tangible plan.

'This request for signatures gives our group specific purpose,' added Clementine.

I cast my eye over the group, gauging who might need further encouragement. Mama hovered at the back of the room, listening intently and giving me support as she always did. 'The more signatures we can provide, the more our voices can be heard. Talk to your friends and family and those in your workplaces about our cause. All we're asking for is for them to sign their names in support, but if they want to learn more, they're more than welcome to join our next meeting.'

Most women were nodding enthusiastically; some, like Mrs Burrows, looked thoughtful but a few were still dubious or stared back with sceptical expressions.

'It's an exciting time for the suffrage movement,' I said, trying to encourage them further. 'With all the societies working together, there's so much we can achieve.'

Clementine and I shared a glance and grinned. A thrill of excitement ran through me. We were part of something bigger now, a national project, and about to undertake useful work that could unite women under a common cause and make a difference to all our lives.

*

Football season had begun and after the success of last year's school program, a school competition had been organised across the district. It gave the boys something to look forward to each week, and it was a good way to encourage them to focus in class. And I was excited to begin the amateur naturalist club Benjamin had approved for the girls when the boys were at football.

In our initial class, I showed the girls how to do a scientific sketch, following the lines and proportions of an object, faithfully reproducing each part and to label those parts with a neatly written title. The aim was to accurately represent true life. Then I asked them to write a description of where the object they'd collected had come from, including colour, texture, smell and size and what impressions they had of their find.

I took the girls to the ancient woodland outside of the village for their first real excursion. It was cool, peaceful and wild; a perfect place to begin our scientific adventures. The trees grew thick; ash, birch and wych elm, their leaves now turning the bright colours of sunset; red, orange and yellow. The sides of the dene were steep and a stream flowed at the bottom, foaming through the gorge to fall into a clear, deep pool below, Minerva's Pool.

'What patterns do you notice?' I asked.

'All the trees grow tall and the plants on the ground don't grow tall at all,' said one girl.

'Why do you think that is?' I asked.

'The trees are trying to reach the sun,' said Jemima.

'Very good. But what about the plants growing close to the ground?' The girls shook their heads, unsure of what to say. 'What do you see?'

'Wood-ruff and dog's mercury,' called Amy Sanderson.

I nodded. 'But what else is on the ground?' The girls frowned. 'Look closer.'

'Leaves from the trees?' suggested Jemima dubiously.

'That's right,' I said, smiling. 'Look and see how the trees and low cover plants are very different in their structure and the way they grow. But they seem to always live together like this in the woodlands. The smaller plants get everything they need from staying close to the ground, protected by the trees above, and they in turn keep the ground moist and allow the leaves from the trees to break down and provide nutrients to the soil, feeding the trees and the plants. They have a special relationship, like a friendship.

'Now find the thing that interests you and explore it,' I said to the girls crouched over the ground cover or looking up into the trees. If I could at least give them the gift of curiosity and learning, then I was happy.

*

My vigilance with the smallpox program continued, fuelled by the worry in Mama's eyes whenever the disease was mentioned.

'How are Samuel and Hattie enjoying the lunch club?' I asked Mrs Morgan one afternoon as we walked together on the street.

'They like comin' to school now,' she said. 'And they want to show me what they've learnt.'

'That's wonderful to hear.' The children who were receiving meals at school were concentrating better in class, were less disruptive and were generally happier, I'd found. And the attendance rate had improved as well. Not only did children want to come but parents didn't feel they had to keep them home for the shame of not being able to provide for their children.

Kitty had become a permanent helper in the mornings too. She was obliging, helpful and so good with the children, and we always made sure she had breakfast and something more to take for her lunch. Coming into winter, the suffrage society had begun a drive, asking members of the community who could afford it to donate unused or outgrown clothing and boots to school children who needed them. I hoped that would ensure children kept attending school through the coldest months.

Mrs Morgan carried a tiny baby, only weeks old. The breath caught in my throat. 'You may already know that Dr Taylor and Dr Jenkins have begun a new vaccination program in the village, and I've noticed that your children haven't been vaccinated for smallpox. Have you thought about getting them done when you vaccinate your baby?'

Her face took on a wariness I'd come to know well. 'What for? We ain't seen smallpox here for years, and nobody can say if the vaccine stops the children from gettin' sick.'

I nodded. The last major smallpox epidemic the village had experienced had been about fifteen years ago and Dr Jenkins had explained that although much of Europe had suffered terribly, England's mortality rate from the disease had been three times lower because of compulsory vaccination. Some people thought that meant we were safe, but Ebberfield was changing and growing, no longer as isolated from the major cities as it had been, and any protection this might have given us in the past wouldn't guarantee our safety in the future.

'But it hasn't disappeared altogether,' I said gently. 'The doctors are willing to give vaccinations to children who haven't had them and the vaccination officer will waive any fines. Surely it's better to be safe and protected rather than hope we never get another epidemic?'

Mrs Morgan took hold of her son's hand. 'My children are strong and healthy.' She stared at me defiantly and I held her gaze for a moment before she looked away. 'But I'll think about it.'

9

I'm constantly fascinated by the way that nature is adaptable, changing to make the best of the surrounding conditions. Survival of the fittest seems to apply to all of the natural world, from the smallest insect or lichen to the largest tree and the most prolific animal of all, humans. Even the suffrage movement didn't gain momentum until conditions were right.

We visited the specialist in Durham a few weeks after Papa's birthday and his slip about Beth. Ironically, he'd been well since then, managing the pub as he always had.

'From what you've told me, you've made the right decision to come back and see me,' said Dr Sloane from behind his large mahogany desk. 'Often symptoms reduce once the patient is removed from the source of exposure, which can lead to a complete cure. But in your case, exposure to manganese poisoning has been protracted.' He looked quickly at his notes and then at Papa. 'You were an engine fitter in a shipyard?'

'That's right,' said Papa. 'Building engines for over forty years. What are my chances of recovery?' Mama grasped his hand.

'You've had a few good years but given your recent deterioration and your long exposure to manganese toxicity, I think your chances of recovery are quite low, unless we find a treatment, and even then it might only stop further decline.'

My breath caught in my throat as panic bloomed through my chest. 'What does that mean?' I asked, trying to remain calm.

Dr Sloane checked through Papa's files. 'Your father's experiencing all the hallmarks of this disease having progressed to the next stage: muscle rigidity; slow, stiff movement; tremors; forgetfulness; as well as mood swings and heightened emotions – much like Parkinson's disease, the shaking palsy.'

'But some days he's fine,' protested Mama.

The doctor nodded. 'That's a good sign. His deterioration may be slow, and as long as he's managing at home, there's little we can do.'

'Are you saying that there's *nothing* we can do?' I asked.

Dr Sloane steepled his fingers. 'We could try some hypnosis to calm the agitation, and belladonna to settle the tremors.'

I frowned. These were short-term fixes, not a solution.

'How much time do I have to live a normal life?' asked Papa.

'Nobody knows. It's still such a new disease and we don't know enough about it yet. Your symptoms will most likely progress until you find it difficult to move and dementia takes hold, but how quickly that will happen, it's impossible to tell. It could be months or it could be years.'

'You're telling me that my wife and daughter have to watch me decline until I become insane?' replied Papa, shaking his head with fury. 'I won't have that.'

'Who knows when a treatment will be found. There's always hope but I suggest you put your affairs in order while you're still well enough to, Mr Todd, and also that you nominate a stage when you know that you won't be able to manage at home and are becoming a burden on your family. That's the time for your wife to bring in additional care for you or for you to agree to be admitted to the Durham Asylum.'

'No!' said Mama, covering her mouth with her gloved hand. 'The lunatic asylum? Not that.'

Papa just looked stricken. I felt dizzy and wanted to vomit.

'I'm sorry to cause such distress, but I find it best to be realistic in these situations,' said the doctor. 'Psychiatric care has improved greatly in the last decade. Private care is costly and while there are a few private asylums and hospitals, they're expensive too and, in my opinion, don't offer superior care. The Durham Asylum is run by the county and has been recently extended and refurbished. It's a modern, caring service with excellent doctors that can best cater to your needs ... It's where I'd send someone I loved once I couldn't manage them at home. And rest assured, I do regular rounds at the asylum so I would continue to look after you.'

'The asylum?' whispered Papa.

'There's no other way?' I asked.

'I'm afraid not,' said Dr Sloane. 'Let's just hope it's a long time before you have to make that decision.'

*

The trip home was quiet, each of us caught up in our own thoughts.

It was no better when we got back to The Ox and Plough. Papa threw himself into the daily routine, Mama did the same and I somehow stumbled through each day with the spectre of Papa's future hovering at the edge of my mind. The only time I felt free was when I first woke in the morning. Those few moments when sleep fell away and I listened to Mama in the kitchen below me; the dustman collecting the ashes from the fireplaces; the delivery of coal to the house and the pub ... Then the horrible truth and Dr Sloane's words would come rushing back and my stomach would clench with grief and fear and what it meant for us all.

My days at school were spent in a daze. I tried to keep busy so I wouldn't think, but I couldn't help it, and thoughts of Papa's decline were inevitably followed by thoughts of my great plans slipping away. Clementine noticed I wasn't myself but I wasn't ready to tell her what had happened. She'd known something wasn't right since she'd seen Papa at the agricultural show but I had avoided the subject with her, maybe because I didn't want to accept Papa's illness myself.

'Are you coming to the winter dance tonight?' Roger asked one afternoon after the boys' football. I'd just returned from an excursion with the girls. 'David, Matthew and I are going.'

'No, I don't think so,' I said as we walked through the schoolyard.

Roger frowned, disappointment moving quickly across his face.

'I'm sorry,' I whispered.

'Is it me?' he asked quietly.

I stopped and grabbed his arm, turning to him. 'No, of course not. It's just ...' I tried to blink away the tears that were forming.

'Is it your father?'

I looked into his bright blue eyes and saw the genuine concern. I nodded. 'We went to see the specialist in Durham and it wasn't good news.'

He took my hand in his as if it was the most natural thing in the world. 'What happened?'

'I don't want to talk about it.' I pulled my hand away.

'Maybe it will make you feel better.'

'I don't know, Roger ... it's too painful, and complicated.'

'Then come to the dance. It will take your mind off your troubles at least for a little while ...'

I imagined laughing around the bonfire and twirling on the dancefloor, Roger in close proximity. Clementine would be at the dance, as would Laura and Benjamin Burnett and Marjorie and Edward Partridge. Maybe it would be good to have a little fun for a change. Missing out on the dance would do nothing to change Papa's health.

'All right,' I said finally. 'I'll see you there.'

*

I walked with Clementine and the Burnetts to the village green, clutching my shawl at my throat to ward off the cold evening air. As we reached the rise in the road, sounds of delight arose like birds taking flight. The green was spread below us, transformed into a wonderland. A large bonfire took pride of place in the centre and oil lanterns cast a golden glow around the two pavilions that had been erected, one for food and drinks, where people milled about the tables, and one for the dancefloor, where a quartet had set up. Papa had missed out on supplying drinks this time and he was expecting a quiet evening at The Ox and Plough. I wondered what the brewery representative, Mr Connolly, would say about that, and made a note to ask Bill to be at that meeting with Papa. And if he couldn't be there then I would be.

I pushed thoughts of Papa's illness from my mind; there'd be plenty of time to contemplate what came next. Soon I was talking and laughing with friends, neighbours and acquaintances, buoyed by cups of beer and partridge pie. I wasn't normally a beer drinker – I found it too bitter and preferred wine myself – but when in Rome …

'Do you know why we have the bonfire and winter dance?' Roger asked as we stood around the fire.

I shook my head.

'It's an old tradition that falls on the eve of All Souls' Day. In the old days, the herder would move the cows and sheep from the summer pastures to the safety and warmth of the stables, and animals were slaughtered for the table and the last of the harvest came in.'

'All ready for the winter.'

'So, we celebrate the successful summer and harvest, and welcome the coming of winter,' he said in my ear against the noise of the other conversations around the fire and the musicians beginning to play. His voice vibrated in my ear and sent hot and cold shivers through me.

'That's ... beautiful,' I managed to say.

He offered his arm. 'Ready for a little dancing?'

'Of course,' I said with a smile, shaking off the feeling.

Roger and I danced in a set with others, following the figure on the dancefloor. At first, I had to concentrate but, before long, I was stepping and twirling, faster and faster, like the locals who had known the dances all their lives.

'It's so much fun,' I shouted to Roger as I grasped his arm to dance with him again.

'And you weren't going to come,' he replied. 'Now I can't get you to stop.'

'Are you telling me you're tired? A big man like yourself?'

'Never,' he said in mock horror. 'I'll keep going as long as you do.'

'Keep up, then.' I nodded with a grin, accepting his challenge before spinning away again.

Finally, when there was a break in the music for the musicians to take their own refreshment, Roger put his hands up in defeat. 'I don't know how you do it, but I've had enough,' he said. 'I need sustenance.'

I laughed. 'Well, we'd better get you fed and watered before you give up the ghost.'

With beer in hand and the last of the pies, we wandered to the edge of the green to find a quiet place to eat.

'Tonight was wonderful,' I said, my cheeks still hot from dancing. 'Thank you for persuading me to come.'

'It was great to see you laughing,' he said, gently tracing the line of my cheek. 'You're beautiful when you laugh.'

I shivered at his touch, and his words. I'd never felt like this before; I didn't think I *could* feel like this. The pie was a heavy lump in my stomach now. 'Tonight, I just wanted to forget.'

'Then let me help you,' he said. 'I'll even get back on the dancefloor if it makes you laugh again.'

I shook my head. 'It won't change anything.'

'Then you'd better tell me about it.'

I gazed at him, realising that I trusted him, and that if anyone could help me, it might be Roger.

Taking a leap of faith, I told Roger about the visit to Papa's specialist.

'We knew Papa wasn't well but it was such a shock to hear the doctor tell us that there's no real treatment for it yet and that he's probably only going to get worse,' I said. My half-eaten pie lay discarded to one side. 'Nobody can tell us how long he has. I hope it's many years, but I just can't believe that when he can't manage any longer, the best place for him is—' I took a shuddering breath '—the asylum.'

'There's no other way?' Roger asked quietly.

I shook my head, tears filling my eyes. 'I can't imagine him there with all those poor disturbed souls. It doesn't seem right ... I can barely think about it.'

Roger took my hand. 'I'm so sorry, Hannah. What will you do now?'

'I don't know. We haven't spoken about it. I suppose each of us is thinking about the doctor's advice before we feel ready to talk about what comes next. You're the first person I've told. But once word spreads that he's sick ...'

'You can trust me. I won't say anything to anyone.'

I nodded. 'I knew you'd understand.'

'I'm about to start work on the extensions to the school, so I'm close by if you want to talk. And if you need extra help at the pub, I can come after work and stay through the evening.' He looked away and I knew what a big thing it was that he'd offered, not just his time and effort, but his friendship too.

'You'd do that?'

'I'm not experienced but I'm a quick learner and I'm sure your father or Bill can teach me anything I need to know. I remember when my father died, everything was so uncertain. The support of those around us helped us get back on our feet.'

I squeezed his hand. 'Thank you, Roger. Your offer means a lot.'

He gazed at me a moment, his blue eyes searching my face. 'Just remember, you're not alone.'

*

Speaking to Roger had been a comfort, and I was reminded again of the friendships I had made in Ebberfield. What I didn't express to Roger, deep from the selfish place in my heart, was that Papa's decline continued to delay my dream to work and live an independent life in the city, and throw my weight in earnest behind the suffragist movement. I could only hope that a cure would be found and Papa would be well again. There was no choice but to carry on so, in the meantime, I threw myself into what I could do in the country. We had signatures to collect for the petition.

After school on market day, Clementine and I found Esther outside the shops along the main street. A couple of women stood nearby, reading our pamphlets about the petition.

'How's it been going?' I asked.

'Good. There's been a steady stream of women taking pamphlets and many of them signing or promising to come to our next meeting.'

Dorothy Duggan stepped out of Mrs Scruton's tea shop. Dorothy was the local washerwoman and sometimes helped Mama and I out when we couldn't get all the linens done for the week. Today she carried a heavy bag, probably containing the soiled linens from the tea room. She smiled at us and Esther handed her a pamphlet and explained what we were doing.

'I already have three daughters who ain't got the same opportunities my two boys got. All me children oughta have a good future,' Dorothy said, patting her swollen belly. I noticed her hands were chapped and red from her work.

With great satisfaction, I showed her where to sign on the sheet. It was one thing for educated and middle-class women to get behind our cause but if Dorothy signed, then many women like her would think about signing too. But then I saw the purple bruises around her wrist and recognised the fading yellow marks on her neck, and my heart dropped. She was exactly the kind of woman who needed the vote, a woman who needed the power to protect herself.

I was handing her a nib pen when we heard an indignant voice call out, 'What's goin' on here? What *you* doin' with me wife?'

We turned to see a man nearly twice our age with a significant paunch striding towards us. Dorothy's husband, Fred Duggan, the brickmaker.

'Fred!' said Dorothy, smiling nervously. 'I was just comin'.'

'You know I don't like bein' kept waitin',' Fred Duggan growled. He ripped the pamphlet from her hand and looked at what it contained. 'What nonsense have these women been fillin' your head with?' he asked with disgust, scrunching the paper and throwing it onto the street.

'It's no nonsense,' Dorothy said, her voice quavering.

He looked at us for the first time and his eyes narrowed with suspicion. 'What you tryin' to get me wife to sign?'

'It's a petition to call for the vote for women,' I said. Fred didn't frequent The Ox and Plough, but I'd seen men like him before, in the pub and on the street, bellicose and full of hot air, and I wasn't going to be bullied.

He took a threatening step forward. 'Nobody asks for me wife's signature without *my* permission. Is that clear?'

The three of us stepped back, shocked at his display of aggression, and he smiled snidely.

'Fred!' Dorothy was pale with mortification.

He shoved her behind him and she stumbled, her bag of washing dropping to the ground as her arms wrapped around her belly to protect the baby.

'Women don't need no vote, all they need is to listen to their husbands.' He moved so quickly that I couldn't react before he snatched the papers out of my hands, throwing them to the ground. Esther cried out in dismay and darted out to pick them up.

'Is everything all right here?'

Roger placed himself between Fred and me. I breathed a sigh of relief. As much as I could handle myself, the situation had escalated quickly and sometimes men like this could be brought down quickest by another man ready to take action.

'These women oughta be taught a lesson, tryin' to turn another man's wife against him,' Fred snarled. His eyes were bulging and his face was red as a beet.

'Nobody's trying to do that,' said Esther hurriedly, returning the papers to me, but Fred just thrust out his chest.

'What kind of man threatens to lay a hand on women?' asked Roger. 'Why don't you pick on someone your own size?'

Esther slipped her hand into mine while Dorothy glanced wildly from her husband to us. I held my breath, worried about what was going to happen next. Fred would either back down or throw a punch. But Roger was younger and fitter by far and there was no doubt who would win a fist fight.

Fred shrugged. 'I only wanted to scare 'em anyway.' He glared at us. 'Leave me wife alone or I'll—'

'Or you'll what?' Roger drew up to his full height and towered over Fred, who stared at him with hatred. 'You'd better move along. And if I hear of you harassing these women again in any way, I'll report you to the police.'

'It's time we were goin' anyway.' Fred grabbed Dorothy's arm.

'I'm so sorry,' I whispered to her before he yanked her away. She shook her head slightly and lifted her chin. He might think he had Dorothy beaten but she still had some fight in her. I hated to think what he'd do to her in private, even though she was pregnant with his child.

'Are you all right?' Roger asked, looking around at us in turn.

'Just a little shaken, I think,' I said, touching his arm without thinking. 'Thank you, Roger. You defused a situation that could have become nasty.'

'It was lucky you were here when it happened,' said Clementine.

'I was going to the butcher on my way home. I received a bonus this week and I wanted to surprise my mother.'

Gratitude filled me. Roger was a good man, and a good friend to me. I was lucky to know him but I felt unsettled, even while my hand itched to touch him again in thanks. We'd been so close since the winter dance and it aroused feelings that wouldn't ease with time. I felt entirely compromised.

'That's lovely,' said Esther with a smile. 'Thank you for intervening, who knows what might have happened.'

'I'm sure your mother will enjoy her surprise,' said Clementine, not even a little abashed.

Roger doffed his cap. 'If you ladies don't mind, I'll keep going before the butcher closes.'

'I've heard things about Fred,' said Esther as we watched Roger walk away, 'but I've never seen anyone behave that way before. He's a brute. Poor Dorothy. She doesn't deserve this – and with a baby on the way.'

'No, she doesn't, but welcome to the real world,' said Clementine bitterly. I wondered what she'd seen or experienced in her past to be so cynical.

'Dorothy is friends with Mrs Scruton in the tea shop, isn't she?' I asked.

Esther nodded.

'Maybe we can tell her what happened and ask her to check on Dorothy,' I said, rearranging the petition sheets and preparing myself to approach ladies as they left the shops. There would always be men who were against what we were trying to achieve, but this was the first real instance of outright opposition. As much as I knew we had to rise above their negativity, even when we were rattled, I hadn't anticipated the consequences.

I wondered for a moment if we were doing the right thing, worried we'd made Dorothy's situation worse, and were putting women like her in danger. There was clearly much work we had to do to change the attitudes in our own village before we'd be accepted. I knew the only way forward was to secure the support of influential men in the township.

10

Since the changes in legislation that improved the status of women, it has been only ten years since married women have had independent and individual legal rights apart from their husbands and for the first time, the possibility of the vote. We are on the cusp of something even greater, I know.

It was early on a Saturday morning when I found her lying on the cobblestones of the alleyway next to The Ox and Plough, curled on her side like a sleeping child. But she wasn't a child. Nor was she sleeping. As I stepped closer, I heard her moan, a soft, low sound, as if she barely had the energy left to use her voice. She was covered in rags, no more than a bag of bones, a destitute girl who had made her way here, perhaps hoping for a warm meal and a place by the fire. My eyes narrowed in the thin light and I realised they weren't rags – her clothes were ripped and shredded. This was a girl in trouble.

I rushed to her side. 'It's all right,' I said soothingly. 'You're safe now.' I saw the thin shoulders shake and the girl began to cry. 'Let me help you up and get you inside.'

I dropped to my knees and went to turn her over, her groans more like whimpers. Blood came away on my hands, slick, dark and warm. 'You've been hurt,' I said alarmed. 'What happened to you?' I moved her carefully, looking for injuries in the early morning light.

'Please help me, Miss Todd,' she whispered. I stared in shock as she pushed herself up and leant against the wall of the building.

'Kitty! Oh Kitty!' My hand flew to my mouth. 'Your head is bleeding. Who did this to you?'

She shook her head. 'I was walking to work,' she pushed through swollen lips. 'Someone was following me ... I was scared. I tried to get to you at The Ox and Plough ... He punched me in the face. I fell and hit my head. And then ...' She looked down at her ruined dress and the scraps of fabric that was left of her drawers and began to cry.

*

I brought Kitty to the privacy of our cottage, bathed her, cleaned the gash on her head and bandaged it, gave her one of my old dresses and hot, sugared tea. Now she slept in my bed as Clementine and I sat in the parlour, discussing what to do.

'She won't tell her family she was raped,' agreed Clementine, as I wiped the tears from my eyes. Only once Kitty was settled could I let my true feelings show. 'She's scared stiff of her father.' Clementine knew the family as well as I did, a very traditional Roman Catholic family.

'She came to me for help and protection. So close and I didn't know what was happening outside these walls.' I dropped my face in my hands, devastated. 'Why did he prey on her? She's only fourteen. Her life is already hard and she has enough problems with her family's circumstances as it is.' I felt sick to my stomach.

'She's young, naive and vulnerable – the perfect target,' said Clementine, clenching her fists.

'She won't say who it was.' I shook my head in frustration. 'I know she's afraid but it could be anyone; a vagrant, a farmer or husband, a stupid boy ... A drunk.'

'Someone who likes the power he has over women,' said Clementine abruptly. She seemed cold, but I knew her well enough to know that she was holding in a steely rage.

I thought about Fred Duggan and men like him, wife beaters who despised women who spoke up for the truth. Could it have been him? Getting to me and the suffrage society through Kitty? Or perhaps the brewery spy, prepared to cause chaos and terror. Surely not. I shook my head. It did no good to speculate. We had to focus on Kitty. I glanced towards the stairs and reassuring quiet of the bedrooms. 'What can we do to help her now?'

'We talk to Esther's mother. With her position in the church aid society, she's seen this too many times to count. She'll know what to do.'

'I'm glad we have someone like her with real-life experience to call on. And now more than ever, we have to push on to get our petition to Parliament. If men believe they can continue to terrorise women in this village, they'd better think again,' I said grimly, my resolve hardened. The image of Kitty curled and broken on the cobblestones was burned in my brain. There was no more wavering in my purpose. Only when women had the vote, could they speak up and change the laws that affected them, especially the *Child Protection Act* and the *Criminal Law Amendment Act* protecting women and girls. Only when women were empowered would men really take notice.

November, 1893

My dearest Hannah,
We are all very well here. I'm sorry it's taken me so long to reply to your letter. George is doing the books from the butcher shop now and he's turned our house upside

down, moving all my correspondence. I lost your letter and only found it again recently. Forgive me.

I was delighted to read about the wonderful celebrations at your school for the royal wedding of Prince George and Princess Mary. I laughed aloud when you described how the children came in paper crowns or bedsheets as bridal trains! It was a sobering thought that a few children dressed in all black as our beloved Queen Victoria. To think that she's still mourning the loss of Prince Albert, thirty years after his death. It must have been a special love.

I wish I'd been there to see it all. But how lovely that you and the ladies of the suffrage society were able to treat the children to a special afternoon tea afterwards at the pub. I'm sure Mama and Papa were thrilled to see the mites so happy.

It seems to me that you are happy and fulfilled yourself. Perhaps Ebberfield has grown on you, as much as you have grown on the people of the village.

Your loving sister,

Mary

'How's Kitty?' asked Marjorie before our next suffrage meeting. It had been a month since she'd been attacked and word had spread quickly among the women of the village.

'Mama says that her injuries are healing,' said Esther.

'That's a relief,' said Marjorie. 'I can only imagine how hard it's been for her and her family.'

I nodded. 'Rory's been very quiet at school and the children can't wait until she's back at the breakfast club.'

Mrs Scruton shook her head sadly. 'She ain't comin' back any time soon.'

'What are you talking about?' I asked.

'You ain't heard? The poor pet's pregnant.' I closed my eyes briefly and exhaled. Poor Kitty had everything against her.

'How come you're always the first one to know?' asked Amelia Brown.

Mrs Scruton shrugged. 'Keep me ear to the ground. Gotta know these things.'

All eyes turned back to Esther. 'Kitty's parents threw her out,' she said quietly. 'She'd only told them she was beaten but when she was forced to tell them the truth, her father blamed her.'

'As if *she'd* brought it on herself?' replied Amelia, incredulous.

'She came to Mama, with nowhere else to go: destitute, no one to support her and no roof over her head.'

Laura frowned. 'But she's only a child. How can they abandon her?'

'An extra mouth to feed, no extra income and the shame of going against the church,' said Clementine grimly.

'Mama sent her away somewhere she can have the baby in relative safety.'

Mrs Scruton laughed bitterly. 'To hide her dirty little secret, you mean? No disrespect to your mother, her hands are tied, but the church won't want her here, showin' off her sinful fruit, or spreadin' fear about a rapist in the village, most likely a church-goin' man. Gotta shut her up and uphold the respectable reputation of this town.' Mrs Scruton was a widow and known for speaking her mind, especially since her husband had passed.

Esther nodded grimly. 'Mama's doing her best. There's nowhere else for her to go except the workhouse.'

'My cousin's daughter went to the workhouse and it was horrible. Brutal, like a prison. Her baby died there,' said

Amelia softly, shuddering at the memory and I shivered in response.

'What will happen to Kitty?' I asked.

'If her parents take her back, it'll be without the babe,' said Mrs Scruton. 'She'll have to give it up to a foundlin' hospital. And if not, find respectable work and lodgin's on her own, place the babe in a baby farm for a small payment each week, otherwise it'll be the workhouse for 'em both.'

'A baby farm?' asked Esther.

'A place where babes are looked after, but notorious for bein' overcrowded and for neglect. You ain't seen the newspapers?' We shook our heads. 'Some women who adopted babes for payment in these places have been executed for infanticide, neglectin' or killin' 'em to make way for new babes.'

I stiffened, horrified. 'Poor Kitty.' She had no control over her fate at all. I felt helpless, the horror of her future colliding with the horror of finding her in the alleyway. Nobody deserved this.

'Isn't there anything we can do?' asked Laura. I knew she was thinking about her own little girls.

'Not for Kitty,' said Clementine, harshly. 'As women, we bear the brunt of life's difficulties, while men, often the cause of our troubles, live with a freedom we can only imagine.'

'So, we tell the women of the suffrage society what happened to Kitty,' said Mrs Scruton. 'Tell 'em to watch their granddaughters, daughters and sisters. Tell 'em to look out for trouble and to talk among themselves. The man who did it is still out there, livin' his life, not a thought for the girl who he destroyed, and he'll do it again, just like the others out there, until we join together and say, "*no more*".'

'I agree,' said Marjorie. 'We're supposed to keep quiet about any violence against our kind, hidden behind power and closed doors. Women have to feel they can talk about it.'

'We have to bring crimes like this out of the darkness and into the light for anything to change,' I said fiercely. 'And we have to keep fighting for the power to protect ourselves. For Kitty, for Dorothy and for all women.'

11

According to the newspapers, infanticide is a very
real problem, with reports of illegitimate babies being
smothered by their own mothers after their birth and
the tiny bodies hidden or disposed of. It's horrific and
unthinkable. Baby farming is despicable enough to
imagine but this is the desperate act of a desperate
woman who has no other place to turn.

November, 1893

Dear Sarah,
I know you've already vaccinated baby Arthur for
smallpox, but I remembered you telling me that many of
the mining families don't see the need for vaccination.
I know how strongly you feel about this issue, like me,
and I felt compelled to write to you, to tell you about our
vaccination program.

   Perhaps you might like to share the enclosed
education pamphlets with other new parents in Trimdon
and see if you have some luck convincing them that
vaccination is essential? The idea of children dying from
something they could have been protected from makes
my blood chill.

   Jenny has been helping Clementine and me with
the literacy classes we're running once a week with the
newspapers, magazines and books that Mr Jones has

kindly provided from the reading room of the Recreational Club. And she's excited to attend the lectures that start soon on a number of popular subjects, like science and history, as well as more practical classes on business and bookkeeping. We have visiting speakers once a month, too, thanks to the help of the Women's Education Union and the involvement of the Durham School of Arts and Science.

Thank you for allowing her to stay with us. She's a great help to Mama and Papa and she and I are as close as sisters—

'Hannah!' I heard Bill call urgently. I was finishing off my letter at the bar while he and Papa were seeing out the brewery representative, Mr Connolly, after their meeting. I looked up to find Bill supporting Papa as he walked across the room. I rushed to help him.

'Not here,' Bill whispered. 'In the kitchen.' He noticed a few old regulars in the bar and said to them, 'He's all right. He just turned his ankle.'

Mama was kneading dough on the bench. She took one look at us helping Papa, wiped her hands on her apron and hurried to his side. 'Come, my love, sit by the window and I'll make you a cup of tea.'

Papa sighed once we had him sitting at the table in the kitchen. 'Thank you, Bill. I wouldn't have managed without you.'

'It's all right,' he said, resting his hand on Papa's shoulder.

It was then that I realised that Papa was trembling. 'What happened?' I asked.

'His legs seized up after Connolly left and he couldn't walk,' said Bill.

Papa waved a shaking hand, as though leg spasms and the pain they caused were nothing. 'The brewery's upset we weren't selling at the winter dance, but there was nothing I could do. The Hare's Foot must have better contacts on the dance committee. I'll have to work harder on my contacts. They want me to make up for it by taking more beer this month, but if we don't use the barrels we have in three days, they'll go stale.' I felt sure that this stress was the cause of Papa's relapse.

'Connolly made it clear that if we can't increase business the brewery will turn its favour on The Black Bull,' Papa continued, stricken. 'Nobody can know about my condition, especially now. If our customers or the brewery find out, they'll abandon us.'

I stared at Papa in shock. Surely not, but then my gaze slid across to Bill and his grim expression told me that it was possible. My chest fluttered; we would be destitute if we lost The Ox and Plough.

'Then we're going to need another barman,' said Bill slowly. 'Someone we can trust implicitly and can call on to do extra hours when you're not well.'

'As tight as things are, I think you're right,' said Papa. 'Do you have anyone in mind?'

'I do,' I said. 'Roger Rainforth.'

I explained my connection to Roger through Anthony and football and told them that he knew about Papa's condition. When I was finished, I held my breath, waiting for a response. I was nervous – would Papa be angry I'd told someone about his illness? My heart was beating nearly out of my chest, and I realised I was willing Papa to say yes to Roger. I knew I wouldn't have felt this way if I'd been talking about any of my other friends.

Bill nodded. 'He's from a good family, a trustworthy lad. I think he's a good choice.'

'Then go and speak to him,' said Papa, 'because I can't guarantee what my condition will do next.'

I let go of my breath. Roger would be Papa's support, but he'd be here for me too.

Roger came straight to the pub and after Bill and Papa had explained the basic workings behind the bar he was ready to work. As the evening progressed, I was glad to see that he was managing to serve the increasingly busy bar area. When Papa was satisfied that Roger would be fine, he went home to Mama to spend the night resting, the first time I'd seen him do that in all the years he'd been the publican.

'You did well today, Roger,' said Bill when we finally closed the doors.

'I'm glad to help,' said Roger.

'Yes, thank you, Roger,' I said, as I wiped the bar down after collecting the last glasses. 'You really got us out of a difficult situation.'

'How is he?' asked Roger.

'Better than he was earlier. Mama's sitting with him.'

He nodded. 'I can come in if you need me in the evenings or after work on Saturdays, and all day Sunday.'

'I'll work out a schedule and let you know. Welcome to The Ox and Plough,' Bill said, extending his hand.

*

The pub was mercifully quiet for a Saturday morning and Clementine, Esther, Laura and I were the only ones in the upstairs meeting rooms.

'The breakfast and lunch club is doing well,' I said as we went over the figures. 'We have consistent numbers, usually the same children each week, and the other teachers are reporting that the children are more attentive in class – and happier.' Any mention of the breakfast club inevitably brought thoughts of Kitty. I couldn't reconcile what had happened with my memory of the smiling girl who had helped the children.

'Edward has invested enough to buy supplies for three months for up to double the number of students,' said Laura, checking her notes.

I nodded. 'We might just need that. With the cold weather setting in, and so many families without work at this time of year, there'll be more children in need. Thank goodness the clothing drive has brought in warm clothing and boots, otherwise we'd lose them until the spring.'

'Let's talk about the petition,' Clementine said. 'How can we reach more people?'

'We organise members to stand outside the hospital and workhouse towards the end of the shifts,' I replied. 'And outside the shops where women work: the grocers, drapers, post office.'

'Especially during the cattle fair,' said Esther. 'Everyone in the district comes into the village whether they're buying and selling livestock or not.'

'Let me write this all down,' said Laura, scribbling furiously.

I nodded. 'That's good. I've also been thinking that we've been lucky so far gathering signatures, but the more we canvass, the more push-back we'll get. If we could persuade Edward to come to meetings or even become a member, it could really boost the petition. We need community leaders, the men.'

'It will be difficult to get them on side,' said Clementine.

I stared at the fire crackling in the fireplace. Then it came to me. I turned back to the others, fizzing with excitement.

'I've got it! We write to the National Society and ask for a high-profile speaker to come and talk at our next meeting – maybe Alice Scatcherd, Elizabeth Clarke Wolstenholme-Elmy or even Clara Curtis Lucas. If our men need more persuasion, we can organise an MP who supports women's suffrage to come and speak as well—'

'Damnation!' The sound of Papa's raised voice coming from the office interrupted our conversation.

'Excuse me a moment. I'll go and see if everything's all right.'

I avoided the gaze of my friends and rushed to the back room where Papa sat at his desk, shuffling through loose papers. 'What are you doing, Papa?' I asked gently.

'I can't find the paperwork for last month's delivery.'

'What do you need it for?'

'I want to check how much beer and soft drink we ordered against this month's delivery. Market day was busier than expected and I might need to order more. I have to keep an eye on what the brewery wants me to sell this month.'

'Here, let me help you look.' I searched through the pile of papers where the paperwork was supposed to be while Papa continued to frantically riffle through the contents of his desk.

'Here it is,' I said, waving the document in my hand before putting it in front of Papa.

'Thank you, my angel,' he said softly. He glanced over the page then at the mess on his desk with dismay. 'I'm sorry. I'm just not myself.'

'It's all right, Papa.' I kissed him on the cheek. 'I don't mind. Just tell me where you want things and I'll write down where I've put them, so that you can find them next time.'

'You're a good girl. I'm lucky to have you and your mother to look after me as well as you do. But I don't want you to waste your life caring for an old man.'

'Don't be silly, Papa. I love spending time with you.'

Papa smiled. 'Like the doctor said, there will come a time when I become too much for you and your mother. I will *not* become a burden. The pub will be enough work for the both of you to manage without me as well.'

My belly clenched at his words. 'We'll get some help. And we'll find a way to stay together, Papa. I won't let you go.' I hugged him tight, sudden tears slipping down my cheeks.

He took my face in his hands and kissed my forehead. 'Let me check the statements and we can tidy the papers later. But we must sit down with your mother sometime soon and make plans for the future. All right?'

I nodded. 'We'll cope, Papa.'

'I know we will, my darling.' He held me tight, just as he had when I was a child and for a moment I felt comforted by his embrace.

I had barely composed myself by the time I returned to the meeting room and I knew my eyes were red from crying.

'Hannah, are you all right?' asked Esther. 'What's happened?'

I slumped in the chair. In a low voice, I told them about Papa's illness and how the future was so uncertain.

They stared at me, horrified.

'What can we do to help?' asked Esther.

'Just talking to you is enough.'

'I knew there was something wrong. Why did you wait so long to tell us? You must be going through hell,' said Clementine.

'I thought that if I didn't mention it, I could avoid it becoming real and wouldn't have to deal with it. But I was wrong. I can't do this on my own.' I squeezed Esther's and Clementine's hands and Laura kissed me on the head.

'We're here for each other. That's what friends are for,' whispered Esther.

Feeling surrounded by love, I let the tears fall. I was lucky to have such kind and strong women in my life.

*

Later that evening, Roger came into the kitchen.

'Bill hasn't had dinner,' he said. 'It's been too busy for him to stop. But I thought I'd come and ask if you have any spare pies or a mutton sandwich.'

I nodded and went to the pantry. Roger followed. 'Have you eaten?'

He shook his head.

I pulled out a couple of pies, a leftover joint of mutton, the crock of butter and half a loaf of bread. 'This is all we have. Sit and have something,' I said, gesturing to the kitchen table, 'and then you can send Bill in.'

I smiled to see Roger sit obediently and passed him one of the pies on a plate.

'Bill's been acting a little strangely tonight,' mumbled Roger as he took a big bite of the pie.

'What do you mean?' I asked.

'It's like he's looking for someone.'

I nodded. 'We think the brewery has sent a man to spy on us.'

'What are you talking about?'

I told Roger about our suspicions while I made mutton sandwiches for him and Bill. 'If we don't find out who it is, I'm afraid it will push Papa too far and make him really sick. He could lose his licence, and we'd lose this place, and then ...' I couldn't say it.

'I had no idea.' Roger sat stunned, the pie unfinished on his plate. 'The brewery can't do this.'

'But they can. It's in the contract, which stipulates that the brewery has exclusive rights to supply us with all their products. They'll use whatever means necessary to get us to buy more beer and soft drink from them.'

He sat for a moment, staring into the smouldering fire. 'We have to find who it is.'

'You'll help us?'

'Of course. Your father is the best publican this town has. We can't lose him.'

'Thank you, Roger. Your help means so much.'

He smiled. 'It's what any decent man would do.' The look in his eyes changed as he gazed at me. 'But I'm not just any man, am I?'

A tugging deep in my belly made me want to move even closer to him. I didn't know what to say for a moment. 'No, you're my friend.'

'I am.'

He leant closer, so that I could feel the warmth of his body, and laid his hand gently on my cheek. The touch of his thumb tracing my cheekbone was featherlight, but somehow it made my skin tingle. I felt breathless and my heart raced, like I was standing on the edge of a cliff. Part of me was terrified of falling but another part yearned for the exhilaration of flying like a bird.

12

December, 1893

Dearest Mary,

I can't believe Millicent Fawcett is coming to this month's meeting of our suffrage society! She's the most wonderful drawcard of all. I never dared hope that the president of the Special Appeals Committee would come all this way from London.

Some of the most influential men in town have agreed to attend. I hope the talk encourages them to become members of our society, especially since Dr Jenkins, Benjamin Burnett, Papa, Mr Hewitt and Mrs Scruton's brother, the grocer, have already joined.

Papa and Mama have been a wonderful support and reminded me that I have a lot to be proud of already with what I've achieved here in Ebberfield, for the children and the vaccination program. I just see what ordinary families go through and how they live their lives from day to day and want to make things better. I felt myself tear up when Papa told me I was a woman of action and courage, just like Mrs Fawcett.

I was almost too nervous to speak when Mrs Fawcett arrived. I wiped my clammy hands surreptitiously on the skirt of my good dress before shaking her hand.

'Thank you for coming to Ebberfield, Mrs Fawcett,' I said, my heart beating hard in my chest.

'It's my pleasure, Miss Todd,' she replied with a smile that reached her eyes. She was older than my sisters and smaller than I remembered but looked crisp and composed after her long journey, immaculate in her dark dress and her hair braided and coiled on the back of her head. 'I always enjoy speaking to the smaller societies in the rural districts. It's much more intimate and personal.'

'Well, it will certainly be that. I first heard you speak about four years ago at a rally in Durham when I was at teachers' college. I've never forgotten how you said that the most important protection a woman could have was the power to protect herself. It really inspired me and made me think about the suffrage movement in a new way.'

'I remember that rally. Lydia Becker and I were speakers and we had a bigger crowd than we expected.' She glanced towards the meeting room, which was filling quickly. 'I believe that this society is in its infancy?'

I nodded. 'We've had some good initial interest but because of your visit, we have many people from the village and surrounding district attending today. I only hope that we can convert their interest to signatures on the page.' I noticed Clementine, Laura and Esther approaching us. 'Let me introduce you to the society's executive before you begin.'

As we stepped into the meeting room, all eyes turned to Mrs Fawcett and a murmur of excitement rose. After I'd introduced her and she began to speak, the room was immediately silent.

She was warm and engaging, speaking with clarity to the needs of every generation and every class. She used personal experience and stories like her stolen purse being returned as the property of her husband to explain the reason women should expect and strive for equality in the laws that governed us. Through the impressive campaigns she and the suffrage society had already supported, which had seen changes to legislation in protecting children from abuse, legal and parenting rights for married women, the rights of women suspected of prostitution, and elementary education, it was clear she understood the complicated machinations of the parliamentary process.

But it was her clear and shining passion about achieving the parliamentary vote for women through democratic means that was most thrilling and her audience was enthralled. She was logical, practical and patient, and in a community like ours, it was a winning combination. I could already tell we'd be adding more signatures to our petition and I was sure the society would soon count most of those gathered as part of its membership.

*

'My daughter Hannah's involved in the suffrage society and is looking for signatures for a petition,' I heard Papa tell the men at the bar as I checked to see if there were any drinks to take to the lounge. Moving between the areas always gave me a good chance to scan the rooms for any odd behaviour. Roger, Bill and I were united in our attempts to find the brewery spy and we'd thrown around a few names but discarded them just as quickly.

'What kind of petition?' asked Mr Bailey, the manager of the quarry.

'A petition to allow the vote for women,' said Papa, pulling a beer.

I hung back a little, waiting to see what reaction he'd get. Roger was down the other end with Bill, both of them busy.

Roger's dark, curly hair fell across his eyes from time to time and he pushed it out of his face with his forearm while he concentrated on pulling the perfect beer, just as Bill had taught him. The gesture was endearing and made me smile.

'Why do women need the vote?' asked one of the farmers from out of town. 'Plenty of men still can't vote, why should women have it?'

'A woman wouldn't know what to vote for unless her husband told her, so it's pointless,' said another man, slurring his words.

'That's not true,' said Papa. 'Would you agree that women know what's best for their children and their education, whether their child needs the doctor?'

The men nodded slowly. 'I suppose so,' said Mr Bailey.

'Then surely it stands to reason that women could know so much more. Look at my daughter Hannah, she's a teacher and is as smart as the smartest men in this pub.'

The men grunted in assent. 'I'll agree with that,' said Benjamin, coming to the bar. 'Sometimes I think she's smarter than me.'

I blushed at the praise.

'Will you sign the suffrage petition, Benjamin?' asked Papa. 'Show the men how important it is to put our support behind the women's cause?'

Benjamin smiled. 'I already have. Laura made a very good argument: that I have to do what I can to give my daughters a better future.'

'See?' said Papa, handing Benjamin a pint of beer. 'Think about your daughters and granddaughters, gents, if not your wives. Supporting the suffrage cause will give them a future where they have the education to get better jobs and help support their families. Nobody wants their children stuck in the kinds of work and conditions we've had to put up with.

It affects us all in some way, in the end. The vote for women is one way to make our lives better, and certainly for our children and grandchildren.'

'What about you, William?' asked Mr Bailey. 'Have you signed the petition?'

Papa nodded and pointed to the sheet on the bar. 'I have, right here. Now it's your turn, gents. Help me support my beautiful Hannah in this month of Christmas. It's a time for giving and sharing and what better gift than the support of our community.'

'All right, William,' said Mr Bailey. 'Give me a pen.'

I'd had to walk away, to the privacy of the kitchen for a few moments, dabbing my eyes with my apron, I was so overcome with emotion. Papa was my greatest supporter.

*

A letter arrived from Millicent Fawcett and the Appeals Committee a few days before Christmas, and I couldn't wait to share the news with Clementine, Esther and Laura. The following evening, we sat around the table in Mama's parlour with a pot of tea and biscuits, away from the noise of the pub. Festivity was in the air, with our tree and decorations and musicians playing in the lounge each night. It was good to sit and have a quiet conversation with my friends next to the warmth of the crackling fire.

I read Millicent's letter aloud while Clementine poured the tea.

> I wanted to say how much I enjoyed meeting you and
> speaking to your suffrage society. Your village was so
> warm and welcoming and I still can't stop thinking about
> your mother's lemon cake. Perhaps you could do me the

honour of sending me the recipe? It warmed my heart
to meet your committee and to see that you're all bright
young women who are passionate about making your
community a better place. I must say, I look forward to
visiting you again, to see how you're faring and of course
to sample your wonderful hospitality.

'Send her the recipe and she'll never make it back here,' said
Laura.

'Send her the recipe and your mother's lemon cake will
soon be the toast of London!' said Esther, laughing.

'Maybe that's how you make your fortune: write a recipe
and cookery book like Mrs Beeton's,' added Clementine.

'All right, very funny.' I was touched by Millicent's personal
message and I would send her the recipe if it meant more
correspondence with her. 'She's already promised to come
and visit us again. But listen to what she has to say about the
petition:

The second reason I'm writing is to inform you that we've
decided to present our petition and signatures with the
Registration Bill to Parliament. This Registration Bill has
now been tabled and includes an amendment for the
enfranchisement for women. We feel that this is our
best chance of showing the groundswell of support for
women's suffrage to voting MPs, with the hope that it
will encourage them to pass this bill. Our Special Appeals
Committee has designated 21 March, 1894, as the deadline
to forward signatures to our office. There we'll compile all
the signatures from across the country into volumes to be
displayed in the library of the House of Commons, ahead
of the first reading of the bill.

'Can you believe that we're involved in such a historic milestone?' I added, a little breathlessly. 'Imagine if we can get the same concessions that men received in their Third Reform Bill. We're going to have the vote sooner than we thought!'

'That's assuming all the items on the amendment are passed,' said Clementine, always practical. 'You know how slippery these MPs can be. They can never really understand our frustration when all they've ever known is power and the ability to exercise it.'

'But this time it will be different. These signatures *have* to make them take notice.' I clasped the letter to my chest, my body tingling with excitement. 'There's never been a pulling together of women all wanting the same thing at a national level. Surely they can't deny us any longer?'

*

It was Christmas Day. Mama had insisted that we spend Christmas lunch at home with Papa. Mary and George and their two boys were coming from Hartlepool, and Sarah and Reg and their family from Trimdon. Jane and Bert and their children had already travelled up from Yorkshire, arriving late on Christmas Eve.

I smiled at the squeals of Jane's children as they discovered the stockings filled with small toys that Father Christmas had left for them overnight. At the other end of the table, Papa lifted the three older children onto his lap as they showed him their presents.

'We miss so much with you living in Yorkshire,' said Mama wistfully. 'The children grow too fast.'

'Bert and I have been talking,' said Jane softly, dipping her toast into a soft-boiled egg. 'Since you wrote about Papa's visit to the specialist ...' her eyes began to fill with tears '... we're thinking about moving back to Hartlepool. We have Mary and Bert's uncle Henry there to help us with the children if need be, until we get on our feet.' She rested her hand on her belly. 'I want the children to spend as much time as possible with Papa and I want him to know this little one too.' She blinked the tears from her eyes.

Mama squeezed Jane's hand. 'God willing we'll all have plenty of time with him still. Now, you finish your breakfast and spend some time with your father. Hannah and I have a few things to do before Sarah and Mary arrive.'

My sisters and their families arrived after we returned from church and the relative quiet of only four children became the shrieks and screams of happy cousins reacquainting, their hugs and chatter bringing a smile to all our faces. They were overjoyed to see their beloved grandfather, who always told great stories and kept hidden little treats and surprises for each of them. When they were hungry, they could turn to their grandmother, who always baked their favourite cakes and sweets. And when all the excitement became too much, they could seek refuge in the arms of their loving aunts.

Jenny had made beautiful placemats and Christmas crackers for us, but soon our focus was on the food that burdened the dining table. Papa carved the Christmas turkey, relishing the performance and drama of being the benevolent head of his large and growing family. But soon the children had finished eating and were restless.

'I think I hear something in the parlour,' I said loudly. 'I wonder if Father Christmas has been.'

The children didn't have to be told twice and raced to the parlour.

'He came!' squealed Isabella, Sarah's five-year-old, rushing to the tree. Underneath sat parcels of all shapes and sizes.

Mama and I had scrimped and saved for months to purchase the perfect gift for each of the children.

Papa presided over the opening of presents soon after, helping the smaller children with their wooden trains and spinning tops while the adults sat sipping punch. The floor of the parlour was littered with wrapping paper but nobody minded the mess.

'Time for dessert,' said Mama when Isabella had opened the last present and shown everyone her new doll. 'Plum pudding, and then we can open the Christmas crackers!'

After dessert, we retired to the parlour. Sarah, Mary and their husbands were out walking, showing Jane and Bert around the village. I'd offered to stay behind and look after the children while Jenny helped Mama tidy up in the kitchen. When everyone was back, we'd sing Christmas carols and play cards and parlour games.

'That's enough now,' said Papa irritably to the five small children trying to climb onto his lap and pester him for another story.

'All right, let's give Grandpa a little break,' I said, shooing them out of the room. 'Go and see if Grandma has any sugar biscuits for you in the kitchen.'

Papa shook his head. 'I can't do it like I used to. I used to be able to spend all day with the children, but now ...' He shrugged helplessly.

'You're in the middle of our busiest time of the year. Don't be so hard on yourself,' I said, moving toys and books from under his feet.

Papa grasped my arm. 'No, it's not that, and you know it. Hannah, I want to teach you how to do the books and look after the business side of things.'

My stomach dropped. 'Papa, please don't worry about that today. Today is for happiness and family.' I didn't want to think about what was ahead. 'Why don't you have a nap until the others get back?' I suggested, avoiding his eyes and reaching for the folded blanket on the arm of the lounge.

He sighed and nodded. 'Just ten minutes. I can barely keep my eyes open.'

I told myself that it was natural that he was tired. It had been a long week. But his words echoed in my mind and uneasiness swirled in my belly.

13

I found an unusually shaped piece of stone on my walk
today. It resembles a blade with thin, sharp edges, a
pointed tip and even hollows to hold it comfortably.
Darwin's *The Descent of Man* suggested that humans had
evolved over time, just as the rest of the natural world and
I wondered if this was an ancient tool made and used by
early humans. Any evidence of our distant past proves
that change comes to all of us eventually.

As I opened the gate behind The Ox and Plough to the rectory
fields, I heard him.

'Hannah!'

I'd enjoyed Christmas with my family, but I couldn't stop
thinking about Roger. On New Year's Day, The Ox and
Plough hosted the Mummers play, a traditional comic play
featuring St George, a duel and the reviving of the loser by a
doctor, representing the end of the old year and the beginning
of the new.

Thankfully Papa was back to his old self and the pub was
full to overflowing, yet I felt Roger's eyes on me whenever we
were in the same room. I'd turn or look up and his intense
gaze connected with mine, and it seemed as though the
hubbub of the crowd fell silent, almost as if it was just the
two of us, alone. I couldn't help but smile or blush; he made
me feel breathless and I couldn't concentrate on my work or
engage with the customers as I usually did. There were a few

times when Mama had to yell at me in exasperation when I'd forgotten to take an order out.

I turned slowly, not sure of myself, and waited for him. There was strength and vigour in his movements, a coiled power in the way he strode towards me. I could see the fire within him, the same fire that burned within me.

'I come here sometimes to think,' I said as we walked along the hedgerow. 'I know I'm not supposed to but it's quiet and I'm not disturbing anyone.'

'If you need time to yourself, I'll take my leave,' he said quietly.

I shook my head, looking up at the naked branches of the ash and elder trees, delicate against the grey sky. When I looked back into his face I saw the yearning in his eyes. We were alone, no one could see us behind the screen of bushes and trees. He was so close. But even though I couldn't forget how the touch of his thumb on my skin had made me feel when last we were alone, I hesitated. I couldn't let this go any further.

But then he dipped his head and brushed my lips with his. They were soft and warm, and it felt so right. I stepped into his embrace and sighed. He kissed me again and this time the kiss lingered, awakening my body with new sensations too strong to ignore. I didn't want to think anymore. I was tired of the biting worry and constant uncertainty with Papa. I surrendered to my body's instincts, wrapped my arms around his neck, and kissed him back. There was no place I'd rather be in that moment.

When we broke away, I stared at him, breathing hard. I'd never kissed a man before. I had never *wanted* to kiss a man before. And the reality of Roger's kiss far outweighed what I had imagined it could be.

'I've wanted to kiss you since the day I met you in Anthony's classroom,' he whispered.

'That was so long ago,' I whispered in return.

Roger nodded, brushing loose strands of hair from my face and tucking them behind my ear. 'It was. I was waiting for the right time and this wasn't how I'd planned it, but I couldn't help myself. Having you so close and you're so beautiful ... Do you mind?'

'I'm still here.' I smiled and reached for his hand. 'I don't know that I would have had the courage to kiss you first but when you kissed me, it felt right.'

He pulled me to him. 'So, you wanted to kiss me too,' he said against my ear, his voice a low rumble, sending barbs of pleasure along the surface of my skin. I sighed, allowing my head to drift back. 'Would you like to do it again?'

I nodded, unable to speak.

This time there was a sense of urgency behind the kiss. My body was pressed against Roger's firm chest, his hands cradling my back and head, but still I felt like I might melt onto the ground. Somehow my body had erupted into flame from the inside out and I never wanted the moment to end—

'We should stop,' he muttered roughly, drawing back. 'Before we get carried away.'

I stared at him a moment, confused. But then the reality of where we were and what we were doing began to seep through. My reputation could be ruined if anyone knew what we were doing, even though it was harmless right now. For the first time, I began to understand how easy it could be to end up doing something that couldn't be taken back. A woman was supposed to be chaste until her wedding day.

But what did that mean for me when I didn't want to marry?

I stepped away, my cheeks flaming with embarrassment. 'I didn't mean—'

Roger caught my arm. 'I know. Neither did I. But I think …
I know I have feelings for you.'

My eyes widened in surprise.

'What do you say to us beginning to court?' He put his
arms around me and kissed me on the forehead. 'I don't want
to lose you because I was too impatient.'

He had feelings for me. He wanted to court me. Where
would this lead? As suddenly as I'd felt the fire in me, now
it felt as if a pane of glass had slid between us, and I could
inspect what was happening. I didn't want to marry, I never
had. I never wanted to be controlled by the institution,
never wanted to be told that I couldn't continue to teach
because I was a married woman. Teaching was my life. And
remaining single and living under my father's roof gave me
the ability to develop the suffrage society. Being married
meant answering to a husband and all the inequalities
that came with that, and being tied up looking after a
household. Inevitably it meant babies and children; having
no independent income if I couldn't teach. I couldn't do
that. I wouldn't do that.

But I liked Roger's kisses. I could still feel the touch of his
lips on mine. I wanted more, and maybe even what came
after the kisses. I wasn't sure I wanted to be chaste all my
life anymore, never knowing the joys of a relationship with a
man.

For the first time, new thoughts and possibilities entered
my mind, making me shiver with their audacity. But unlike
some of the girls at teachers' college who had whispered about
their trysts, I didn't think I had the courage to deliberately
step over that invisible line and risk pregnancy. A baby would
destroy every dream I'd ever had for my future. No, I'd rather
be content with those two kisses.

I looked into Roger's bright blue eyes and touched his cheek, rough with stubble, and found I couldn't say no; not yet.

'Let me think about it.'

*

A letter arrived from the Special Committee and Millicent Fawcett a few days later, just over two months before the March deadline. I read it out to Clementine, Laura and Esther in our parlour one evening.

> I'm sorry to inform you that the Registration Bill that our petition was to accompany is no longer being presented to Parliament.

I looked up in dismay.

'What?' exclaimed Laura, her face paling.

'All that work,' said Esther. She looked as dejected as I felt.

'This happened with the last petition too,' said Clementine, shaking her head with disgust.

'What will you do now?' asked Mary. She had come to visit and she and Mama were sitting with us as we enjoyed a pot of tea and a light supper. It was a quiet night at the pub. Papa was working with Bill and Roger with Polly serving in the lounge and Jenny in the kitchen and scullery, giving me a rare night off.

I shook my head. 'I don't know.'

'Read on,' said Laura. 'Surely they'll present it anyway.'

> Our deadline of 21 March still stands as we're investigating suitable opportunities to put our petition before the Members of Parliament. We want to get as much

exposure for our cause at a time that support from such men can and will make a practical and real difference to the lives of women.

I know this setback is a blow but I still believe that the process of parliamentary reform is the best way to bring about lasting change. I'll keep you informed of our progress.

'See? Where there's a will, there's a way,' said Laura, ever the optimist.

'So, it's not over,' said Esther. 'I didn't know how we'd be able to tell all the women who organised signatures that the petition wasn't going to be used.'

'Thank goodness we don't have to,' I said, dropping the letter onto the small side table. 'We can't afford for even one woman to stop believing in our cause.'

'We need to be seen as doing something, taking some kind of action,' said Clementine, leaning forward in her seat. 'Perhaps politely allowing men to push us to one side isn't helping our cause at all.'

'What are you suggesting?' asked Mary with a frown. I could see she was angry, determined to protect me from any criticism, but she didn't understand Clementine, whose ideas for social change went far beyond mine.

'Make some noise to start with. Marches through the streets, demonstrations, just like the Chartists did fifty years ago to help ordinary working men in their fight for the vote. Let the men in power know that we're not going anywhere, that women have found their voices and we're here to stay. So they'd better start paying attention to what we're saying.'

'That's a bit radical, isn't it?' asked Esther in awe.

Clementine shrugged. 'Not as radical as the strike action the Chartists took after parliament refused to look at their petitions. Women have been campaigning for their rights for nearly thirty years without any change. The Chartists might have been violent but they made people sit up and take notice, they brought attention to their cause, even if it was quashed in the end. They were instrumental in over half of all men now having the vote.'

'She's right,' I said, smiling grimly at Clementine. She was like a warrior angel, a real champion of those who were disadvantaged, and I loved her for her outspoken bravery. But I believed that the suffrage movement had evolved since Chartism. Much progress had been made in improving the rights of men, women and children since those days through rational argument and evidence, like the petition. The world was a different place now I knew humanity was destined to evolve. Progress was inevitable in my mind. 'Nothing's changed for us right now, but remember it's an important moment in our struggle too – this is the first time women have come together at a national level. Let's give logic and reason a chance.' I squeezed her hand. 'We need to keep collecting signatures until March and see what Mrs Fawcett and the Appeals Committee can do to get our petition the attention it deserves. Agreed?'

All three of my friends nodded. I prayed that Mrs Fawcett's efforts would bear fruit soon.

'That's our Hannah,' I heard Mary whisper to Mama, who nodded, her face suffused with pride.

*

When Mr Jones attended the next suffrage meeting, I wondered if his drinking with the group at The Ox and Plough a few nights before had been just a coincidence. He worked for the rectory and looked after the Recreation Club.

He'd been with mainly farmers from beyond the village but with them was Trevor Carter, a friend of Mr Franks; Mr Morgan; Mr Bailey, who managed the limestone quarry; and Fred Duggan. Mr Jones was a tall, thin, balding man with spectacles perched on the end of his nose, and most found him sour and disagreeable, except for possibly Reverend Mason. In truth, a most unlikely brewery spy.

'I don't have any problem with your lunch clubs, libraries and reading groups,' said Mr Jones after I'd explained the setback to presenting our petition to Parliament. 'But women's suffrage is something I can't endorse. Give up this fool's errand. Women are not at all suited to the masculine pursuits of logic and reason.'

'Maybe it's a sign,' called Mr Franks. I found it a bit odd that he'd come to a meeting for the first time after many invitations over the previous months. 'We all know women are better off at home, lookin' after their husbands and children. It's in their nature to be emotional and easily influenced, and that's why their men vote for them. Askin' women to vote will be askin' for trouble at home.'

My blood was boiling but everyone was watching for my reaction – I had to remain calm. I plastered a brittle smile on my face. 'Thank you for your opinions, gentlemen. We're committed and resolved and won't give up after one obstacle. And we're as suited to logic and reason as any man. Ask any schoolteacher what they observe in the classroom and they'll agree.'

Mr Jones's face did not budge from its bland expression. I didn't know if he was the spy but I certainly had enough reason and logic to find out the truth. I turned to address Mr Franks.

'A woman with husband and children will undeniably focus her attention on them, they are her family and part of her life, but surely a woman can focus on more than one thing, such as business or academic pursuits. You are quite capable of running The Rose and Crown, managing your business affairs and remaining attentive to your own family and household. Many women have proved that they're just as able. Our own Queen Victoria manages to rule our great empire.'

'And look at Mrs Scruton and Mrs Adams, running their own businesses here in the village,' said Esther, despite her face flooding with colour at speaking out. Mrs Scruton nodded, sitting a little taller, clearly pleased she'd been mentioned, and Mrs Adams, the draper, dipped her head shyly.

'So,' I said, 'it must follow that if it's a woman's duty to do everything in her power to look after her family, then it's imperative for her to be able to vote about issues that affect a subject she knows so intimately. Wouldn't you agree?'

Mr Franks stared at me, first in surprise at my argument and then, when he realised he had no reasonable reply, with loathing. 'You think you're so smart,' he snapped. 'But see how smug you are when you don't have this place as your soapbox.'

'What are you talking about?' I asked before I could stop myself.

'You think you know it all, but you know nothin'. If I was you, I'd be lookin' after what's closer to home than your fanciful ideas.'

Was he threatening The Ox and Plough? Maybe he was the one trying to destroy us.

'That's enough!' Edward stood abruptly. 'This meeting is for civil conversation and discussion. Personal attacks are not acceptable. I think it's time for you to go,' he said to Mr Franks.

'Do you agree with this nonsense?'

'I do. All men and women deserve the right to have a say in what happens to them and, in this country, that right is enacted through our parliamentary process and the ability to vote.'

Mr Franks shook his head. 'Some people are stupid and selfish. I see it every day.' He gazed around the room belligerently, daring someone to tell him different.

Edward sighed. 'And I've seen many things in my time as magistrate on the district sessions and often it's desperate men and women who don't believe they have any other choice than to break the law who end up in front of me. If they were part of the solution to the problems that affect them, as Miss Todd alluded to, I doubt our courts would be as overwhelmed. People make stupid, selfish decisions when they have no other recourse.'

I smiled in amazement. Edward was a humanist like me, and believed in the innate human desire of people to better themselves. We were lucky to have him and Marjorie to support us.

'Well, I don't need to hear any more of this mumbo jumbo,' he sneered, looking around the room. 'When you all come to your senses and want to do somethin' about everyday problems come and see me at The Rose and Crown.'

There it was. It was as bald an attempt as possible to discredit the society – and our pub. Mr Franks was only here to campaign for himself, to be the most popular publican in the village and for his pub, The Rose and Crown, to follow suit.

My head was spinning. I couldn't wait to tell Roger and Bill what had happened.

14

I prize logic above all else. I can't endorse the Chartists' methods for achieving their aims. Violence cannot be the answer to women's enfranchisement: we will win with reason.

School had finished early and my class and I had joined the entire village to witness the annual spectacle of the Shrove Tuesday folk football match. The school gate at the west end of the village and the gates of the poor house at the eastern end were the designated goals. It was a medieval version of our modern game with the entire village as the field, where a goal was awarded only when the ball was tapped three times against either gatepost and then the ball would return to the village green to begin again.

'Who do you think will win?' asked Jemima as we waited for the game to pass us.

'The farmers, of course,' said Rory, craning his neck to see if any of the players were coming down the street.

'No, the tradesmen's team,' said Anthony, giving Rory a little shove. 'All of my brothers are on that team. You know they'll win.'

The crowd erupted as men ran towards us. One player had broken away from the huddle, holding the ball as he sprinted towards the school gate goal. I sucked my breath in at the sight of an athlete in full flight. It was David Rainforth and I could see why he was wanted by more than a few teams and was such a talent.

'Come on, David, you can do it,' screamed Anthony. Rory was yelling in encouragement too. Then a group of burly men came from nowhere, seeking to block David's run to goal, and a collective shout escaped from the crowd around me. This game was much rougher than normal football and I was worried they'd hurt David. But in a sudden motion he flicked the ball to Roger, who came from behind. All hell broke loose as David was mobbed by the opposing team and Roger shot ahead towards the goal.

'Run, Roger, run!' I screamed along with the children. He was magnificent as he ran, long limbed, his hair pushed back, magnifying the look of fierce determination on his face.

Jemima clutched my arm as Roger reached the gate but I didn't think he had enough time to tap the post three times before the opposition reached him.

'Do it!' shouted Anthony. It was as though Roger moved in slow-motion as he tapped the ball against the stone gate post once, twice, three times.

I jumped up and down, screaming until I was hoarse.

The ball returned to the green to begin again and I made my way back to The Ox and Plough to help prepare for the evening rush. The game would go on until it was too dark to see and then people would seek the warmth of the pubs to relive their favourite moments and soothe sore throats from too much yelling.

As I entered the pub, I was drawn to the smell of cooking and discovered Bill at the kitchen table devouring a plate of golden pancakes.

'Sit and eat,' said Mama. 'Everything is done. I'll help Papa while things remain quiet. Take the break while you can.'

'Thanks, Mama,' I said, kissing her cheek before removing my coat and joining Bill at the table.

When I put the first forkful of silky, buttery pancake in my mouth, I realised how hungry I was. Roger joined us not long after to help on the evening shift, leaving the others to finish the game. Mama loaded him up with the last pancakes, hot from the stove, as we congratulated him on his goal.

Sitting with Bill and Roger, I told them about Mr Jones and Mr Franks at the suffrage meeting.

'He spoke to you that way? If your father had been there, he wouldn't have dared,' growled Bill.

'I think that's the point. Bullies are cowards most of the time. But I've been working here long enough to know what men like that are about and how to deal with them,' I said.

'You stood up for yourself,' said Roger. 'Good for you.' He shook his head and smiled ruefully. 'No one will make the mistake of thinking that you'll step back and accept what the old crusty men in this town want, which is for nothing to ever change.'

'That was when the penny dropped,' I said, pouring more tea for each of us. 'I think he's come to a few of the meetings to see what we've done to The Ox and Plough and to learn how Papa's helping me with our community projects. He doesn't want to miss out on anything, customers especially.'

'It makes sense,' said Bill, frowning, pushing his large, weathered hand through his brown hair. It was more peppered with grey than I'd realised. 'Perhaps it's Franks himself who's the brewery spy, using one of his men to get extra information when he can't.'

Roger whistled and shook his head.

'Perhaps,' I said. 'I can't help but think the suffrage society is connected in some way. Mr Jones seems to be more against the suffrage work but accepts the community projects we're doing. Neither Mr Franks nor Mr Morgan, Trevor Carter or Fred Duggan hold any kind of regard for me, but maybe they wanted to know more about the suffrage society from Mr Jones to find a way to stop the work we're doing, as well as bring down The Ox and Plough.'

'It could be as simple as one of them being offered money to spy on us,' said Bill, ever the pragmatist.

'I don't know,' said Roger. 'I think Hannah's onto something. What if they're all linked? Someone who hates the suffrage society, wants to hurt The Ox and Plough or see the other pubs thrive, and is willing to be paid to act as a spy.'

I pushed my plate away with a sigh. 'It could be anyone.'

*

'It's time to teach you about the business,' Papa said one day when I joined him at the desk in his office. 'I've been meaning to show you for weeks.'

The sick feeling in my stomach hit me. I didn't want to learn because it meant I had to accept Papa was ill. I'd much rather believe that he would perhaps get a little worse but still remain well enough to stay with us, running The Ox and Plough, even from an armchair.

'But what about Mama or Bill?'

'Bill will have enough on his plate running things. You have to understand the business if one day he leaves. Your mother's happy to continue doing what she always has, but she hasn't had to deal with figures for years. You're the natural choice. Arithmetic is easy for you.' He opened the ledger in front of him. 'I'll be by your side as you learn. I won't be able to hide my illness forever and the day will come when you'll have to put your name up when the annual liquor licence has to be renewed.'

His words felt like a physical blow. I felt disjointed, somehow distanced from myself. I had never considered the possibility of running the pub myself, with my name on the papers. I had only been waiting for Papa to be well again so that I could really begin my life, the life I'd always dreamed of.

'Don't speak like that Papa,' I said, finding it difficult to speak. 'You'll be here for years yet. Once the brewery relaxes the pressure on you, you'll feel much better, I'm sure. And if Dr Sloane can find a treatment, you won't get any worse.'

Papa sighed and folded his hand over mine. 'But I can't base your and your mother's futures on ifs. I have to be prepared for the worst. We could lose everything otherwise: our income, the pub and our home. We'd have nothing. I know this scares you, but you won't be alone. You'll have Bill to guide and advise you and your mother, and if I'm not wrong, young Roger Rainforth to support you. He's here more than he is at his own home, not only the shifts that Bill asks him to do, but the many hours he stays to give me a hand or to help out around the pub.' He raised an eyebrow. 'Tell me I'm wrong.'

'He just wants to help,' I murmured, blushing.

'I spoke to Elizabeth Rainforth when I last saw her in the village to assure her that I'm not using her son.'

'You know her?'

Papa nodded. 'I know just about everybody in the village now. The Rainforths are good people, caring and kind. But she knows what Roger's like. He won't be told what he can and can't do ... a bit like you really.' He smiled then patted my hand and continued. 'He's doing it for you, you know. His mother told me that he feels something special for you. The question is, what do you feel for him? Do I teach him about running the pub with the hope that one day he'll be the support that you need?'

'Papa, I ...' I hesitated, trying to find the right words, shocked to be talking about Roger and my future in the same conversation and worse still, with my father. 'Roger's a lovely man and a good friend but you know how I feel about the restrictions on a woman once she's married. I wouldn't be able to teach and I'd have to defer, legally, to my husband. If I stay single, I can continue a life of independence and respect on my own terms.'

'But what about a family and having children? Don't you want that?'

'You know I love children. The children at school feel like my own. I pour my heart into teaching them and doing what I can to ensure they have the best opportunities to improve their lives. I have enough nieces and nephews to satisfy the urge to kiss and cuddle children, give them love and affection.'

'Are you sure this is the life you want?'

'I'm sure, Papa. Between teaching, the suffrage society and helping Mama and Bill look after the pub, I already have a full and busy life. I'll be content.' I couldn't tell him about my hopes to eventually work and live away in the city. And I certainly couldn't tell him about the feelings I had when I was around Roger, my secret yearnings to be in his arms again. They were simply physical desires that I'd have to overcome, a small sacrifice for a lifetime of independence.

'I know you're strong willed but I just want to make sure that you're happy and that your future's secure ...' He blinked furiously. 'If you wish to remain unmarried like you say, it's especially important to ensure you have a steady, secure income to supplement your teaching. I want to provide for you, give you what you deserve – a good life.' He took my hand. 'Do this for me and take the burden off your mother's shoulders.'

I gazed into his eyes, green, gold and brown. I had no choice. I had to do this for him, to ease his mind. My darling Papa.

I took a shuddering breath, feeling a door closing. 'All right, Papa. Where do we start?'

I spent many long evenings in the office with Papa, going over the expenses, reconciling the accounts and learning when stock orders needed to be placed. I accompanied Papa and Bill to the brewery to meet the manager, Mr Worthington, and began to attend the meetings with the brewery representative, Mr Connolly. Learning the business was more complex than I'd first thought but Papa and Bill were patient with all my questions and soon I got the lay of the land.

I was surprised to find that talking to Papa about Roger had clarified my thoughts. Papa's questions had forced me to make my position clear to myself and in theory, that was all well and good, but reality was another matter.

*

It was Valentine's Day and Mama handed me an envelope as I joined her for a cup of tea and a quick bite before school.

'This came for you,' she said. 'I found it slipped under the door.'

I used a knife to gently open the envelope then pulled out a card with a beautiful drawing of red roses and blue violets on the front. I opened it to find a carefully written message.

Dear Hannah,
You know the verse. But elm and hawthorn have more meaning to me.
My heart is yours. Today, tomorrow and always.
Your Valentine

I closed the card quickly, the kiss against the hedgerow came back to me in a rush. I blushed, my heart racing.

Roger had made his declaration, now it was all up to me.

'A Valentine's card then,' said Mama with a short, satisfied nod.

'It's nothing,' I said, flicking my hand in dismissal, but I couldn't look her in the eye. Now I felt terrible. All I could think of before I fell asleep at night was Roger's arms around me and his lips on mine. But for the sake of the life that I wanted, I knew I should tell him that I wasn't looking for marriage. I couldn't lead him on. He was a good and respectable man and despite the promise I'd made to Papa to learn the business, I still harboured dreams of leaving Ebberfield one day.

Mama remained silent, but I felt her gaze on the back of my head as I left the room.

I was in The Ox and Plough's kitchen, tidying up after the day's cooking, when Roger brought in the washed and dried pots and pans from the scullery.

'Did you get my card?' he whispered.

'I did,' I whispered in return. The busyness of the day fell away.

'Did you like it?'

I closed my eyes and sighed. 'I didn't know you could draw, and so well too. It made my day.'

'Just your day?' I knew he was smiling.

'Well, maybe my week.'

My eyes flew open as Roger twirled me around to face him, mock indignation on his face.

'Just your week?'

I grinned, impishly.

Then his expression softened and he touched my cheek. 'Maybe I need to remind you of that day.'

He was very close, just as I'd dreamed. I stared into his eyes. He was so beautiful.

'Maybe you do,' I whispered, and slipped my hands around his neck. I knew I shouldn't. I knew I should step away. It was so confusing to go against what I knew was right, what I'd decided I wanted. But then his hand cradled the back of my head and he bent to kiss me. I'd been imagining this moment for weeks and it was better than I'd remembered. Every nerve in my body was humming. How could I ever refuse this?

'I meant what I wrote in that card,' he said as we broke away.

It took me a moment to pull myself from the intensity of the moment, but when I did the reality of what we were doing broke though, and I stepped away. If I didn't tell him now, I didn't know if I ever would.

'Roger, I don't know what you expect ... I know we're friends, but you do more for me than you need to and I don't know that I can give you anything in return.'

Roger took my hands in his. 'I'm a patient man.'

'Any relationship besides platonic friendship has to lead inevitably to marriage. You know that, don't you? I have my reputation to protect, especially as a teacher in a small village.'

'I know.'

I swallowed hard. 'I ... I can't allow our relationship to head in that direction.' I pulled my hands away and looked down at the wooden floor.

'Is that because you're opposed to marriage or me?'

My head jerked up as I looked at him in surprise. He knew me too well.

'I've never wanted to marry,' I said bluntly. 'A woman's identity disappears or becomes secondary to her husband's once she marries. I wouldn't be able to continue teaching and I value my independence too much to lose it.'

'So, it's just marriage then.'

'I didn't say—'

He caressed my cheek. 'I'm not sure you're opposed to me at all, otherwise you wouldn't be standing here with me now. Just so you know, I'll always respect you, whether you want to marry me or not, but if you do, I'd worship the ground you walk on. You're a modern woman and I understand your desire for independence and your own identity. I've seen how my own mother has had to struggle. I want a woman who knows her own mind and carves her own path through life, not some docile girl who does whatever I bid her.'

'But—'

He put his fingertips gently on my lips. 'There's no rush. I promise I won't propose marriage but if you decide that you're game to step into the future with me, I'll be ready and waiting.'

15

March, 1894

My dearest Mary,
My heart is heavy as I write to you. Kitty has had her baby,
born in the middle of the night. There was some suspicion
that she smothered the child, but it was born much too
early to survive. She was never accused or arrested but
her parents refused to have her home. It seems likely she
will go to the workhouse unless we can find work and
lodgings for her.
I hope she will be in your prayers as she is in mine.
I must do all I can to ensure this never happens again.
Your loving sister,
Hannah

Despite the tragedies circling around, I put all of my energy
into collecting signatures for the petition, the deadline fast
approaching. I felt sure that Mrs Fawcett would find a way
to have our petition presented to the House of Commons. So
it was with great hope that Esther, Laura, Clementine and I
reminded our members to bring whatever they'd collected to
our March meeting while Dr Jenkins, Robert Sanderson and
Mr Hewitt, Mrs Scruton's brother, all agreed to help us as
we did the rounds of the village to gain as many last-minute
signatures as we could. Marjorie persuaded Edward to join

us, as much to gather more support as to be a buffer for any attacks or conflict.

'No one deserves to be verbally attacked like you were in our meeting,' Marjorie said to me when we met in the village to gather final signatures.

'Growing up and working among these types of men, I understand where they're coming from,' Edward told me as we set up pamphlets and signature sheets outside the shops. 'They feel their beliefs are being challenged – and their very way of life. Here in Ebberfield they've never come into contact with the modern world, and some will do anything to preserve what they're used to.'

But change is inevitable, I thought. We all have to adjust and evolve or, as Darwin suggested, we'd be left behind.

'That doesn't make it acceptable,' Marjorie said, the feathers on her hat quivering as she shook her head.

Edward took her hand and kissed it. 'I know, my love, but I learnt a long time ago that if you can understand how those who oppose you see things, you can work out the best way to deal with them and bring them around to your way of thinking.'

'That's why you're here, to reassure them,' I said, half to myself.

The evening before our suffrage meeting arrived and, feeling relieved that we'd done everything that we could, I sat in the parlour at home to go over my notes and the past minutes in preparation for the following day.

'Roger's been looking for you,' said my mother, popping her head around the door. 'He has something to give you.'

I nodded. 'All right. I'll go across to the pub in a minute.'

'No, dear, he's here.'

'He's here?' I gave my full attention to the conversation.

Mama nodded. 'Waiting in the entry. He's determined to give it to you himself.'

'You'd better let him in then.' I quickly put my hands over my hair, pushing loose strands into the coil at the back of my neck, and stood, straightening my skirts and smoothing my blouse. I couldn't imagine what was so important for Roger to come to the house.

'Hello, Hannah,' said Roger, looking uncomfortable as Mama ushered him in. 'I'm sorry to call on you at home but I thought I'd find you at the pub tonight.'

I frowned. 'Is everything all right?'

'Yes, but I had to get this to you before your suffrage meeting tomorrow.' He handed me an envelope.

'What is it?'

'Open it and you'll see.'

I opened the envelope and pulled out a single folded page. I stared at what the page contained – row after row of signatures. Roger's mother, sisters and brothers had signed their names at the top of a long list that included Roger's name.

I looked at him, bewildered. 'Your whole family. You asked your whole family to support my cause. There must be forty names on this list.'

'Fifty-one,' he said softly, looking pleased. 'Everyone in my family asked people they know to sign the petition. And my mother and my sister Alice are coming to the meeting tomorrow and want to become members.'

'Really?'

He nodded.

'Roger, how can I tell you how much this means?'

'You don't have to. I can see it clear as day.'

'That's very kind of your family,' said Mama. 'Maybe your mother and sister will stay for supper after. I've been waiting to have a good conversation with your mother. It will be a good opportunity to sit and talk without any other distractions.'

'I'm sure they'll be delighted,' said Roger. 'Well, I'll be off. I should try to get home for dinner on time at least one day a week.'

'Thank you, Roger,' I said, wishing we were alone so I could fling my arms around him in gratitude.

He only nodded and turned to the door.

'That young man is trying hard with you,' said Mama once Roger had left.

I sighed. 'I know, but he's wasting his time.' The page was almost an unofficial declaration of approval from his family and made Roger's intentions clear to me and to my mother. And that scared me.

'Is he?' Mama's expression was sceptical. 'I've seen the way you look at him too. Don't tell me he doesn't mean anything to you.'

'I don't want to marry,' I said flatly.

'You want to end up a spinster?'

I glared at her, feeling the anger churn in my belly. Mama had lived independently and worked as a dressmaker from the age of nineteen when her father died, and didn't marry Papa until she was twenty-nine. I thought if anyone would understand, it would be her. 'What's so wrong with that?'

'Is this suffrage talk?'

'Don't, Mama!' I said sharply. She just didn't understand that I wanted a different life, a life where I could choose how I lived it.

'Do you want to be like Mrs Fawcett? She married and had a child before she was widowed. She knows the joy of motherhood and marriage.'

'No, Mama!' I exploded. 'It's not because of Mrs Fawcett.'

Mama sat there unmoved and I immediately regretted my outburst. She had always had a calm pragmatism that I wished I had.

I shook my head, frustrated, and took a deep breath, trying to start again. 'Besides, her daughter, Philippa, is a similar age to me and hasn't married. She's dedicated herself to her academic career at Cambridge University. There's nothing wrong with a woman giving her life to her work. Not all of us aspire to be model wives and mothers. Teaching is my passion, and I've trained so long and hard to become a teacher, I don't want to give it up.' Mama, my sisters and even Mrs Fawcett, were of an older generation, and their experiences of life were different from those of Philippa and mine. The world was changing fast as we crept towards the new century with the internal combustion engine Esther showed us making machines more efficient and convenient, the development of the telephone enabling people long distances apart to talk to each other and advances to electric arc lights used in city street lights that could now be found in some wealthy homes. We were immersed in new modern ideas and opportunities. I for one was determined to evolve to live the life I wanted – an independent life in the city where I could choose to do whatever I wanted, whether it be attend rallies, visit the theatre or spend all night with other passionate individuals making plans to improve the lives of women and children, especially the vulnerable.

Mama nodded. 'I see you've made your mind up.' She stood, smoothing her skirts. 'But let me tell you that life doesn't always go the way you plan. Your views might feel more important than the views of those who know and love you, but remember that anything rigid can break more easily than something that has some give. Don't focus all your attention on one path or course of action, at the exclusion of all others. I don't want you to regret passing up the opportunities in your life without first examining their merits.'

I stared at my mother a moment, her blue eyes piercing, and knew that she could see straight into my soul, like she always had. That made me afraid, because she was the one who would make me face my own truth. 'I don't want to be like Jane and Sarah, tied to husbands who constantly struggle to provide for their families, and believing more children will give them the satisfaction and identity that they crave, in a life they have little choice over,' I said hotly.

'Don't you dare,' whispered Mama, her face white. 'Don't you speak that way about them. You and Mary had the privilege that Jane and Sarah never did. They had to work as servants from a young age away from home while you and Mary got to stay at school so you could take advantage of better jobs close to home.'

I dropped my head, ashamed of my words, tears pricking my eyes at my mother's harsh assessment. I rarely saw her angry like this. 'I'm sorry, Mama. I didn't mean to belittle their choices.' I loved all my sisters but they were so different from me.

'And how do you know that your sisters aren't happy, wouldn't choose the life they have if they had the chance to choose again?'

'I don't,' I muttered.

'No, you don't. You don't know the first thing about real life. You're only twenty-three and your father has always spoilt you. But your sisters do know what the real world is like.' Her face softened and she touched my cheek. 'I won't tell you what to do, but any choice you make will bring its joys and challenges, even the seemingly glamorous, independent life of an unmarried woman. True love is a rare gift, not something to throw away without thought or consideration. And I see that Roger loves you and I think you might love him too. Just don't cut off your nose to spite your face.' She kissed me on the forehead. 'I'm going to prepare your father's dinner. Come and help me when you're finished with your work.'

I couldn't work after Mama left the room. I felt terrible for saying those things about my sisters, even though I believed they were true. But my sorrow wasn't about them at all, it was about my own conflict and my own fears.

I stared at the envelope containing the Rainforth signatures and felt heat rising in my cheeks. It was getting harder to deny the attraction I felt towards Roger and the certainty that he felt something serious for me. But did I feel love? I didn't know. What I did know was that the fear of losing my independence and everything I'd worked so hard for was stronger than any feelings I might feel towards him. I remembered something I'd heard in one of the Fabian Society lectures about equality in marriage, and wondered what a world might be like where men and women were equal. What kind of husband would Roger be behind closed doors? Would he give me the freedom to do what I needed?

But Mama was right. I was lucky to have a choice – many didn't – and whatever I chose, I also had to face the consequences of that decision. If I wanted to be an agent of change, it was time for me to step into the real world and accept things the way they were.

*

The following evening, a large group of women congregated in the meeting room of The Ox and Plough. All our usual supporters and members were there, as were many others, curious to see how many signatures we'd collected. I was relieved when I didn't see Mr Jones or Mr Franks. But, true to Roger's word, I noticed Elizabeth and Alice Rainforth arrive, as did a very pregnant Dorothy Duggan. I hadn't expected to see her at a meeting after her husband's performance on the street. She was clearly a tough woman and although she appeared to be well, who knew what remained hidden under her high collar, long sleeves and skirt?

The meeting went well and I was proud to announce that we had well over three hundred signatures ready to send to London. I couldn't wait to hear how many signatures had been received across England and how Mrs Fawcett's Appeals Committee was going to use the petition to ensure it got the attention it deserved.

After the meeting concluded, Roger's mother and sister waited, chatting to Clementine and Esther while Mama and I ushered the last stragglers from the room. When Esther had gushed enthusiastically about the Rainforths and their contributions to the petition, Clementine had merely raised a knowing eyebrow. We'd spoken about my reservations concerning marriage and, like me, Clementine valued her independence above all else, was committed to remain unmarried too.

'You're in a fortunate position, Hannah. You have a choice,' she'd said as we walked home from school one afternoon. 'Many women would fall over backwards to be in your shoes with a suitor like Roger. He's dependable, intelligent, handsome, and clearly adores you – and you feel something for him in return. Most marriages are based on a lot less.'

I valued Clementine's opinion but since we both had the same dream, I knew she'd understand whatever decision I made.

'Thank you for coming this evening,' I said to Roger's mother and sister as we walked into the cottage.

'I've been wanting to attend for a while,' Elizabeth said with a smile. 'But with one thing or another, I just haven't made it. Roger told me how important this meeting was and when he promised to stay home and help Anthony with his homework, Alice and I had to come.'

'Well, I'm glad you both came tonight. And I greatly appreciate all the signatures your family collected. They've made a big difference to our overall numbers,' I said, taking their coats and hats. 'Come into the parlour where it's warm.'

'Mama and I believe in what you're doing,' said Alice once we were seated by the fire. 'I work as a housemaid for a chemical engineer at the iron works in Birtley and, the family is kind and fair, but some of the other girls in domestic service have it tough.'

'I know what you mean,' I said. 'My sisters Jane and Sarah worked as domestic servants before they were married, both for vicars, and they said much the same thing about some of the other girls they met at the markets.'

'This is my favourite part of the day,' Mama said as she joined us. 'When I get a few moments to myself. I don't have much of a chance to entertain, so I'm very pleased that you could stay this evening.'

'That would make two of us,' said Elizabeth with a smile. 'With the four boys still at home, it seems that I don't get a minute to myself.' She glanced at me. 'Although Roger is very good to me and tries to ease my load. But there's only so much he can do.'

Although in her late forties, Elizabeth's hair was still dark, just like Roger's, and only threaded with grey, despite the terrible hardship and loss she'd experienced. She was still a beautiful woman, tall, elegant despite her well-worn dress and softly spoken, and I wondered why she hadn't married again when it might have eased the strain on her and her family. Perhaps remaining a widow was a conscious choice, even though it meant sacrifice and hardship.

'You need me back home, Mama,' said Alice softly.

Elizabeth squeezed her daughter's hand and smiled. 'Perhaps when Anthony finishes school.'

My heart clutched at those words. I was hoping to keep Anthony at school for another couple of years at least, to give him every opportunity to get a better job. But it was harder for women to get work in a small village like ours and Elizabeth couldn't afford to keep Alice as well as Anthony. Another reason for me to remain single and in control of my own destiny.

*

It was April, nearly the end of the football season, and I was determined to give the girls one last big excursion along the coast. We stopped by the scrub on the clifftops to draw the gorse bush, linnet finches and Common Blue butterflies, before making our way down to the sand. The girls had created an impressive collection of various types of local butterflies with their beautiful colours and patterns, each pinned carefully to a board and labelled clearly. It was a favourite exhibit at school.

The girls had come so far. They were enthusiastic amateur naturalists, learning to not just accept whatever they were told but to question and explore theories and explanations – the perfect foundation to higher learning. There were a few girls in this group who I had high hopes for but scholarships were few and far between.

'What do you girls hope to do when you finish school?' I asked as we walked along the sand with our bare feet.

'Work on my family's farm until I get married,' said one girl.

I nodded. Many girls didn't expect much more than that. 'Have any of you thought about going to high school?' Some of the girls frowned. 'You could get a job with better pay and security, like a shopkeeper or clerk, or even go to university,' I explained.

'Can women really go to university?' asked Jemima, a wistful expression on her face.

'They can and I hope that one day soon, women will be awarded degrees, the same as men.'

'I'd like to become a doctor,' whispered Jemima. She had the ability, all she needed was the opportunity.

'I want to be a solicitor like my father,' said Amy Sanderson, emboldened by Jemima's admission. 'Mama told me about the work the suffrage society does and if I can understand the law, then I can help people.'

'Maybe you'll be a Member of Parliament one day,' said Jemima, squeezing her friend's hand. 'Then you can change the law.'

I smiled. 'You never know what's possible until you try.' I looked around at the other girls. 'If you could do or be anything at all, what would that be?'

'The prime minister!' cried Amy, her hair whipping across her face in the stiff breeze. I grinned. What would I be? The thought came to me immediately. *I'd be exactly as I am now.* I felt a shock of surprise. Ebberfield was clearly making a home in my heart. And then I felt gratitude for the rare fortune that my life was just as I wanted – for now, that is.

All the girls began to call out. 'A dancer, own a department store, be like Charles Darwin, be an explorer, travel the world, be an actor, visit Africa ...'

'I'd be a princess!' yelled one girl with glee.

'No, I'd be a queen!' shouted her friend, splashing her with water from the shore.

Suddenly there was splashing, shrieking and laughing, as the girls released their exuberance, running into the water or up onto the sand. There would be soggy and sandy clothing before long. But this was what girlhood should be about: joy, dreams and freedom to imagine.

16

I feel I might not write much tonight; my hands shake
from the shock and sadness at the news of Kitty's death.
She was sent to the workhouse after the birth and within
days she had childbed fever. When Mrs Burrows learnt of
it, Kitty was too unwell to embark on the journey back to
Ebberfield. She died alone in that friendless place.

Roger and I stood outside The Rose and Crown on market
day regarding the large advertisement for the freak show. He
thought it might keep me focused on something else, the news
of Kitty's death having left me hollow and raw for weeks.
Bearded ladies, savage Zulus, an Amazon queen and snake
people were the main attractions. We had learnt about The
Rose and Crown hosting the freak show a few weeks earlier
and knew we had to see what it meant for Mr Franks' business.

Once inside, we were swept along with the crowd towards
the back of the inn where the performance was about to
begin. I tried to force my way to the main bar but it was
useless, so I craned my neck, taking in my surroundings. All
I could see were the heads of excited people, ready to view
the human curiosities. I knew how popular these shows were,
the fascination many held for those who were different, but
it wasn't until the showman was on the raised platform in
front of us, explaining the story of how the heavily haired
man beside him who had been discovered in the wilds of
Africa was the 'missing link' of evolution, that I understood

the appeal. The people around us were shocked and titillated, shaking their heads and gasping.

Revulsion rose in my throat as the curiosities were displayed. Small people were introduced as living dolls and a tall woman dressed in exotic clothing as the giant Amazon queen; some appeared to have medical conditions or diseases, like the bearded ladies, or deformities, like the Siamese twins and the snake people, who had no arms or legs. But all had been given false or exaggerated stories and all were being exploited by the showman. This was humanity at its worst. Maybe we hadn't evolved at all.

'I have to get out of here,' I whispered desperately in Roger's ear.

I turned and forced my way through the press of people with Roger following close behind. I noticed the signs on the walls for cheap drinks – cheaper than ours – just for those who stayed after the show, and I wanted to scream. The Rose and Crown was big but it was a labyrinth of small, poky rooms and I took in the signs of age and neglect and the smell of stale beer that permeated the place. Mr Franks hadn't spent any money on the pub for years. This was a place with no heart and was nothing compared to the comfort, warmth and conviviality of The Ox and Plough.

Roger grabbed my arm. 'Look,' he whispered in my ear.

I turned to peer through the opening of a partly closed door and couldn't believe my eyes. Huddled together in deep conversation with Mr Connolly, Papa's brewery representative, were Mr Franks, Trevor Carter and Mr Bailey, the quarry manager.

'The Ox and Plough won't be able to recover,' said Mr Franks with a short laugh.

'I didn't sign up to this,' said Mr Bailey miserably, shaking his head.

'You'll keep tellin' us what they're doin' if you know what's good for you,' growled Mr Franks. He glared at Mr Bailey and then Mr Connolly. 'I pay you both well for your services.'

I stood rooted to the spot until Roger pulled me away. We couldn't afford to be seen. We raced out of the pub, my heart pounding through my chest, and didn't say a word until we'd reached the street.

'It can't be,' I said, pressing a shaking hand across my mouth. I looked into Roger's face, as pale and wide-eyed as I knew my own would be. 'Mr Bailey's the brewery spy.'

'And he's working with Mr Franks, *and* Connolly. He's cut a deal with them both.'

'They think they've got us cornered … What if they know about Papa's illness? If we lose the pub, we lose everything. We'll have nowhere to go.' Cold fear shot down my spine.

'We have to tell Bill and your father,' said Roger urgently.

I shook my head. 'Not Papa. I don't know what it will do to him.' Papa had dismissed any suggestion of looking for a spy. He believed that if we worked hard to build up customers and paid our loan on time each month, there was nothing the brewery could do to us. 'Let's talk to Bill first and work out a plan. We can't let them ruin us.'

April, 1894

Dear Hannah,
Bert and I are settled into our new place, just around the corner from Mary and George. It's taken some time for Bert to find work. Mama kept suggesting we ask George, but she forgets that he doesn't own the butcher's business, only works there. Now Bert has a job as a contract cartman and we can both breathe easy.

Little Eliza is beautiful. I'm lucky to have her at my age. Some women I know are grandmothers at thirty-six and this pregnancy was difficult. I'm sure she'll be my last baby and I want to take every moment to remember these special times. The children are a handful and I'm finding it hard to manage at the moment, especially with Eliza being fretful.

If you could come for a few days to help, I would be so grateful. I feel like I could sleep for a week.

Your loving sister,

Jane

Jane needed me, but I couldn't pretend to myself that I hadn't wanted to escape Ebberfield for a moment. Papa's relapse, the discovery of the spy, my confusing feelings for Roger and Kitty's death were all closing around me, threatening to topple me over. I felt like a coward.

Jane and I were in her bedroom where I'd been helping her change the baby and rock her to sleep in her cradle when she asked me about Roger.

'What did Mama tell you?' I whispered, annoyed.

Jane shrugged. 'She didn't have to say much. Just that he's helping out as a barman. But why would he do that when he already has a job?' She folded her arms and raised an eyebrow at me.

It was my turn to shrug.

'Mama told me that his mother and sister have visited for supper. You can't lead him on, Hannah' she said softly.

'What are you talking about?' I snapped. I turned quickly, worried I'd woken the baby, but she hadn't stirred.

'You're allowing him to think or even hope that you'll marry him.'

'I'm doing no such thing,' I said hotly, grimacing when Eliza grizzled.

Jane began rocking the cradle again until the little girl relaxed into sleep. 'I've seen how you look whenever his name is mentioned. Have you kissed him?'

I felt my face flame. 'I—'

Jane sighed and sat on the bed, gesturing for me to join her. 'That's how it starts. If you don't put an end to it, you'll lose control.'

'Don't be ridiculous,' I said, but I sank beside her all the same. I had already had thoughts of more, my body craving things as I imagined being in Roger's arms.

'You can't hide in a small village, not like the city. Sooner or later, someone will find out. You'll be ostracised and lose your job and the respect you've worked so hard for. And for what? A moment's pleasure?'

I began to rise. I didn't want to hear any more, but Jane grasped my arm.

'What happens if you fall pregnant? Have you thought of that? Nobody will want you running the suffrage society or working at the school or even The Ox and Plough. The men of the village will make sure you don't. You can't be a woman in a position of influence and flout the rules with Roger. You can't be pregnant *and* unmarried.'

'I haven't done anything, so I won't fall pregnant,' I said between clenched teeth. But Jane was right. Unless we played by the rules, women had no chance of being recognised. But they weren't our rules. We didn't make them. I felt the familiar fire of rebellion rise in my belly. It just wasn't fair.

'I've heard that before,' she said. 'Do you really think you're so different from everyone else? I can tell you that you're not. You're lucky – you have a good life, but that can change in an instant. A kiss can lead to so much more in the heat of the moment and it's something you can never take back. It only takes once, you know. That's the harsh truth. *Once,* and you can't do a thing. It happens to women everywhere, abandoned by the men who make them pregnant. If you have a rich family you might be sent away to have your baby in secret, perhaps adopted out or brought home for their mothers to raise, but women like us don't have that kind of luxury. Women like us are cast out, left to fend for ourselves, with no job and no friends to support us.'

My blood was boiling now. 'How dare you make assumptions about me,' I hissed. I was so angry I wanted to scream. 'What would you know? And don't lecture me. I can't bear it,' I ground out.

Jane only sighed. 'I've seen it more times than I care to count, here in Hartlepool but also in Yorkshire. Women end up in the workhouse, some die during childbirth, but it's rare for an unmarried mother and child to stay together on their own when they're destitute. All for a few minutes of passion.' She rested her hand on her new daughter, her eyes softening. 'Having a baby changes everything, but imagine how much harder it would be on your own.'

We sat silently for a few minutes, the fire in the grate crackling. She was right. She was a mother of five and had seen far more hardship than I ever had. Of course she was right. As my heart slowed, the anger in me abated and I gazed at the sleeping child breathing softly in her cradle. I loved her fresh baby smell, her boneless warmth when she'd fallen asleep in my arms.

I sighed and felt a tug of longing. A baby would be lovely, but I was dedicated to a life of greater purpose. And I knew that if I ever decided to go further with Roger, I had the self-control to stop.

I looked at Jane and smiled, ashamed of my outburst. 'Sorry,' I whispered.

She kissed my cheek. 'From what I've heard, Roger's a good man. If you don't intend to marry him, and I still don't understand why you wouldn't, then you have to tell him there's nothing waiting for him. You can't give him false hope.'

'You're right,' I said, nodding, then noticed the dark rings around her eyes. 'Why don't you sleep while the baby's sleeping? I'll make dinner and look after the little ones.'

She touched my cheek and smiled. 'Would you? You're a love.'

*

A letter from Millicent Fawcett was waiting for me on my return to Ebberfield.

> My dear Miss Todd,
>
> Thank you for your lovely letter that accompanied the wonderful collection of signatures for our petition. We've received over 248,000 signatures from women across the country, making this the largest parliamentary petition since the Chartist petition of 1842. You, your committee and the members of your suffrage society can feel proud of the mighty contribution you've made to this extraordinary national response. Our Special Appeals Committee feels renewed in our efforts to ensure this petition is used in the most effective way possible.

Hundreds of thousands of signatures! There couldn't be any doubt now that the parliamentary vote was what women wanted. This good news was a welcome relief and I couldn't wait to share it with our members.

I have to say that thoughts of your mother's wonderful lemon cake along with a nice cup of bracing tea have made me want to rush home and bake a batch large enough to keep everyone in the office going as they organise the signatures by county.

The other wonderful news I wish to share with you is about the new *Local Government Act*. One of our founding members, Ursula Bright, has been instrumental in ensuring that this bill, which grants some concessions to women, has been passed. Single and married women who own property are now eligible to register to vote in the district council elections, the local parish elections and the election of local guardian and school boards. This means that women will now have a say not only in who is elected but who can seek to be elected themselves in the parish and district councils, as poor law guardians and to the school boards. I know it's not ideal, as it leaves out so many women who should be included, but it's a start.

The first elections will be held later this year in November and with the support of the Women's Local Government Society, of which I'm a member, I'd like to speak with you about your involvement in your local elections. Perhaps we can look into your eligibility to stand for election—

I dropped the letter in shock. Millicent Fawcett wanted me to stand for election? A smile spread across my face as the idea sank in. I retrieved the letter and kept reading.

But if this doesn't suit or isn't possible—

'Doesn't suit!' I exclaimed, throwing my hands in the air. I'd never reject such an offer.

I'd like to discuss further opportunities for you within
our national organisation or even seek your involvement
in further education reforms. The Royal Commission
on Secondary Education, chaired by Member of
Parliament James Bryce, has begun its review and
the recommendations need support to ensure they're
enacted into practical and useful laws. I'll write to let you
know when it's possible for me to travel north again,
otherwise if there's any chance you might be able to come
to London for a couple of days, I'd be more than happy to
talk you through my proposal then.

I screamed out loud and jumped up and down. I couldn't
believe that Mrs Fawcett wanted to speak with *me* – and
about a future in government and the educational reforms I
was most passionate about. My deepest dreams were being
realised. I could see myself living and working in London as
clear as day. If Papa's health remained stable, I could commit
myself to my new life.

Mama came running to the parlour. 'What's happened?
What's wrong?'

I threw my arms around her and hugged her tight.
'Millicent Fawcett wants me to go to London to discuss
further opportunities.'

'What are you talking about?'

I waved the letter in front of her face.

'I can't see it like that,' she said, exasperated. 'Let me read
it properly.' She took the letter from my hands.

'It's more than I ever imagined,' I said when she'd finished
reading.

'But what about your teaching?'

'I can do both. It's the perfect mix. I'll write back and let
Mrs Fawcett know I'll come to London. I'll ask Mr Burnett

for a day off from school and take the train down.' I took her hands in mine. 'Just think, Mama, I can help improve the lives of women and children in our district and maybe even across England.'

'What will you tell Roger?'

Her words were like a slap in the face. There was no room in my life for a husband, especially if I had these kinds of opportunities. I took a shuddering breath. 'I'll have to tell him that I've made up my mind.'

It was going to be difficult. I trusted Roger and we would still have to work together in The Ox and Plough. Mama and Elizabeth Rainforth had become friends, and after our supper together, I'd decided I liked Elizabeth and Alice very much. They were a family of kind, nurturing people, accepting and generous. If I was ever going to consider joining another family, it would have been with Roger and the Rainforths.

*

Papa's face broke open with a huge smile when I found him in the cellar and told him my news.

'Well, you must go,' he said. 'I'm so very proud of you. I always knew you'd do something important.'

'I've learnt from the best,' I replied. 'From you. I remember you with your men from the shipyard. You did everything to help and support them.'

He sighed. 'I wish I'd been able to do more for them with my engineering society but things were different back then. Not everybody was accepted as a member. I've seen how much things have changed when I listen in to some of the meetings Roger's trade society have here. They're a new breed of men. They're more organised than we were, they don't just want benefits but want to see real change at work – and at home.' He kissed my cheek, his eyes glistening with tears. 'I have high hopes for you. I know you'll make a difference.'

There was so much to do. Since Kitty's death I'd experienced overwhelming feelings of despair. The violence committed against her had affected me deeply. Surely as a species we could rise above such base actions? But despite all the reforms that had already been achieved, the evils of victimisation and exploitation were still rife. In a perfect world I could have it all – go to London, do my suffrage work, teach ... and be with Roger. Heat still flamed in me whenever I thought of him, and he was unlike any other man I'd met, but I knew my reaction was only physical. And now with Mrs Fawcett's belief in me I felt I could do just about anything for the cause ... and for Kitty.

*

It was a relief when we finally decided to confront Mr Bailey. I couldn't wait to put an end to the spying matter, so I could go to London, confident that the weight would finally be off Papa's shoulders and his health could improve again. I wouldn't be able to make any decision about my future until I knew he'd be fine. Roger and I waited for Mr Bailey outside the quarry. As he locked the gates he looked tired and drawn, his shoulders slumped, and when he saw us, his faced paled with shock.

'We know about you, Bailey,' growled Roger.

'I ... I don't know what you're talking about,' Mr Bailey stuttered, then turned swiftly to leave.

Roger grabbed him by the arm.

'Let me go, or ... I'll go to the police,' Bailey said desperately.

'You do that and I'll tell them what you've been up to,' said Roger softly. Mr Bailey's face turned red and then grey.

'I think you'd better sit down, Mr Bailey,' I said.

Roger marched the man to a low stone wall.

'I didn't want to,' Mr Bailey groaned as I sat beside him.

'I know you're a good man,' I began, putting my hand on his shoulder. 'I understand why you did it. Things have been tough at the quarry.'

'Yes, I only want to look after my family.' He was shaking.

'Just as I want to look after mine,' I said. 'My father is a good man too and only wants to bring the community together. He's never done anything to hurt anyone ... not even Mr Franks.'

'I know.' Mr Bailey hung his head.

'He just wants to make a living, but we're doing it tough too.'

'I never meant to hurt your father. At first, I was asked by Connolly, the brewery representative, to find out your prices and numbers of customers. I thought it was harmless. Then it was anything that you and your father were doing or talking about. I listened to conversations in the bar and lounge and talked to customers.'

'You took that information back to Franks?' Roger stood over him ominously.

Mr Bailey nodded. 'I want my own pub one day ...'

Roger snorted. 'You do know that Connolly and Franks have no control over that? They're exploiting you and your desire to own a pub.'

'I do now ... I don't want anything more to do with them. I won't be part of destroying your family. And they won't stop with The Ox and Plough. Next it will be The Black Bull.'

'What are they planning to do?'

'If they make it harder and harder for Mr Todd to get ahead and make ends meet, they think they can force him out and put in someone who will be to their benefit. I thought that was me ... until they started talking to Trevor Carter.'

'What about Worthington – the manager of the brewery? Does he know about this?' Roger asked.

Mr Bailey shook his head. 'He doesn't know about me at all. He thinks that Mr Connolly is just trying to help him build the business. And he doesn't know the pressure your father's under.' He glanced tentatively at us both.

'What is it, Mr Bailey?' I asked gently.

'I overheard someone say that your father is ill and soon won't be able to manage the pub. And ...' he took a deep breath, 'I told them before I knew they were going to double-cross me. I'm so sorry.'

The breath was forced from my chest as the world began to spin. The damage could be irreparable.

'Put your head between your legs,' said Roger, pushing my head down. 'Now breathe slowly.'

I did as he suggested and slowly my vision returned to normal. 'Thank you,' I whispered.

I gazed at Mr Bailey, who looked ready to kneel at my feet in apology. I had to think and act quickly.

'Everyone deserves a second chance, and you can still help us, Mr Bailey.'

'Anything,' Mr Bailey muttered.

'You need to tell them you were wrong, that there's nothing wrong with my father. And then we'll find a way to mitigate their plans to destroy us.'

17

Mama's words have stayed with me. 'Love is a rare
gift, not something to throw away without thought or
consideration.' But what do I know of romantic love? I
can only turn to my books, to the poets and writers, and
perhaps extract some meaning from their pages.

I was ready to go to London. I spoke to Benjamin and booked
my ticket before I finally had the courage to speak to Roger.
One evening, I waited in the scullery for him to return from
the cellar, where he was moving empty barrels for Papa, ready
for the drayman to collect the following day.

'Have you got a minute to talk?' I asked him. 'Come into
the kitchen where we won't be disturbed.'

'What's wrong?' he asked, reaching for my hand. 'Is it
Mr Bailey?'

I shook my head. 'No, no. And I'm so grateful for your
help when we confronted him.' I pulled my hand away. 'But
don't touch me. You can't touch me.'

Roger frowned. 'Have I done something to upset you?'

'No, you've been the perfect gentleman, kind, patient and
everything I would want in a man except ...'

'Except what?' Roger's eyes bored into me and I felt my
heart shrivel at the hurt I was about to inflict on him.

'Except that I've made up my mind. I can't think about a
future with you – or anyone, for that matter.'

'Ah! The marriage thing.' He looked a little amused and a shock of white-hot anger shot through my body.

'Don't, Roger!' I hissed, furious. 'I can't do this.'

'We make such a good team,' he said more gently. 'Look what we've been able to achieve together.'

'I know, but I mean it, Roger. I've been asked by Millicent Fawcett to become more involved as an activist at our local elections later this year and with the national suffrage organisation. I'm going to London to discuss my future with her next week.'

'Hannah, it doesn't have to be this way.' He reached out again to caress my cheek and his touch made me want to forget my resolve and step into his arms for even a few minutes.

I stepped away. 'Don't you see? I have to remain above reproach if I want to earn the respect of the people I'm trying to persuade, as well as those I'll be working with.'

'So, this is it? It's over between us?' The hurt in his eyes was almost unbearable.

I nodded. 'Unless we can just be friends.' I clenched my hands together to stop myself from throwing my arms around him.

'But I don't want to be just your friend.'

'Then I can't see you anymore,' I whispered. Tears slid down my cheeks. 'I'm sorry, Roger, but we just can't be.'

I watched as his face closed, his eyes becoming flat and hard, before he nodded once and left. My tears came freely then. I'd expected to feel liberated, free and light with the prospect of my new life about to begin, but I didn't. A dull ache throbbed inside my chest and guilt and loss weighed heavily on me. But this was the sacrifice my mother had spoken about and this was the pain I'd have to endure to embrace the life I wanted.

*

To stop thinking about Roger and what I'd done to him, I buried myself in preparations for my meeting with Mrs Fawcett. Although Esther and Laura were excited for me, it was Clementine who understood what I most needed. I'd told her that I'd rejected Roger and she agreed that it was probably for the best, in light of the opportunities ahead of me and the life I wanted to live. She was supportive in more practical ways, helping me find extra background information on the previous successes of the suffrage movement. The more I knew, the better prepared I'd be and the better I'd understand what further changes were needed. I wondered if I could ask Mrs Fawcett to let Clementine join me. With my passion and her knowledge of activism and campaigning, we made a good team.

Three days before my trip, I was going over my travel plans in my mind while I made tea and toast for breakfast. I'd never travelled that far before, the furthest I'd ever gone was to Guisborough in Yorkshire to see Jane. And London was a lot bigger than any city I'd ever been to. I'd dreamed of going as a little girl when Papa told me about the archaeologist from the museum and again in teachers' college after the suffrage rallies and hearing the other girls talking about beginning new lives there. I couldn't wait to walk through Hyde Park and see the Crystal Palace that Prince Albert had created, Buckingham Palace where Queen Victoria lived, visit the British museum ... and maybe even go to the theatre.

'Wait a moment, William,' I heard Mama call from upstairs. 'I'm coming.' She insisted on accompanying Papa down the stairs in the mornings. His movements were getting jerky and uncoordinated when he first arose, but he always forced his body back into working order before he'd enter the pub.

I heard the top stair squeak with Papa's footfall and stopped what I was doing to listen for Mama's quick steps joining him at the top of the stairs. But instead, I heard him grunt loudly.

'Papa?' I called.

I rushed out of the kitchen just in time to see Papa tumble down the stairs. I tried to reach him but it was as if everything was happening in slow motion. He was like a rag doll, arms flailing as he tried to grab on to anything but helpless to break his fall. The image of his eyes wild with fear and shock was horrifying. I screamed for my mother.

Papa landed at the bottom of the staircase in front of me, arms and legs askew and eyes wide and unblinking. At first, I thought he was dead but then he took a deep, gasping breath and cried out in pain.

I fell to my knees. 'Don't move, Papa,' I whispered.

Mama reached us in an instant. 'William, my love, stay still.' She rested a hand lightly on his chest.

Jenny gasped from the top of the stairs and Mama and I glanced up at her.

'It's all right, Jenny,' I said. 'Go and fetch Dr Taylor or Dr Jenkins. Tell them it's your grandfather and to come quickly.'

'Where does it hurt, William?' Mama gently felt over his body and Papa groaned when she touched his ribs and his leg.

'I'm sorry, Ellen. I should have waited for you,' he murmured. 'All I've done is cause you more trouble.'

Mama kissed his cheek. 'Never, my love.'

I wiped the sweat from his forehead. I wished I knew how to help him. 'Don't worry, Papa. The doctor will be here soon and he'll get you right in no time.'

Papa just nodded and grasped my hand, holding it tight.

It wasn't until Papa was resting comfortably in bed and had been treated by Dr Jenkins that I could breathe a sigh of relief. His cracked ribs were bound tightly and the break in his leg cocooned in plaster bandages that had set hard. He'd been given a draught to ease his pain and help him sleep.

'He was lucky,' said Dr Jenkins, packing away the last of his supplies into his bag. 'There seems to be no damage to his organs but we'll continue to watch for any changes. The ribs might be painful but they'll heal without any trouble. The leg may take longer but I'm not sure how his condition will affect his recovery.'

'You know how he loves the pub,' said Mama. 'Will he be able to return to work?'

The doctor nodded. 'He might feel disoriented for the next few days and I think we should expect him not to feel himself for a week or two. But as soon as he's up to it, I don't see why he can't go back to the pub, as long as he stays off that leg.' He looked around the room. 'You may want to move his sleeping arrangements to something suitable downstairs. He won't be able to manage the stairs and we don't want another fall. And it might be easier for him to get around in a wheelchair to start with.'

'Thank you, Dr Jenkins, for coming so quickly,' I said.

'You did the right thing calling me,' he said, smiling 'It could have been a lot worse.'

I sat in the chair beside Papa's bed while he slept, reading a novel that Clementine had bought me for my birthday, wildflowers, harebell, daisies and centaury, dried and pressed within the pages. *The Heavenly Twins* by Sarah Grand was about the 'New Woman' who was educated, working and independent, an activist and suffragist, and who challenged the double standards in conventional marriage. The protagonist was much like Clementine and like me, I realised.

'Ellen! Is that you, Ellen?' Papa's voice was thin and reedy.

I held his hand. 'It's Hannah, Papa.'

He pulled his hand away. 'But where's Ellen? I swear I saw her a moment ago.'

'Mama's downstairs. How are you feeling? Do you remember you fell down the stairs this morning?'

'I fell down the stairs?'

'Are you in pain?'

'I want to go home now.' His eyes had glazed over and he was staring into nothingness.

'All right. Here, have a drink and a little rest first. You've hurt your leg.' There was no point arguing while he was like this. I put my arm under his neck and helped him to sip the medicine Dr Jenkins had left for him, just like a small child. 'Close your eyes for a bit and when you wake up, we can go.' I pulled up the blankets around him. 'I'll sit here and wait.'

Papa nodded and he stared at the ceiling until his eyes began to get heavy and closed.

Over the next two days, Mama, Jenny or I sat with Papa while he slept and cared for him. But as each new day dawned, I realised there was no way I could go to London now. With a heavy heart I knew that none of my sisters were able to come at short notice, and Mama needed me – she couldn't run the pub while I was away with May Day festivities to prepare for. I knew I'd fret and worry all the way to London and be a nervous wreck when I got there. Someone had to go in my place.

'It has to be you,' I said to Clementine when I went to see her. I felt wretched enough after pushing Roger away and then Papa's fall and I could barely believe I was having to give up the opportunity to go. But the next worst thing was to let Mrs Fawcett down.

Clementine shook her head vigorously. 'No, Mrs Fawcett wants you, not me.'

'That's not true. You're perfect for the work she's talking about. You're a born activist.'

She blushed at the compliment. 'But I can't just show up. It wouldn't be right.'

I grasped her hands. '*Please*, Clementine. Imagine what it will do for our society and our community. You have to go.'

Clementine gazed at me, unmovable. She was so stubborn sometimes, but I knew that pushing her towards this meeting was the right thing, even though I wanted to scream with frustration. 'I'll only do it to tell Mrs Fawcett what happened to your father, and to bring back whatever we talk about. Then you'll be ready when you do go to London.'

'Clem, I know you want this as much as me,' I said, gripping her hands tighter. We'd both shared our dreams of a big future in London. We knew what it meant to each other. 'And whatever happens, we'll do it together. We can work out the details after you get back and we know more. Agreed?'

Clementine smiled wryly. 'Agreed.' She picked up her teacup. 'Here's to our partnership.'

I clinked cups with her. 'To our great partnership. Now, you'd better get ready to go to London.'

It was only later that night in the privacy of my room that I allowed the devastating blow to hit me, crying bitter tears of disappointment until I fell into an exhausted sleep.

*

As Dr Jenkins had predicted, it took Papa a week to start feeling a bit better. Thankfully, there seemed to be no other injuries from of his fall, apart from Papa being upset that he'd been the reason I didn't go to London. I reassured him that I would go when he was feeling better, but I was glad to be busy rearranging the drawing room to prepare his new bedroom. The task kept my mind off my crushing disappointment and kept me out of the pub and Roger's way. Seeing the reproach on his face, when I was barely coping with Papa's fall and the fact that Clementine was in London and not me, would have been too much.

Dr Jenkins came to see Papa every day and by the end of the week he agreed it was time to move Papa to his new room. Papa had experimented a few times with the crutches Dr Jenkins had brought over, but he was still in a lot of pain from his cracked ribs.

'What is this?' asked Papa, rapping his knuckles against the plaster on his leg.

'Plaster bandages,' said Dr Jenkins, helping Papa stand. 'Dr Taylor learnt about them when he was in Crimea. Much lighter and more effective in treating broken bones than heavy splints and braces. It shapes the leg and immobilises the area so the bone can heal as straight as possible.'

Papa nodded. 'Lucky for me you learnt about them but I still have to get downstairs without using my leg.'

'Leave it to us,' said Dr Jenkins. 'Hannah and I will manage it.' He flashed me a smile of reassurance.

Getting Papa to the stairs was slow and my heart began to thump as we carefully made our way down, one step at a time, Papa's knuckles white as he held the banister tight. He was shaking with the effort by the time we got to the bottom and collapsed into the wheelchair we had waiting.

'This will be your new bedroom until your leg heals and you can manage the stairs again,' said Dr Jenkins as I opened the door to the drawing room. It had always been Papa's space, somewhere he could relax and entertain, and Mama, Jenny and I had tried to leave it as much as we could, using screens to block off one side of the room where a bed, a cupboard for his clothes, a comfortable reading chair and small table now sat.

Papa nodded, his jaw clenched. 'It will have to do. And we won't have to worry about me falling down any stairs.'

'Dr Jenkins patted him on the arm. 'You can use the wheelchair to come and go to the pub as you please. But make sure you have someone with you. Another fall might not be so lucky.'

'I can go back to work?' He looked between the doctor and me in disbelief. I nodded, knowing how important it was to Papa to prepare for May Day.

'There's no reason why you can't. You'll have to supervise your staff from the wheelchair and keep your leg raised until the bone begins to knit. Then you can start to put weight on the leg, until you're walking normally again.'

'Normal ... I don't think I'll ever be normal again.'

'Don't say that, Papa. You have to give it time.' He'd get better, I knew he would.

'You've managed so far. It's all about adapting.' Jenkins smiled encouragingly. 'You have the most supportive staff and family around you, Will.'

'Thank you, Dr Jenkins,' Papa said. 'I'm tired. I think I'll rest now.'

*

Clementine returned the following afternoon and I could hardly wait for her to tell me how the visit had gone, unable to focus on the lessons I was preparing.

It seemed like I'd waited forever before the knock at the door had me jumping to my feet in my rush to open it.

Clementine followed me to the kitchen, where I put on the kettle.

'How did it go?' I asked almost breathless with anticipation.

'Oh Hannah, London was astonishing,' she said, her eyes bright.

'I thought it would be.'

'So many people everywhere. I went on the underground railway. It was hard to believe that we were travelling through tunnels under the roads, but not only that, I rode on trams through the crowded streets too. It took no time to get across the city. I even got to spend time wandering through Harrods. I've never seen so many beautiful things.'

'It sounds incredible,' I said, trying my hardest to push the jealousy aside. Unlike Clementine, I'd lived in Hartlepool and Durham, two big cities, but London was something else and I could only imagine how much bigger and grander it was.

She sat at the table and reached into her bag. 'Here, I bought you a little something from Harrods.'

'Really, Clem, you didn't have to,' I said, taking the package.

'It's only something small to cheer you up after missing the trip and your father's fall. How is he?'

I smiled, feeling touched. She really was the best friend. 'On the mend, at least physically, but he's been very quiet … It's almost like he's given up or something.' Papa's mood was worrying.

Clementine squeezed my hand. 'It might just take time.'

'Yes, he'll get better. He always does.' I sat beside her and opened the parcel. 'A paperweight! It's beautiful.' I turned the glass object in my hand, looking at the coloured picture in the centre.

'It's the Houses of Parliament,' said Clementine with a smile. 'As inspiration. The important work we do will eventually reach Parliament and one day you'll sit in the ladies' gallery and listen to the debate.'

'I love it,' I said and hugged her quickly. 'I'll keep it on my desk at school, so I can see it every day.'

'I'm glad you like it.' She patted my shoulder. 'Mrs Fawcett was disappointed not to see you but she sends her best wishes for your father's recovery.'

'Thank you.' I put a plate of biscuits on the table, my heart beating faster. 'What did she have to say?'

'As you know, she's also a member of the Women's Local Government Society who support women to stand in local elections and she wants to arrange another meeting soon to discuss the parish and district elections and how we might support a female candidate of our own. Unfortunately, neither of us can vote because we don't own property or pay rates.'

My dreams weren't dead, only on hold. And there was still important work to be done here in our county. 'Does she have anyone in mind?'

'I suggested Esther. She owns property through her grandparents. I know we'd have to coach her, but we could work well with her. Esther knows what issues we want to promote and she's local.'

I nodded as I thought this new idea through. Esther was a good choice, and although not a confident speaker, she was passionate about the work we were doing. 'All right.'

'But that's not all. Mrs Fawcett wants to know if you're interested in speaking around the district.'

I could feel my cheeks flushing. Speaking in front of our small society was one thing – speaking to people I didn't know was another. I became suddenly restless and got up to put the tea into the teapot. 'About what?'

'Women's suffrage, higher education for girls and education for working people.'

'She wants me to speak at events? You're the knowledgeable one.' I felt flattered, but I didn't understand why Mrs Fawcett hadn't asked Clementine. I was good at doing and organising. Clementine was the one who knew exactly what to say, how to answer a question.

Clementine smiled. 'No, Hannah, you're the stronger speaker. You're empathetic, you're warm and persuasive. People listen and respond to you because you care so deeply.'

I paused, the spoon suspended above the teapot. 'You really think so?' Even though Clementine was my friend, she had always been a straight talker and this was high praise.

'I do. You'll be fine. But even better, she also mentioned speaking to teachers' groups about the importance of secondary and university education so that girls aren't obliged to study cookery and needlework when the boys can do science and study electricity and chemistry.'

Excitement surged through me. If Clementine and I worked together with the backing of Millicent Fawcett, there was no telling what we could achieve. 'There's the Royal Commission on Secondary Education coming up – we'll have to make sure we know about all the issues.'

'She's already thought about that.' Clem smiled. 'She wants you to meet with two advocates who can help you understand the issues and campaigns. Emily Davies has been on the London School Board and Maria Grey has been heavily involved in the Women's Education Union.'

I took a sharp breath, the honour not lost on me. Emily Davies was another well-known suffrage supporter and famous within the teaching community for co-founding Girton College at Cambridge University, one of the first colleges for women, and for her work in advocating for the admission of women into universities. And I knew all about Maria Grey, who'd helped found the first teachers' training college for women.

I sat beside Clementine again, letting the tea infuse. 'But what about you? You've been following the changes in education much longer than I have.'

'Mrs Fawcett wants me to support you and Esther until the elections are done at the end of the year. Then she says that there's work for me at the National Society.'

'What kind of work?' I felt bad that Clementine was being asked to stay in the background when she was so qualified.

'I don't know yet.' She patted my hand. 'Don't worry, Hannah. There's more than enough to do for the moment and I'm excited for the three of us to be working together.'

I rubbed my thumb over the smooth glass of the paperweight. She had to be disappointed. I knew how ambitious she was, what potential she had as a campaigner. 'As long as you're recognised for your talents and skills and you have your moment in the sun too.'

'You know me well enough to know that I will. I'm persistent, like a dog with a bone.'

I kissed her on the cheek. 'Thank you, Clementine. None of this would have happened without you, but when your time comes, I'll be there to support you too.'

18

Despite being a place for families and neighbours to
come together, even our own pub promotes a visible
divide between men and women. Women aren't allowed
in the main bar and can only order drinks in the lounge.
As much as I dream of changing this rule, nobody would
come if women were suddenly able to drink in the
main bar.

It was Sunday morning in late June and Papa had asked us to
stay after breakfast. Jenny had gone home to see her parents
and would return with Sarah, who was going to stay for the
midsummer celebrations here in the village.

'What is it, William?' asked Mama. 'What do you want to
talk about?'

Papa nodded, as if gathering his thoughts. 'It's been a
couple of months since my accident and it's clear that I'm
getting worse, not better.'

'No, you're not,' I interrupted in annoyance. His plaster
had been removed and we were doing everything to make
sure that his leg regained some strength and mobility and
that he could manage around home and the pub. But there
were some days when he still used the wheelchair because he
couldn't manage with the walking sticks and didn't want to
ask for help.

He raised a shaky hand. 'Let me finish. My leg is healed
but who knows if or when I'll be able to use it properly again.

I can't walk without someone helping me and that's not likely to change. We have to face the facts: I can't manage on my own and one day not even your help will be enough. I won't be a burden on you.'

Papa was running the pub from an armchair in the bar, supervising the staff and making sure all the daily tasks were done but the pain of the badly damaged leg took it out of him, and he'd fall asleep in his chair at the end of the day before Mama had even brought him his tea. Bill, Mama, Roger and I always made sure one of us covered for him but it would take time until his leg was strong again. I still hadn't managed to mention Mr Bailey's role as the brewery spy to Papa, but at least I knew Mr Bailey had taken back what he'd said about Papa's health.

'You're not a burden,' said Mama hotly, 'and you're doing fine.'

Papa reached for her hand across the table. 'Ellen, you know that's not true. There's no way I'll ever return to our bedroom upstairs.'

'Then we'll move our bedroom downstairs. We'll find a way around all the obstacles.'

'How?' asked Papa, his face creased with anguish. 'What can you do about my hands? I can't hold a glass, let alone pour a beer, they shake so much, and if I try to write anything, nobody can read it.' The belladonna drops had helped only for a short time. But I didn't think he'd really get better until the issue with Mr Connolly and the brewery was resolved.

'That's what you have Mama and me for,' I said gently. 'And Jenny, Sarah, Mary and Jane will help.'

He pulled his hand away from Mama's in frustration. 'You all have your own lives to live. For goodness' sake, Jane's just had a baby.' Tears filled his eyes. 'This was never how it was supposed to be.'

'But we want to be here to help, Papa.' I couldn't bear to see him so upset and I didn't want to be having this conversation. I only wished that all of this could disappear, that neither of my parents had to suffer through this impossible situation.

'What don't you understand?' he replied, raising his voice. '*I don't want you to!*'

Mama and I shared a look of fear. Papa could be stubborn when he wanted to be.

His shoulders slumped. 'It's time, Ellen. I've made my decision.' Pain, sadness and regret darted across his face and he opened his mouth to speak but closed it again, his lips pressed tightly together.

'What decision, Papa?' I whispered, fear shooting through me.

'I'm going to the county asylum.'

I watched the blood drain from Mama's face as she swayed in her chair. I could barely breathe, and had to force my lips to move. 'What?'

'It's for the best. I've spoken to Dr Taylor and he agrees. This is the time to do it, while I'm still lucid. I've written everything down, instructions for the pub, my wishes for when I can no longer think for myself and for after my death. A letter detailing the management of The Ox and Plough and my estate and naming my receiver has been overseen by the solicitor Mr Sanderson and will be sent to the Master of Lunacy once I enter the asylum. It will provide sufficient legal grounds to allow you to continue to run the pub in my absence.'

'You can't do this, William, not now,' whispered Mama. The look of devastation and hurt on her face nearly broke my heart.

'Don't you think I know what this condition is doing to you all? I won't torture you any more than I already have. My fall prevented Hannah from going to London. I won't have you stop your lives because of me.'

'Please, William. We're all right. You can't help it.' Tears were streaming down Mama's face as she reached for Papa's hand. 'We can look after you here and if we need, we can hire someone to help care for you.'

He patted Mama's hand gently and sighed. 'I've thought about this long and hard. We can't really afford to hire someone, it's too expensive and who knows how long I'll need help. It's not that I want to be away from you but I'm better off somewhere that can give me the care I need. There are more treatments available in the asylum. It's close to Sarah if I need anything, and you and Hannah can visit. And hopefully, if the treatments help, it won't be forever. I can come home when I'm well and go back in when I need more treatment.'

'Then don't go now. You still have time,' I pleaded.

Papa shook his head. 'No, I don't. I know what Mr Franks at The Rose and Crown and Trevor Carter are planning.'

I started in shock. 'Papa—'

He put his hand up to stop me. 'Bill told me how you wanted to let me know, but with everything ... What you did saved us but we're out of time. The vultures are already circling. Mr Connolly has persuaded the agricultural and village committees to sponsor The Rose and Crown for the upcoming festivals and shows. Faith in me as a publican will only decline, so if I stay, we're done for.' He spread his hands on the table, pressing them down to force them to stop shaking. 'I have to retire, Hannah. Everything I've done, insisting on your education, sending you to teachers' college and your training here, has prepared you for this. You'll have plenty of help from Bill and Roger, but you're ready and more than capable.'

'What are you talking about? Papa, I can't run The Ox and Plough.' This couldn't be happening. Papa had always backed my activism, to change the world – that's what my education had been for – but here he was tying me to this place, forcing a future on me that I'd never wanted. I'd only agreed to learn the business to reassure him, to help him, not take over.

Was this what he'd wanted for me from the very start, when he first considered buying The Ox and Plough? I tried to speak but no more words came.

'You have to, for all our sakes,' said Papa grimly. 'I can continue to hold the liquor licence as owner of the premises and business, but not if I stay and run the pub. Franks and Carter will make sure of that and I won't leave this decision until it's too late. We'd lose everything.'

I stared at him, the reality of his words hitting home like a punch to the gut. He had no choice … and neither did I.

'You know the others will complain,' pressed Mama.

'Let them,' said Papa with a flick of his wrist. 'I still own The Ox and Plough, nobody else. While I live, the pub remains in my name and Hannah will run the business. I've set down my wishes, so there's no doubt.'

'William—' Mama pressed a trembling hand to her mouth.

'Of course, Papa,' I whispered finally, feeling light-headed. I couldn't believe we were discussing plans for a future without Papa.

'You're better off here,' sobbed Mama. 'This is where you belong, with those who love you best.'

Papa slammed the table hard. 'Stop!' he yelled. 'I've made my decision and you're not going to change my mind.'

'I won't let you go,' Mama moaned. I put my arms around her, wanting to shield her from the pain.

'I leave in a few days,' he said more gently. 'Dr Taylor has arranged it.'

'A few *days*?'

'There's no point delaying the inevitable. The sooner this is done, the sooner we can make the change official on my licence and nobody can force us out.'

Papa was right and I knew there was nothing I could do to alter his decision. He was doing this to save us and The Ox and Plough.

*

The next few days were spent in a flurry of activity, preparing for Papa's departure. He had more energy than he'd had for weeks, going over the accounts with me one last time, making sure I understood what needed to be done, talking at length with Bill, who promised to help me manage the pub, giving me guidance as I needed. The looks of disbelief on the faces of Polly and Reg when Papa told them he was going away to a sanitorium to recuperate and that I was taking over as manager mirrored Mama's and my feelings of being caught in a terrible nightmare.

Bill told Roger, who just looked stunned. I could only nod when his eyes met mine, turning away from the comfort I knew he wanted to give me. I had to stay strong and I was afraid that if I spoke to him now, I'd break down. But the hardest part was helping Mama pack Papa's things, thinking about what he'd need, what he'd want to have with him to remind him of home and to help him feel close to us. It all passed in a blur and I felt numb as we ticked off the list of things that had to be done before he was locked away. My sisters arrived to help in any way they could and to spend time with Papa, but it didn't take long for him to get short with them as they tried to persuade him to stay, even though the order had been signed.

The night before his departure, The Ox and Plough was full of customers, which gave Papa the send-off he truly deserved. Even though we hadn't broadcast his situation, news of him leaving temporarily to let his leg heal had spread. I soon discovered that Laura, Clem and Esther were behind that story. I was more than grateful for their love and support.

Mr Franks and Trevor Carter had taken the bait about Papa not being ill, which was a small blessing. Now they were too late to take action and the new details on Papa's licence had been lodged with the licensing register. The pub was safe. The Ox and Plough could remain our haven, a place for the suffrage movement, a refuge for all women.

It was late when we closed. After we'd cleaned up and everyone had gone home, Papa and I sat quietly in the main bar.

'You know I don't want to leave you like this,' he said. 'But you understand why I have to do it.' He looked exhausted, the dark smudges under his eyes tell-tale signs that he hadn't been sleeping. I knew that he'd been pushing himself almost to the point of collapse and that the pain in his leg had flared up with the extra activity and periods of standing and walking.

I nodded, swallowing the lump in my throat. 'I know, but I wish there was another way.'

'There's not. I've investigated all the options and thought long and hard. This is the only sensible decision. I know you can do it.'

I shook my head. 'I don't know if I can.'

'But I have no doubt.' He squeezed my arm. 'Look after your mother. This is going to be hard on her.'

'I will.' I furiously blinked the tears away but one escaped down my cheek anyway.

Papa gently brushed the tear away. 'Don't cry. I've been lucky to have been here as long as I have with you and your mother. I've been blessed to see your sisters' families grow. And I know you'll be fine, whatever you do with your life. You're strong like your mother.'

'But what about you? How will you cope there?'

'I'll manage, knowing that you're both looked after, that I've done the right thing. It will give me strength.'

The tears came faster now. 'But I can't bear to think of you there. You love The Ox and Plough.'

He looked around the room, his eyes soft with memory. 'I'll miss this place more than I can say.'

'It won't be the same without you, Papa.'

He shook his head. 'It's time for a new chapter, fresh blood and new ideas. You were made for this place. And it can give you a good life, whether you remain teaching or not.'

I wanted to shout that this was not what I wanted. I didn't want the responsibility of looking after The Ox and Plough, no matter how much I'd grown to love it. This was Papa's dream, not mine. But I couldn't. He was doing this for us.

'We'll all visit as often as we can, Papa. And ...' I had to force the words out now '... I won't let you down.'

Papa kissed me on the cheek, both our faces wet with tears. 'I've never doubted you, my beautiful girl.'

And I knew then that despite all my doubts, I would do anything to keep my promise to him. The Ox and Plough was his legacy, and after tonight, the best way everyone would remember him.

*

Early the following morning, we saw Papa off, accompanied by Dr Taylor in his carriage. I clung to Papa. His thin frame through his clothes that smelt of the tobacco that he used in his pipe; his soft cheek against mine and the fine tremor that had become constant whenever he was worried or upset. Then he was gone, the carriage disappearing down the street. But I couldn't bear returning to our parlour with Mama and my sisters in tears, and retreated to the pub where there was plenty of work to push away my sorrow. But everywhere I looked I saw evidence of Papa and the only thought I had, pounding like a tattoo in my brain, was how could Papa have done this to himself, done this to us? Leaving Mama and me when he didn't have to. The rational part of me knew why he did, but all I could feel was loss and abandonment.

When Roger came into the kitchen to help me after closing, I tried to tell him how adrift I felt without Papa. How he had always been my anchor, and I didn't know how to centre myself. I was overwhelmed with the responsibility now on my shoulders. But the words wouldn't come out. I was so tired. I leant in towards him instead and he put his arms around me as if it was the most natural thing to do. I gazed into his face and my eyes rested on his lips. Then I was kissing him and it felt so good. The world dropped away, all my worries, hurt and pain receding, and I allowed myself to fall deeper into the moment.

I wrapped my arms around him, one hand in his soft hair, and pulled him closer, registering the gentle grazing of his rough evening stubble against my skin. All I wanted was to forget, if only for a little while. His kisses were long and slow, igniting a fire within me that had my body burning for him. I wanted to burn.

He broke away, leaving me breathless, only to kiss the sensitive skin on my neck and throat. I took his hand and slid it over my shirtwaist to cup my breast. When his thumb began circling so that even against the thick fabric of my corset, my nipple stood erect, I gasped. Even as I pressed my hand over his, overwhelmed, part of me wondered how much more pleasure might be possible.

'You'd better go,' he whispered. 'Before we go too far.'

'But I don't want to go.'

'Neither do I, but it's easy to get carried away in the moment. I don't want you to regret what we've done and hate me tomorrow.'

'Roger, I could never hate you.' I felt dazed, my skin still on fire from his kisses.

'Maybe not, but I don't want to take the risk of losing you altogether.'

I nodded and sighed. He was right. 'Mama and my sisters will be wondering where I am. But I don't know if I can face their sadness.'

'I know the burden is heavy but remember you're strong. Whenever the grief and pain get too much, maybe the memory of our kisses will take you away to a happier place until you feel you can cope again.'

I smiled. 'I like that.' My forehead rested against his.

'Come on then,' he said, taking my hand. 'Let's finish up and go home.'

19

At teachers' college, I'd gone to the talks of the Fabian Society and agreed with their central idea of equality for all, the tenets of humanism and the beliefs that all life was sacred.

My sisters returned home in the days that followed and Mama and I were left with a gaping hole in our lives. It was painful not seeing Papa each day and too quiet without him at The Ox and Plough. Mama wrote to him each night after we'd had our dinner, telling him about our day. She focused on our visit to him, once he had settled, putting together a list of what she'd need to make his favourite biscuits and her famous lemon cake. I tried to support her as best I could when I wasn't at school. But I could see how much she was hurting and there was little I could do.

'She pretends that everything's all right,' I said to Clementine as we walked home from school, 'but it's the little things I see. The absent gazes at Papa's chair at the dining table; the misty eyes whenever she makes his favourite dishes; how she delays going to bed at night because he isn't by her side.'

'It's going to take time to adjust, for the both of you,' said Clementine. 'But I know you'll do it and it won't be long before you can go to visit your father.'

I nodded. Roger had said much the same thing. It was easy to cross paths with him during our daily activities. He was still working on the new school buildings but it was getting harder to remember not to touch his hand or stand too close to him. I didn't want to set tongues wagging, but the truth was that I couldn't stay away from him. He was the only one who kept me on an even keel and the thought of seeing him kept me going. I knew I was sending the wrong message to him and what we were doing wasn't right, but I couldn't stop thinking about him, wanting to be near him.

I was tired of being the responsible one. I was tired with how tight the corset felt. The future I'd imagined for myself was moving further and further out of reach. I was learning that life wasn't as absolute and certain as I'd thought. It was changeable and uncertain and nobody really knew what was ahead of them. I still felt single-minded in my purpose, but now everything seemed restrictive: so much harder to achieve and my successes smaller. I had my duty to my parents and to the continued success of The Ox and Plough, to our suffrage society and the people of Ebberfield. But I felt suffocated and overwhelmed with all of that responsibility on my shoulders.

Ever since Papa's departure I had the undeniable urge to rebel against reality. Late at night in my room I'd started contemplating even further intimacies with Roger. I thought about the dangers – to myself and to Roger's feelings – but I knew how we could be careful, so I'd never fall pregnant. At college I'd read some of the pamphlets from the Malthusian League which promoted contraception, and some of the girls had mentioned that although Indian rubber letters were available under the counter for men, those women who used the new contraceptive devices which could be expensive, inconvenient and uncomfortable, were still labelled in the same category as prostitutes. They talked about the ancient withdrawal method still being the most effective. But I wondered what a relationship with a man might be like if pregnancy could be reliably avoided. For one thing, I would be less cautious and wouldn't have to hold myself back from Roger. If women had the same sexual freedom as men, a relationship would be more equitable. Perhaps one day.

'Esther and I have been talking,' continued Clementine, breaking into my thoughts, as we crossed the street. 'We want to help you and your mother any way we can. Perhaps we can come into the pub on a Saturday afternoon or after church on Sundays to help with the cleaning, or even help with serving when you're busy.'

I stopped outside the rectory and clasped her gloved hand. 'What would I do without you both?'

She nodded and looked away.

'What is it?'

'I know this isn't a good time, but we still have to talk about the local elections before you reply to Mrs Fawcett. The election is only four or five months away and there's a lot to do to prepare Esther and her campaign.'

Clementine and I had approached Esther after Clem's trip to London and with much persuasion, she had agreed to run. We'd begun preparations for her campaign and platform with Mrs Fawcett's guidance but now she wanted to arrange a time for Esther, Clementine and me to come to London to talk further and for me to meet Emily Davies and possibly Maria Grey, despite her ill health.

'To be honest, I haven't given it any thought since Papa's departure. Everything else has been pushed straight out of my mind.'

'Of course.'

'But we can't keep Mrs Fawcett waiting. Why don't you and Esther come over after church on Sunday and we'll talk more about the elections? It will be a good distraction for Mama too. And with summer holidays around the corner, we'll be able to work out a time for the three of us to get to London.'

*

The final days of the school year passed in a blur. I was sad to see my class go, many leaving school and entering the world as labourers or young apprentices. Benjamin, Clementine and I handpicked the oldest students we thought could benefit from another year of schooling. Many of their parents agreed to send them back to school in the autumn but some didn't see the value or just couldn't afford not to have another income, like Rory's parents, but perhaps Kitty's death had only made them want to keep their remaining children close.

I felt the familiar fire in my belly at the thought of Kitty's life cut short, unnecessarily so, and decided to discuss with Clementine, Esther and Mrs Fawcett what we could do to promote raising the compulsory age of schooling and increasing opportunities to attend higher schools and even university for those in our district. No one deserved a workhouse fate. I was thankful that Elizabeth Rainforth had agreed that Anthony could return to school.

With the summer break, I turned my attention to the pub. There was a lot to catch up on. Bill and Roger pitched in however they could, I continued to serve, do the books and help Mama in the kitchen. And through it all, I kept a burning secret from everyone, something of my own that no one could take away. Night after night, as we closed up the pub, what had started as a few kisses had developed into something more. The more intimate Roger and I became, the more I contemplated going further with him. I wanted to know him fully, I wanted us to be one.

One evening, I knew the time had come to step over that invisible line. Papa's departure had broken me open. It was as though all my tightly held emotions had risen up to overcome my logical brain, and reason had lost its mooring to submerge beneath the tide. Now all I wanted was to feel joy, happiness and pleasure. I wanted to feel the thrill of Roger's touch on my body, and of my own on his. I wanted to rebel and break the rules. If I was discreet, I could do whatever I wanted. I could be free.

'I'll finish up here, Bill,' I said after closing, decision made.

'No, I'll stay,' Bill insisted. 'You do it every night, go home, Roger can help me.'

I nodded, my gaze holding Roger's for just a moment. 'I'll see you both tomorrow then.'

Once Mama and Jenny had retired for the night, and I knew Bill had left, I slipped back into the pub.

'Finally,' I said, stepping into Roger's arms and shivering with anticipation.

'I've been waiting all day for this moment,' said Roger, dipping his head to kiss me. It surprised me how quickly we'd become familiar with each other; the way my head tucked under his chin and how our bodies fitted together so seamlessly. We'd become more and more daring with each meeting, exploring each other's bodies in a jumble of clothes, hands and mouths, eagerly seeking but never consummating our desire. We had discussed how to prevent pregnancy, so we both knew what we would do if we lost ourselves in our ardour. Roger had even offered to go to Hartlepool to buy Indian rubber letters from a discreet barber shop but in the end, we agreed to try the simple, age-old method that had been recommended to me.

'For this moment?' I asked, grinning cheekily, as my hands slid lower to rest on his firm behind.

'Well, I'll take any moment I can get with you.'

It amazed me how our few stolen hours of kisses, tight embraces and wandering, urgent hands had changed the whole nature of our relationship. I was able to tell him things I'd never told anyone, about my hopes and dreams, about my fears and insecurities; and he'd wept as he told me about his darkest days after his father had died. I was moved by the sight of this big, strong man with tears running down his face, who'd trusted me enough to be raw and vulnerable. I'd never met a man like him before: behind the tough exterior, he was honest, sensitive and thoughtful.

'Ahh, but the night is young. We have plenty of moments to spend together.' I pressed myself against him and felt the hardness of his body between us. 'And I intend to make the most of them.'

Roger squirmed. 'Keep doing that and I don't know if I'll be able to control myself.'

'I don't know what you're talking about,' I said, my eyes wide with innocence before taking his hand and leading him to the couch in Papa's office. 'Besides, you're getting good at slipping away before things get out of control.'

'Let's take things slowly then.' He sat on the couch and settled me on his lap before kissing me again. The room around us disappeared and it was just Roger and me.

'I want to be like this always.' I sighed.

'If I had my way, we would be.' He smiled wolfishly and I shivered in anticipation at the thoughts that I knew were going through his mind. I settled my hand over the hard ridge between us, which jumped to attention at my touch. 'No, not yet,' he groaned, 'or I'll never last.' Instead, he took my hand. 'Help me undo your corset, so I can pay homage to your beautiful breasts.'

*

Sometime later, after we had discarded most of our clothes, Roger allowed me to look at him by the light of the old paraffin lamp that we'd lit. It was the first time I'd ever seen a man completely naked. He was beautiful: long limbed, tall and sculpted like the illustrations of ancient Greek warriors I'd seen in my history books at college. I traced my fingertips across his warm skin, marvelling at the dark springy hairs on his chest and the way his nipples hardened at my touch, just as mine did with his. His hands twitched, and by the longing etched on his face, I knew he wanted to touch me in return. His lips were swollen from our kisses, and his eyes were bright. He held still, watching me with an intensity that made me want to explode somehow.

It was only when my hand strayed between his legs, and the surprisingly soft skin became firm, that he took in a sharp breath and caught my hand.

I looked into his face, unsure. 'Have I done something wrong?'

He shook his head. 'Let's just say that I'm finding it hard to contain myself.'

I was about to step away, feeling a little silly that I hadn't been able to read the signs, but he took my hands, bringing them to his lips.

'It's all right. Just give me a moment to settle.' His blue eyes held my gaze and he smiled reassuringly.

I could see the question in his eyes, the deeper vulnerability. *Do I meet your approval?*

'You're magnificent,' I whispered.

'Let me see you now.' He reached towards me, kissing my bare shoulder, my chemise the only thing between Roger and me.

I swallowed, suddenly shy and nervous. He smiled at me

and I stood, finding my courage, and dropped my chemise to the floor.

'You're breathtaking,' he whispered. 'Perfection itself. Just as I knew you would be. There are no secrets between us now.'

I nodded, his words making me feel powerful. I sat beside him and embraced him, relishing the new sensation of skin on skin. We couldn't be much closer.

'I love you, Hannah, and I know I'll love you till the day I die.'

I drew back and searched his face but there was no guile, only a deep honesty. I was safe and loved. And I realised with surprise that I loved him too.

'Is this what you want?' he whispered.

'I want you.' I kissed him again and allowed myself to surrender to the exquisite sensations that overwhelmed me.

When Roger finally slid home, I was beyond reason, unable to heed caution, driven by desire despite the sudden, searing pain.

'Are you all right?' he asked, pausing. 'Are you sure you want to do this?'

'Don't stop now,' I whispered, clinging to him.

'We'll have to be careful,' he murmured, beginning to rock.

'I know.'

We were as close as we could be, joined as one. It seemed so right and perfectly natural. How had I ever lived without this before? But I knew the answer. I hadn't met Roger and I'd never fallen in love until now. I was swept up in a crescendo until suddenly Roger pulled away, and collapsed beside me.

'Are you all right?' I asked after a moment.

Roger nodded. 'I am now, but that was a bit close.' He kissed my throat. 'And how are you?'

'I'm fine.' The truth was I felt a little raw but blissful.

'You drive me wild,' he said, kissing me again deeply. 'I could do this with you all day and all night.'

'Then we'd never get anything done.'

'I don't care. I only want to lie by your side.'

I shivered. He wanted to do this again and he wanted to be with me.

'I love you,' I whispered finally.

But when I gazed into his face, his eyes were closed and his breathing was deep and regular. He was asleep.

20

The Fellowship of the New Life taught that sex was a natural part of life to be enjoyed between a consenting man and woman. It feels deliciously wicked, but they believe that sexual freedom is an essential part of a women's rights and, with an understanding of birth control and contraception, there is no reason a woman shouldn't choose for herself.

Finally, about a month after Papa had left and he had settled in, the day arrived when Mama and I were able to visit him. His letters home had assured us that he was beginning to find a routine, working in the garden in the morning and playing games in the hall in the afternoon. But I couldn't wait to see him for myself, to gauge how he really was and to assess his surroundings for anything Mama and I might do to improve his comfort.

The Durham Asylum was a fairly new establishment on a generous country acreage. Its grand entrance made me feel we'd arrived at a large estate, and I could see some of the tension ease in Mama's shoulders. Perhaps it was a much nicer place than we'd thought. The main building sat at the end of a tree-lined road like a proud manor house, and was surrounded by gardens and cultivated farmland. We were greeted by asylum staff inside the reception hall, where Mama and I had to sign the visitors' book before we were taken to a nearby room where Papa waited for us.

He was sitting at a table by a large window that overlooked the garden, the summer sunshine streaming in. Papa seemed well and he stood, beaming from ear to ear, when he saw us.

I was in his arms in a moment. 'Papa, I've missed you so much,' I said.

'I've missed you too.' He kissed Mama and was holding us both tightly to him. Tears welled in my eyes. 'Come now,' he said. 'Sit down and tell me everything that's been happening.'

'First of all, tell us how you are,' said Mama.

'I'm fine.'

'No Papa, how are you really?' I peered into his face. He looked like he always had, like my beloved father. His eyes were bright and keen as he waited eagerly for news of home.

He nodded. 'As you can imagine, there's been a period of adjustment. At first it was hard being away from you both, not waking up next to your mother and seeing your smiling face, but knowing what you were doing gave me comfort and strength.' Mama squeezed his hand across the table and Papa smiled reassuringly. 'But soon, I began to know the men in my ward, the attendants on duty each day and finally other residents as I learnt the new routine.'

Mama frowned. 'New routine?'

'Yes, my love. We get up at six, have a wash, get dressed and have breakfast. Then we can go outside to enjoy the gardens. I've been given a small plot to grow vegetables that I tend during the morning, along with the flowers growing in the greenhouses, before we come in for tea. My leg's getting stronger all the time and I can do more with each passing week. In the afternoon, we can spend time in the recreation hall, reading, playing board games and cards or just talking to the other men. After supper, we go to bed. And on Sundays, after the chapel service, we take a walk through the fields, pastures and woods. I've been able to go a little further each time.'

'So, you're getting better?' I asked, tentatively.

Papa nodded. 'I am. Perhaps the treatment Dr Sloane has prescribed is working.'

'What type of treatment?'

'Fresh air, exercise, a relaxed environment and a special medicine to help relax my muscles.'

I smiled. 'That sounds promising.' The modern philosophy here at the asylum and Papa's holistic treatment made me hopeful. Being away from the worries of the brewery and growing the pub while keeping it afloat had no doubt helped. Perhaps Papa had made the right choice for his health.

'What about your meals?' asked Mama.

'The food's not as good as yours, my love, but it's still decent. We have meat or fish with our vegetables, as well as bread and cheese most days and pudding sometimes and there's always beer, tea or cocoa to wash the food down.'

'How's the beer, Papa?'

'It's not bad, but ...' He smiled. Then he became more serious and businesslike. 'Is Mr Connolly giving you any trouble?'

I shook my head. 'No, he's not changed or increased any of the products. Bill seems to have him well in hand.'

He nodded. 'Good but make sure you keep an eye on Mr Franks, he's an untrustworthy snake.'

'Don't worry, I will, Papa.' I was determined to take this burden off his shoulders. I began to nurse some small hope that Papa would return home to us.

'Find a way to change the brewery and the committee's mind about their sponsorship decisions. We have to give them confidence in our ability to continue as we have done, as the heart and soul of the township. And get in early for the festivals. It pays to be prepared and organised.' He sighed. 'I wish I was there to help you.'

Mama suddenly put her hands over her face and began to shake with silent tears.

'Don't cry, Ellen,' whispered Papa, looking stricken. He reached out to touch her face.

'It's all right, Mama,' I said, putting my arm around her. 'Papa is fine. As you can see, he's well cared for.'

She nodded and brushed the tears from her cheeks. 'I know,' she said, sitting tall once more, steeling herself against all the things she couldn't control.

Papa seemed unsure for a moment and then reached across the table and took both our hands. 'Tell me about everything. How are the girls and the grandchildren? How's The Ox and Plough? And what's happening with your suffrage society and Millicent Fawcett?'

I told him about Esther running for local council and our plans to go to London to see Mrs Fawcett.

'You'll go far,' he whispered, kissing my hand. 'Make the most of every opportunity, but most of all, do what truly makes you happy.' I felt a stab of irritation but held my tongue. Papa's version of happiness was me staying in Ebberfield to run the pub in his stead. 'Now, remember every little thing until I see you both next, especially about your trip to London, Hannah. I want to hear it all. And anything you need to talk about before then, send in a letter and I'll answer you the very same day. But now, it's time for you to go.'

*

Bill and I took Mr Bailey to meet Mr Worthington at the brewery. After my conversation with Papa, I knew it was something I had to do for the good of the pub, to make sure we had the brewery on side and reduce the negative influence of Mr Connolly. Together we told him about Mr Connolly and his association with Mr Franks and how they'd been plotting against us.

'Mr Connolly has been forcing us to buy more beer and other brewery products, taking his commission and misleading you about our position,' I concluded.

'I assure you, I knew nothing about this arrangement,' said Mr Worthington, his frown deepening. 'This brewery has a reputation to uphold and at no time would we ever approve such underhanded tactics as what you say Mr Connolly has employed.'

'I have all the evidence you need to confirm my story.' I placed the ledgers on the desk in front of him which showed the discrepancy between the larger orders from the brewery and smaller amount of alcohol we sold each week. His eyebrows rose in surprise.

Mr Bailey twisted his soft cap in his hands. 'Everything Miss Todd says is true. Mr Connolly and Mr Franks want to ruin The Ox and Plough for their own gain. I can only feel regret for my part in the whole sordid affair.'

'All we want is what is fair and reasonable,' said Bill. 'Mr Todd and now his daughter have been good managers of The Ox and Plough, growing the business and trying to make a living. Greed and jealousy have been the motives behind the collusion between Mr Connolly and Mr Franks.'

Mr Worthington stood and reached for the door. 'If you'd like to wait while I go through your books and check your claims against our own information? I'll have tea brought in for you.'

I nodded. 'Thank you,' I said. There was no need for Mr Bailey to stay, so Bill and I followed the secretary into a small room where we sipped hot tea and chatted while we waited.

Finally, we were ushered back into Mr Worthington's office where he flipped through the paperwork I'd prepared, shaking his head. 'The brewery has only ever wanted what was agreed in your contract. I can't do anything about Mr Franks as he has no tie to this brewery. But from what you've shown me, Mr Connolly will no longer be our representative or deal with any of our tied-houses.'

'Thank you, Mr Worthington,' I said. 'We can deal with Mr Franks, provided he no longer has Mr Connolly and the power of the brewery behind him.'

'We don't want an association with anyone who tarnishes the reputation of this brewery,' said Mr Worthington, standing. 'We look forward to continuing our business with you, Miss Todd.'

'As do I,' I said, shaking his hand. It was a relief to have this problem resolved. And any trouble Mr Franks could inflict on us was now limited.

The Ox and Plough could continue to grow and contribute to the life of our community, just as Papa had intended. Protecting the pub was my first act as manager and I felt strong and proud.

*

I had to see Roger again before I left for London. We'd agreed to meet at the beach after closing on the last day of July. Everything was ready for the Lammas festival the next day where loaves baked with the first grain of the harvest would be blessed at church and a village fair would follow. The moon was bright as I crept out onto the dark, deserted streets and cycled along the country lanes, the silvery light dappled across the fields, casting everything in deep shadow. It was beautiful, so peaceful, and I felt as free as a bird.

I abandoned the bicycle at the top of the cliff and walked down to the beach. It was empty, the only sound the waves breaking gently on the shore, soothing the pain of seeing my father in the asylum. Roger wasn't there yet and so I decided to surprise him, undressing and dropping my clothes piece by piece as I made my way down to the water's edge. I stood there for a moment, stretching my arms in the air, the gentle sea breeze caressing my naked skin like the whispers of a lover. Breaking the rules felt wonderful and exhilarating. I couldn't resist stepping into the water and allowing the sea to hold me in its embrace. As I floated, staring up at the stars, pinpricks of silver and gold in the silky blackness, I surrendered to the night and felt so very blessed to be alive.

Then I felt warm arms around me and reached up to kiss the mouth above me. I'd know his touch anywhere. We were skin on skin, buoyant in the salt water and I could feel his urgent desire, but even still he paused, waiting for my consent, as I slid my hands around his shoulders and down the hard muscular planes of his back, before his slippery warmth, delicious against the refreshing cool, was inside me.

'Surprise,' I whispered, as I melted into him.

In that moment, I could forget everything else. The world was my oyster and I could do anything I wanted.

21

I loved the exciting range of ideas that I was exposed to
in the university city of Durham; egalitarianism, positivism,
the ethical movement, socialism, the co-operative
movement, trade unionism and politics. There was no
turning back for me.

I'd never seen so many people before. Crowds of men and
women walked in all directions as Clementine, Esther and
I finally alighted at King's Cross Station. I couldn't believe
how big it was. According to Clementine, there were over ten
platforms, connecting lines to Leicester, the suburban services
and the underground trains that went all over London. Esther
and I followed Clementine out onto Euston Road.

'Are we staying there?' asked Esther, pointing to a grand
building that looked like the Houses of Parliament. Lavishly
dressed people followed porters carrying suitcases and
luggage coming and going from the magnificent entrance that
boasted three ornate stone archways.

'The Midland Grand Hotel,' I read from the sign.

'No, it's too expensive, and I don't think voters would
appreciate if we stayed here in the lead-up to the campaign,
even if your parents are putting us up,' said Clementine as we
continued to walk.

'I don't think so either,' I said.

Esther shook her head regretfully. 'Maybe we can stay
another time when it won't matter,' she said wistfully.

'Of course.' Clementine smiled reassuringly at her. 'In the meantime, I've found us a little lodging house nearby where we can stay. It's not far to Mrs Fawcett's in Gower Street.'

After freshening up, we made our way to Mrs Fawcett's home. It took only minutes for us to arrive in Bloomsbury by tram. A young housemaid ushered us into a parlour, where we waited for Mrs Fawcett. I felt honoured to be received in her home and hoped she'd like the small gift I'd brought: some of Mama's recipes, carefully copied, and her lemon cake.

'This room is beautiful,' whispered Esther.

Clementine nodded. 'Mrs Fawcett's sister is a house decorator.'

'But it feels so comfortable as well,' I said. Colourful rugs were scattered around the room, the seats were easy to relax in and the room didn't seem overcrowded with ornaments, as was the fashion. A well-used bureau was tucked into one corner, covered with neat piles of paper, but it didn't look out of place at all.

'It's utilitarian,' said Clementine, finding the word I'd been looking for.

Mrs Fawcett came into the room, smiling broadly. 'So wonderful to finally have you all here,' she said. 'There's so much to talk about regarding the campaign and the projects I'd like you to consider helping us with.'

'We're so happy to be here,' I said, excitement rushing through me. 'Where do we start?'

*

Despite the thrill of the work we'd achieved with Mrs Fawcett, my head was aching by the time we left that evening. I was more than happy to flop onto the bed at our lodging house.

'Come on,' said Clementine. 'Let's go out! I know somewhere we can get a cheap meal.'

I shook my head. 'I don't think so. I just want an early night. You two go ahead.'

Esther nodded. 'You're probably right. It's been a long day and we should all have an early night. Besides, it's not respectable to be out without a male chaperone.'

'What's wrong with the two of you?' exclaimed Clementine. 'This is London and we're here together. There are plenty of places we can go without a chaperone, Mrs Fawcett told me of a few last time I was here. Let's make the most of it!'

'Please, go and enjoy London, Esther. I have a bursting headache and need to sleep,' I said.

'With everything going on with your father and the pub, it's no wonder,' said Esther.

'All right,' conceded Clementine. 'You haven't stopped for weeks. Rest up. But be warned, tomorrow there'll be a lot to see.'

I smiled. 'I promise I'll be ready to take on London tomorrow.'

I awoke refreshed but Esther and Clementine were a little sluggish. I hadn't heard them come in but evidently it had been a late night.

'We went to the Dorothy Restaurant, a ladies' only dining room,' said Esther, her eyes sparkling. 'Women were smoking and drinking, relaxing without the curious stares of men. It was wonderful, but I'm paying for it now.'

'We'll be fine, Esther, after a little breakfast and a brisk walk,' said Clementine, already dressing for the day.

'I don't know how you do it,' whispered Esther, shaking her head.

'By doing it all again,' said Clementine, grinning. 'We've got a lot of sightseeing and shopping to do before we go home tomorrow.'

'We most certainly do,' I said, suddenly invigorated. 'Let's make sure we have the time of our lives.'

We made the most of our freedom. After we'd finished our meetings with Mrs Fawcett and Emily Davies, Esther suggested we visit Tower Bridge.

'It's just a bridge, like any other bridge,' said Clementine. 'I have to take you both to Harrods.'

'But you don't understand,' said Esther as we walked along the busy street, 'it opened just over a month ago. It's an engineering marvel, the first of its kind, with two suspension bridges spanning the banks of the Thames with a bascule bridge in the centre.'

'A bascule bridge?' Clementine raised an eyebrow in question.

'Two arms of the bridge raise using steam-powered hydraulics to allow the ships through to the port facilities. It's quite innovative.' She looked at us pleadingly. 'I just have to see it in action while we're here.'

'Of course!' I said. 'How can we deny you something that means so much to you?' I nudged Clementine, whose face softened, and she smiled.

Esther beamed. 'The best way to get there is to ride on the underground. I've been wanting to see the subterranean stations and tunnels for so long.'

Clementine and I laughed. 'We come to London and you want to see bridges and tunnels,' said Clementine, shaking her head. She took Esther's elbow. 'Let's go then. There's so much to see.'

I was glad we rode the underground and walked across the Tower Bridge, standing on the walkway suspended high above the river as the bridge opened beneath us to allow a clipper entrance to London's port. I wondered what exotic part of the world it had come from and whether it brought tea, wool or sugar from the far-flung parts of our glorious empire. On the north and south sides of the river, boats were docked at the various wharves unloading their goods into warehouses. The dome of St Paul's Cathedral dominated the London skyline.

'I feel like I'm on top of the world!' I cried out, watching the ship sail through. Horses and carriages, omnibuses and foot traffic all waited like tiny ants clustered around sugar for the bridge to close again.

'I feel free as a bird,' said Esther.

'We're the powerful queens of all we survey,' I declared, arms outstretched. 'Up here it feels like I can do whatever I want.'

'Because we can,' said Clementine. 'We can do anything,' she shouted, through the latticework, her words carried away by the wind.

'Let's tell the world,' I said, suddenly inspired, running across the walkway. 'Nobody can hear us up here.' Very few had ventured up the countless stairs to the walkway.

Clementine and Esther followed me down the stairs and back onto the bridge. 'We are women and we can do anything!' I shouted, leaning across the railing and over the river. Clementine and Esther were right behind me, echoing my mantra. The wind was against our faces, whipping the hair from our pins to fly from under our hats and around our faces.

'Get off there,' said an official-looking man walking angrily towards us. It was then that I noticed the looks of horror of the pedestrians at our recklessness were interspersed with disapproving expressions.

The three of us glanced at each other, and with a single shared thought we ran away, careering back across the bridge until we collapsed against each other laughing.

'I think they got the message,' wheezed Clementine.

'That was so much fun,' gasped Esther.

I grinned at my friends. 'I've never felt so alive.'

From there, we walked back along the Thames until we reached the majestic Palace of Westminster, which housed Parliament.

'It's much grander and more imposing than I'd imagined,' I said as I stared at the ornate Gothic architecture, the intricate spires and the three stately towers. 'Soon we'll walk through the entrance with the petitions and sit in the gallery as the Members of Parliament debate the bill to admit equal rights for women.'

A loud booming split the air around us and we jumped. I could feel the vibrations through my body.

Esther pointed above us. 'It's the clock tower,' she shouted over the noise. 'Big Ben's chiming the hour.' We were silent, taking in the resonant ringing of the bell.

I vowed that I'd return to Westminster to play my part in gaining suffrage rights for women and I'd stand here as I was now, listening to Big Ben chime the hour when the law had been passed.

But it was evening when we were able to really relax, spoiling ourselves with a steak dinner in the ladies' grill room at the well-known Holborn Restaurant before enjoying the delights of the city. Mrs Fawcett had suggested that we take in a show and we made our way to the West End, to the Tivoli Theatre of Varieties on The Strand.

'I can't believe that George Robey, Lottie Collins and Vesta Victoria are the headline acts,' I said as I looked at the program for the evening's performances. 'I've read about them in the newspaper and I think we're in for a treat.'

'What's so special about them?' asked Esther. She wore an evening dress with a low-cut neckline and bare arms while Clementine and I were in good day dresses. With her parents' social calendar, Esther had more need for evening wear. She looked beautiful in a gown that actually flattered her curvaceous figure and showed off her full bosom, rather than our everyday clothing, which covered us from neck to foot.

'Both Lottie Collins and Vesta Victoria have risen to stardom because of the songs they sing ...' I tried to think of the songs. 'One of them is "Daddy Wouldn't Buy Me a Bow Wow".' Esther and Clementine giggled. 'And George Robey is a comedian. He's quite famous.'

'So many acts,' said Clementine, reading the program and shaking her head with wonder. 'Over twenty!' We were seated in the pit, the cheaper seats on the floor of the auditorium. Above us, lining the theatre, were the more expensive balcony stalls. The space was lit by electric lights, so different from gas lighting or the flickering oil lamps of home. I'd never been anywhere so fancy before, not even in Durham.

'I feel like we're sitting in one of the Queen's palaces,' I whispered.

Clementine clutched Esther's and my hands. 'Imagine if we lived here. We could enjoy everything London has to offer whenever we wanted.'

A surge of excitement swept through me. After her last visit to London, Clementine had talked about one day transferring to a school here. Mrs Fawcett had talked about important committee work here in London after we were finished with Esther's campaign. Being here, my own dream of leaving Ebberfield suddenly felt more tangible than it had for many months. Maybe Papa would finish his treatment and come home again ... I let my imagination run wild. Perhaps the three of us could live together, as Mrs Fawcett did with her sister and relatives. I could teach as well and Esther could study engineering and even find related work in the city.

Nothing was impossible. Mrs Fawcett's sister, Elizabeth

Garrett Anderson, was the first female physician in Britain, and had founded the London School of Medicine for Women and the recently opened New Hospital for Women on Euston Road. I couldn't wait to tell Jemima Johnston about her. Her dream of becoming a doctor *was* possible. London was opening my eyes to so many new ideas and opportunities.

Soon the lights dimmed and we became engrossed in the performances. We laughed at the sketches performed by the comedians and mimics, and were entranced by the dancers, acrobats, musicians and singers. I could see why George Robey was such a star. But it was Lottie Collins who caught my attention with her daring performance. She sang the song she was most famous for, 'Ta-ra-ra Boom-de-ay!' At first I thought it was a lovely performance but nothing terribly memorable until she reached the chorus and a collective gasp went up around the auditorium when she began a dizzying skirt dance, lifting and moving the long layers of fabric while kicking her legs high, showing off her stockings and even her bare thighs above glittering garters.

'Did you see that?' whispered Esther to us, looking scandalised. We nodded, none of us able to look away.

'Astonishing,' I whispered back. Hundreds of strangers could see her legs and bare skin with each performance.

'She's aiming for shock value,' murmured Clementine. 'It's time that women pushed the boundaries. We have legs and a body, just like men. Why should we have to hide them?'

I was no longer surprised by Clementine's comments. She was a modern woman. I thought Lottie Collins epitomised what we all wanted to do: push the boundaries of what was acceptable, to bravely confront and shed light on the archaic values in our society.

*

I came home full of grand plans and lofty ideas. My commitment to Esther's campaign and the work we were doing as activists was stronger than ever. Clementine, Esther and I launched straight into our suffrage society meeting and the announcement of Esther's campaign. With school on summer holidays, it was a relief for Clementine and me to have the extra time to spend on fine-tuning our plans and itinerary with Esther, even though we'd discussed it all at length with Mrs Fawcett and other members of the committee in London.

But coming home was also a harsh return to reality. Mama wasn't cut out to handle all the responsibility of the pub alone even with Roger's and Bill's help. It was as if some of the spark within her had faded. It reminded me that she was also getting older. Most people didn't want to take on an enterprise like this in their sixties. Papa was excited for me when I told him about London but was determined to explain the steps of barrel conditioning again and reminded me to ensure The Ox and Plough was seen favourably for upcoming events.

I called on Edward Partridge at his estate, Dalleymoor, and explained our position with The Ox and Plough and the lack of confidence from the festival and show committees.

'I know that Mr Franks has friends on the committees,' Edward said, leaning back into the large leather chair in his study. 'Probably people he's paid off or who he has something on, but I'll remind the committees what you and The Ox and Plough have done for this community.'

'Thank you, Edward,' I said. 'You and Marjorie have been great friends to us.'

'We can't imagine what you and your family have gone through with William's absence.' He stood and gestured towards the long hallway with black and white marble flooring. 'Marjorie's waiting in the parlour to take tea with you.' He put his hand on my shoulder, and a shiver of disquiet ran through me. 'Leave it with me.'

*

The hardest part of spending so much time at The Ox and Plough, however, was seeing Roger. I was drawn to him like a moth to a flame, my body aching for his touch, but my trip to London had shown me a different kind of life I could one day have for myself if I was more disciplined. Lately Jane's warnings about being careful had started ringing in my mind and I realised what a dangerous game I had been playing.

'Are you trying to avoid me?' Roger whispered as I slipped behind the bar and out into the scullery one evening.

I shook my head. Roger glanced at Jenny washing and drying glasses but I was too busy to stop and went to the kitchen where the leftover pies sat under a clean tea towel.

'I've barely seen you since you've been back from London,' he said, catching my arm. 'Is something wrong?'

I stared at him a moment, my gaze dropping to his mouth. I wanted nothing more than to kiss him and to step into his arms. 'We can't continue like this,' I said in a low voice.

'Why not?' The challenge in his blue eyes made me want to give in. His dark hair was rumpled and his nearness made me want to forget about everything but him.

'Because the longer we continue, the higher the risk of being found out. My reputation will be in tatters,' I replied, holding my resolve.

He took me in his arms and kissed me before I could protest. 'Then marry me,' he said when he stepped back. 'We can spend every night in each other's arms without any hint of scandal.'

The pit of my stomach fell and I shook my head so vigorously that hair slipped loose from my pins. 'I told you, I can't marry you.'

Roger's face drained of colour. 'So you want to end this.' The pain etched in his eyes was almost unbearable to see.

'I don't want to, but I have to. We're finished for good this time. I'm so sorry, Roger.' I covered my face as the reality of not spending another night with him hit me. 'I have to go,' I whispered, wiping my eyes with the edge of my apron.

I darted out through the scullery before he could stop me.

22

London is the centre of it all, where new ideas become reality through action. I can't wait to see what more it has in store for us and our plans.

'You look pale,' said Mama one morning as I came into the kitchen. She put the kettle down and peered into my face. 'You have dark rings around your eyes. Haven't you been sleeping?'

I shook my head, almost overwrought with emotion.

Mama frowned. 'Come and sit down, my darling. Maybe have a quiet day today, just resting with a book? Perhaps look through your pressed flowers or your interesting collections?'

'I've got too much to do,' I said, but I sat at the table anyway.

I'd buried myself in my work ever since I'd ended things with Roger, keeping to Papa's office upstairs when Roger was working, even though it reminded me of our nights together, and working the floor when he wasn't behind the bar. Clementine and Esther had long stopped asking me about our relationship after my denials that there was anything between us. I felt like part of my heart had been ripped away and even though I knew I'd done the right thing for my future, I had the feeling that I'd made a terrible mistake. I didn't dare tell them the truth. I missed being able to confide in them and share my misery. And they had taken the opportunity to enjoy the last weeks of summer, Esther with her parents at the seaside in Scarborough, Clementine in Staffordshire visiting her parents, and Laura with her family in their hometown in Sussex, before school began in September. Without them and Roger, I felt bereft and worked harder than ever, poring over the ledgers for the pub until my vision blurred.

I began to burn the midnight oil, trying to write speeches for farming and mining communities across the district. Somehow, I needed the locals to see that education was a useful tool to help raise their children out of poverty and provide opportunities for better jobs and a better life. I continued to work on Esther's campaign and even began preparing classes for the oldest students returning in the new school year.

Mama nodded. 'I know, but it doesn't all have to be done today.' She put the kettle on to boil. 'Have a cup of tea and something to eat.'

'I'm not hungry,' I said automatically. I felt wretched and miserable, my eyes felt like sandpaper, and all I wanted to do was crawl back into my bed and disappear into oblivion.

'Well, I'm not taking no for an answer,' said Mama, setting a pan on the stove. 'I'm making pikelets. Jenny hasn't eaten either and I think the three of us can enjoy breakfast together before we attend to our chores.'

'All right,' I said, resigned to Mama taking over. In fact, it felt good, letting her fuss over me a little, just like when I was a child and pikelets smothered in butter were a rare treat. 'But let me help you.' I stood and my vision swam. A wave of dizziness overcame me as I saw black spots and then nothing.

I woke on the kitchen floor with Mama and Jenny watching over me anxiously.

'What happened?' I croaked.

'You fainted,' said Mama in a strained voice. 'Are you sore anywhere?'

'I don't think so,' I whispered. I touched my head gingerly, feeling the lump that was beginning to rise. It was only then that I realised my head was resting on a cushion from the parlour.

'Grandma was worried you'd hit your head on the corner of the table,' said Jenny.

'I'm all right.' I felt foolish but I was still light-headed as I tried to get up.

'No, you don't,' said Mama, putting a restraining hand on me. 'Jenny and I will help you up to bed, where you will stay for the rest of the day. You've overdone it. Don't think I haven't seen the light under your door all hours of the night.'

She glared at me as I began to protest. Mama was a force of nature when she put her mind to it. The truth was that my head ached and I had no energy to fight with her anyway.

After being served tea and breakfast in bed, which Mama watched me eat, my eyelids became heavy and I was surprised to wake some hours later to find Sarah sitting in my reading chair.

'Well, good morning,' she said softly.

'What are you doing here?' I pushed myself upright, wincing as I remembered the knock to my head.

She was by my side in an instant, fluffing the pillows behind me. 'How are you feeling?'

'Besides a sore head, I'm fine.'

'You gave Mama and Jenny a scare. Don't you remember I was coming to see Jenny today?'

I shook my head and immediately regretted it.

'I arrived not long after you fainted. After Papa's fall, they were understandably a bit jumpy. Mama wanted to call the doctor but I told her to let you sleep and we'd see how you were when you woke.' She sat on the side of the bed. '*Should we call the doctor?*'

I took a deep breath, taking a moment to process what she'd said. 'No, I just haven't been sleeping well and I've been working late into the night. There's nothing to worry about.'

Sarah nodded. 'It's not like you, Hannah. What's going on?'

'Nothing.' But that wasn't true. Tears welled in my eyes. I couldn't start crying now or I feared I'd never stop.

She took my hand. 'Is it Papa? Or did something happen while you were in London?'

The touch of her hand on mine felt comforting, and suddenly I felt like I wanted to tell her what was happening in my life. I sighed. 'Oh, Sarah, I don't know where to start.'

'What is it?'

'It's been so hard with Papa gone. Visiting him was wonderful but seeing him in the asylum ... I don't want to let him down.' I blinked away the tears.

Sarah squeezed my hand. 'You won't. Papa adores you.'

'And then London was incredible, and I'm excited about the work we discussed with Mrs Fawcett. It's just that when I came back, between the campaign, the pub, teaching and Roger—' I glanced at her, not sure how much to tell her.

'Roger Rainforth, the barman? Mama told me that his mother and sister came for tea. What's going on between you?'

'Nothing.' I didn't have the energy to tell her about it.

Sarah frowned. 'It doesn't sound like nothing. Jenny tells me that the two of you spend time together, walking home from school and talking in the kitchen of an evening.'

I dropped my head, the pain of Roger's loss blossoming in my chest. 'Not anymore.'

'Did something happen?'

I swallowed the lump in my throat, wanting to share my burden with someone. 'He asked me to marry him.'

'And what's wrong with that? From what I've heard, he's a decent fellow.'

'You know what's wrong. I can't continue to teach if I marry and I don't want another man making decisions for me, telling me what I can and can't do. I have a degree of independence while I'm single, I can live the life I want. Being in London showed me what's possible.'

Sarah put her arms around me and kissed my forehead. 'You've always seen everything in black and white.'

'But it's the life I want, Sarah.' I put my head in my hands as the tears began to flow.

'Do you love him?'

'Yes, I think so,' I said wretchedly, thinking of how strongly I'd felt when I'd said the words on our first night together. 'I think about him all the time, wondering what he's doing, wishing I was with him ...' My nights were filled with him: when I wasn't dreaming about him, I was imagining we were together, remembering our nights of passion.

Sarah grasped my hands and waited for me to continue. 'He's not like anyone I've ever met. He's kind, thoughtful, shares my vision of a better world and he supports my work. He's helped me cope with Papa's decision to go to the asylum.' I felt the heat rise to my cheeks, and I turned my face away so she couldn't see me blush. 'I don't know what I would have done without him.'

Sarah drew away, her face filled with consternation. 'I don't know why I didn't see it before.'

I frowned. 'See what?'

'When did you last have your courses?'

'What?'

'Have you missed your last bleed?'

I stared at her a moment as I tried to think. 'They're a bit late, but I've been so busy, and with all the worry about Papa ...'

Sarah sat very still. 'How late?'

'Maybe two or three weeks, I can't be sure.' A wave of uneasiness rolled through me, making me nauseous.

'Hannah, have you been intimate with Roger?'

I couldn't even be outraged by the question. I stared at her, Jane's words rushing back to me again. We'd been so careful. Even that last time in the sea, the night before Lammas.

She sucked in a breath. 'Oh, Hannah, I think you might be pregnant.'

'How can you be sure?' I whispered. She had to be wrong. I couldn't be.

'You've been dizzy and nauseous, especially in the morning, haven't you?'

I nodded slowly.

'And you're tired and cry at the drop of a hat?'

'Sarah, I can't be.'

'I had all the same symptoms with each of my pregnancies,' she said gently. 'My breasts became tender at the beginning every time too.'

My hand strayed to my bosom, sensitive to the touch. 'No, there must be some other explanation. I still feel like my courses are ready to come.'

Sarah nodded. 'The bloating lasts a couple of months.' She took my hands again, ice-cold now. 'I think you should prepare yourself.'

I felt like I was far away, distant and removed from reality. There could be many different reasons for the way I was feeling but, deep in my bones, I knew that she was right. I felt like a heavy weight was pressing down on me and suddenly I couldn't breathe.

Sarah enfolded me in her arms and I took a deep breath, still feeling overwhelmed.

'How did this happen?' I whispered to myself.

Sarah kissed my cheek. 'Todd women are fertile. We only have to look at the bed and we fall pregnant.' She squeezed me tightly. 'It only takes once, one fleeting moment of passion.'

Roger and I had had more than one moment. 'What am I going to do?'

'The only thing you can do. Marry Roger as soon as is practical, so your child is born legitimately.'

Marry him? I felt dazed and numb as I stared out the window to the church across the road. How many weddings that had been performed there over the centuries had been pre-empted by pregnancy? Could such a situation lead to a happy and successful marriage? That chance, no matter how remote, was far better for many women than the alternative of being shunned by society and their community and ending up destitute and in the workhouse. I knew that Roger loved me and, even though I never wanted marriage, I loved him. I was more fortunate than most.

'If you love each other, you can still have a good life,' said Sarah, reading my mind.

'Maybe,' I whispered. I wasn't sure of anything.

Sarah left me to gather my thoughts and went to help Mama at the pub. I was grateful for the peace and quiet and the undisturbed time in bed. But no amount of reworking my thoughts changed anything.

How could I have been so reckless?

*

It was with a heavy heart that I faced my mother at dinner. Jenny was at the pub so it was just the three of us. Sarah smiled encouragingly as I sat at the table.

'Are you feeling better?' asked Mama, her faced creased with concern.

I nodded. 'I had a good rest.'

'You gave us a scare.'

'I'm sorry,' I whispered.

'There's nothing to be sorry for, you couldn't help it,' said Mama frowning. 'You just have to stop working through the night.'

I couldn't ignore Sarah's pointed stare. She wanted me to tell Mama now. I took a deep breath. There was no way out of this. 'Maybe it wasn't just the late nights.'

Mama raised her eyebrows quizzically.

I gripped the edge of my chair tightly. 'Sarah thinks I'm pregnant.'

'What?' Mama's eyes widened with shock and fear.

'She has all the signs,' said Sarah. 'It's Roger. Did you know that he asked her to marry him?'

Mama shook her head, her face pale. 'You're going to marry him, aren't you?'

'No, Mama,' I whispered. 'I turned him down. I don't want to get married. I love my teaching and I love my life just as it is.'

She could only press her hands over her face.

I'd disappointed her terribly. This couldn't be happening. I dropped my own head in my hands and began to sob. 'All my dreams ... Everything's ruined.'

'No, my girl.' I heard Mama push her chair back. 'Nothing's definite.' I felt her arms around me and then kissing my cheek.

'What do you mean?' I lifted my head and frowned at her in confusion.

'Mama's right,' said Sarah slowly, exchanging a knowing glance with her. 'I've never had any problems but Mary lost a few pregnancies early on.'

'And so did I,' said Mama, smoothing my hair.

I breathed out slowly, drying my eyes with my sleeve, as I clutched at the small glimmer of hope. Nothing was certain, even if I was pregnant.

'You still have time,' said Sarah. 'A couple of weeks, maybe. But if it's certain, you'll have to make a decision before you're too far along.'

'But what if Roger changes his mind?' I looked down at my still-flat belly. 'Neither of us were expecting this.'

'Roger's a responsible man, family oriented. He'll do the right thing and look after you,' said Mama.

'It's not such a bad thing,' said Sarah with a wave of her hand. 'They love each other. Hannah might not be able to go back to teaching in the classroom but she can still tutor and I'm sure all her misgivings will disappear when her little bundle of joy arrives.'

Anger rushed through me at the injustice of it all. I couldn't even imagine a baby in my life. 'But I didn't choose this for myself! And there's nothing wrong with a married woman teaching, even a woman who has children. Just a man's stupid sensibilities.'

'Don't be so naive,' said Sarah, her voice hardening. 'You've always thought you're special and Papa encouraged it, pampering your every whim, but you can't deny what's right in front of you. This is the reality of being a woman. It's a precarious business at the best of times, and at the worst it can destroy your life.'

I felt like I'd been slapped, brought into line like a naughty child. But Sarah's words only made me more furious. I wasn't a child. 'I won't be pushed into something I don't want!' I yelled across the table.

Sarah took a deep breath rather than scream back at me. 'What are you going to do?' she asked quietly. 'Bring up a child on your own? Do you know how lucky you are to have a man as devoted as Roger, a man who loves you? You were probably too young to remember what Jane went through when she had Lizzie at eighteen.' Tears filled her eyes.

'Lizzie?' I shook my head in confusion, then realised what Sarah was saying. 'Jane had a baby at eighteen?'

She nodded. 'She was sent home in disgrace from the vicarage where we were both working. The father didn't want to know anything about her and refused to marry her. She told me that she was in love and she was heartbroken.'

Mama closed her eyes as though to block out the memories. 'Sarah, stop. It's all in the past.'

'No, Mama. Hannah has to hear this and understand how fortunate she is.' Sarah turned back to me. 'Jane had to endure the shame and the smear to her reputation and I remember the looks that Mama and Papa would get.' She shook her head. 'It was wrong, but that didn't stop it from happening.'

'She never told me.' I thought back to my conversation with her. She had been speaking to me from personal experience.

'She married Bert a few years later, but Lizzie fell ill and was too sick to travel down to Yorkshire with Jane and Papa for the wedding. Jane was devastated, leaving her daughter behind, only for Lizzie to die in Mama's arms days after the wedding. I don't think she ever got over it.'

'I didn't know,' I whispered. My poor, poor sister.

'My point is that you have a man who loves you and wants to marry you and you clearly love him back. Life can be hard, but it's better shared with someone you love and who supports you. Don't be stubborn and stick to some impractical idea of what you think your life should be like. You have to put your grand ideals behind you now and be realistic. You might have got the order back to front but it's not the first time that's happened in our family.'

'You have some time to think through all your options,' said Mama. 'You could do a lot worse. Roger comes from a good family but if you truly don't want to marry, we'll find a way to work things out, just as we did with Jane.'

I looked into my mother's face with a mixture of surprise and relief. 'Really?'

'Of course,' said Mama, hugging me tightly. 'I only want you safe and well.'

But over the next few days it didn't take long for me to realise that I couldn't raise a child on my own without my teacher's pay. Running the pub was hard enough but a child under foot would put Mama and me under greater pressure, and customers would voice their disapproval of the manager being an unmarried mother. Then there was the disappointment I knew I'd cause my father. He'd expected so much of me and it could all amount to nothing.

*

Sarah had gone back home, and with Clementine, Esther and Laura still away, I continued to bury myself in my work, hoping I wasn't pregnant. But I darted back and forth between thoughts of marriage, which seemed unthinkable without my teaching, and the idea of being a single mother and even of having my child in London and finding a way to live there.

In my darkest moments I thought about getting rid of the pregnancy, but immediately dismissed that option with a feeling of loathing and disgust. It was inconceivable. I felt trapped. Instead, I waited.

Mama said very little, just kept an eagle eye on me, making sure I was eating properly and finding any excuse to give me a reason to rest. I realised I was all Mama had left. She lavished on me all the care and love she would have given Papa, or my sisters had they been close by. Every morning, I woke knowing that my fate was becoming more certain. Any escape from this nightmare was disappearing fast and I'd soon have to face it. I was terrified of telling Roger. I already knew I loved him deeply and passionately. But how could I reconcile following my heart with the logic of the life I needed to fulfil my purpose? Could I somehow do both? I couldn't imagine not teaching. It was my very life's blood. How could I let go of my dream of living and working in London, when it had felt within reach only weeks ago? And if I did choose a life with Roger, what if he turned away from me after my rejection of him? My thoughts and fears went round and round in my head.

'I'm going to have to tell Roger,' I said to Mama one evening a few weeks later. We were in the parlour waiting for Jenny to come in from The Ox and Plough. 'I think this baby's here to stay,' I said as I smoothed the fabric over my belly. Now that I'd said it and accepted what was ahead of me, I felt strangely content, and remembered the yearning I'd felt when Sarah and Jane had had their last children. Soon I was going to have a baby of my own. Soon I was going to be a mother.

She put down her embroidery. 'Then you'll have to do it soon,' she said. 'And you'll want to be married before you begin to show.'

I nodded. 'First I have to tell him and let him get used to the idea.'

'Are you going to marry him?' she asked, tentatively.

My heart clenched at her words. I opened my mouth to tell her that I hadn't decided, because there were sacrifices whatever I chose, but found I couldn't. Roger was everything I'd ever want in a man: love, trust and he shared my ideas about the way of the world. Fate had delivered to me what I truly desired, buried so deep beneath my ambitions to make the lives of women and children better. But now that the scales had dropped from my eyes, I felt the horror that I had lost him anyway.

I grasped her hand and kissed it. 'We'll see.'

She just nodded. 'When will you tell him?'

'Now I've made the decision, I think the sooner, the better.'

23

Working-class women who become pregnant out of
marriage have very few options: to marry the father, seek
compensation through the courts, and if these are not
possible, enter a workhouse.

I met Roger at closing time that night, clenching my shaking
hands tight. I felt my whole body quivering with nerves and
wondered vaguely if my disquiet was clear for everyone to see.

'I have to talk to you,' I said as he was cleaning up behind
the bar.

'I didn't think we had anything to talk about,' he said
coldly.

'Please, Roger. It's important.'

He nodded abruptly and continued until he was done, then
walked through to the kitchen. He stood rigid against the
table, the pots hanging orderly on their hooks behind him,
and the breath caught in my throat. What if he hated me
now? I knew I'd hurt him deeply.

'What is it, Hannah?'

'I'm so sorry for everything,' I whispered.

'You came here after all this time to tell me that?'

His look of disbelief made me want to walk out the door.
Maybe this was a bad idea. I'd find a way to raise this child
on my own.

I shook my head. 'No. I've been just as upset since your
proposal.'

He laughed mirthlessly, making my blood boil. I had to make him understand.

'There's more at stake for a woman and she has to sacrifice so much more than a man ...' I stepped towards him but he recoiled. I tried to hold back the tears. 'Don't you see? I wanted it all. I wanted you and I wanted the life I already have. I didn't want to choose. Maybe it was a mistake,' I said.

'That's right, because you've made your decision already. I can't take any more of your backwards and forwards. Every time you get my hopes up, you dash them again.'

My shoulders slumped as the fight in me drained away. There was no way to make this conversation better. Maybe he'd never really understand my reasons for rejecting him. I could never regret what we'd done together or the choices I'd made. I'd carry the joy of being with him always, now embodied in our child. I just had to tell him.

I took a deep breath. 'I'm pregnant.'

'You're what?'

'I'm pregnant,' I repeated, lifting my head and looking him in the eye. 'Two months along.'

'I thought we'd been so careful,' he said, stricken. His face was pale with shock, but I couldn't expect any other reaction. I'd been the same.

'I did too. I've waited, to be sure, but there's no doubt now.'

'We're going to be parents?'

I nodded woodenly. 'We have to decide what we're going to do.' I wound my hands tightly in my skirt. I couldn't believe I was allowing my fate to rest in someone else's hands – and a man's at that. But no, I couldn't think like that. This was Roger.

He glared at me with mingled exasperation and anger. 'What we're going to do? So, I'm good for something now you're pregnant?'

'No, Roger, it's not like that. You know it's not.' I couldn't bear his disdain. 'I love you. Giving you up was the hardest thing I've ever had to do.'

He walked to the window and looked out into the darkness. Then he turned towards me and sighed. He took my hand. 'Do you truly love me like you say you do?'

'I've loved you for longer than I care to say. Something happened the first time I saw you in the classroom doorway. And that feeling has grown ever since. I just didn't want to admit it to you or to myself.'

'But why? I've always been so clear about the way I feel about you.'

I thought a moment. 'Because it's something I couldn't control and I had set plans in place for the life I wanted to live. But the first time we came together I knew I was in trouble because I wanted you with a passion greater than anything I could imagine. Since that day, I've never wanted to be apart from you and that feeling overwhelmed me and made me afraid that I was losing the life I had planned. Afraid that I'd lose everything I ever thought I wanted.' I looked into his eyes, my own vision blurry with tears, searching for his trust and forgiveness and feeling more vulnerable than I ever had being naked before him. 'And now I'm afraid of losing what I'm certain I want: you.'

'Then say it to me again.'

'I love you, Roger,' I whispered, a tear trickling down my cheek.

He gently wiped the tear with his thumb, his touch like a balm for my heart. 'I love you, Hannah, and have done since the day I met you. I've always known that you're a singular woman who knows what she wants, who's strong-headed and determined. It's one of the things I love about you, and I'd never try to stop you from doing what you feel passionate about.'

A sob broke from my lips as he got down on one knee and took my other hand.

'I knew one day we'd be together. I just had to be patient and wait for you to be ready. This isn't the way I expected, but I'll have you all the same.' He looked up at me, his eyes bluer than I'd ever seen them and as vulnerable as I had been a moment earlier. 'Hannah Todd, will you marry me?'

I cupped his beloved face. This was a man who truly loved me. And I loved him just the same. He was what I wanted, to the depths of my soul. I was both my purpose and my love for this man and I had to embrace the two halves of myself if I was ever going to be whole. I'd tried to separate my head and my heart, but with Roger I could be all of me. With mutual love and respect, we'd find a way to give each other what we needed.

'Yes, Roger Rainforth, I'll marry you.'

Roger was on his feet, pulling me into his arms, in an instant. We were both crying.

'Two of the happiest moments of my life in one day,' he murmured. 'I'm going to be your husband and a father.'

'You really want a family so soon?'

'Oh, Hannah, I just want to be with you. But this as well … nothing could make me happier.' He bent his head to kiss me and in that moment, nothing else mattered except that we were together.

*

Elizabeth Rainforth couldn't contain her joy. The moment she stepped into the cottage to have morning tea with me and Mama, she hugged me tight. 'Congratulations, my dear,' she said. 'I can't tell you how happy I am at hearing your good news.' She drew away and appraised me, tears in her eyes.

'You're glowing. Double good news. I've waited so long for this happy occasion.'

'It was a bit unexpected but—'

'It happens to the best of us but I've never seen a more perfect couple than you and Roger. There's already a strong love between you, a rare and special thing, and a child will only deepen it further. You'll be wonderful parents to my first grandchild.'

I glanced at Roger and he smiled reassuringly.

'Come and have tea,' said Mama, hugging Elizabeth and Roger warmly. 'We have much to discuss.'

I could only sip my tea as we talked of the future.

'We still have time to call the banns if we do it soon,' said Mama. 'They could be married within a month.'

'I'd like to ask for Mr Todd's blessing,' said Roger, holding my hand. 'If we could arrange to go and see him as soon as possible?'

I smiled. 'I'd like that.'

'All right,' said Mama. 'But the sooner you're married, the better. Let's set a date.'

'I can't wait until I can tell everyone that you're getting married,' said Elizabeth.

Roger nodded. 'You'll have a few weeks back at school at least. I'm sorry that you can't continue teaching once we're married. It's a senseless rule.'

'I know,' I replied, deflating. No matter what I'd decided, there would have been sacrifices. In the face of the life-changing consequences most of my choices had carried, stepping away from teaching was the least harrowing prospect. But it didn't make it right and it didn't change the terrible heartache when I thought about it. There was no logical reason I couldn't do both.

'You have the chance to say goodbye to your students,' said Mama softly.

'And you'll still see most of them in the village,' said Elizabeth.

I dropped my gaze, twisting the fabric of my skirt around my fingers. I knew they were trying to make this easier for me but nothing could take away the painful disappointment I felt.

*

Now we'd made the decision, there was a lot to do. It was September and the new school year was about to start. My first visit was to the Burnetts to speak to Benjamin.

'Roger Rainforth,' he said, surprised. 'I knew that the two of you were friends but Laura told me that it was nothing more.'

'It wasn't at first but with Papa leaving, we began to work together at the pub more and I realised how much he means to me. Marriage makes sense. The Ox and Plough's getting too much for Mama to manage on her own and this way I can do what I need to keep it running.' The support of Roger's income meant I could devote myself solely to my role as manager of The Ox and Plough for at least the next six months.

'I'm so sorry to see you go but I can't help thinking how proud your father must be, committing yourself to the pub that was so much a part of his life.'

I nodded as a stab of guilt shot through me. I wasn't sure how proud Papa would be.

I met with Laura, Clementine and Esther later that evening in our parlour, steeling myself to tell them my news. Laura and I sipped our tea while Clementine and Esther regaled us with stories of their summer holidays.

'The resort was almost as busy as being in London itself,' said Esther. 'We ate ice cream and took a tram ride along the cliffs to get away from the crowds. The view out over the North Sea was spectacular. But the highlight was going to the beautiful new concert hall and watching a performance of a musical comedy touring from London, *A Gaiety Girl*.'

'I think Hannah's had some excitement while we've been away,' said Laura, softly.

'What? What is it, Hannah?' asked Esther, her face a mask of worry.

I took a deep breath, the blood pounding in my head. 'I went to see Benjamin this afternoon because I wanted to give him as long as possible to find a replacement for me at school.'

Clementine dropped her pastry onto her plate, eyes wide. 'You're leaving the school?'

I nodded. 'I'm leaving teaching.'

'But you love it, it's your passion,' she said, incredulous.

'I've decided to marry Roger.'

'You've what?' Esther stared at me, perplexed. 'But you haven't been interested in him for months.'

'That's not strictly true,' said Clementine with an arched eyebrow. 'She's never stopped loving him but decided in the end that doing the work we discussed with Mrs Fawcett was more important. Things have changed then?' She looked at me pointedly.

'I'm still committed to my work with Mrs Fawcett,' I said, turning my head away. I couldn't look at the shocked faces of my dearest friends. 'But something happened while you were away and I've had to make the most difficult decision of my life without you all.'

Laura put her arm around me. 'It's all right, Hannah. I'm sorry we weren't here when you needed us, but you can tell us now.'

I lifted my head, tears welling in my eyes. 'After Papa went to the asylum, Roger was there to comfort me ...'

Realisation dawned in Clementine's eyes. 'You're pregnant?'

I nodded.

'And you didn't think to tell us?'

'I thought you'd be sick of hearing about it. He asked me to marry him when we got back from London but I told him we were finished, for good this time. I only realised I was pregnant after you'd all gone away. I didn't know what to do when I found out. I never imagined I'd have to make such a decision. None of it feels real.'

Esther grasped my hand. 'You're one of the few lucky ones who can marry for love. I've known Roger and his family a very long time and I know you'll make each other very happy. Congratulations.'

'We're so happy for you,' said Laura. 'Everything will fall into place, just you wait and see. Becoming a mother will fill you with that same sense of purpose and fulfilment you have with teaching. You have a man who loves you and you're surrounded by friends and family and a community who love and support you both. You can achieve anything with stability and security like that.'

Clementine looked at me for a moment, and I was afraid that she was going to reject everything about my new life since we had shared the same dream. 'We're going to be aunties!' she said, her face breaking into a grin. 'So, are we invited to the wedding?'

'Of course,' I said warmly, her words filling me with relief. 'I couldn't do any of this without the three of you.'

24

Although I run a pub, I agree with the temperance
movement. I am against the terrible things that drunk,
entitled men do to women. Violence against women is a
very real problem that still isn't taken seriously enough by
society or by officials.

Only once Roger had visited Papa to ask for permission to
marry me, could I think about planning a wedding. I'd been
worried about telling Papa that I was pregnant and getting
married but rather than being disappointed, he was overjoyed
for me. He reminded me that when life took unexpected
directions, it opened the door to exciting new possibilities. It
gave me something to think about and I hoped he was right
because I was stepping into the unknown, so far removed
from the life I had imagined for myself.

But our plans were almost ruined as soon as they were
made when Mama learnt that the church was closing for
repairs and restoration work within the month. Mama,
Elizabeth, Roger and I all went to see Reverend Mason.
Only by pleading with him and reminding him that Papa
was returning home for the wedding even though he was
still unwell, did he agree to fit our wedding ceremony in on
the day before the church was due to close. The banns were
called and by the time I returned to school for the new year,
everyone at school and in the village knew that I was getting
married.

'I can't believe you're leaving,' said Anthony as I was tidying up at the end of the school day. He and Amy were in the class that I'd been teaching.

'Me neither,' I said. 'But I'll still see you all the time.'

'I always knew you were going to be part of our family one day.'

'How could you know that?'

Anthony shrugged. 'I don't know. I just did.'

'Well, I'm very happy that I am. Now, you'd better go to football training before you're late. You don't want to be yelled at by your own brother.'

Anthony grinned. 'All right, but I'm used to being yelled at, even if I'm the fastest player on the field.'

I stared after him as he left the classroom. There was so much I was going to miss: the children; the teaching; the staff; all the challenges and moments of fulfilment and satisfaction. I'd achieved many of the things I'd set out to do when I first started and attendance at the school was at an all-time high. But how could I leave the breakfast and lunch club? And watching the children's joy reading books they'd chosen from our new library and the girls' wonder and excitement during their naturalist excursions. How could I leave when there was still much to do?

I dashed the tears away as the room began to blur. Clementine had organised a farewell afternoon tea – well before my last day – with the blessing of Benjamin and I didn't want to turn up in front of my colleagues red-eyed and weepy.

Three weeks was long enough to plan a wedding, especially since we were having the reception at The Ox and Plough. But as the days slipped by, I wasn't sure it was long enough for me to get used to the idea of how much my life was going to change.

Mama insisted on making me a wedding dress. We'd visited the draper's emporium in Hartlepool, where Mary used her expertise and connections to get me a beautiful champagne silk satin and some pieces of ivory lace.

'Have you decided where you'll live once you're married?' asked Jenny, holding Mama's pins and scissors during a fitting in my bedroom. Mary was pulling and tugging on the bodice to get it to sit right with my growing bustline while Mama pinned the back as I stood still so I didn't get pricked by the pins and ruin the fabric. Sarah was trying to decide where to place the pieces of lace that were going around the neckline and on the cuffs of the leg-of-mutton sleeves.

'We'll stay here,' I said. 'I have to help Mama, so it makes the most sense.'

'Jenny, I'd move downstairs rather than stay across the hall, if I were you,' said Mary, grinning. 'It might get a bit noisy and disturb your sleep.'

I felt the blush rising up my chest. My sisters knew that I was pregnant but not Jenny.

'Don't go putting those kinds of ideas into her head,' said Sarah, elbowing our sister.

'It's a natural part of life,' retorted Mary, dodging Sarah's wicked aim. 'And don't tell me she hasn't heard you and Reg at it.'

'Enough, girls,' said Mama. 'We're all old enough to know what happens in the bedroom after marriage, even Jenny.'

'What about Roger?' asked Sarah, changing the subject as she bent down to straighten the hem of the skirt and draped the small train to one side. My belly was still relatively flat and Mama felt confident that the skirt would still fit well on the wedding day. 'Will he begin work on the restoration of the church or spend more time working behind the bar?'

'He'll work on the refurbishments until they're finished and help me and Bill at night, on Sundays and whenever he has gaps in the building work.' It was a relief to know that he would have work for at least a year, giving us good financial security until well after the baby had arrived and I could do more at the pub.

'You'll need to redecorate your room before you're married then,' said Sarah, standing and looking around the bedroom. 'Roger won't want to sleep in a small bed with you and you might need more cupboard space for his clothes.'

'We'll manage,' I said, waving a hand in dismissal. I'd already decided we could move the extra single bed and closet from the spare room before converting it to a nursery when the time came.

'It's time we make some changes,' said Mama, coming to the front to survey the results of her adjustments. 'I don't need such a big room to myself, so I'll take your room and you and Roger can take my room.'

'I can't do that, Mama,' I said, shaking my head. I didn't want to force Mama from the bedroom she'd shared with my father. And it would feel strange to be moving into the bed they'd slept in. 'And what about when Papa comes back home? The treatment is already helping him.'

Mama gazed at me with an unwavering and determined expression. But I could see the sadness beneath her steely blue eyes. 'You can and you will. Papa and I can have the smaller room. You'll need the bigger one. Add your own touches so it feels like your room.' She rested her hands on my shoulders. 'There, I think the dress sits well now. It won't take long to do the finishing touches and then you can try it on again with the veil and shoes and see how it all looks together.'

Mary shook her head, caught up in the excitement of the moment. 'Let's do her hair and veil now, so she has an idea of what it looks like before the last minute.' She threaded her fingers through my hair, pulling it back and into a coil. 'Pass me some pins,' she said, gently loosening the hair around my face, before pinning the rest into place.

'That looks beautiful,' said Jenny, giving Mary more pins.

'Let's put the veil on,' said Sarah, reaching for Mama's tulle veil. I only glimpsed the lace headpiece – which I knew had been Mary's – before Sarah secured it to my head.

'It's perfect,' breathed Mary.

'Can I see now?' I asked, scowling at my sisters.

Mary looked at Mama, who nodded.

Jenny and Sarah picked up Mama's mirror from where it rested against the wall and placed it in front of me.

I gasped. I almost didn't recognise myself, dressed in such fine fabric with the veil draped down my back. Even the way Mary had done my hair looked somehow sophisticated. 'I love it. I don't want to change a thing.'

'Wait until it's finished,' said Mary, smiling smugly.

Mama kissed my cheek. 'You'll be such a beautiful bride.'

'Thank you, Mama.'

*

Suddenly the wedding day was upon me. I stood inside the vestibule beneath the ancient Norman bell tower of the church.

'Are you ready?' asked Papa. It was his seventieth birthday, but he'd insisted we get married on this day, surrounded by family, and explained that my wedding was the best gift he could ask for. He'd been determined to walk me down the aisle, even though the walk across the street and up the path to the doors of the church had been laborious for him. But now we were here and I couldn't be prouder that he was giving me away.

'I am,' I said, smiling nervously. All the frantic plans and last-minute preparations had led to this moment. I thought back to my first day in Ebberfield. It seemed so long ago. I'd never imagined standing here but I was so different from the girl who'd arrived: older, wiser, stronger.

'Take a deep breath and relax,' whispered Papa. 'I can't tell you how very happy I am to be here by your side and, don't tell your sisters, but I think you're the most beautiful bride I've ever seen, besides your mother of course. This is your moment – enjoy it.'

I squeezed Papa's arm. 'Thank you. It means more than anything to have you here. And you look very handsome too.' Papa still cut a distinguished figure in his dark suit and new bowler hat, his eyes shining with energy and excitement.

Mama stood ahead of us with Roger, beautiful in a dress she'd repurposed with Mary's help. Roger seemed calm and relaxed, straight and tall in his morning coat and suit and the top hat he'd borrowed from his best friend and groomsman, John Duffield. We'd decided to choose friends for our wedding party so we wouldn't have to choose between our siblings.

Part of me couldn't wait until this day was over and the formalities were complete. Roger and I hadn't spent a moment alone in weeks and the memories of our previous encounters had never been far from my mind, even with the daily nausea I now experienced, a constant reminder of the results of our passion. My face flushed at the prospect of what this evening might bring but all thoughts were dispelled as Roger's groomsmen and my bridesmaids began to walk down the aisle.

The faces of the villagers and friends blurred as I focused on the long, stained-glass windows behind the altar and Papa's steady progress. It didn't matter how long we took to reach the rector, only that Papa managed in a dignified manner.

Then I was standing beside Roger and Papa had stepped away, finding his seat with Mama in the pews decorated with wildflowers from the nearby fields. I stared into Roger's eyes and the moment he took my hands, I felt his calmness flow into me. It was just the two of us, repeating our vows, and nothing else mattered. He slipped the wedding band on my finger and we were married, husband and wife.

I'd never expected to become a married woman but here I was, ecstatic to be starting a life with Roger.

*

I stood face to face with my husband, blissfully alone in our new bedroom, with only the muted laughter and shouts of the reception continuing next door to break the silence.

'I've waited for this moment for weeks,' said Roger, caressing my cheek.

I closed my eyes at his touch. 'You have no regrets?'

'Never. You're all I'll ever want. I still don't know how I've been so lucky to have you as my wife.' He pulled me to him and held me tight. 'And you? Any regrets?'

'No. I've loved you for so long but I needed a push from the hand of fate to see what I would have lost.'

'You can still have your dreams, and a husband and family who adore you too.' He slid his hand over my belly. 'Our child will grow up understanding the importance of following your passion and helping those unable to help themselves. You want to make the world a better place and I'll support you in any way I can.'

I sighed, leaning into him. 'Oh, Roger, how did I get so lucky to have you?'

'Oh, I don't know,' he said, his hands moving lower to cup my bottom through my skirt. 'But I think this dress has to go so I can show you how lucky you really are.'

I laughed and then kissed him. Knowing I could now do this whenever I wanted made me want him even more. I stepped away, grinning like the Cheshire cat. 'But you have a few buttons to undo before we can get started.' I turned to present the row of tiny buttons running down my back.

Roger groaned. 'We could start now,' he murmured, grabbing me around the waist and sliding his hand up my leg, 'and worry about your dress later.'

I gasped as his fingers found their mark 'All right. We have all night, after all.'

Surrender wasn't always a bad thing, I'd discovered.

25

I've been naive to think that I can separate my heart from
my mind. Both love and my work are what sustain me and
I've been foolish to think I can do one without the other.
Somehow, I'll find a way to balance the two.

Roger filled my every day. It was a joy to wake each morning
with him by my side, sometimes still enfolded in his arms, just
as we had fallen asleep. He insisted I stay in bed when he arose
in the dawn light to get the coal stove alight before bringing
me a cup of tea and a dry biscuit to help settle my stomach.
Thoughts of him were with me throughout the day as I worked
with Bill in the pub, with Mama in the kitchen, or in Papa's
office with the ledgers. Often my eyes would stray to the
church across the street. Sometimes Roger would come home
for a bite of lunch, a brief interlude of joy in my day, otherwise
it was his footfall on the stairs of the pub of an evening or his
presence in the doorway of the parlour that brought a smile to
my face.

I looked forward to our time alone in our bedroom, the
time we could talk – about our fears, frustrations, worries and
about the future ahead of us – and show what we meant to
each other before drifting off into a deep and dreamless sleep.

When Roger and I officially announced news of my
pregnancy to our families and friends, it didn't take long for
the news to spread. I'd been feeling tiny flutters in my belly
for a week or two, and according to Laura, they were signs

that the baby was truly there. I imagined it doing somersaults inside me and somehow that thought made me smile every time. At the next suffrage society meeting, I was overwhelmed by congratulations and good wishes, before we turned our attention to Esther. Her campaign for the parish election was gearing up. We now had a solid platform and policies in place, ranging from health and sanitation to education and protection of local agriculture.

'What about our water supplies here in the village?' asked Mrs Scruton. 'How do you propose to keep our water safe to drink?'

'But disease is in the air,' called a farmer's wife.

'Disease is definitely in the air,' called a new voice. I looked to the back of the room to see Trevor Carter and Fred Duggan smiling snidely. They were here to do Mr Franks' dirty work, clearly. Edward had told me that Mr Franks was running in the election too, so of course he had to present as a respectable candidate.

Trevor Carter walked down the centre of the room between the chairs. 'But there's one disease that was right here that none of you knew about,' he said pointing to the meeting room's carpeted floor.

'What are you talking about?' asked Mrs Burrows. All eyes were on Trevor now, while Fred Duggan glowered, an ominous presence at the back of the room.

'I'm talkin' about lunacy,' Trevor said softly.

I went cold.

'Oh, go away! You're interruptin' this meetin' with nonsense,' said Mrs Scruton, standing and shooing the man with her hands.

'No, hang on a minute,' said Fred Duggan, stepping forward. 'We have the right to speak like the rest of you. And trust me, you'll want to hear this.'

My heart began to race and my mouth was dry. Could they know about Papa?

Trevor waited until he had the room's attention once again. 'William Todd ain't in a sanitorium for his leg, he's in the Durham Lunatic Asylum. He's gone soft in the mind.' He leered, triumphant, at the shock on the faces around the room

'Probably the pox. Todd's gone gaga with it.' Fred pointed at me. 'I wouldn't trust a word this woman says. She's a lyin' cow!'

The room erupted in exclamations of shock and I couldn't breathe. How could they besmirch Papa's name with the slur of syphilis?

'Get them out of here!' yelled Dr Jenkins, rushing to my side. 'Take some deep breaths,' he said to me, peering into my face anxiously.

I shook my head. 'No.' I stood slowly, still feeling woozy. But as I watched Trevor and Fred frogmarched from the room by Mr Sanderson and Mr Jones, I felt fire build in my belly. I would not let them destroy everything we'd achieved. 'I have to face this.'

'Is it true?' asked Mr Morgan, a belligerent expression on his red face.

'It is true, but it's not syphilis,' I said, standing tall. I felt the support of my friends behind me and the reassuring faces of those who knew in the audience. 'My father has an illness caused by the many years of inhaling toxic fumes from welding steel. It has progressed and causes poor coordination and forgetfulness. It's how he fell down the stairs and broke his leg.'

I gazed across the room. Many faces were hostile and closed off; I'd lost their trust. But I continued to tell them about Papa, how he'd tried to stay as long as he could and how he'd chosen to go for the sake of Mama and me and The Ox and Plough.

'I'm here to continue his legacy, to make this place the heart and soul of the community, to try to live up to his legend. I want to do him proud but I can't do it without you all. If you support me the way you all supported my father, I will do all I can to make this a place you can be proud of too.'

'You know Hannah and William,' said Mrs Scruton. 'Would any of you have done different? Will we condemn them for wantin' a little privacy, after all the good they've done for Ebberfield?' She eyeballed every person in the room. Some nodded, some dropped their heads in shame but only a handful still glared with distrust and anger. 'Then let's give Hannah and Ellen our support.'

'Thank you. I won't let you down,' I said.

*

The rigorous schedule of the following weeks, as Clementine and I followed Esther and her mother around the district on the campaign and I spoke at meetings and rallies, meant I couldn't accompany my mother to visit Papa. We were only ever away for a couple of days but I found I was bone tired whenever we returned and I always missed Roger, his calm, solid and unruffled manner and the feel of his arms around me. I couldn't stop thinking about how I missed teaching and seeing the children every day, either. It had been my vocation, knowing I was encouraging and shaping minds for the future, and I felt its loss like a gaping hole in my heart. I was still involved with the meal club, the clothing and classroom resources drives through the suffrage society but it just wasn't the same as being in the classroom.

I tried to console myself with this new work and kept busy, advocating for the changes that would most help in all the areas that Esther was promoting: girls in high schools; equal education for girls and boys; university access for women; and improving literacy for working people. I only hoped we'd cover all constituents before voting day and that the women we'd spoken to would convince their husbands, brothers and fathers of the merits of Esther's position and the benefits she'd bring as councillor. And I hoped the men we'd reached would see the logic of Esther's policies as the best way forward for our district into the future. But Mr Franks was campaigning too, against progression; feeding the fears of the older men in the community.

One Sunday, rather than a morning of cleaning at The Ox and Plough, Roger whisked me away on a surprise picnic in the woodland valley outside the village.

'You've been working too hard,' he said, glancing at my growing belly as we settled on a rug under the shedding ash and wych elm trees.

'So have you.' I looked up at the golden leaves against the dark twisted branches, listening to the whistling calls of the thrushes in the trees around us and, in the background, the gentle sound of the waterfall as it fell into Minerva's Pool. It was bliss. 'Peace and quiet and alone with you at last.'

'We have plenty of time to do whatever we like,' he said with a grin.

'Whatever we like?' I asked. Roger nodded and leant in to kiss me. 'Well then, I think I'd like you to massage my feet.'

He looked at me with mock horror. 'Your feet?'

I shrugged. 'Maybe after we've eaten. I'm starving.'

While we ate cold pies and roast beef sandwiches we talked about Esther's campaign, Roger's work on the church, The Ox and Plough and, inevitably, Papa's condition. 'Mama says that Papa is doing well. I feel terrible that I haven't been able to see him as much as I'd like but the elections are just around the corner,' I said as I lay with my head on Roger's lap. 'I can't believe Mr Franks is standing as well. Edward thinks he has a better chance of winning than Esther but we have to prove him and everyone else wrong.'

'Stop worrying and don't listen to Edward. He can be obnoxious and thoughtless sometimes, full of his own self-importance. You have so many people supporting you and Esther and even if Mr Franks wins, you just keep going and run again in the next election.'

'Quick! Give me your hand.' I grasped his hand and pressed it to my belly. 'There, can you feel that?' The baby's kicks were getting stronger with each passing week. I watched as the look of anticipation on his face changed to a beatific smile.

'She's a strong one,' he murmured.

'She?' I gazed into those blue eyes and wondered how he could possibly know when I didn't. Would the baby have his eyes or mine?

He nodded. 'It's a girl, and I know she'll be just like you. Strong, independent and passionate.'

'Well, it sounds like we'll have our work cut out for us.'

'Probably,' he said, leaning to kiss me. 'But let's worry about that later.'

*

The day of the election arrived. I met my friends at The Ox and Plough before the voting booths were open. We'd had fierce competition from The Rose and Crown and The Hare's Foot to host the booths, but in the end, none of us had received the honour. Instead, the school hall had been transformed into a polling place.

'I don't know if I can do this,' said Esther with a deep breath. She was the only woman running for council. If she made it on the annually elected parish council, she could become well known in the community for her policies and advocacy before trying for the next district elections in three years.

'Of course, you can,' said Clementine shortly. Clementine believed in Esther's ability without question.

'You're the best one for the job,' said Laura soothingly. 'Man or woman.'

Esther shook her head. 'I just want it to be over.'

Clementine took Esther's hands in hers. 'Come on, one last push and then we can all relax.'

'Here,' I said, pouring strong, dark tea into Esther's cup. 'This is what you need. We're all behind you. But whatever the outcome, this is only the beginning. There's always next year. A door for women has been opened so that our voices can be heard and we'll make sure it's never closed on us again.'

Esther nodded. 'There's nothing more we can do. Let's see if our district is ready for a woman's voice.'

On the day the results were released we gathered together in our parlour to celebrate my twenty-fourth birthday: Esther, Laura, Clementine, Mama, and Elizabeth and Alice Rainforth. Roger and Jenny were working at the pub and were joining us later.

'Are we ready?' I asked excitedly, opening the newspaper. Esther had insisted that we have tea and birthday cake before we looked at the results. Everyone leant in across the table. It would be the best birthday present if Esther was elected and a wonderful boost for our suffrage society. I could imagine the celebrations already.

Esther clasped my hand. 'Let's see,' she said, craning her neck as we scanned the page.

I frowned and read the words again. 'It can't be,' I whispered.

'I didn't win,' said Esther leadenly.

'But Mr Franks did,' said Laura, incredulous.

I felt sick to the bottom of my stomach, disgusted, and wondered how many bribes and threats it had taken for him to succeed.

'I'm so sorry, Esther,' said Mama.

'Maybe it's just as well.' Esther pushed her plate away with the half-eaten remains of her piece of cake. 'I couldn't imagine having to work with those men who think they know it all and everything should be done their way, like Mr Franks. How much would I really be able to get done as a woman on my own? They'd join forces, not because they might be opposed to my policies, but because I'm a woman and they wouldn't want to be associated with me.'

'Don't say that,' said Laura.

'But it's true,' said Esther. 'I've been around men like that all my life. I only have to look as far as Mama's brothers. They think they're entitled and that they have all the power over women. Even those I once thought of as kind and generous boys grew up to be just as obnoxious.' I thought about Roger's words and wondered if Esther had heard Edward's rather vocal opinion about the likely outcome of the election. Along with many on the old rural sanitary board, Edward had won a position on the district council.

'Then we have to take our own power back,' said Clementine. 'Any way we can.'

Esther shook her head, her frizzy ginger hair slipping from its pins to surround her head like a halo. 'Don't you see? It doesn't matter how much we lobby and advocate for change to women's rights if we can't get the men who vote for and implement change to see us as their equals, and to see merit and worth in what we say. Until then, we won't achieve anything.'

'But what comes first? The law which gives us equal rights or the respect we deserve from men?' I asked. They were able to show respect to Queen Victoria, nodding to her portrait on the wall of our meeting room, but not to us. I understood Esther's frustration; we all felt it. Leading into the election I believed we'd be victorious.

'We won't get men to change their views on women, not in our lifetime,' said Clementine scathingly. 'Unless we do something to demand the laws change. Only when they say we're equal will men be forced to change the way they see us.'

'But how do we do that?' asked Laura.

Clementine leant forward, her eyes sparkling with passion. 'Maybe we have to join together with all the women who feel the same as we do. There must be many thousands of us across Britain as well as all our supporters. We make sure we're heard by Parliament, through our collective noise, with protests and rallies and even strikes.' She'd recently joined the Women's Emancipation Union, which promoted much more radical resistance to inequality.

'But the Chartists didn't get what they wanted,' I said. 'Voting rights for men didn't come for another twenty years.'

'But maybe that's where women will be different. We'll learn from their mistakes,' she said with a determined set to her jaw.

'Maybe.' But I couldn't see how that would be any better. Violent protest would only alienate those in power further. I shook my head firmly. 'No, we can't stoop to that level. Men expect us to be irrational and emotional, that's part of the reason they don't believe we're capable of voting. We have to remain respectable, reasonable and logical.'

'I disagree,' replied Clementine, hotly.

An argument between us wasn't going to get us anywhere but Mama was ahead of me.

'Who would like more cake?' she asked.

26

*Carrying my first child brings my thoughts back to Kitty.
She and her child gone, bright sparks of life snuffed out:
victims of our heartless system, victims of patriarchy.
I will continue to fight for the voices of women and the
disadvantaged with her in my heart and burned in my
mind. We have to make sure that women have the power
to protect themselves.*

Roger rose with the dawn as usual one crisp April morning.
I'd had a restless night, unable to get comfortable with my
protruding belly, and was wide awake. I watched him pull
off his nightshirt and marvelled at how beautiful he was. I'd
never seen another man naked but I doubted that few men
would have as perfect a body as Roger. His back was long
and elegant, the muscles that rippled over his shoulders and
down his back, strong and well defined from the hard physical
work he did every day. I'd never get tired of looking at him.

The ache in my back had returned and lying here wasn't
going to help it. I sighed as I struggled out of bed. Surely this
baby would come soon.

Roger turned at the sound of my sigh, glorious in his
nakedness. 'Stay in bed,' he said, kissing me on the lips. The
warmth of his body and mouth made me reconsider. Perhaps
I could persuade him to join me under the covers before he
had to leave for work. It might take my mind off my back.

'Only if you stay too,' I murmured, kissing him back.

'You know I can't. It's an important day for the church. We're lowering the floor.'

'Whatever for?' I asked.

'The restoration work of forty years ago raised it and we're going to return it to the original twelfth-century level.'

'Ah,' I said absently. 'Come on, just a few minutes. I'll make it worth your while.' I wrapped my arms around his neck, pulling him towards me and he collapsed on the bed beside me.

Roger grinned. 'Will you now?'

I slid my hand down his taut belly. 'I want you,' I whispered.

Roger drew back. 'No, we shouldn't. I don't want to harm you or the baby.' We'd been avoiding intimate relations over the last few weeks on the advice of Dr Taylor after I'd begun spotting.

'I'm fine now. Whatever it was has settled.'

'Are you sure?' His frown of concern made my heart melt. Not all husbands were so considerate, I knew. I still couldn't believe that this was my life.

I nodded. 'We may not get many more opportunities before the baby arrives.'

Roger kissed the skin at the base of my throat. 'I'll be gentle but it might be quick. I don't think I can hold back.'

'Come to me,' I murmured and sighed with pleasure as he slid home.

*

I couldn't stay in bed after Roger left for work. The back pain had eased, replaced by a pleasant ache from our morning activity, but I still felt restless. I went downstairs to find a pot of tea already brewing. Somehow, he'd found time to start the fire and boil the water. Mama and Jenny would be up any minute, so I pulled out three cups and saucers from the cupboard and opened the tin of oat biscuits. We'd eat a proper breakfast after we'd cleaned the pub and finished cooking pies for the customers.

A sudden gush of wetness flooded my drawers and I swayed as a wave of fear washed over me. Perhaps this morning had been a mistake after all. Grasping the edge of the kitchen table, I touched the wet fabric and withdrew a shaking hand, expecting to see bright red blood. Instead, it was a clear, sweet-smelling liquid. Then I remembered. Sarah had warned me that labour could sometimes start like this, before the pains had even begun.

'Are you all right?' Jenny stood in the doorway, white-faced with worry.

'I think it's beginning,' I said. I wasn't sure what to do next.

'I'll go and get Grandma.'

The pains came on not long after, beginning as minor and infrequent cramps.

'Nothing to worry about,' said Mama, pouring tea into my cup. 'There's no doubt that the baby's coming. I'll let Roger know soon but it will be a long while before we have to call the midwife.'

'But what do I do until then?' I asked. I'd read what I could about the subject of birth, but much of it was academic and gave little practical insight. I'd turned instead to my mother and sisters for advice but now I was here, I realised there was still so much I didn't know.

'While you're still comfortable, continue as normal. Some even say that it helps bring the baby on and makes the process smoother.'

After sitting with Mama and Jenny for a cup of tea and nibbling on an oat biscuit, I felt stronger and reassured. The ache in my back had eased and the pains in my belly hadn't worsened – they were noticeable but nothing that stopped me in my tracks. Things still had to be done. I joined Mama and Jenny at the pub and, at Mama's insistence, helped only with light cleaning and cooking of the pies. It took my mind off what was ahead, and standing and walking felt more comfortable than sitting or lying down. But by mid-morning, I was struggling to focus on even simple tasks like cutting the pastry for the pies as the pains became stronger and closer together. I gasped as a fresh pain tightened around my belly, the force of it taking my breath away.

'Go and rest,' said Mama, wiping her hands on her apron. 'Your time isn't far off and you'll want all the energy you can find.'

'How long until it really starts?' I asked weakly after the pain had ebbed away.

Mama guided me to a chair, frowning. 'I think I'll send Jenny for the midwife now.'

I clutched her hand. 'How long Mama?'

'It's hard to say, but if things continue as they have been, I think it will get serious soon.'

I nodded, not sure whether to be excited or afraid. 'You think the baby will be born today?'

'There's a good chance.'

When the midwife arrived, she examined me.

'The babe is comin' today,' she said, straightening. 'But likely not till later this afternoon.'

My heart sank. 'That long?'

She patted my hand at the look of disappointment on my face. 'When the waters break first like they did for you, labour can come on quickly, but you're birthin' for the first time, so the body takes a while to learn what to do. You're only in the early stages and I suggest you move around. Unless your mother's worried or you feel like pushin', I'll be back after lunch.'

The day dragged on, my world expanding and contracting with the pains in my belly, but I was grateful that Mama stayed with me, leaving Jenny to finish cooking the pies and continue her work in the pub. Mama was my strength and comfort. She'd seen this many times before with my sisters and knew what to look for, making me pace the room when the pains were bad or helping me get comfortable when I had a moment or two to rest. If my sisters were anything to go by, this birth wouldn't be long. All I had to do was rely on instinct and allow my body to take over.

Mama sent word to Roger and Elizabeth that the baby was on its way and soon Elizabeth had joined us.

'You need to sustain yourself,' she said, carrying a tray of food into my room. 'It's only light, so it won't make you nauseous.'

I wasn't hungry but the aroma of the broth made me realise it had been a long time since the oat biscuits early that morning.

Listening to Mama and Elizabeth talk about their experiences of birth made me realise that it was a natural process, nothing to fear. They were a good distraction to while away the minutes but I wanted to see Roger more than anything, to share this with him.

Soon word had spread and friends and neighbours came to our door to ask after me. Mama and Elizabeth took it in turn to receive our callers, who thankfully didn't stay long, but when I heard the sound of a second pair of feet on the stairs, I knew that Roger was home.

Suddenly I was in his arms. 'How are you?' he whispered.

I drew away, clinging to the foot of the bed as a fresh wave of pain rolled through me. They were closer together and more intense now. I breathed through it like Mama and Elizabeth had instructed. Then it ebbed away and I sighed.

'I'm all right,' I said, smiling weakly. 'Better now that you're here.'

'Is it bad? What can I do?'

'Not so bad. I'm getting used to it.'

'There's nothing you can do, son,' said Elizabeth softly. 'She's in good hands and is doing well.'

'Is it because of what we did this morning?' he asked me in a low voice, his face turning red. 'Because if it is, I'm sorry.'

I shrugged. 'I don't know. Maybe. But perhaps it was my body's way of telling me that it was time. My waters broke not long after you left.'

'The midwife will be back soon to assess her progress,' added Mama, picking up the tray. 'Do you want some lunch, Roger?'

He shook his head. 'No, I have to get back soon. I just wanted to see that Hannah was all right.'

'Your mother and I will make you something to take with you,' said Mama.

'A moment just to ourselves,' said Roger, taking my hands in his once they'd left.

'They've been wonderful. I don't know how I'd have managed without them.'

'I know but I also know that a birthing room is the domain of women and once the midwife arrives, I doubt I'll get to see you again until the baby's born.'

'Just hold me, Roger.' He enfolded me in his strong arms. 'I'm afraid. What if I can't do it?'

'You're the bravest person I know. You can do anything.'

I rested my head against his chest. I could hear the steady beat of his heart and I found it calming. 'I wish you could stay with me.'

'I wish I could too, but there's nothing I can do to help you and I'd just be in the way. Our mothers know what they're doing.' He kissed my forehead. 'I'll be thinking of you and the baby for the rest of the day, and after work I'll be waiting downstairs, pacing the hallway until I'm allowed to come up to see you and meet our child.' He cupped my face and kissed me on the lips. 'We'll be a family soon.'

The rest of the afternoon passed in a blur. The midwife stayed after examining me and I knew then that it wasn't going to be much longer. But rather than feel relieved or elated, I felt irritated.

'Why is it taking so long?' I snapped between the pains. They were coming hard and fast, leaving me gasping. I grasped Mama's hand so hard that I could feel the bones grind together.

'It won't be long before you want to push,' said the midwife once the contraction had passed. She was the picture of calm and serenity. All I wanted to do was slap her across the face. I was tired, cranky and I'd had enough.

But I was surprised to find a new level of strength and energy once the pushing began.

'Come, it's time to get into squattin',' said the midwife. 'Opens up the birthin' passage and makes the most out of every push.' She helped me squat over the towels on the floor. 'Take her arms to support her,' she said to Mama and Elizabeth.

The urge to push was overwhelming, my body taking control without any conscious thought of my own. But now I was determined and focused. This baby was coming out and soon. I rode the waves of each push, screaming with the effort, as though somehow it might help release the baby into the world. A ring of fire burned with the pressure of the baby's head and my legs shook with the exertion. I rested between pushes on the edge of a chair, just long enough to gather my strength for one more push. My nightdress clung to my skin, soaked in sweat.

'Nearly there,' said Mama, as the urge took me once more.

My voice was hoarse from screaming but I couldn't stop. The pressure was enormous and I wondered if I would split in two.

'I can see the babe's head,' said the midwife.

'Really?' I gasped, as I leant on the chair.

She nodded. 'Reach down and touch it.'

I looked at Mama, her faced etched with exhaustion, but lit with excitement. I placed a shaking hand between my legs and felt the wet, downy head. 'It's happening,' I whispered in amazement. I could do this. I would do this.

'Two or three more pushes and your babe will be here,' said the midwife, smiling encouragingly.

Three pushes were all it took for the baby to come sliding into the world and into the hands of the midwife.

'You did it,' breathed Elizabeth.

Mama kissed my head. 'I'm so proud of you.'

While the midwife checked the baby over, Mama and Elizabeth helped me onto the bed. I was exhausted and sore but elated. I'd done it.

'Here's your babe, a healthy little girl,' said the midwife, putting her into my arms. I stared at her, so small and delicate, big blue eyes staring back at me. I felt something I didn't recognise rush through me. A fierce protective instinct flooded my body. I would do anything for her and anything to make sure the world she grew up in was a place of optimism and hope.

'Congratulations,' said Elizabeth. 'She's beautiful.'

'She looks like you when you were born,' said Mama, her voice husky.

Tears welled in my eyes. She was perfect and everything that had happened up until now, all the pain, heartbreak and suffering, disappeared. She was my new beginning, my reason for living.

*

We called her Annie, after Papa's mother. Roger and I took her to see her grandfather a month after she was born.

'Congratulations, my sweetheart,' said Papa, as we embraced. He was moving with difficulty today I noticed with shock. But Mama had assured me he was doing well with each of her visits.

'Meet your new granddaughter, Annie,' said Roger, after Papa was sitting again. He placed her, tightly swaddled, in Papa's arms.

'She's beautiful,' whispered Papa, tears in his eyes. 'She's got so much hair,' he said, stroking her head. 'You were like that, I remember.'

'You remember, Papa,' I said with a smile.

He nodded. 'I'm forgetting a lot of things, like what I had for dinner yesterday, but not things that happened so long ago, not that.' He planted a kiss on Annie's forehead like a blessing. 'My mother, your great-grandmother, was a strong woman,' he said to her. 'Your mother's a strong woman and I know you will be too.'

I was overcome with emotion, just as I felt milk draw down in my breasts. Mama had said that milk always arrived with tears. I hastily blotted the tears from my eyes. I wasn't going to cry, not here, not now. 'Thank you, Papa,' I said, my voice wobbling.

Roger took my hand. 'Looks like I'm surrounded by strong women,' he said.

Papa gazed at the baby, who had worked her little arm free of her blanket, punching the air in victory. 'Look, little Annie's ready for the world.' He smiled and passed her back to me. 'You watch, your children will be the making of you,' he said, touching my cheek, before his hand fell to his lap.

27

Esther has turned to her other passions after the
loss of the election. She's corresponding with Hertha
Ayrton after reading her articles in *The Electrician*
about electric arcs, which as Esther explained it to me,
is where electricity flows between two points. Hertha
is an inventor, mathematician and engineer but also a
suffragist.

'It will pass,' said Laura, rocking Annie to sleep while I made
us tea one morning. 'The first few months are the hardest,
especially with babies who are fretful. Soon she'll be smiling
and taking more interest in her surroundings and you'll be
able to enjoy her more.'

'Are you sure? Some days I don't know if I'm doing anything
right.' Laura was the only one of my friends who understood
what I was going through.

Motherhood wasn't what I'd expected. Annie cried lots and
slept little. I drifted through a constant fog of exhaustion,
feeling a great sense of achievement if I was able to wash or
spend an hour checking the books at the pub. Roger and I
seemed like ships in the night. When he wasn't spending long
hours working on the refurbishment of the church, he was
working at the pub. I often woke to Annie's cries to find him
sound asleep next to me.

Laura nodded. 'Just keep doing what you're doing and let
your mother and Elizabeth take her and help when they can.

I wished I'd had my mother or even Benjamin's mother nearby when I had the girls. Being in a new place with no friends or family was much harder than I'd imagined.'

I felt bad, not being able to manage by myself. Mama and Elizabeth were busy too and although they had been helpful, they tended to hover in the background, not wanting to interfere or overstep. I'd always found it hard to admit that I was struggling but maybe it was time to surrender and ask for their help.

I touched her arm. 'Thank you, Laura, for being such a good friend and for being here for me.'

'Any time. I'm glad to help.'

With the support of my mother, sisters and friends, as well as Elizabeth and Alice, I was able to slowly reclaim some of myself. But there was always the pub, waiting like a jealous lover to hungrily devour every spare minute I possessed. At least it allowed me to see more of Roger, who helped me go through the books and updated me on what we needed to order.

'I've missed you,' he said one afternoon when we'd finished discussing business.

I looked around Papa's office, the very place where Annie had been conceived nearly a year earlier. I was still amazed at how overwhelming having a child could be, how every waking moment was devoted to her, either caring for her, thinking about her or waiting for her cries.

'I miss you too.' The nearness of him and the memories of those early days stirred something in me. I kissed him. His lips were warm and soft.

'It's been too long,' he murmured. 'I wondered if you didn't want me anymore.'

I drew away, frowning at the thought, and saw the pain flash across his face. 'How could you think that?'

He shook his head. 'I know you've been tired but some of the lads at work have mentioned how their wives never wanted to touch them again after the birth of their children.'

'Oh, Roger, it's nothing like that.' Laura had spoken about Benjamin feeling unloved and shut out when their girls were babies, but I hadn't expected Roger to feel this way already. 'It's just that I'm always so exhausted and most of the time I don't know where my body ends and Annie's begins.'

'We can do something about that,' he said, sliding his hand along my thigh.

'I can't think of anything better,' I whispered breathlessly. I wanted to feel like a desirable woman once again, a woman separated from her role as mother, if only for a little while. We were blissfully alone in a quiet room and that was arousing enough for the both of us. 'You have always made me burn and you always will. There will never be a day when I won't want you.'

*

Clementine, Esther and Laura met me in one of the meeting rooms at The Ox and Plough one evening a month later to discuss the agenda for the upcoming meeting of our suffrage society. Annie had been fed and was sleeping in her crib next door with Mama watching over her. I was free for a couple of hours and excited to extend my mind beyond talk of babies and motherhood, and to bounce ideas off each of my friends, to become a collective creation between the four of us. We were good together and I'd missed the intellectual conversation and camaraderie between us.

We discussed the proposal for a new isolation hospital that Dr Jenkins had brought to us and how we could aid the submission to council. The village had expanded so the hospital was no longer on its outskirts, as required by law. As much as Ebberfield had been lucky in recent years, outbreaks of infectious diseases still occurred, and Dr Jenkins wanted to remove the stigma of isolation in the old mill building with a modern facility where patients would receive the best medical care available. Education and changing outdated attitudes was key to the evolution of our community and its survival into the new century.

Marjorie joined us after visiting Becky, and Edward arrived halfway through our meeting, popping his head in to let her know he'd wait for her downstairs.

'Please stay,' I said to him. 'The report on the Royal Commission on Secondary Education has come out and I'd like you to hear the recommendations and perhaps give us your thoughts on how it relates to us here.'

Edward nodded and took a seat.

'How do you know the report has been released?' asked Clementine, holding her glass of wine mid-air in surprise.

'I have my ways,' I said with a grin. I might be busy with a baby, but I was determined to stay abreast of the progress that was happening in London. I'd received a letter of congratulations on Annie's birth from Mrs Fawcett and she'd told me about the reports and petitions that had been presented to the House of Commons. I lifted my milk stout to my mouth. I wasn't a great beer drinker – I didn't enjoy the bitter taste – but Mama and Elizabeth had sworn that dark beer, especially milk or oatmeal stout, was nutritious for nursing mothers and good to improve milk supply and had insisted I have a glass every day.

'But do you have the *whole* report?' Clementine asked, smiling mischievously.

'What, you have it?' I breathed.

She nodded and held up a thick bundle of pages. She must have received a copy from one of the committees she was working with at the Women's Emancipation Union. She was getting more involved with their political activities and the four main rights they were targeting for women's equality: civic rights and duties; education; workplace and career choices; and marriage and parenting rights. She leant forward and pushed her glass away, a sure sign that she meant business.

'What about girls' education and teacher training?' I asked.

'The report mentions the low numbers of secondary school placements for girls and the inadequate education of secondary schoolteachers.'

I nodded and picked up the pages, turning them until I found what I wanted, the statistics that Clementine had underlined. I read them out.

> Only one third of students over the age of fourteen
> is female. And for every one thousand of population,
> secondary school is available to only ten children. In 1868
> there were thirteen secondary schools across England,
> now there are eighty.

I looked up and shook my head. 'There has been progress in the last twenty-five years, but not nearly enough. We'll have to do more to get girls in secondary school. Scholarships to the schools that do exist and advocating for more secondary schools to be opened in the county. If the Welsh and the Scots can have coeducational secondary schools, then so can we.'

'We can work on that plan with the suffrage society and Benjamin,' said Laura.

'And if we can get you, Edward, and James Duffield on board ...' I lifted my eyebrow quizzically.

Edward nodded. 'We can take your proposal to the county council.'

'We might have a chance at getting even a few more schools,' I said, getting excited now. If we had more opportunities for girls at secondary school, they'd have more chance of being accepted into university. Although Cambridge still awarded university diplomas to women, London had admitted women to the same university programs as men for over ten years and female students at my old teachers' college had recently been given permission to apply for degrees.

I sat back in my chair, wondering if I would have studied something else if I'd had the opportunity. I loved teaching, but I would have studied for a three-year degree instead of the two-year offering.

'The last point the report makes is that there aren't nearly enough higher-grade elementary schools to cater for the demand in science and technical studies, and it recommends adding literary studies too, and giving scholarships to gifted elementary students to go to secondary school,' finished Esther, reading over my shoulder. She'd recovered quickly after the local elections and Clementine was encouraging her to try again at the next elections, held annually and scheduled for the following April. But for now, Esther was occupied with her studies in science and engineering, despite her mother's objections.

I nodded. 'It's a great start!'

'Benjamin has already introduced higher grades to our school, but what if we can persuade the other schools in the district to do the same?' asked Clementine.

'There'd be more chance for children to develop a love of learning and want to further their education at high school,' I said. 'But we have to make lawmakers, school principals and influential men understand the importance of improving the opportunities for everyone to have a secondary education.' I read from the report again:

There is an acceptance of the narrow ladder that exists
from the gutter to university.

'Not everyone agrees with your ideas of education for everyone,' said Edward, drinking his scotch. 'There are many who believe that "overeducating" the working class is unwise and unnecessary, because they don't need secondary education for their jobs or work. We should only educate those who show an above average aptitude.'

Marjorie frowned and shook her head. 'But how are we ever going to widen the ladder when outdated attitudes like that exist?'

'We keep on with the small changes we can make, like keeping children in school longer, through our library, the breakfast and lunch program, clothing drives and the higher top classes. And we lobby Parliament to make the legislative changes necessary,' I said.

'We're not the only ones,' said Esther. 'There are more and more people across the country making their own contributions to improving education for everyone, like Margaret McMillan, who campaigned for similar changes to these recommendations in the Bryce Report.'

I nodded. 'The Royal Commission highlights what teachers already know about the problems in our education system and the inequalities for working-class and female students,' I said. A buzz of excitement rushed through me. 'Surely with enough voices behind this report, the government has to listen?'

'But will they? With Bryce no longer in government, I wonder if real change will happen.' There was a growing edge to Clementine's voice, an impatience and dissatisfaction with the slow progress of our fight.

28

An underground explosion in one of the nearby coal
mines has left wives without husbands and children
without fathers. It has been a terrible shock to the district
and the suffrage society is planning a fundraising concert
to support the women and families in their time of
unimaginable loss.

I stood in the lounge of The Ox and Plough, filled with members of the public, rooted to the spot in horror by the coronial inquest taking place.

'The fire was caused by a paraffin oil lamp, knocked over while alight,' stated the coroner.

I glanced at the grieving family of the three little girls who had died in the house fire, burned almost beyond recognition. I couldn't imagine what they were going through. It was horrible to hear the details; all I could think about was little Annie and how I'd feel if it had been her.

I stepped out of the lounge and took a deep breath, trying to dispel the horror. It had been a battle to secure this inquest. With Mr Franks on the parish council, he had been able to persuade the committee members that The Rose and Crown was best placed to host most of the community events. But I had begun to win back some support since providing village refreshments at the May Day festival and showing the councillors how The Ox and Plough did things. We were big hearted, generous and community minded, but we still needed customers in the door. Many would stay after the inquest to discuss its findings over a pint and to support the family in their loss and I wanted to make sure that everything was ready.

'Annie's still crying and a letter came for Grandma,' said Jenny as I came down the corridor, thrusting the screaming baby into my arms and handing me an envelope. She was frowning and looked harassed, like she wished she was anywhere but here.

'Where's Grandma?' I shoved the letter into the pocket of my skirt and held Annie's hot little body close to my chest.

'She's in the kitchen, getting out the last of the pies. She asked me to watch Annie but I just don't know what to do.'

I nodded as I hurried towards the main bar, jiggling the crying baby in my arms. 'Go and help her and make sure all the food is ready and I'll be there in a moment.' Annie had been unsettled through the night and hadn't stopped crying all morning. Elizabeth had told me that her children had been the same at this age with colic. I'd been careful with what I was eating, keeping to plain foods, but it wasn't helping.

'Everything all right?' I asked Bill behind the bar.

'Everything's under control here. You don't need to worry. It looks like you have your hands full.'

I breathed a sigh of relief and nodded before turning towards the kitchen. I didn't know what I'd do without him.

Mama and Jenny were putting pies on platters. 'I'm going to give her a quick feed and change her nappy,' I said, sinking onto a chair by the window. I opened the front of my bodice, unbuttoned the nursing flap of my corset and adjusted Annie on my lap. She latched onto my nipple and there was immediate silence.

'Did you give Grandma that letter?' asked Jenny, placing the last platter on the table.

I shook my head and fished it out of my pocket with my spare hand, feeling the wet patch on my clothing. Annie had soaked through her nappy. I only hoped it was wet and not dirty too. 'It's a telegram,' I said in surprise, looking at the envelope, 'and it's addressed to you, Mama.'

'Who would want to send me a telegram?' Mama waved her hand in dismissal. 'Open it and tell me what it's about while I cut the sandwiches.'

Dear Mrs Todd,
I regret to inform you that your husband, Mr William Todd, passed away through the night. His death was sudden and unexpected. Dr Sloane has attended him and pronounced the cause of death as apoplexy.
    Our deepest sympathies are with you and your family at this difficult time.

I stared at the page, the words blurring as I heard a roaring in my ears.

'Hannah, Hannah!'

Someone was shaking me and the sound of Annie's cries brought me back to the painful present.

'What is it, Hannah?' asked Mama, her face etched with fear. 'Are you all right?'

I glanced from her to Jenny with Annie in her arms, feeling dazed. 'I'm so sorry, Mama,' I whispered, my face crumpling. 'It's Papa.'

'No.' She took the paper from my unresisting hand. 'No!' she moaned again, reading the words. 'My love ...'

Somehow, I was on my feet, holding her to me, before her knees gave way. Great gasping sobs were ripped from her chest.

I rode the wave of Mama's grief as I held her in my arms, feeling nothing but a searing pain in my heart. Maybe I was burning from the inside out ... I pushed every thought away. There was just Mama and me, fused together in our pain.

Sometime later, it might have been minutes or hours, the sound of Annie's howling reached me. Numbly, I allowed her to blindly rootle around until she found my nipple.

Roger found me huddled round the warm and sleeping form of our daughter. It was only once I was in his arms that my own tears began to fall.

*

Papa was buried in the asylum graveyard. Mama and I wanted to bring him back to Ebberfield to be buried in the graveyard across the road from The Ox and Plough, so he could be close to us but the cost of bringing him home to bury was far more than we could afford. It was heartbreaking to say our final goodbyes with my sisters and their families in the cemetery chapel, before we gathered around Papa's grave – watched as he was lowered into the ground.

I had been strong until that moment, for Mama, but I began to shake uncontrollably as I realised that I had wasted the last few months, not visiting him every chance I had. I would never again kiss his cheek, hear his voice or talk to him about anything and everything. I couldn't imagine feeling separate from him and the spark of humanity and joy that had suffused him during life. But with each spadeful of dirt thrown onto his coffin, he disappeared from us, until he was gone. I sobbed like a child, barely noticing Roger's arms around me, lending me his strength.

We were determined to celebrate Papa's life in a way that would never be possible with an asylum burial. A wake at The Ox and Plough was a fitting memorial. Friends, neighbours, acquaintances and anyone who knew him came. The pub was as full as I'd ever seen it and rather than the sombre mood of a funeral, stories about Papa brought joy, laughter and inspiration to us all. It was the perfect send-off for him. He was well loved and would be long remembered: truly the heart of our community.

Only after closing, when the last patrons and well-wishers had finally left, did I suddenly sense my father's presence, so strong that I turned towards it, feeling his love and joy for just a moment. Then it was gone. 'Goodbye Papa,' I whispered into the night.

*

Through the haze of grief after Papa's death, I continued to put one foot in front of the other. Annie needed me, her demands forcing me to push through my loss, as did The Ox and Plough.

Papa had left everything to Mama and now the liquor licence and register had to name her as the new owner of the pub. His last wishes requested that I carry on as manager. We were two women carrying the responsibility of The Ox and Plough, carrying our own future in our hands. I felt like I had no choice except to step up and take that responsibility. Mama couldn't do it, nor wanted to at her age. But it meant that my dreams of someday moving to London, even now with Roger and Annie, had turned to dust. The hope I'd harboured all these years, no matter how dim, was now finally extinguished. And all I could feel was numb.

29

Dear Sarah,

I still can't believe Papa is gone. His loss feels like a shard of glass in my chest. I'm glad he met Annie. It was the last time I saw him and while he had deteriorated physically, he was completely lucid. With everything that was going on, Mama told me that she wanted to protect me from the truth of his condition. She knew he was never coming home. I feel a fool for not realising.

Some days I want to just let my grief take over but there's so much to do. We were waiting for the annual sitting of the district licensing committee, which approves transfers and new licences and renewals of liquor licences. My name is already on the licence but the official register has to be changed to include Mama.

But Mr Franks and Mr Yule, the publican of The Hare's Foot are opposing the renewal of our liquor licence and now a special session with all parties present has had to be arranged. I shouldn't be surprised at their attempt to kick us while we're down. It's the last thing Mama and I need, but without the renewal we can't trade.

'I don't know if I can do this,' I said one evening. Roger was closing up, Annie was asleep and I had joined Mama for a cup of tea in the parlour before bed.

'Do what?' asked Mama.

'All of this.' I sighed, a long, deep exhalation of exhaustion. 'Be a mother, a wife, run the pub and continue my work with the suffrage society.'

'But you already are,' she said gently. Mama had aged in the month since Papa's death. The dark smudges beneath her puffy eyes told me that she didn't sleep much and still cried every day for him. Outwardly she was as stoic as ever, helping in The Ox and Plough and looking after Annie. I didn't know what I would do without her.

'I don't want to let Papa down. I want to do him proud, build on the legacy he's left behind, but ...' I shrugged helplessly. 'When Papa was here, I knew I could always turn to him for advice, but now I don't know if I can do it. The responsibility feels like a heavy weight around my neck.' I put my head in my hands as the load on my shoulders became too heavy to bear. I missed him so much. Even on his bad days, his presence had been reassuring; I hadn't been alone with this burden.

'Hannah!' I felt Mama's hand resting on my head. 'I know you can do it. Papa had faith in you and so do I.'

I lifted my head and blinked the tears from my eyes. 'Really?'

'If anyone can make a success of The Ox and Plough, it's you.' She took my hand in hers. 'You are your father's daughter and there's nobody better suited to bring the community together. You are already doing him proud.'

'But the scavengers are out in force now that Papa's not here.'

Mama frowned. 'When has a bit of opposition ever stopped you? You've always been the first one to step up in the face of resistance.'

'I know but this is different. I don't know if I have the energy or the fortitude. It's too much.'

'You are a courageous woman. You've faced and overcome so much in your life already; shaping your dreams of life in the city around the reality of life in a small village; facing the objections and opposition to change with grace and persistence; taking over the managing of this place at the age of twenty-three and taking that terrifying step into the unknown with Roger and becoming a family. You can do it again.'

I closed my eyes to shut out the world. 'I don't know, Mama. This time I feel so unsure and I'm so tired.'

'I've never understood why you wanted such a different life from your sisters and for a long time, I worried about your choices to go to teachers' college and not to marry and have a family.'

'And yet here I am,' I whispered.

'I know this was never the life you wanted,' she said, kissing my forehead. 'But you're still doing everything you set out to do, to help create change, not just here in the school and the village, but in the district and London too, and because of that, you'll make a better place for all of us to live in. Just as your father would have wanted.'

'But I have so much to do here, sometimes I feel I'll never have the chance to create meaningful change.'

Mama shook her head. 'Your father understood that working in The Ox and Plough would give you opportunities to see where the real problems lie within the community and where the change has to happen.' She put her arm around me and pulled me to her. 'Just keep walking forward, through the troubles and the joys. You have it all now: the blessing of a family; a husband who encourages your dreams; your suffrage society; and The Ox and Plough to provide you with security, inspiration, love and the support of your village. Your father and I couldn't have hoped for more.'

I knew Mama wouldn't lie to me. She was always forthright and honest, sometimes brutally so. My heart felt somehow lighter and the darkness that had been suffocating me began to lift. I could do it – I *would* do it. If not for myself, then for my parents, who had put their hopes and faith in me.

*

A few weeks later, Roger, Mama and I arrived at the special session of the licensing committee held at the petty sessions court in Bishopdene, a neighbouring village. Mama and Roger were already inside the courthouse waiting for me to return from the washhouse where I'd had to replace the sodden flannel nursing pads inside my corset.

As I approached the courthouse, I saw Fred Duggan, Trevor Carter and the erstwhile Mr Connolly loitering by the entrance.

'Women don't belong on a liquor licence,' said Fred in a low voice as I passed. 'It's time you learn your place.'

'Say goodbye to The Ox and Plough,' said Trevor.

Mr Connolly just stared at me with what I supposed was the most withering expression of disdain he could muster.

I smiled coldly. 'We'll see about that.' I stood tall and walked past. Instead of fear, I found myself filled with fury and determination. We would prevail and when we did, these men could do nothing to stop me from proving that women could do as good a job as any man. Sometime soon, they'd rue the day they underestimated me.

There were five Justices of the Peace on the committee, including Edward Partridge and James Duffield. It might have been intimidating for some but I was relieved to know that we had supporters. I glanced at Mr Franks, who stood stiffly in front of the bench.

'I object to the renewal of this licence,' he said. 'Mrs Todd and Mrs Rainforth ain't fit applicants to hold this licence.'

I glanced at Mama. She was pale with mortification. I clenched my hands in my skirt. My blood was boiling already and we'd barely started.

'Mrs Todd is of good character and has been by the side of the publican, her late husband, Mr William Todd, these last five years,' said the chairman of the committee.

'That don't make her daughter an appropriate choice as publican,' argued Mr Franks. I wanted to slap his smug face but the onus was on him to prove his case, not on us to defend ours. The licence would be renewed unless Mr Franks could present a valid reason for it not to be.

'What's your objection to Mrs Rainforth?' asked Mr Duffield.

'She's an agitator, a troublemaker. She turns women against their husbands and promotes women congregatin' in the public house when they should be home with their families.'

Roger grasped my hand and squeezed.

'That has nothing to do with her managing a public house,' said Mr Duffield. 'Women are allowed in public houses, unless you're talking about in the main bar or drunkenness?'

'That's right.' Mr Franks nodded. 'Drunkenness.'

'Where's your evidence that she allows drunkenness in women?' asked Edward.

Mr Franks shook his head sullenly. He had none. 'Everyone knows The Ox and Plough is becomin' a hotbed of female unrest.'

I dropped my head to hide my smile.

'Are you saying that Mrs Rainforth conducts a disorderly house on the premises?' asked one of the committee members.

Mr Franks stared at him.

'You can't make such accusations without proof. Now, for any of the offences you're suggesting, a police constable is required to enter the premises to find evidence of the charges. Only after repeated offences can a licensee become disqualified.'

'I'd expect God-fearin' believers of temperance like yourselves to take this seriously. But of course, she has you both in her pocket,' Mr Franks said, pointing at Edward and James.

'Are you accusing a member of this committee of bribery and collusion?' asked the chairman, removing his glasses to glare at Mr Franks.

Roger, Mama and I had been to see Mr Sanderson the solicitor for legal advice before this session and he'd explained that any Justices of the Peace associated with the brewery industry were prohibited from joining any licensing committee. This meant that Mr Franks had no leverage with his brewery contacts. Many committee members were also followers of the temperance movement and were strict on not providing licences to those they believed would flout the drinking laws and allow or promote drunkenness in their establishment.

'No, of course not,' he said hastily. 'But no respectable person is goin' to go to a public house where the owner and publican are both women.'

'And why not?' asked another committee member.

'It only leads to disreputable types frequentin' such a place – unruly men and women.'

'Both Mrs Todd and Mrs Rainforth are respected members of the community,' said Edward.

Mr Franks spread his hands in regret. 'Women can't be expected to understand the inner workings of a drinkin' establishment, especially respectable ones; the seedy underbelly, the business side of dealin' with breweries and their agents. They most likely will be preyed upon by those who wish to take advantage of two naive ladies. None of us want that. I would think it's the duty of this committee to protect Mrs Todd and Mrs Rainforth from such a terrible position.'

I took in a sharp breath. The hide of him. I was livid, shaking with fury. I'd been doing it all since Papa left for the asylum over a year earlier. But all I could do was show no reaction to his words.

'The committee has heard your argument, Mr Franks,' said the chairman. 'We will deliberate now and then come to a decision.'

The five men whispered briefly between themselves, nodding in assent.

'The liquor licence for The Ox and Plough is renewed to you, Mrs Rainforth, with Mrs Todd as the owner. Mr Franks, your objection is dismissed.'

I hugged Mama. It was the first battle of many, I suspected, but we were safe for now. The pub was ours and could remain a warm haven of community and respite.

*

It was a fine October afternoon when the circus arrived in the village. The sound of beating drums and trumpets grew louder as I finished placing the clean glasses on the shelves under the counter.

'It's going to be busy,' said Mama, peering through the window.

'Not as busy as we're going to be over the next couple of days,' said Bill, checking the beer taps were running well after we'd connected the lines to the new barrel.

'We have to be prepared,' said Mama. She was feeling anxious because this was the first event that stretched over days since she'd become the official owner of The Ox and Plough.

'We'll be fine,' I said. I had gone over the orders, checked the paperwork and made sure I had everything organised. We were prepared for a full house on all three days the circus was in town.

A cheer erupted outside and I joined Mama at the window. A large crowd had gathered along the road, children and adults alike climbing the embankment in front of the graveyard and lining the street in front of our pub to better see the parade. I wondered briefly if Roger had stopped his work on the church to watch too. The excitement was palpable. Although I'd seen a few circus parades, I never ceased to be amazed and excited by the spectacle. The procession of wagons with colourful pictures of clowns, acrobats and circus animals painted on their sides was pulled by horses in feathered headdresses. Clowns, acrobats and animal handlers, all in bright costumes, followed behind, along with elephants and camels, and lions and tigers in cages on the back of carts, monkeys and pygmy ponies led by their trainers, and a small brass band playing well-known showground tunes.

As the parade passed, the crowd dispersed, some coming into the pub, others returning home, but most following the procession to the village green. I turned my attention to the busy afternoon ahead.

'Let's go to the circus today,' said Roger the following morning as we lay in bed. It would soon be time to get up and begin the day. Annie was six months old and although she was sleeping better and I'd only got up to her a couple of times through the night, I was still bone weary.

'We can't,' I said automatically.

He rolled onto his side and kissed my bare shoulder. 'You haven't stopped in weeks.'

I opened my mouth to answer him but a yawn came out instead.

'Come on, it will do you good. It will do us both good.'

I yawned again and this time stretched. If I didn't move now, I would burrow under the blankets, close my eyes and fall back to sleep. 'I want to, I really do. It's just that ...'

'I know, we need customers through the door.'

I nodded. It was still a fine balancing act, paying off the loan to the brewery, paying higher prices on their products and making enough to cover all our costs and also live on. At least we no longer had the pressure to buy beer we didn't need or weren't going to use.

'But we've done everything,' Roger continued. 'It's all prepared. It won't be busy until after the performance so Bill can manage behind the bar until we get back. And the more people who see you out, the more will think to come to The Ox and Plough.' He shuffled closer and put his arms around me, warding off the cool morning. His warmth was better than any blanket. 'Please?' he whispered in my ear.

We stepped out onto the street later that morning. The pub was quiet, Annie was with Mama, and Jenny was in the kitchen. I felt like we were delinquent children, sneaking off for an exciting excursion as I gazed over the village from our vantage point at the top of the hill. Often it was covered with a mist at this time of morning, especially in October, but today it was clear and I could see red roofs and whitewashed buildings, the patchwork of green grass and the short golden stubble of harvested fields behind them all the way to the coast. It was a glorious day and I felt weightless. I looked up at the sky, not a cloud in sight, and my gaze came to rest on the sign above The Ox and Plough. *H. Rainforth: Licensed Victualler.* That was me. My name was above the door. I broke out into a wide grin. I would never have imagined it five years earlier. Papa would be proud.

Roger and I were immediately ambushed by Anthony and Rory.

'Good morning, Mrs Rainforth,' said Rory enthusiastically. 'Have you seen the circus today?'

I shook my head but before I could reply, he continued talking. 'The tents were up when we got there this morning. But best of all they were putting up the big circus tent and now everything's hidden behind the canvas. It looks like a magical showground. You wouldn't know that it's our green.'

Anthony nodded vigorously. 'It's a place where anything can happen – wild beasts jumping out at you, acrobats flying through the air ...' His face became wistful. 'I wonder what it would be like to run away with the circus ... or pretend to be pirates and search for lost treasure like Tom Sawyer and Huck Finn ...'

'You don't know how to be a pirate or search for buried treasure, and what circus skills and tricks can you do?' asked Rory. 'You'd end up shovelling animal dung.'

Roger laughed. 'I can't see you doing that, little brother.'

Anthony nodded. 'You're probably right. We have to go and meet Jemima and Amy,' he said, pulling on Rory's arm.

Roger smirked as we watched the boys run off towards the village green. 'I don't think he wants to be seen dead with us.'

I smiled and threaded my arm through his as we followed the children to the green. What I loved about this age, hanging precariously between childhood and adolescence, was that children still clung to their imagination and sense of hope. It wouldn't be long before they lost much of their innocence and joy, especially when they finished school and were thrust into the world. Memories of the daring acts and strange sights would stay with them for weeks as they talked about the show with their friends. Their lives would be transformed for a little while, the glitter of the circus falling on their shoulders like stardust. If only we could harness this imagination and hope as adults, allowing us to have the courage and vision to make change for the world we lived in.

Roger and I joined the line of people jostling impatiently to enter the circus tent. Soon we were seated on raised wooden benches, looking out over the circular performance area with tightropes and ladders fixed high in the air. Many came to the circus to see popular curiosities such as the bearded lady, giants, dwarves and Siamese twins – like the people who had featured in that terrible 'freak show' held at The Rose and Crown – but for me, it was about the incredible skill of the performers. I could have sat there in stunned amazement for hours, watching the antics of the clowns, the daring acts of the riders on horseback, the flips and tumbles of the acrobats flying high in the air, the steadfast poise of the tightrope walkers and the tricks of the various animals led by their bravehearted trainers.

It was over too soon but my heart felt lighter as we left the tent. I blinked as we entered the real world, my eyes watering from the blazing sun overhead.

'Time to mingle a little,' said Roger. I nodded and we made our way to the cages of exotic animals, greeting neighbours, friends and customers along the way. I hoped to see Esther and find out how her preparation for the parish council elections was going. She had six months to campaign before the beginning of the annual term in April.

'Thank you for persuading me to come,' I said, leaning in to him as we stood by the tiger cage. 'You're right, it's good to get out, just the two of us.'

Roger kissed the top of my head. 'He really is spectacular,' he said softly, entranced by the tiger. The exotic gold and black creature prowled the confined space, flicking his tail with impatience. He was magnificent but his contained strength, power and ferocity were even more apparent in the small cage. A part of me was sad that he wasn't running free through the jungles of India, as nature had intended.

I turned my attention to Roger. We were both in our Sunday best. Roger looked handsome in a waistcoat, jacket, tie and bowler hat; his shoes shined to a gleam. He exuded confidence and quiet power; someone to take notice of. As spectacular as the tiger before us. But I preferred him in shirtsleeves and his workman's clothing; his muscles visible as he performed his labour, his dark hair a riot of curls as he broke a sweat that beaded on the skin visible under his open-necked shirt, the fierce concentration on his face as he worked.

'Hannah!'

My appraisal of my glorious husband was interrupted by a hand on my shoulder.

'I hoped I'd find you here.' Emily Duffield kissed me on the cheek. She and John had married not long after Roger and me. It had been good to share those early experiences of marriage with each other and we had become friends.

'Where's John?' asked Roger.

'He's around here somewhere,' Emily said with a wave of her hand. 'It was near impossible to get him here, weaning lambs and calves, but I managed it.' She smiled and placed her hand over her belly. 'I wanted to share our news today.'

'You're pregnant?' I asked tentatively.

She nodded and drew me away towards the elephant enclosure. 'Four months along. I have so much to ask you. My mother and aunts have glossed over the details but you're the only one of my friends I trust to tell me the truth.'

'Of course.' I hugged her. 'Congratulations!' I tried not to laugh at the thought that, somehow, I'd found myself in the position of advisor and expert on pregnancy, childbirth and motherhood, subjects I'd never imagined I'd ever be knowledgeable about.

When it was time to feed Annie, Emily and Laura joined me for tea at the cottage, leaving the men and children at the circus. Laura had advised me through my pregnancy and motherhood and I knew she could help Emily too.

'It's so good to sit and relax,' I said with a sigh. 'But Annie isn't going to wait much longer.'

'How do you feed her while still wearing a corset?' asked Emily with a frown.

'I'm wearing a nursing corset,' I said. 'There's a flap that I can unbutton.' I put my tea down. 'Why don't I show you?'

Emily glanced nervously towards the door of the parlour as I removed my shirtwaist and corset cover. 'Aren't you worried someone will see you like this?'

I shrugged. 'Who's going to see me? I'm in my own home and I'm not expecting anyone. Come on get comfortable and relax too. You're not in a maternity corset yet, are you?' She shifted uncomfortably on the lounge and shook her head. 'This is our private space. I'm sure that if men were the ones who were pregnant or nursing, that they wouldn't wear such restrictive clothing.'

'I can't,' she said, the blush rising to her cheeks.

'Why not?' asked Laura with a grin. She flicked her shoes off, rolled down her stockings and removed them, wriggling her bare toes with relish. 'I feel freer already.'

'Well, I do feel like I'm going to burst out of these clothes,' admitted Emily. She undid the buttons on her bodice, the fastenings on her corset and the waistband of her skirt. 'That's better,' she sighed. 'I feel like a ripe fruit that's exploded.'

'It only gets worse,' I said, and Laura and I giggled at Emily's expression of horror.

I picked Annie up from the bassinet, unbuttoned the nursing flap and folded it down. 'See, it's really quite simple.' I settled her on my lap before her little searching mouth found what she was looking for and latched on and began sucking. I closed my eyes and sighed at the deep tugging sensation. 'It's the most wonderful feeling of release when the milk draws down.'

'You mean the milk isn't already there?' asked Emily, intrigued. 'I've never seen a woman nursing up close before.'

'Oh no, not until the baby is ready to nurse,' said Laura.

'I've got so much to learn,' said Emily, shaking her head.

I shot a wicked grin to Laura. 'Well, did you know that sex can bring on the baby when it's close to time?' I asked with a confidential whisper. Laura's brows rose but her eyes glittered with amusement.

Emily's eyes widened. 'No!'

I nodded. 'Yes, and it was some of the best I've ever had.' Laura and Emily roared with laughter at my scandalous comments.

'That's something to look forward to then,' said Emily, wiping the tears of laughter from her eyes.

30

Germ theory has been researched and has been cutting-edge science for some years now but when I try to explain to villagers here in Ebberfield that tiny organisms, invisible to the naked eye, are responsible for disease and are passed from person to person, they look at me as if I'm mad.

'Finally!' I shouted with glee, throwing the letter from Mrs Fawcett into the air. I grabbed at it as it began to flutter to the floor. I had to read it again to make sure.

February, 1896

My dear Mrs Rainforth,
I'm excited to tell you that our appeal and petition will finally come before Parliament in May, accompanying Mr Begg's Parliamentary Franchise Bill and its extension to women. All the hard work that went into acquiring and putting together the signatures, over 250,000 of them, is about to pay off. We've been given permission to display the petition in Westminster Hall before the debate and I'd like to extend an invitation for you and your suffrage society committee to join us as we speak with MPs to ensure they understand the wishes of women right across the country and to attend this very special sitting of Parliament.
My best wishes to you and your family,
Millicent Fawcett

It had taken two years to find another opportunity to present our petition. When we were first asked to find signatures I had never imagined it would take so long but I'd since learnt that finding the right supporter took patience and stamina.

I pressed the letter to my chest. This was our chance to change everything. In a few months we could be on the way to achieving the parliamentary vote for women. Excitement fizzed through me and I couldn't wait to tell everyone. My mind raced. It wasn't long until the next suffrage meeting. I didn't want to take the spotlight off Esther's campaign for the next upcoming parish elections but this news was too wonderful to sit on.

I glanced out the window over the back of The Ox and Plough and our cottage next door with its line of clean nappy cloths hanging out to dry. My heart sank. I would have jumped at the opportunity to go to Parliament back then but now it would be impossible. I was three months pregnant, still nursing Annie, and hadn't left her for more than a few hours before and even thinking about the organisation it would take for me to be away from The Ox and Plough made me tired. But this opportunity was the culmination of all the work our society and community had done.

I placed the letter next to my collection of colourful feathers on the office desk. My thumb ran across the smooth surface of the paperweight Clem had given me. I remembered the promise I'd made myself when I'd stood outside the Palace of Westminster. I had to see it through.

A few hours later, I was still buzzing with excitement when I saw Dorothy Duggan coming out of the grocers.

'Hello, Dorothy,' I said as I approached her.

She turned her head away but I knew that she'd seen me.

'Dorothy? Are you all right?' I was right in front of her now and she couldn't avoid me.

'Hello, Hannah,' she replied, her face in shadow under her broad-brimmed hat. 'I'm sorry, I didn't see you.'

I frowned but decided that perhaps I was mistaken. 'I wanted to tell you about some good news I just received. Are you coming to our next suffrage meeting?'

'I won't be comin'.' She paused. 'Actually, don't know if I can come again.'

I stared at her, the pit of my stomach suddenly cold. 'But why?'

'I just can't.' I touched her arm and she flinched. And then I saw it. The purple bruises and the swollen wrist that had been hidden under the sleeve of her dress. Exactly the same as the first time.

'Dorothy, what happened to you?'

'I fell,' she murmured.

'Was it Fred?' I whispered.

Her eyes widened. 'No,' she said quickly.

And then I realised that the bruises weren't just on her arm. One side of her face was red and swollen, purple blooms beginning to surface on her cheek. Nothing had changed for the better since the day I first met her, getting signatures to our petition over two years earlier.

'You should see the doctor,' I said in an even voice, although I wanted to scream at her to leave her husband and never go back to him. I knew from what I'd seen and heard in The Ox and Plough, as well as talking to women in the lounge, that a violent husband never needed much excuse to beat his wife and if he beat her enough, usually she would do what he wanted, just to survive.

'I'm all right.' Her eyes slipped from my face to something across the street. 'I have to go.' She started across the path and then stopped and turned to me. 'I'm sorry, Hannah. I wish it could be different.'

I watched her walk away, her slight limp telling me there were other injuries too. I shivered, feeling somebody's gaze on me, and looked across the street to see Fred Duggan on the steps of The Rose and Crown.

*

It didn't take long for my excitement about London to diminish into insignificance. I was in the parlour with Mama when we received Mary's frantic letter. Her son, Nicholas, was sick with diphtheria.

Mama read it out to me.

> As soon as the doctor realised what it was, more than the sore throat and fever we first thought, he sent Nicholas to the isolation hospital. I went with him and helped to settle him into bed. My poor, poor boy couldn't stop coughing, a terrible barking sound, and afterwards struggled to get his breath. I stayed a few hours with him but then I was told I had to leave. It was the hardest thing I have ever done.

I was frozen in my chair, unable to move as I watched Annie crawl across the parlour floor towards the rattle I'd dropped.

> But I know it's for his own good and that the doctor and nurses will treat his illness and care for him in ways that we cannot at home. Every time I see Nicholas's empty bed next to Christopher's, I want to cry and run to the hospital to take him in my arms. I so want to bring him home. But Christopher has become lethargic and George and I are worried that he may also have contracted diphtheria. The doctor will come tomorrow to check him.

George has gone around to Jane's to let her know before
sending this letter on the overnight post and I'll stay by
Christopher's bed through the night. Thankfully we are
still well and I pray that we remain so. Otherwise, we can't
look after our boys.

Mama clapped a shaking hand across her mouth, looking as
horrified as I felt. Nausea swirled in the pit of my stomach.
For Mary to be separated from her sick child like this ... I
remembered when Nicholas was as small as Annie. And if
Christopher had it too ...

'I can't imagine what she's going through,' I whispered,
dread curdling in my belly. This reached to the very heart of
the fear that all mothers felt, the fear of your children struck
down by sickness or disease. Worst of all, the fear of losing
them.

'I have to go to her,' said Mama. Her face was pale. We
all dreaded a day like this but for Mama, with what had
happened to Beth and then losing Papa ... I didn't know how
we'd cope with this as well.

'I'll come with you.'

She shook her head. 'No, you won't,' she said vehemently.
'I don't want you there. You'd put Annie and the baby at risk.
I won't have that.'

I touched her arm, understanding the reason for the
intensity of her response. 'It's all right, Mama.'

'No, I don't want any of you to come to Mary's – you,
Sarah or Jane.' Her face was rigid, like a mask carved of
stone. But even stone could shatter.

'But what about you?'

'I'll stay with Jane and visit Nicholas in hospital until
we know what's happening with Christopher. Mary won't
want to leave his side.' She stood. 'I'll take the next train to

Hartlepool. I'm sorry I have to leave more work for you and Jenny, but I know you'll manage.'

I pulled her into an embrace, suddenly afraid. 'They're strong. They'll be all right'

*

Mama wrote every day, and each day the news seemed more dire. Jenny and I sat in the kitchen and read her letters when they arrived, taking solace in being together.

> Christopher has been in hospital two days now and Mary was taken last night too. I'm allowed to go to the hospital to see only one of them each day. I'm made to wear protective clothing, a form of mackintosh, when I sit with them, but I'm not allowed to touch them or the bedding. I take comfort in being in the same room, being able to talk to them, even though they're both too sick to reply. But Nicholas is getting worse, a tube sticking out of his throat to help him breathe, and I can't offer him comfort of any kind, only watch him through a closed window as he struggles.
>
> There's a new medicine available but it's in short supply and the hospital is waiting for more doses. It's supposed to stop the sickness from getting worse but I only hope it comes in time.

Jenny started crying. 'Are they all going to die?'

I put my arm around her. 'I don't know.' It was a miracle that George was the only one who hadn't contracted diphtheria. Nicholas had gone to the docks with a school friend and his father to see one of the new steam cargo ships put to sea for the very first trials. The other boy and his father were in hospital too.

'Isn't there anything we can do?'

I shook my head.

But Jenny's words stayed with me and when Dr Jenkins and I met to discuss expanding the vaccination program, I told him about Mary and her boys. 'Can you tell me about this new medicine the hospital's waiting on?' I asked.

'It's a new development, only a few years old, called serum therapy.'

'Like a vaccination?' We'd made such progress with smallpox that there had to be something for diphtheria too.

'Not exactly. It's an antitoxin.'

'A what?'

He steepled his fingers. I'd noticed he often did this when he was explaining a medical process. 'The bacterium that causes diphtheria releases a toxin in the body of the host. An antitoxin is cultured from the blood of horses infected with the bacterium, which is then used to treat diphtheria.'

'What does the antitoxin do?'

'It seems to reduce the severity of the disease and the mortality rate, but unfortunately it doesn't prevent the disease or its spread, like a vaccine does.'

Hope surged through me but desperation followed close behind. What was the point if we couldn't get it to Mary and the boys? 'I'm worried that my sister and my nephews will die if they don't get the antitoxin.' I reached across the desk and touched his arm.

He looked at me in surprise. I knew it wasn't seemly, although we knew each other well but I had to make him understand how important this was to me. 'Isn't there anything we can do to get it to them?'

He covered my hand with his own. 'Perhaps I can help the hospital find the doses they need. Let me see what I can do.'

Tears welled in my eyes. 'I'll collect them myself if I have to.'

Dr Jenkins patted my hand. 'My dear Mrs Rainforth. There's no need for that.' He stood. 'I'll scour the country for the antitoxin and send word if we can secure the doses any sooner.'

'Thank you, Dr Jenkins.'

I found it hard to concentrate for the rest of the morning. What if there was none to be found? It set my nerves on edge and made my stomach twist in knots. Sarah arrived with her two youngest in the afternoon, worried about Mary, the boys and Mama too. Jenny cried when she saw her mother, soothed only by Sarah's embrace and comforting presence.

I was cooking dinner while Sarah bathed the younger children and listened out for Annie asleep in her cot, when I heard a knock at the door. I wiped my hands on my apron before opening the door.

A boy held out an envelope. 'A message from Dr Jenkins,' he said.

I took the paper from his hand and nodded, barely noticing him leave. Holding my breath, I slipped the note from the envelope.

I'm sorry I was unable to deliver this message personally but I've been summoned to an urgent house call and I wanted you to know immediately. The president of the British Institute of Preventive Medicine, Dr Ruffer, has been able to source the antitoxin that the hospital needs and the phials are on the overnight postal train to Hartlepool. I've contacted the doctors there to let them know.

Wishing you, your sister and her family all the best of luck.

I climbed the stairs, two at a time, unable to contain my excitement. I had to tell Sarah.

'He's done it,' I yelled. 'Dr Jenkins got the antitoxin!'

Annie started crying but, for the first time, I didn't mind that her sleep had been disturbed. I scooped her up from the cot, kissing her warm and slightly damp face and head.

Sarah emerged from the bathroom, a child wrapped in a towel in each arm. 'What's happened?'

'Mary and the boys are going to be all right.'

'Thank the Lord,' she whispered.

Mary and the boys received their first injections the following morning and Sarah went home a couple of days later. Mama continued to write daily to tell me of their progress. Mary and Christopher improved quickly.

But the antitoxin had arrived too late for Nicholas. The disease had raged through his body for too long and nothing could be done to help him. He hovered between life and death for days with only the doctors and nurses caring for him and Mama and George looking through the window of his room.

Then the news I'd been dreading arrived from Mama.

I begged the doctor and nurses to show some compassion. It was clear that Nicholas was in a pitiful state and Mary was making herself sick, beside herself at not being able to see him. Screaming for her boy, refusing to eat, wretched and rake thin, with barely enough strength to even stand. I thought my heart would break to see her like that. But somehow, I found the strength to calm her, to tell her that we'd find a way. I spoke to the director of the hospital and finally they relented.

Mary sat by Nicholas's bedside last night. He knew it was her, I saw it in his eyes. Then she held him in her arms, although she was not allowed, tight against her breast, whispering words of comfort to him. I watched them through the window until our sweet boy breathed his last shuddering and painful breath. Then he was very still.

They gave Mary time alone with him and when the nurses finally pried him from her arms, I saw my girl broken in two. My heart did break then, because I could do nothing to comfort her. I remember the feeling of holding Beth, dead in my arms. It will never leave me. But I could not hold my grieving, breathing and living daughter in my own arms and tell her that I understood, give her what comfort I could. She was sent back into her isolation and I could only call to her through the glass to hold on for Christopher.

I was sick of heart. But in my grief, I recognised that it was always women who bore the brunt of life's hardest trials. And I understood once again, that only with a woman's unique understanding of matters that were close to her heart would the laws change to support women and families in any meaningful way. Women needed to have the vote. Nicholas's death and the short supply of life-saving medicine was one more reason to continue my fight with all the energy I had.

31

Though I miss teaching dearly, it's valuable to me to keep abreast of educational developments. Margaret McMillan, director of the Bradford School Board has led a deputation to Parliament, campaigning for legislative changes to child welfare and education; improved layout of furniture in classrooms, ventilation, meals to be provided by the school for those who don't get breakfast or lunch.

The results of the local parish elections were in. Once again, we gathered in the parlour of the cottage, Esther, Clementine, Laura, Alice, Emily, Marjorie and I, bolstered by Mama's cakes and tea.

'Are you ready?' I asked Esther, as I opened the newspaper.

'I feel sick,' she whispered.

Clementine squeezed her hand. 'You can do it.'

'I don't know what I'll do if I've failed again.'

'You keep going,' said Clementine.

'Whatever happens, we're here and we love you,' said Laura, smiling encouragingly.

I turned to the page and began reading. 'Looks like all the same names as last time ... Mr Franks is there ... No wait, not quite. Here you are! "*Miss Esther Burrows*",' I read. I looked up, feeling my mouth stretch wide. 'Esther, you've done it! You're a parish councillor.'

'I've done it?' Her eyes were glassy and she looked dazed. 'Are you sure?'

'Look here.' I pointed to her name in the paper and everyone crowded around to see.

'Congratulations Esther,' said Clementine, hugging her tight.

As everyone congratulated her, I scanned the paper for the results of other parishes in our district and shook my head with amazement. 'Esther, you're the first female councillor in our entire district.' Everyone turned to me.

'The first?' asked Esther, frowning dubiously. I nodded, feeling like I was floating. We had achieved something monumental. 'I can't believe it.' She broke into a wide grin. 'I'm the first woman in the whole district in local government,' she shouted, jumping up and down. She held her arms out to us all and we came together in a tight huddle of unity and joy. 'We've done it,' she sobbed. 'We've done it!'

April, 1896

My dearest Sarah,

I can't believe Nicholas is gone. Mary is finally home with Christopher, but they are still weak, especially Mary, who is worn down by illness and grief. Mama is with them and will stay to look after them both, until Mary is on her feet again.

I'm so tired with this pregnancy and looking after Annie, but as much as I'm grieving, I must persevere. Bill and I are running the pub, and now Roger is working on building the new isolation hospital outside of town which has finally been passed by council. Dr Jenkins has suggested that after what happened to Nicholas, now is a good time to expand the vaccination program to revaccinate children at the age of ten and then anyone who received their vaccination more than ten years ago.

He tells me that the new research has shown that the
vaccine becomes less effective in protecting against
smallpox after this time.

Esther is embracing her new role as the first female
parish councillor, and soon we will go to London to watch
our petition being presented to Parliament. I feel the
conditions are finally right for the suffrage movement.

I will write again when I return.

I was already five months along and with everything that
had happened in the last few months, I couldn't believe how
quickly my second pregnancy had progressed. At first, I had
felt dazed to be pregnant so soon after Annie, but I couldn't
deny the bubble of joy Roger and I felt once I was sure. Now
it wouldn't be long before we'd be welcoming this new child
into our expanding family.

To add to my excitement, on the back of Esther's success,
we had one of our largest turnouts at the suffrage meeting
before the trip to London. We'd spread the word that the
petition was finally being presented to Parliament, and our
members and many in the community were excited. We
talked about our visit to Parliament and what we hoped to
do, and answered questions from enthusiastic members and
from those who were merely curious. But we had double good
news with Esther's success and we also gathered together to
celebrate her win.

'Women are forging ahead across the north with elected
positions on school boards and as poor law guardians but
Esther's election is a major milestone for us,' said Clementine
with pride.

'And we've just learnt from Mrs Fawcett and the Women's
Local Government Society that Esther is one of only two
hundred female councillors across the eight thousand parishes

in Britain,' I announced. The audience broke out into cheers and applause and Esther had turned beetroot red but was beaming from ear to ear.

'Thank you,' said Esther. 'Thank you for your support and your votes. Wins by women, like these, can only lead to greater awareness of our ability and our sensible and logical goals. I'm excited to begin working towards improving women's lives and the lives of everyone in Ebberfield.' We were all on our feet, clapping and whooping. Clementine, Laura and I smiled, happy that Esther was receiving the recognition and love that she deserved. I hoped that this was a sign of things to come, that soon the national vote would be ours.

'How's your sister?' asked Mrs Scruton, stirring the tea in the large pot at the celebratory gathering after the society meeting. Funny how she automatically stepped into the role.

'Getting better each day,' I said, placing a platter of sandwiches on the table.

'London will be good for you,' she said, patting me on the shoulder.

'I did think about not going.'

'You have to go; you owe it to yourself. You're the one who's been pushin' this petition and it's only right you're there when it's presented.'

'Of course she will be,' said Edward Partridge. 'Even if I have to take her there myself.' He smiled widely as he presented his cup to Mrs Scruton for her to fill with tea. I wondered if Marjorie did that for him at home. I did for Roger sometimes, but he was quite capable of pouring his own tea. I was disappointed not to see Marjorie. Edward had told us she'd decided to remain at Dalleymoor at the last minute because she was unwell with a cold. She had been considering joining us in London, but now we wouldn't see her until we returned.

'Thank you, Edward, but there's no need. We've booked the train and nothing short of a disaster is going to stop me from going.'

'I only hope it's a worthwhile trip,' he said.

'What do you mean?'

'Private Members' bills can take some time before they're discussed on the floor.' He sounded almost dismissive.

Everything took time. I'd come to understand that. But we had to start somewhere. 'Well, we'll just have to persuade the Members of Parliament that it's a worthy bill – the signatures of over 250,000 people should help.'

Others started to join us around the table.

'What do you think will happen when the bill is passed?' asked Alice, who had returned home to Ebberfield and was soon to be married.

'Women will be free ...' said Sybil, Mrs Adams' daughter, picking up a sandwich.

Mrs Adams shook her head, handing her daughter a lemonade. 'No, they won't. Nothin' will change at the beginnin'.'

'That's right.' Emily had brought John's elderly mother to the meeting, along with her new baby. Mrs Duffield had had some experience with politics through her father and her husband. 'Women's groups will have to decide on which issues they want to pursue and choose a Member of Parliament who will take their causes to London. Legislation will have to be drafted and parliamentary committees formed before the bill can be discussed in the House of Commons.'

I pulled out a chair for Mrs Duffield to sit on at the end of the table and placed a cup of tea and a plate with a sandwich and a piece of slice on it next to her.

Sybil frowned. 'Then we can get what we want?'

'No,' said Esther with a smile. 'It's voted on and if it's passed, then it goes to the House of Lords, where, if approved, it can be made law.' We were over the moon for her but she had yet to sit in a council meeting and work with the men, including the re-elected Mr Franks.

The girl nodded thoughtfully. 'It's a long process.'

'But what would we change first?' asked Amelia Brown. It was a good question with no simple answer.

Calls came from around the room.

'Independence from our husbands.'

'Custody of our children.'

'Temperance and banning alcohol.'

'The same pay and workin' conditions as men.'

It gave me goosebumps to hear how invested these women were in change for themselves and their children.

Clementine shook her head. 'No. It's easy ... Equality between men and women.'

I took her hand and squeezed it. 'Exactly. But that's just the start.'

*

Clementine, Esther, Laura and I took the train to London a few days before the bill was being presented to Parliament. By now I was six months pregnant, cumbersome and uncomfortable, and still plagued by the guilt and anxiety I felt at leaving Annie, even though she was with her Granny Elizabeth during the day and Roger at night. The horror of Nicholas's death still gnawed at me. Annie was vaccinated for smallpox but I couldn't do anything to prevent her getting sick from something like diphtheria. The threat of an epidemic spreading had dissipated with only a few still in hospital in Hartlepool. Roger had assured me that Annie would be fine until I returned and reminded me how disappointed I'd be if I didn't go.

'She was happy and smiling when I left her,' I whispered to Laura, who had left her girls too. Clementine and Esther were in the seat opposite us. Esther was asleep, her head lolling on Clementine's shoulder, travel hat askew and slightly squashed, while Clementine, unable to move, rested with her eyes shut. Even the gentle rocking of the train that had lulled Esther to sleep hadn't been able to soothe my anxiety, although talking with Laura helped. 'But I know that by this evening she'll miss me and by bedtime, she'll be crying for me.'

'I remember the first time I left Eleanor ... it was like ripping a piece of my heart away,' replied Laura.

I nodded, looking out at the fields of gold that rushed past. 'It feels just like that. And I only have one. How can you leave all four of them?'

Laura patted my hand. 'The first time is always the hardest. It gets easier after that and they get used to it too. Now my girls are older and understand that I'm coming back. They consider this an adventure, time with just their papa. It's only Maisie I worry about, but she's in good hands with Mrs Cartwright during the day.'

'Motherhood's so much more complicated than I first thought. When you're with them, you wish you had time to yourself but when you're away from them, all you want is to be back with them.' I had a much clearer understanding of what my sisters had told me before I'd had Annie, about the realities of being a woman and the difficult choices we had to make. But the women of my generation had more choices because of the trailblazers who came before us and we had to continue this evolution of women. But when I thought about what Jane had gone through leaving Lizzie to go to Yorkshire, to have her daughter die while she was away ... I could feel the visceral horror of it.

'But remember why you're doing this. Not just for your own sanity and sense of self but for Annie. We're doing this for the future of our daughters. One day they'll understand and be proud of what we've done, no matter how difficult it might have been for us. And we're the fortunate ones, with understanding husbands who support what we're doing.'

My thoughts turned to Dorothy. Fred wasn't the only husband to disagree with his wife's involvement with the suffrage society and the work we were doing. Nor was she the only wife to suffer from her husband's displeasure. People were often resistant to change, I understood that, but men like Fred, Trevor Carter and Mr Franks were bullies and brutes, cowards who used their physical strength to beat and incite fear in those they believed weak. Forward-thinking men like Roger, Benjamin and even Esther's father were a rarity, to be treasured and thankful for.

*

It was a special moment when we arrived at Westminster Hall. I gazed up at the ceiling space with awe. It was the most eye-catching part of the room with its intricate medieval timber arches spanning the width of the hall. I remembered reading that it was nearly a thousand years old, the oldest surviving part of Westminster Palace. The hall had always been used for ceremonial purposes and occasions of state. In times gone by, the coronation banquet of each new monarch was held here, as well as the lying in state for royal funerals. But most importantly, it used to hold the highest law courts in Britain before they were moved to a glorious new building, the Royal Courts of Justice. I only hoped that the long history of the law deeply imbued in the walls of this hall would influence the MPs, men who held all the power, to look to Britain's future and support the vote for women.

The hall was a flurry of activity, long rows of tables set up in one corner, the massive volumes of signatures spread across the space, divided into the various constituencies. Women delegates from all parts of England, Ireland and Scotland milled around their tables, making sure everything was just right before the MPs arrived.

'Imagine if we can do this,' I whispered to Clementine as we walked towards our table, where women from other societies in our district already congregated. The statues of fifteen kings watching us, the women of Britain, in their sacred space might have been intimidating to some, but not to me. Britain had been ruled by men for centuries but two of the longest reigning monarchs were powerful and influential women: our own Queen Victoria who had ruled the British empire for the last fifty-nine years and was still going strong, and Queen Elizabeth who remained unmarried so she could shape the Tudor world to her vision. It was a wonder that women's ability to vote was still called into question at all. The world was changing and it was time for women to have a say in how our country moved into the twentieth century. It was time for the nation to evolve or to be left behind.

'This is our best chance,' Clementine said, her lips drawn into a determined line. She saw this as a battle we had to fight and win but I saw it as an exercise in reason. The large volumes filled with the signatures of those who supported our cause could hardly be denied. And we had the rest of the day and the evening to persuade Members of Parliament, especially the members for our own constituencies, that the vote for women was the next logical step in the evolution of our glorious legal system.

'Why should we consider your petition?' asked an MP, flicking through the pages of signatures.

'Well, women already have the right to vote in local government elections, they sit on councils, school and education boards, parliamentary committees and advise on royal commissions,' I said.

'Yes, I understand that. But are women fit to fulfil the full duties of citizenship? The campaign trail of those seeking election to Parliament is rigorous and brutal. For women it would be degrading,' he said in all seriousness.

Esther tried a different tack. 'We're half the population, and as you can see from these volumes, thousands of women support the idea of female enfranchisement.'

'That might be true,' said his friend. 'But unlike men, women can't bear arms or defend their country, and therefore don't deserve the vote.'

'I've heard all the reasons why women shouldn't have the vote,' said Clementine tightly. 'Women aren't intelligent enough, are too emotional and easily influenced, we're physically and mentally unfit, we don't need the vote because the man of the family will vote for us. Giving women the vote is as absurd as asking men to engage in women's work ... or as absurd as giving the vote to horses or dogs ...'

The shock on the MPs' faces made me want to laugh. It was an unconventional approach but I could feel my spine tingle. These were forbidden conversations, a woman speaking up about men's attitudes towards us, but if we didn't have them now, with the men who were making decisions about women's futures, then we wouldn't have done everything we could. 'But have you heard all the reasons we *should* have it?' I asked. The men shook their heads, looking very uncomfortable. It was difficult not to see how farfetched and ridiculous these excuses were and how stupid the reasons for denying women were.

My friends and I explained all our reasons again, providing logical arguments and empirical evidence for each; women in positions of administration, at university, voting rights granted to women in some of the colonies and our special understanding of issues concerning women and family.

'Giving women the vote will bring so much more to our government, provide another important perspective, and alternative solutions to issues. It's a government and country that will only be made stronger with the input of women,' I concluded. 'Your support not only helps us and our country, but will bring you a whole new demographic of voters – women.'

I glanced at the circle of men that our discussion had attracted, each looking thoughtful and many nodding in agreement.

'It does seem counterintuitive not to include half the population in the governance of this country,' said one MP.

'Your arguments have been most illuminating and thought provoking,' said another.

'We'll certainly consider your petition,' said the MP who had first examined our volumes of signatures.

'Thank you for your consideration,' I said gravely. But once the MPs were gone, I broke out into a broad grin.

'It's as good a commitment for support as we're likely to get,' said Esther squeezing my hand in excitement.

32

Some of Esther's scientific journals summarise the experimentation on animals in extracting ground-breaking medical developments. While I am thrilled by progress, I feel compromised by its cost. Must all movements come with a price?

The next day we made our way to the House of Commons filled with anticipation and trepidation. It was 20 May 1896 and Mr Begg, a non-ministerial Member of Parliament, serving with the conservative government, was to present the petition to Parliament, finally. Had we done enough to turn the tide? Was this finally our time?

'They can't pretend we don't exist,' I said to my friends as we walked towards Westminster. 'Women all over the country want a voice, they know that much now.'

'Do you really think we can do it this time?'

I understood Esther's reservations. I hoped that the MPs present today were more progressive or at least smart enough to realise that they could harness the votes of another large section of the community.

I took Esther's hand. 'We're about to find out.'

'Time to join the others in the Cage,' said Clementine as we entered the House of Commons. I'd heard about the Ladies' Gallery, situated on the upper level of the chamber, but it wasn't until I reached the small, enclosed and poorly lit space myself that I truly understood the nickname. A brass trellis screened our view onto the floor below, giving only a partial perspective from any of the small diamond-shaped openings, making it difficult to see what was going on.

'It's like looking through a kaleidoscope,' I said, squinting to see the men sitting on the benches. 'And I can't even see the speaker of the house.' The speaker's chair was almost directly beneath us with the Table of the House in front of it.

'It's so the men can't see us and be distracted,' said another woman, rolling her eyes.

I shook my head, noticing the open and well-lit balconies across from us for men who came to listen to the parliamentary proceedings.

'It's not ideal,' said Mrs Fawcett, joining us at the window. 'Be prepared for an almighty headache by the end of today's session. But it will be worth it if we get the numbers we need. Hopefully today's the day.'

I repeated the words silently, like a prayer to the Lord above, hope burning in my heart.

But the morning's high excitement was eroded as the hours dragged by in the stuffy environment of many women crammed into a small space as items of government business seemingly more important pushed Mr Begg's bill to the back of the queue. I fell into a stupor, and was only prevented from falling asleep by a pounding headache and the solidarity of the women surrounding me. My heart sank as I watched the looks of disappointment deepen on the faces of the Appeals Committee.

And then the session ended and Mr Begg's bill still hadn't been presented. Our opportunity was gone, ignored by the men who ruled our land. We hadn't even voiced our aspirations.

'We never had a chance,' said Esther as we filed down the stairs. I wondered if she too would be disregarded or ignored in the parish council meetings. Everything we'd done had only led to lip service by the MPs who'd looked over our petition and signatures. Would powerful men ever let women in? I shook my head to dispel those morbid thoughts.

'If the bill had been presented and voted on,' Laura said, 'we'd at least know one way or the other how much support our cause has attracted.'

'It's not enough,' said Clementine bitterly. 'Our voices will never be heard this way.'

'It's been a complete waste of time,' said Laura. I knew she was thinking about the time she'd been away from her daughters, and I had to agree.

'I'm so sorry,' said Mrs Fawcett, as we gathered outside. 'You've come all this way and worked so hard to help us get to today's sitting but, unfortunately, other government business has taken priority. Sometimes it happens this way.'

'So what now?' I asked. I felt drained and demoralised, exhausted by the effort of the last few days.

Mrs Fawcett shook her head. 'I'm not sure. But what we have gained here is the coming together of the Central Committee and the National Society, as well as many of the large suffrage societies from across the nation. It seems we can work well together for a common cause. We'll have to regroup and work out our next move, maybe find another way to lobby Mr Begg's bill, so that it will reach Parliament again and be presented.'

I nodded. 'We all feel honoured to have been involved. Thank you for asking us to join you.' But the months of effort and preparation she and the committee had put into this ... To come away without the bill being presented was a blow.

Mrs Fawcett took my hands. 'Your group is so passionate about our cause. I only wish we had more like you.' She smiled at the four of us and then her gaze rested on my protruding belly. 'I remember feeling quite tired at this stage of my pregnancy. I'm sure you want nothing more than to get home. I'll write when I know what our next steps will be. I look forward to hearing your good news.'

*

We gathered dejectedly at The Ox and Plough on our return. We'd sent word to Marjorie and Alice Rainforth to join us, but Marjorie was still unwell so Edward came instead.

'What a disaster,' said Clementine. She was drinking whisky and I understood why. We were like injured dogs, withdrawing to lick our wounds.

'I still can't believe it didn't even get a mention,' said Alice.

'It was never going to work,' said Edward, drinking his scotch.

'But why?' asked Esther, leaning forward in her seat. 'Our petition and Mr Begg's bill had been tabled for that day.'

'You have to understand how Parliament works,' he said, sighing irritably.

Clementine slammed her glass on the table. 'Don't patronise us!' she said sharply.

'Well, clearly you don't understand about Private Members' bills,' he said harshly, with a dismissive wave of his hand.

I frowned, surprised at his short temper, and wondered if his behaviour was because he was worried about Marjorie.

'I think we do,' I said calmly, before Clementine could speak again. Mr Begg had explained to us at the end of the parliamentary session that bills presented by a Member of Parliament to the House of Commons didn't carry the same weight or need for discussion as a proposed public bill presented by government ministers and supported by the government. And we couldn't get the support of a government minister.

'Then why did it come as a surprise?' Edward asked in a hard voice.

'We thought it might have a chance with so many signatures,' said Esther.

'If you want to achieve anything, you have to be more realistic and less naive.' Edward was always direct but I didn't like the tone he was using or his opinions turned on us.

'We expected some degree of respect for the work we put into the petition and that Mr Begg put into the bill. The least they could have done was acknowledge it. It was disrespectful,' I said, my anger flaring.

'Welcome to Parliament,' said Edward with a short laugh. 'It's a pit of wolves and they don't care about your feelings.'

'Then what would you suggest we do?' I replied icily.

'We should do what the Chartists and the trade unions did,' said Clementine. 'We have to make them listen the only way they will, through noise – strike action and public rallies and protests. Disrupt the status quo, make them uncomfortable until they're forced to do something.'

Esther shook her head. 'That isn't the answer. You don't know how the authorities will react. What if they put us in prison like they did with the Chartists?'

I sighed and leant back in my chair, rubbing my swollen belly. 'I agree that we can't alienate the community with extreme measures because then we'll achieve nothing, but if there was something else we could do to push the parliamentary process along ...'

'If you can't agree on your strategy, you'll never get anywhere,' Edward said.

Esther turned to glare at him. 'Stop criticising. You can be pompous and arrogant but I've never seen you this belligerent.' She pressed her lips together as soon as the words were out of her mouth.

'Belligerent, is it? I'm trying to make you see sense. I don't want the good works you're doing in this community to be tainted with this ... this embarrassment.'

'You think we're an *embarrassment*?' I exclaimed in shock.

He shook his head, hands raised in denial. 'No, you know I don't. But it's men like Reverend Mason, Mr Jones, Mr Franks and others on the parish and district councils who will take every failure and disappointment you experience and twist them to their advantage to prove you're not fit to continue the stellar works you do here.'

I hadn't considered that. We couldn't risk the projects already underway in our county.

'You mean the works *you're* involved in. You don't want to be associated with our failures.' Clementine stared at him, realisation dawning on her.

'It's been a long few days and I think everyone's tired and overwrought,' I said quickly. 'Edward has been a great supporter and benefactor. He's only trying to help us by playing devil's advocate. It's what he always does. It can be a little harsh sometimes but it has always been useful advice.'

Edward nodded. 'I apologise. Marjorie tells me that sometimes I come across too abrasively, but there will always be opposition to progress and change, and to avoid the resistance, we have to be one step ahead.' He rose from his chair. 'I must go now. I have a meeting with Reverend Mason and Mr Jones about refurbishing the Recreation Club.'

'He thinks he can control us because he funds some of our projects,' said Clementine once he had gone. She leant in. 'My bet is that he didn't *let* Marjorie come to London. He doesn't want her involved in the suffrage petitions to Parliament.'

'Surely not,' I said with a laugh. 'We all know that his heart is in the right place. And he would never forbid Marjorie from joining us in London. It's like saying that Roger or Benjamin would do something like that.'

'No,' said Clementine, doggedly. 'Edward doesn't think we'll succeed and he doesn't want either of them associated with our failure or to have the negative feelings of the township directed at them.'

'He can be a pompous ass when he lets the power get to his head. Edward wants everyone to love him,' said Esther with a bitter edge to her voice.

'I think you all need to go home to bed,' said Alice. 'None of you are making sense now.'

'You're right,' I said with a sigh. The baby was restless and beginning to kick me hard. 'I'm not looking forward to telling everyone the news, but sitting here and dissecting the facts doesn't change them. Maybe we all need a little distance before we can look at what we do next with clear heads.'

But privately my anger at the bill not being presented had now been tempered into cold, hard steel. Even though we weren't victorious, I didn't believe my trip to London had been a waste; I'd been involved with the parliamentary process, seen what promoting our cause to those who could change the law was like and how politics worked.

Although it might be years before we could effect change, I was at the coalface for the first time and I found it exhilarating.

33

I've heard from Dr Jenkins that many women in the cities
are now having their babies under medical supervision in
a hospital, but I'm not sure that's progress. The doctors
are men and though they have the medical knowledge if
something goes wrong, they know nothing of childbirth.
Another reason why women need the vote.

The baby was born in August, at the height of summer. It was
two weeks early, and in a hurry to come into the world, not
even waiting for the midwife to arrive. Laura was downstairs
watching over Annie playing with her youngest, Maisie, when
it pushed its way into Elizabeth's outstretched arms.

'It's a boy,' said Elizabeth, watching him intently.

Mama squeezed my hand and it seemed that the three of
us were suspended in time while we waited for the baby to
take his first breath. In the pause, I could hear Annie's faint
laughter and the buzzing of an insect outside the window, feel
the sweat trickle down my neck and back. I noticed how the
small shaft of sunlight that snuck between the closed curtains
hurt my eyes with its brightness. Then my son cried, a strong
and lusty cry, announcing to the world that he was here and
ready to make his mark.

Elizabeth brought him to me, his arms wide and face
screwed up. 'My first grandson,' she said, her face alight with
joy as she put him into my arms. Elizabeth's eldest daughter,
Maude, finally had a healthy baby daughter and Alice,

recently married, was pregnant with her first child. I thought of Nicholas. Holding him for the very first time, Mary would never have imagined that his life would be cut so short. I pushed the raw pain of that thought and the bone-deep fear for my own children away. 'He's a strong one.'

'Just like you were,' said Mama, gazing at her new grandchild.

As soon as he lay in my arms, his skin against mine, he stopped crying, as though he knew I was his mother and he was safe and protected once more. 'Hello, my sweet boy,' I whispered. He opened his eyes then, the clearest blue eyes I had ever seen, and something passed between us. An unbreakable bond had formed between us and I thought my heart would burst with the love I felt for this tiny child.

In those early days of new motherhood, my life shrank down to caring for my new son, who we named Thomas after Roger's father. Annie was intrigued by the baby, watching as I fed him in my rocking chair and wanting to climb up on my lap too. The times I treasured most were when Annie and Tommy were both asleep on my lap. Looking down on them made my heart squeeze with more love than I could have ever imagined: Annie's curly blonde head resting against my chest, looking like an angel, and Tommy tucked into the crook of my opposite arm, replete, his soft rosebud mouth still covered in milk and his shock of dark hair making me smile every time I saw it. Elizabeth had told me that Roger had been blond as a child, like Annie, but according to Mama, Tommy was like me. I wondered if he'd keep his dark hair into adulthood as I had. Often, I'd drift off to sleep with their heavy weights warm against my body. I felt like I was living inside a bubble surrounded by God's grace.

Only when Roger joined us did I feel even more complete.

'We're a proper family now,' he whispered as we lay in bed in the pale dawn. Annie lay between us, limp limbed and deeply asleep after a restless night. Tommy was on my breast, the rhythm of his suckling slowing. He would soon drift back into sleep.

'We were a family before,' I murmured sleepily. But I knew what he meant. One child made a family but two children was something else. The relationships between the four of us were more complex now.

Roger was wide awake. 'This is all I could ever want.' He reached across and found my hand, intertwining his fingers with mine. 'I still can't believe how lucky I am to have you as my wife. I never believed it would be possible when I first met you and here we are with two perfect children.'

I watched him caress Annie's cheek, his eyes moist with fierce love and pride.

'Seeing us like this, I sometimes still can't believe it either. I have to pinch myself to make sure I'm not dreaming. I denied that I wanted you for so long. Thank God Annie came along when she did to make me see sense. You're the love of my life and I can't imagine my life without you.'

He brought my hand to his lips and then pressed it against his cheek, rough with bristles.

August, 1896

Dear Mrs Rainforth,

First, I'd like to congratulate you on the birth of your son, Thomas. I'm glad you and the baby are well after his early and speedy arrival. I look forward to seeing your growing family again when next I visit the north. Second, I wanted to inform you that the Central Committee and the National Society have proposed a special fund to finance

a lecture campaign to run over the following months. If
your society could make a modest contribution to this
fund, it would be much welcome.

But the main reason I mention this to you is that we'd
like you to speak about our projects across your entire
district. I know this may not be possible with your current
situation, but if you're indisposed, perhaps Miss Foster or
Miss Burrows would be interested?

I shook my head with dismay. With Clementine's
encouragement, I'd realised I enjoyed public speaking. It
helped fill the void within me that was left after I'd stopped
teaching; at the rallies and meetings I could almost see the
passion sparked by our ideas ripple through the audience. But
Tommy was too young to leave and Annie was a handful.
Bill had been unwell and without him, the workload at
The Ox and Plough had become insurmountable. I sighed.
I couldn't leave any time soon. Maybe it was best Esther and
Clementine did the lecture circuit, especially as Esther was a
parish councillor and wanted to run for the district elections.

Third, the Central Committee would like to invite you
and your suffrage society committee to Birmingham in
October for a national conference where we'll decide
the future direction of our organisations. The agenda is
attached, but the main item is to explore if we should
amalgamate with the National Society and become one
national body. You'll be pleased to know that we've also
been involved in forming a parliamentary sub-committee
to lobby for Mr Begg's bill.

Good. Amalgamating seemed the natural progression. If we
were going to achieve anything worthwhile, we had to be

united. It was gratifying to see the special fund being raised and support returning for Mr Begg's bill. I knew it was only a Private Members' bill but there didn't seem to be any other way of bringing women's suffrage in front of the House of Commons. If the bill was heard in Parliament, our chances of being heard were also improved. But I was glad that our appreciation of his support was helping his cause too.

I felt the excitement rise within me once more. The idea of a national conference was an exciting one: everyone together in one place to discuss our aims and the best way for us to achieve our goals.

Mrs Fawcett's news was received with great excitement at the next suffrage meeting.

'Have you seen Marjorie Partridge?' asked Clementine, holding a small sandwich at refreshments after the meeting had concluded. 'Apparently, she's supposed to be here with Becky. Esther's looking for her. She wants to talk to her about ways to help the families of tenant farmers.'

Marjorie had come to visit after Tommy's birth, confiding that she'd miscarried around the time of our trip to London. She'd cried when she held Tommy and I felt so sorry for her. I was disappointed that Edward had kept the truth of Marjorie's condition from us but his obnoxious behaviour after our trip made more sense. He and Marjorie had been grieving.

I shook my head and my gaze alighted on Marjorie's sister. 'Becky's here,' I said, pointing.

'I'll let Esther know.'

My attention was captured by Amelia and Mrs Scruton.

'I'm very sorry to hear that the bill didn't get heard in Parliament,' said Amelia. 'But all those signatures surely won't go to waste. Look at the support we have. And now with Esther on the parish council, we'll have a woman's voice and we can get some of the changes we've been wanting in the village.'

'If women had a say in even half of what's done in this village, things would be done better and quicker,' said Mrs Scruton, waving around her sandwich. 'Women just get it done. They ain't got a choice, when they look after children, keep house and hold down a job. Men only think about themselves and goin' to work.' Amelia laughed and I grinned.

'How's Anthony?' I asked. Anthony was doing an apprenticeship with Mr Hewitt the grocer, Mrs Scruton's brother.

'He's good with numbers and the accounts, I hear. Courteous, respectful and helpful to customers and me brother too.'

Clementine tapped me on the shoulder. 'I'm sorry to interrupt. Esther's spoken to Becky. Marjorie was supposed to meet her today but after some altercation with Fred Duggan in the village—'

'Ain't you heard?' asked Mrs Scruton. 'I hate to think how that poor woman is tonight.'

'Marjorie?' I asked.

'No, Dorothy.' She shook her head sadly. 'She was in me tea room this afternoon after deliverin' me clean linen and I suggested she stop and have a spot of rest. She looked worn out, poor pet, so I made her a cuppa tea and she started chattin' to Marjorie, waitin' for Edward and Becky to arrive.

'Fred stormed in like a dark cloud, took Dorothy by the arm and roared that he expected her to be ready when he was. Scared the livin' daylights out of Marjorie. Dorothy begged him not to make a scene and then, to me complete surprise, Marjorie told Fred to leave Dorothy alone, that he should be ashamed of the way he treats her. But he just stared at her, couldn't believe a woman dared to tell him what to do. He called her terrible names, which I won't repeat, before draggin' Dorothy out the tea room.'

My heart sank and I sighed, shaking my head in disbelief. 'I saw Dorothy not long ago and noticed the bruises on her then. I wanted to do something to help her but she was so afraid. I wish I'd been able to persuade her to come with me.'

'We were yellin' at him to stop but it made not a spot of difference. We ran out into the street after them, but he just bundled her onto that cart and they were gone. That's when Edward came back from the post office. When he saw Marjorie so pale, he rushed to her side. I brought her a fresh cuppa tea and told him how proud he'd have been to see Marjorie stand up to the brute with such courage but Edward was horrified and took her straight home to Dalleymoor. Marjorie only had time to ask me to apologise to Becky, tell her she wasn't comin'.'

'He's a bit overprotective of her, isn't he?' added Amelia, the drink in her hand forgotten.

'He treasures that girl, to be sure, but she's stronger than he thinks. He has to give her space to breathe. She hardly comes to the village anymore,' said Mrs Scruton.

'And then we have women like Dorothy, who the law should be protecting,' I said bitterly. Men like Fred were unlikely to ever change but we needed laws to protect the vulnerable.

'This is where the change has to start,' said Clementine. Her voice began to rise. 'Where's a woman's right to stand up to an abusive man without fear of reprisals, destitution or stigma? Men know they can beat or belittle their wives and children, and manipulate the law in their favour. Judges and magistrates look down on women who fight back. How can women be respected by men in power, men we expect to change the law to give us equal rights, when that attitude is everywhere?'

I nodded. I couldn't have said it better myself. We had to make sure that women had the power to protect themselves. I thought about Kitty. If she'd been supported by the law and magistrates, she may well have named her attacker. He would have been brought to justice and there would have been no need for her to hide away in shame. She and her baby may still be alive. Poor Kitty ... And poor Dorothy.

Amelia stared at Clementine but I wasn't sure if it was in shock or awe. 'You're right, of course,' she said finally. 'Women deserve respect.'

Mrs Scruton nodded. 'Respect is all well and good but I worry it'll be too late for Dorothy,' she said grimly.

34

I know that the New Woman is the future. The Angel of
the House is a figment of the past.

As much as I'd have loved to have gone to Birmingham for
the conference, Bill continued to be unwell, meaning I had
to work more. Tommy was fretful, too, not sleeping more
than half an hour each time I put him down. Clementine
and Esther had agreed to go, and while I was disappointed
I wasn't joining them, the days flew and before I knew
it, they were back and telling Laura and me all about the
conference.

'It was good to see many of the women we met at
Westminster,' said Esther. 'They send their congratulations
on Tommy and were sorry you couldn't be there, but they
hope that they'll see you at the next conference.'

I nodded, rocking Tommy gently as I walked around the
parlour. He was quiet now and hopefully would nod off any
minute. Thankfully, Annie was already in bed and Mama
had made us all tea.

'Amalgamation was agreed on, we're to be part of
the National Union of Women's Suffrage Societies,' said
Clementine. 'It won't happen formally for another year, but
the wheels are in motion.'

'What about the individual societies? Are there any major
changes to the way we operate?' I asked, feeling bolstered by
our unified collective.

'The National Union will only act as an umbrella organisation for the local societies to start with. Each society maintains its own autonomy and overall the Union will remain neutral, but the primary aim is to win the parliamentary vote for women, equal to the rights of men,' she said.

'That's good news,' I said. I glanced down at Tommy, his tiny body limp in my arms, and sighed.

'Finally asleep?' asked Laura with a smile.

I nodded but I didn't dare to sit just yet, continuing my path around the lounges and table. 'What about the projects for the year ahead?'

'First of all, a generalised campaign over the autumn and winter to inform as many people as we can about our new organisation and what we do, through the lectures and talks Mrs Fawcett wrote to you about,' said Esther. 'Clementine and I will cover this district and do some lectures in Durham as well. But if you want to take on any yourself ...'

I sat carefully next to Esther, not wanting to disturb Tommy. 'Thank you, Esther. I've thought long and hard about this, but it's still busy here and not likely to get any easier. I think it's best that you and Clementine do them. Besides, it will be good exposure for your campaign for the local elections next year.'

'It will fit in nicely with the shift in focus towards working-class women in the north,' said Clementine. 'Each local society is urged to prepare a list of supporters in the new year and put pressure on the local MP to support our cause. Esther's bound to get more support as we show that what we're doing isn't just for the rich upper-class or educated women but for all women.'

I realised now that I could never be an active part of the national push. A cold lump formed in the pit of my belly. This was my greatest fear, to be denied the chance to make a difference on the national stage. But my responsibilities to my children and The Ox and Plough had to come first.

'We have to change the image of "The New Woman",' I said, returning to the matter at hand. 'She isn't some bloomer-wearing, bicycle-riding academic far beyond the reach of normal people, someone who's out of touch with the real world, she's a woman just like any of us here in the village. She lives with the challenges of everyday life but embraces the modern world to improve her life, and her family's.'

Clementine nodded, her eyes bright. 'A working woman is just as capable of contributing to the decisions in her own household and her community and workplace. Even the national government!'

'That's what being a suffragist is all about,' said Esther. 'We're all capable of doing so much more.'

Clementine and Esther were inspiring. I knew I had to hand over the national fight to them. They would do what I could not.

'Well, we have a big job ahead of us, but I'm up for the challenge,' I said with a grin. 'Here's to making the "New Woman" every woman.'

But inside my heart was breaking.

*

The Ox and Plough had been successful in its application to supply food and drinks for the winter dance despite Mr Franks trying to bribe his way onto the committee to block it. Bill was back at work but still not himself and I'd sent him home to rest. I was down in the cellar making sure we had enough barrels tapped when a wave of dizziness overcame me and I sat on one of the boxes until it passed.

I could hear Mama in the kitchen, making the pastry for the pies we'd have to cook fresh the next day. Jenny was watching Annie and Tommy, who would wake for another feed soon. He was thankfully an easier baby than Annie had been, but I was struggling to keep up with his needs. I thought a moment. I hadn't eaten since breakfast or had enough to drink to build my supplies of milk. I could feel my corset rubbing against my skin. I'd already laced it as tightly as I was able but the fact was I was skin and bone from nursing, and working long hours. Something had to give.

'I don't know what to do, Papa,' I whispered into the cool darkness of the cellar. I put my face in my hands. The burden of responsibility weighed heavily around my neck.

'Hannah?' Mama's voice wafted down from the scullery.

'I'm down here,' I called.

'What are you doing? What's the matter?'

I lifted my head to see Mama's concerned face in the light of the oil lamp.

'I'm just tired …' Tears began to seep from the corners of my eyes.

'Have you finished down here?'

I nodded.

'Come up to the kitchen and I'll make you some tea.'

'Tea isn't going to fix this, Mama.'

'What is it?'

'I can't do it all, Mama. I have to let something go.'

She put her arm around me and nodded. 'I know.'

'I have to step back from the national suffrage work. I can't manage it with the children and this place. But I can't give up everything I've worked for.'

'Who said you have to give it up?'

I shook my head. 'But it's this place as well. With Bill not right and Roger working around his building and me around the children, nothing's functioning. I want to give my full commitment to everything I do but I'm afraid of losing it all, everything I've dreamed of, all my plans.'

'But you have everything right in front of you. You've worked hard to get here and now you can decide what you want to do. Many women don't have that kind of opportunity.'

'I feel like it will all slip away.'

'No, my girl. You just have to be brave as you have been every time you've faced difficulty.' She took my face in her hands. 'Look what you've achieved. You've faced every challenge head on with strength and courage. You can do the same again.'

'The children have to come first.'

Mama kissed my forehead. 'Like most women with children, you have some difficult decisions to make. But it won't be forever, and when they're older you can do more.'

'I want to continue with the work we've started here in the village but I don't want to let Papa down either. Maybe it's time for Roger to get more involved.'

'He's as committed to this place as you are,' said Mama softly. 'And you're not letting Papa down. Roger can stop juggling the two jobs and see more of the children and you. That's if he wants to take it on.' She rubbed my back in solidarity and comfort. 'My brave girl. What we have to decide as women … You can still have it all, just not all at the same time. You have to choose your battles and conquer them one by one.'

Mama was right. It was a balancing act, like a circus juggler throwing balls into the air. I could choose how many balls I was juggling at any one time. It would take timing, balance, precision and steely determination, qualities I understood and knew well.

I spoke to Roger that night when we were readying ourselves for bed.

'What do you think about working full time at The Ox and Plough?' I asked tentatively. 'I can't do as much as I used to with two children and Bill's illness ...'

'That would mean giving up bricklaying and building and tying our entire livelihood to the pub,' he said. 'I'll admit, manual labour isn't something I want to be doing forever. Running the pub is something I'd like to do and it will give you more time with the children and to do your suffrage work.'

I shook my head. 'I'm stepping away from the national work. I know Mrs Fawcett will be disappointed but Clem and Esther are good choices to carry on with the next stage.'

'But you love it.'

'It's too hard with the children and the pub. But I'll continue with the projects we have in the township – there's so much to do here.'

'Of course. It's part of who you are. It makes sense then. I can be closer to you and the children and give you time for yourself and your community work.' He gathered me into his arms. 'How long have you been thinking about this?'

'Since before Tommy was born, but it's clear that I need more time for the children. Mama's not getting any younger and we can't ask your mother all the time. I can continue with the books and help with the business, but it's the day-to-day chores and decisions ...'

'Are you sure you want to do this?' he whispered, our foreheads touching.

I stared into his deep blue eyes. There was no judgement or pressure, only love. I was afraid because I knew that once I stepped back and allowed Roger to be the publican, I could never ask him to return to bricklaying.

'I think it's the only sensible choice, Roger. You're just as invested in this place as I am.'

'We have to do this together. Your name is above the door as licensed victualler, where it will stay, and I'll be the manager. You do the books, and together we'll make decisions about the business.' He frowned for a moment. 'Will your mother agree to this? To our partnership?'

'She agreed that it makes sense for us to do this together, however it works best for us.' I took his strong, callused hands in mine. 'Imagine what we could achieve. We'll take The Ox and Plough from strength to strength and—' I put my arms around his neck, my body pressed against his naked chest. '—we have the added benefit of spending more time together.'

Roger chuckled. 'That clinches it then.' He kissed me, the weight of promise behind the soft tenderness.

'Come to bed,' I whispered. 'I'm not dead on my feet for once.'

Roger took me in his arms. 'You don't have to ask me twice.'

35

I'm so lucky to have brave women around me, continuing our efforts for suffrage while I focus on issues closer to home. I have to stay sharp juggling the new vaccination push, women's education classes that I host at the pub, our mothers' groups and outreach programs for struggling families ... and the proposal for a new water supply for the township. So much to do.

It was a clear summer night and The Ox and Plough was filled to overflowing. People had come from all over the district to celebrate Queen Victoria's Diamond Jubilee, marking sixty years of her reign, the longest reigning sovereign in British history. The newspapers had reported that heads of state, their representatives and troops from around the British colonies had arrived to attend the festivities, which would continue for the rest of the week. According to the papers, it was a celebration of empire, an impressive display of the wealth, might and glory of Britain.

I joined my friends in the lounge for a few minutes after bringing them drinks.

'It was such a lovely afternoon and evening,' said Marjorie with a sigh. Edward, John Duffield and Robert Sanderson were talking about the trouble with the Boers in the British colonies in southern Africa at another table. 'It's a shame that Emily and Alice had to leave early. I would have loved to talk to them more about their pregnancies.'

I smiled, feeling so happy for Marjorie. She was pregnant again, about five months now, and all was progressing normally. When she'd been unwell early in this pregnancy, Edward had insisted on bedrest until the danger period had passed, even though Dr Jenkins hadn't thought it necessary. I'd found Edward's behaviour a little obsessive but I could understand why he felt so protective of her. He was worried she'd miscarry again.

'You can talk to Becky,' said Esther.

Marjorie shook her head. 'Talking to my sister is one thing, but Jemima is twelve now and her youngest is already six.'

'Congratulations on a successful event,' said Clementine, raising her glass to Esther.

'Even Mr Franks was no match for you,' I said, grinning.

The parish council had convened a month before to appoint the committees to organise our Jubilee celebrations. Mr Franks had volunteered to sit on the finances committee but Esther knew that, with his underhanded financial dealings and bribes, it was asking for trouble and somehow had managed to manoeuvre him to the sporting and games committee, much to his disgust. Esther had been instrumental in arranging everything: the afternoon's parade from the school to the village green; the streets decorated in red, white and blue bunting and flags of the Union Jack; the official ceremony and the planting of two sycamore trees on the village green. The festivities had concluded with the lighting of a bonfire at dusk and fireworks at nightfall. All the pubs had been given special permission to stay open until after midnight and many were making the most of the opportunity to celebrate.

I returned to the main bar, touching Roger on the shoulder. 'I checked the cellar a little earlier, and the barrels we've tapped should be enough for tonight,' I said into his ear. It was hard to hear with the noise in the room, packed with men talking more loudly with every drink they imbibed.

Roger nodded, pulling on one of the hand pumps and filling a glass without spilling a drop, all while continuing his conversation with the customer at the bar. Roger hadn't worked as a bricklayer for over six months and was masterful now. Bill still came in a couple of times a week, perhaps more out of habit and company than need, but he was family and we were grateful for his help on the busy days like today. But more than anything, I felt I could breathe again. I had time for the children, time to work through the ledgers and to plan for each week and month ahead, and I had time to devote to the ever growing list of community projects.

'All right,' I said, raising my voice above the noise. 'I'll be in the kitchen if you need me.'

I felt Roger's hand at my waist, lingering a moment before patting my hip. I rested my hand over his and smiled into his eyes. I squeezed his hand briefly before slipping away.

It was mercifully quiet in the kitchen, although still hot from the ovens. The platters of pies were empty now – customers had been peckish after the community meal that had been served hours earlier. I checked the sandwiches, which were nearly gone too, and wondered if it was worthwhile making more. I liked to have plenty of food on offer on a big night like this – if customers ate, they were less likely to get drunk, at least not so quickly. I checked the larder, scanning the shelves for bread and fillings.

'Aunt Hannah?'

I turned to find Jenny in the doorway. She was nineteen and a grown woman now. I thought back to the young girl who arrived to help us four years earlier, shy and unsure of herself and now she could calm unruly customers with a firm word and manage everything from a hot kitchen to a busy market stall at a festival. I was grateful for her help and her friendship, but I had a feeling that she insisted on staying with us rather than returning home or finding work in Durham or Hartlepool because of a boy she was interested in, Tom and Amelia Brown's son, Robert.

'What is it?' I asked sharply, noticing her pinched expression.

'There's a disturbance in the lounge.'

I nodded. It was to be expected on a night like this. 'Tell Reg to fetch the policeman on duty. The sooner it's dispersed, the better.'

'But it's Fred Duggan,' she said, looking afraid. 'He's drunk and shouting at his wife for talking to Marjorie and Esther and I don't know what he'll do before the police get here.'

Fear surged through me. Fred was much worse with drink in him.

I nodded and removed my apron. 'Go and tell Reg and I'll see what's going on.'

At first, I didn't notice any trouble in the lounge. The buzz of loud conversation and laughter seemed normal. Then I heard Fred's voice raised in anger.

'Leave me wife alone, you shrew!'

I saw them in the middle of the room. Fred was grasping Dorothy's arm tightly while towering over Esther and Marjorie, who were sitting together at a table. The customers nearby had stopped what they were doing, some affronted by Fred's language and others eagerly watching to see what would happen next. I scanned the room for Edward, John or Robert Sanderson, but they weren't to be seen.

'She ain't done anythin', Fred,' pleaded Dorothy, trying to squirm free.

Fred turned his glare on his wife. His face was flushed from too much drink and his eyes were glassy. 'I told you to stay away from that lot. They're trouble.'

'What lot?' asked Marjorie, rising from her seat.

'You lot who don't know your place and think you're as good as us men,' he sneered. 'I ain't having me wife infected by your grand delusions.' He pushed Marjorie roughly so that she fell against the table, her belly noticeable against the taut fabric of her skirt, and an audible gasp rose from customers nearby.

'Everyone, please calm down,' I called, catching Esther's eye as she helped Marjorie to her seat.

Fred laughed harshly. 'You're another one.'

'Come on, Mr Duggan,' I said soothingly. 'Everyone's having a good night. How about you let your wife go? You might be hurting her.'

'I won't. And the welfare of me wife ain't your business.'

'Please, Fred,' whispered Dorothy, beginning to tremble. 'You're makin' a scene.'

'I'm makin' a scene? I forbade you from speakin' to them. I ain't the one who caused this. You did.'

He had to go. I glanced around the room to make sure I had support. There was enough. 'I think it's time for you to leave, Mr Duggan.'

'Who do you think you are? You can't tell me what to do. I'll stay as long as I like.'

'I've called the constable. Do you want him to escort you out?' I asked. 'Maybe spend the night in a police cell?'

Fred stared at me, unblinking. The naked hatred on his face was plain to see. 'Fine,' he said finally. 'I only came here to get me wife.' He lurched forward, still holding Dorothy.

'Dorothy, do you want to stay?' I asked.

She seemed to quail at the question, looking from me to Esther.

'She's comin' with me,' roared Fred, pulling on his wife's arm and making her stumble.

Edward strode into the room, his focus on Fred. The look of ferocious intensity on his face reminded me of a statue I'd seen of Mars, the Roman God of war. He was terrifying.

'I believe you just pushed my pregnant wife,' he growled.

'She don't know when to shut her mouth. Maybe you should control your wife better,' said Fred.

Edward advanced on him. Fred took a few steps backwards, letting Dorothy go. He wasn't so brave faced with someone his own size. But it was too late. They scuffled, the fight punctuated by the sound of breaking glass as an oil lamp fell, before Edward punched Fred in the face, knocking him to the ground.

'Don't *ever* touch my wife again,' he said quietly.

A flame erupted from the broken lamp, igniting the edge of a tablecloth that hung too close to the ground. Customers screamed as the fire spread quickly along the path of the spilt oil. The bucket of sand we kept for such accidents was in the scullery. I searched the room, desperate for something closer to put the fire out with.

'Give me your jacket,' I said to Edward, but he only stared in horror at the fire. I removed my own jacket. My shirtwaist was visible but that was too bad. I threw my jacket over the fire, smothering the flames before stamping them out. It had taken only a moment but my heart was pounding as though I'd run a mile.

Reg arrived, closely followed by the policeman.

'Fighting isn't tolerated here,' said Constable Peters, taking in Fred sprawled on the floor and Edward standing over him. 'These two men cannot stay.'

I explained the situation as he helped Fred to his feet. Edward ignored the constable, moving to Marjorie's side instead.

'Do you want to leave, Mrs Duggan?' the constable asked.

She shook her head imperceptibly, refusing to meet Fred's gaze.

'Time to go, Mr Duggan,' said Constable Peters.

'Not without me wife.'

'She'll leave when she's ready,' said the constable, not taking any more nonsense.

'What about him?' Fred pointed accusingly at Edward, who had his arm around Marjorie, speaking quietly to her. 'He hit me. Ain't you gonna do somethin' about him?'

'I'll deal with him, but it's time for you to go.'

'One more drink in the public bar.'

'No,' said the constable. 'You've had enough. Go home and sleep it off.' He took hold of Fred's elbow. 'Mr Partridge, I'm sorry, but you have to go too. No matter the reason or provocation, we cannot allow anyone who has been involved in a fight to stay.'

I watched as Edward's face first went pale with mortification and then red with indignation.

'Not so high and mighty now, are you?' jeered Fred.

Edward's hands clenched into fists, whether to hit Fred again or to keep from shaking with anger, I wasn't sure. 'I understand, constable,' he said. 'I apologise for the disruption. Of course, I'll leave now.' He turned to whisper something to Marjorie, who shook her head. A flash of disappointment crossed his face before he rose with as much dignity as he could muster and walked out of the room ahead of the constable.

'It's for the best, Edward,' I said firmly, following him into the hall. I was still shocked that he had given in to Fred's provocation, had lost control and had hit him.

He only nodded sharply.

I watched Constable Peters escort them out of The Ox and Plough and heaved a sigh of relief. I couldn't have fighting here. It would only invite more trouble.

I turned my attention back to the lounge, where it seemed almost as if nothing had happened. Jenny and Polly had cleaned up the mess where the fire had been and a fresh cloth was now on the table. It was frightening how quickly the fire had started. People had returned to their conversations, heads bent towards each other or bodies leaning back casually as they listened to an amusing story. But Dorothy stood dazed in the centre of the room, Marjorie by her side. Esther had her hand on Dorothy's shoulder, trying to comfort her.

'Are you all right, Dorothy?' I asked as I joined them.

'He'll punish me for this,' she whispered.

'He has no right to stop you from talking to your friends,' said Esther indignantly.

'But he'll punish me anyway.'

'Come and sit down,' I said, guiding her to a chair.

'I should've gone with him. What am I gonna do?' She put her face in her hands.

'Can you go and stay with someone tonight?' asked Esther. 'Wait until Fred is sober and has calmed down before you go back home?'

'Go back home?'

I turned to find Mrs Scruton sitting nearby.

'I saw everythin'. You can't go back to that good-for-nothin' husband of yours, pet. Go back and he'll beat you till he kills you.'

'But I have to. The children need me. I have to get home to them.'

Mrs Scruton took Dorothy's hand. 'You and the children, come stay with me. I could use your help at the tea room.'

Dorothy shook her head. 'I don't want to trouble you. I'm sure Fred will go to The Rose and Crown. I have time to get back home and lock him out until he's sobered up. I know what to do when he's like this. In the mornin', he'll be calmer.'

'Constable Peters will escort you home,' I said. 'If Fred comes back and causes trouble, send one of the children and I'll direct the constable to your door.'

'Good idea,' said Mrs Scruton. 'And you know where to find me.'

'Thank you.' Dorothy rose from her seat. 'I know you think I'm stupid, but Fred's my children's father. He loves them and when he ain't drunk, he's a good father. He loves me too, in his own way.' She looked at each of us beseechingly, pleading with us to understand.

'Of course,' said Marjorie, placing her hand on her belly. 'Only you can know what he's truly like.'

Dorothy nodded. I accompanied her to the door and made sure the constable could escort her home.

'Mr Duggan has gone to The Rose and Crown,' he said. 'He's been allowed entry, I'm not sure how long for, but he won't be bothering you for a while.'

I shook my head with anger. Of course he'd been let in.

'Thank you for your kindness, Hannah,' said Dorothy, squeezing my hand before turning away to join the constable.

I returned to the lounge to make sure that everyone was settled and still enjoying themselves.

'You look tired, Marjorie.'

She sagged in her chair and nodded. 'It's been a long day. All I want is to rest my feet. Thank goodness Becky's place is a short walk. Edward has gone to his mother's and I told him I'd meet him at Becky's after. I didn't want to go when I know how much his mother doesn't like me.' Clementine's eyebrows rose and Esther looked taken back. This was news to us.

'Why wouldn't she like you?' asked Esther, frowning.

'Edward told me she wanted him to marry someone from a better family, someone with a pedigree befitting a gentleman,' she said bitterly. She looked into Esther's eyes. 'Someone like you.'

Esther flushed with embarrassment and shook her head. 'That's ridiculous.'

'He told me that you were friendly before he left for London. His mother had high hopes, but when he returned after his uncle's death, we were already married.'

'I promise you, I had no idea,' Esther said. I was surprised at this revelation. I thought I knew most things about the village but clearly not everything. It made me wonder what else I didn't know.

Marjorie squeezed Esther's hand. 'I'll go to Becky's and have a cup of tea with her. I'd much rather her company than Edward's mother's anyway.' She smiled.

'Why not wait until the constable returns?' suggested Clementine.

'He could be a while yet and I really want to spend some time with Becky before Edward comes,' said Marjorie.

'Take Reg,' I said. 'Edward wouldn't be happy for you to go out at night without a chaperone.'

'I'll come with you,' said Esther. 'I'll tell Reg to ask Papa to come around to Becky's to collect me.'

I watched Reg accompany Esther and Marjorie until their lanterns disappeared over the rise then began collecting glasses from the lounge.

'I hear you were involved in making the new reservoir a reality,' said Mrs Mason, the rector's wife, as I moved around the room. 'I went to the official opening and it's so wonderfully modern.'

I smiled. 'Yes, a lot of thought went into the planning. Dr Jenkins helped us get the project approved.' Finally, we had a clean source of water available from street taps, supplied from the reservoir via gravitation. 'But I think we have to thank our parish and district councils. Isn't that right, Mrs Burrows?'

Mrs Burrows held her drink in mid-air, her cheeks ruddy from the warm night and perhaps a little too much wine. 'That's right. Esther told me the councillors work long and hard to make sure our new buildings and infrastructure are exactly what we need.'

Things had changed a lot between Esther and her mother. Since Esther had been made councillor, Mrs Burrows couldn't help but tell anyone she met about all the good works that her daughter was involved in. Now Mrs Burrows was an integral part of our suffrage society and was warming to the work we were doing for the vote. But I wondered how long it would be until she'd accept Esther's studies and research in science and engineering.

'Did your Esther have anything to do with the filling in of that disgraceful pond?' asked Mrs Mason.

'She did.' Mrs Burrows beamed.

'I've heard they're working on plans for the new pumping station,' I said. I was interrupted by someone pulling on my sleeve.

'Aunt Hannah, you have to come. It's Reg,' whispered Jenny into my ear.

'Excuse me, ladies, there's something I have to attend to,' I said, before following Jenny from the lounge.

'What's wrong?' I asked in a low voice.

'He's out the front with Constable Peters. He won't come inside.'

'What's happened?'

'I'm not sure, but he looks banged up and says that he was attacked.'

My hand flew to my mouth as I hurried out onto the street. 'Reg, are you all right?' I held up the lamp to find his eye swollen and his nose and mouth bloody, and gasped.

'Don't worry about me,' he said urgently. 'We have to find Mrs Partridge and Miss Burrows and make sure they're all right.'

My heart pounded hard in my chest. 'What happened?'

'Fred Duggan was waiting in the dark outside. He must have been watching for his wife to leave. We didn't see him until he was upon us. He attacked Mrs Partridge, trying to drag her away. She fought against him and I tried to stop him, but then he landed a punch on me and knocked me out. When I came to, they were all gone. I looked up and down the street but couldn't see them anywhere and it was quickest to come back here to alert Constable Peters.'

'No,' I whispered, horrified. I should have seen something like this happening. I'd seen the raw hatred on Fred's face.

'Nobody could have known, Mrs Rainforth. But we'll find them,' said Constable Peters. 'We'll see if they're with Mrs Partridge's sister before we raise the alarm.'

I turned to Jenny, who had followed me out. 'Go back inside and find Mrs Scruton and Clementine, discreetly, and ask them to join us out here.' Mrs Scruton had once been a nurse and if Marjorie was injured, she'd know what to do, and I wanted Clementine by my side. They were both clear-headed and calm under stress. 'Knock on Dr Jenkins' door. Tell him what's happened and ask him to see to Reg then meet us in our parlour.'

'I can manage this on my own,' said the constable.

I shook my head, my lips pressed tight in determination. 'We're coming. If anything has happened, they'll need us.'

36

Love, security; it didn't matter why we chose to be with someone, what mattered was how we made our peace with those choices. Love could be wondrous with the right man, but with the wrong man it could be disaster.

Under different circumstances, it would have been a beautiful night for a stroll, especially after the day we'd had. It was quiet and the salt-tinged breeze from the sea was cool and invigorating after the press of bodies inside the pub. Lamplight spilled from between the drapes at the windows and under the doors of homes. We lifted our lanterns and scoured the shadowy corners and alleyways on our way to Becky's house. With my heartbeat rushing in my ears, I repeated a fervent prayer under my breath, over and over: *Please let them both be safe and well at Becky's.*

The look of confusion on Becky's face when she answered the door made my heart drop.

'I haven't seen Marjorie. What's this all about?'

'Mrs Partridge and Miss Burrows are missing,' said Constable Peters. He quickly explained what we knew.

'I told her to be careful,' she whispered, reaching a trembling hand to her mouth. 'We have to find her.' In her panic, she tried to rush out the door without shoes and with her hair loose around her shoulders. Her state of panic worried me. Was there something I didn't know?

'No, Becky,' said Mrs Scruton, putting her arms around her. 'Let Constable Peters do his job.'

'We'll look for her, but I need you to stay here in case she turns up,' said the constable softly.

Becky nodded. 'Please find her.'

The gate creaked as Clementine and I made our way into the nearby graveyard. Constable Peters and Mrs Scruton were still out on the street, asking locals if they'd seen anything. Holding the lantern above my head, I scanned the yard and peered towards the stand of oak trees on the far side but saw nothing unusual.

'Let's look between the gravestones,' whispered Clementine.

I nodded, a cold shiver running through me as we stepped over the dead. This was hallowed ground and I was by no means superstitious, but dread rose within my belly. Most of these graves were old, some hundreds of years, many abandoned and forgotten by those who lived in the parish now. I swallowed my fear and lifted my chin, peering into the blackness.

A guttural groan rose from the earth and I froze, my heart pounding, not sure whether I had imagined it.

'Did you hear that?' I whispered to Clementine, clutching her arm.

'It's coming from over there,' she said, pointing to a large gravestone. I held the lantern high but all I saw was darkness.

'Come on,' she hissed. 'It could be Marjorie or Esther.' She grabbed my hand and we crept towards the sound.

'Careful,' I murmured. 'It could be an injured animal, or maybe Fred himself.' I was trying to be pragmatic and brave but my head was thumping to the sound of my heart.

And then I saw it – a shape in the shadows. And then another cry, but this time I recognised it for what it was: a woman's call of both relief and despair.

'My God, it's Marjorie!' I said.

We rushed to her side.

What we discovered made my blood run cold. Even in the light of the lantern, her face was a bloody mess, and brought images of Kitty in the alleyway flooding back. As my eyes travelled over her ripped and dirty clothing, I realised her skirt was covered in blood.

'Marjorie,' I whispered, cradling her head in my hands. 'We're here now.'

'The baby ...' she mumbled. Her hand reached down to her skirt, wet and sodden with blood. Tears ran down her cheeks. I glanced at Clementine and she shook her head. Marjorie had been badly beaten. Without a word, Clementine ran back to the road to alert the others.

'Don't move,' I urged. 'Help is on its way.'

'Esther?' she whispered. 'Is she all right?'

'We haven't seen her.'

'She saved my life ...' She closed her eyes.

'Marjorie, do you know where she might be?' I asked urgently. 'Marjorie?'

She opened her eyes slowly. 'She was here with me ... When I woke, I was alone.'

'They're coming,' called Clementine, rushing back to our side.

Marjorie began to tremble. 'I don't want anyone to see me like this. Not even Becky.'

'It's only Mrs Scruton and the constable,' I said, smoothing her hair from her face.

Mrs Scruton took over as soon as she saw the condition Marjorie was in. The constable lifted her carefully to carry her back to our parlour, where I knew Dr Jenkins would be waiting.

I pulled Clementine aside. 'I think Esther's here somewhere too.'

'What if he's killed her?'

I put my arms around her. She was shaking like a leaf. 'We'll find her.'

We scrambled between the gravestones, calling Esther's name.

'We shouldn't have let them go,' said Clementine, anguished.

'Reg was with them, Clem. None of us knew this would happen.' I pushed my own guilt aside for now.

Again my eyes rested on the stand of oak trees. 'Let's go up to the trees. It's a little higher and maybe it will give us a better perspective of where she might be.'

When we reached the trees, the light from the lantern seemed to barely penetrate the darkness between them. I cast the lantern over the yard below but it was difficult to see anything through the gloom.

'We'll never find her this way,' said Clementine, staring into the darkness. 'We'll have to ask Marjorie if she remembers where Esther was before she blacked out.'

'Maybe she's not here at all.' I couldn't voice the one thought that persisted: maybe she was unconscious, dying or already dead.

We trudged back along the fence line, calling Esther's name, looking more methodically. The longer she waited to be found, the worse her injuries might become.

'Hannah! Clementine!'

I started at the sound of our names, a shock of hope rushing through my body, making my skin tingle. It was faint, but I'd know that voice anywhere. I lifted the lantern towards the fence.

'She's here!' shouted Clementine. We rushed towards the sound. 'Esther! Where are you?'

'I'm here,' she sobbed. 'Help me!'

Clementine and I followed her voice until we found her, crumpled against the fence. We knelt beside her.

'We're here, my darling,' cooed Clementine as she would to a small child.

'Are you hurt?' I whispered. Her face was smudged with dirt and her hair was unbound, the wispy tendrils flying around her face.

'My ankle. I can't walk on it.'

'Here, we'll help you up.' Clementine and I took her by the arms but Esther cried out with pain. 'What is it? Should we stop?'

'No, get me out of here,' she said hoarsely. She was shaking badly and, now that she was standing, I could see that her blouse was torn and she held her arm over her ribs. Dread swirled in my belly.

'What did Fred do to you, Esther?' I asked gently. 'Your clothes are torn.'

'I don't want to talk about it.' She refused to look either of us in the eye. 'Nothing happened. I tried to get help for Marjorie but turned my ankle in the dark and fell. It hurt too much to walk, so I crawled until I reached the fence.' Esther took a shuddering breath. 'Have you found Marjorie?'

Clementine and I nodded.

'I thought he was going to kill her.' She closed her eyes.

'He has to pay,' said Clementine darkly.

'Mrs Scruton is with her,' I said. 'She's alive but we're worried about the baby. We'll go to the pub, Esther – Dr Jenkins is waiting in my parlour.'

Esther shook her head. 'I'm fine. I don't need any treatment.'

'What about your ankle?'

'I'll wrap it up and I'll be good as new in a few days.' She was trembling and ice cold. 'I just want to go home,' she whispered.

'You can't go home like this,' said Clementine. 'Come back to Hannah's first.'

'You can have a bath and a cup of tea,' I said.

She was silent for a moment, then nodded. 'Not a word of any of this to anyone,' she pleaded.

'All right,' said Clementine. 'If you're sure.'

They both turned to me. Esther was a councillor and local gentry. Even the hint of a rumour could damage her reputation and ruin her future. I nodded. As much as I wanted the whole world to know what Fred had done, I had no choice but to keep what had happened here between us.

*

We brought both Marjorie and Esther back to our cottage. While Dr Jenkins examined Marjorie in the parlour with Mrs Scruton holding her hand, Clementine and I took Esther to undress and bathe. She cried at the sight of the marks on her body. Her tears were silent at first, then, as her damaged and swollen skin touched the warm, soapy water, she began to whimper. When she finally sat, holding her ribs for the pain, the sobbing came, her fat tears falling into the bathwater.

Dr Jenkins was worried about Marjorie and while Clementine stayed with Esther, Mrs Scruton and I gently removed her clothing. She moaned as we washed the blood and dirt from her face and body and I had to use all my strength to stop my hands shaking and from the tears welling in my eyes. The application of stitches and plaster bandages and the red and purple bruising blooming on her pale skin were nothing compared to the continued bleeding that made us worry about the health of her baby.

Edward arrived, fetched from his mother's, and stood in our parlour, pale with shock and worry, watching Dr Jenkins' ministrations while Mrs Scruton and I assisted.

'Will she recover?' he asked quietly.

'I think so, given time,' said Dr Jenkins, focusing on the fine stitches he was using to close one of Marjorie's wounds.

'What about the baby?' Edward's voice broke and I could see the horror in his crumpled face. To lose another baby when he'd done everything to keep Marjorie safe ...

Dr Jenkins put a hand on Edward's shoulder. 'I can still hear a heartbeat but she has lost a lot of blood.'

Edward's shoulders slumped but he reached for Marjorie's hand. 'The baby still lives,' he whispered to her, his face alight with hope. She nodded, then turned her head, tears escaping the corners of her eyes and trickling over her ruined face.

'Let me take her home to Dalleymoor, where I can have the best nurses looking after her around the clock,' he said to Dr Jenkins.

'I can't agree to that,' said the doctor. 'Her condition is too delicate. There's still a high risk she'll lose the baby over the coming days. I don't even dare move her to the hospital or my clinic to treat her more easily. I've brought everything I need with me. If we're to maximise the chances of your baby surviving, Mrs Partridge will need to remain here until the danger has passed.'

'What about the care she needs?'

'There's not much we can do except watch and wait. I'll return to see her morning and evening and Mrs Scruton and Mrs Rainforth have agreed to watch over her until her condition stabilises and you can take her home.'

'Marjorie and I owe you a debt of gratitude,' he said, turning to me.

'It's the least we can do,' I replied. 'We'll do everything we can to make Marjorie comfortable. I'll have a bed made up for you to stay the night too.'

He nodded, blinking the tears from his eyes. 'Thank you.'

Mrs Burrows had been informed of Esther's fall, cracked ribs and twisted ankle and had taken her home in fresh clothes with her ribs and foot bandaged. And soon after, Clementine left too, her mask of efficiency slipping and the strain showing on her face. I knew she'd cry, alone in the privacy of her room, and I was grateful that I had Roger.

Mrs Scruton and I settled Marjorie in Jenny's room while Roger remained with Edward in the parlour, comforting him as best he could. Dr Jenkins gave Marjorie a sleeping draught before he left and, with Mrs Scruton watching over her for the night, Edward retired to the drawing room and Roger and I to our bedroom.

'How can something like this have happened?' asked Roger.

'The signs were there,' I whispered, cuddling up to him. I wanted to feel close to him, his body against mine. He put his arm around me. 'We've all seen the way Fred treated his wife. I've seen the bruises on her arms. But nobody wanted to make it worse by saying something to him – except Marjorie, and he resented her for calling him out. If only I'd done more.'

Roger planted a tender kiss on my temple. 'You can't think like that, my darling. The whole village knows what Duggan is like. He's always been a bully. I've had more to do with him than many, and he's always trying to cheat me whenever I buy bricks from him. Unfortunately, he makes the best bricks in the district.'

'How has Dorothy existed all these years?'

'Well, I'm sure she thought he was a good man at first. Bullies can be charming. Then, when the children started coming, I suppose she believed she had no choice but to stay.'

I thought about Marjorie and Edward and of his mother's disapproval of his choice of wife. If Marjorie had gone with Edward to visit his mother, none of this would have happened. Then I wondered what would happen to Dorothy and her children once Fred was arrested. She'd be better off, I had no doubt.

I kissed Roger's chest, the coarse hairs tickling my nose. If I'd loved the wrong man, my life would have been so different now. I sent a silent prayer of thanks to the heavens, reminded how precious my relationship with Roger really was.

'How's Marjorie now?'

'She's asleep, but I don't know how she'll feel in the morning. After what they went through last year and Edward's devotion with this pregnancy, if she loses the baby, I don't know how he'll take it.'

'I'd like to beat the living daylights out of Duggan myself, so I can hardly imagine how Edward feels. I only hope he's arrested first thing in the morning. It'd be better than if Edward finds him first.'

'I'm sure Edward's not a violent man. I doubt he'd jeopardise his position on the district council or as Justice of the Peace and magistrate.'

'It's easy for a man to be in control of his emotions when an event doesn't concern him, but threaten a man's family or his wife, and you'll see a different person.'

I nodded. I thought about Edward's attack on Fred. It had been justified, but it had been a shock to see Edward lose control. If Roger had been in the same situation, I was unsure he would have acted with restraint either. The thought made me shiver. 'Fred will come to justice and Dorothy will be safe and free of him, but she'll need support. I only hope Mrs Scruton can give her and some of her children work, like she promised.'

'Mmm,' he said, sliding his hand down my back. 'Maybe we can take one of them on once Jenny leaves. According to Tom Brown, it won't be long before his son proposes to her.'

'That's a good idea. Do you think Fred will go to prison?'

Roger sighed. 'It's hard to say. Reg didn't see the whole thing. But when Marjorie presses charges and reports what happened, there'll be more chance of him being jailed for longer, especially as the wife of a district councillor. Add Esther's testimony and Fred won't be back for a good while. It will give Dorothy a chance to begin a new life.'

'I don't know.' Cold dread had settled in my belly, bringing a squeamish discomfort with it. I'd promised Esther I wouldn't say anything, but Roger was my other half. I couldn't keep secrets from him. 'I think Fred attacked Esther too,' I said quietly. 'She has cracked ribs, cuts and bruises that suggest she didn't just fall, she was beaten.'

Roger jerked. 'What?'

'I don't know what happened for sure, she won't speak of it and made us promise to say nothing about what we saw, but I think he retaliated after she tried to stop him hurting Marjorie.'

'He has to be brought to account,' Roger growled.

'I know. If only we could show the entire village exactly how we'd seen Esther and Marjorie tonight, everyone would understand that men like Fred must be more harshly punished under the law.' For Kitty's sake, too, I told myself. 'But it's not that simple. After what Marjorie and Esther have been through, I don't think they want anyone to know what happened. It wasn't their fault, but people talk and the shame and the stain on their reputations will follow them around anyway, ruining their lives.'

'You may be right. They have suffered already. Perhaps the police will have enough to charge Fred with only Reg's statement. Let's see what happens in the morning.'

I wrapped the bedclothes around my clenched fists to contain the fury and feeling of futility that rose within me. 'Yes, let's see,' I whispered, suddenly exhausted.

37

The Diamond Jubilee was an impressive display of
imperialism but there has been talk at the pub about
about rising tensions between the Boers and British, and
their struggle for power and influence in the gold-rich
colonies of southern Africa. Perhaps British imperialism
isn't as mighty as we are all led to believe.

The month following Marjorie's and Esther's attacks was
difficult and I'd seen little of either of them. I'd heard through
Becky that, despite surviving the danger period, Marjorie
had still lost the baby. She was inconsolable and Edward had
not left her side since he'd taken her home to convalesce at
Dalleymoor. I'd sent Marjorie flowers and a note with my
condolences, asking if she'd like me to visit, but I hadn't heard
back. Perhaps she wanted to grieve in private. Esther also hid
away from the world. She didn't even want to see Clementine
and me.

The police had been prepared to apprehend Fred Duggan
for assault on Reg's testimony but Fred had disappeared and
they were still searching for him. Dorothy was undoubtedly
relieved that he was gone but without Fred's income she was
all but destitute, her work as a washerwoman not nearly
enough for her and her children to survive. Thank goodness
Mrs Scruton was true to her word and gave Dorothy and
a couple of her daughters work at the tea room. We had
promoted Reg to cellarman and one of Dorothy's boys,

Bobby, had taken up the position of potman. The Duggans would keep a roof over their heads and put food on the table, and in a home where Dorothy no longer had to fear.

Although Esther and Marjorie were constantly on my mind, life had to go on, and I was kept busy preparing for the events held in our meeting rooms and a family celebration for Tommy's first birthday.

'Have you seen this?' I asked, pulling a pamphlet out from among some papers as Mama and I sat in the kitchen having breakfast. I was feeling tired and Mama had insisted I rest. Perhaps I'd press the wildflowers I'd picked during my walk with the children the day before.

'What is it?' Mama was spooning porridge into Tommy's mouth, his little hands around the spoon trying to do it himself, so that most ended up smeared across his mouth. Annie was eating quietly, after Mama poured a dash of treacle over her porridge. At two years and three months, Annie could take what seemed like hours to finish eating.

I read aloud for Mama.

Help end compulsory vaccination. Vaccination devastates health and lives. It introduces pus from sick cows infected with smallpox. It is unsanitary and poisonous. Not only can it produce intense discomfort to your child but it may transmit other diseases from the animal into their system. Many have suffered from syphilis, mania, consumption as well as smallpox itself after vaccination. It is wrong, unjust and tyrannical for the government to enforce this poison into our precious children

'Who wrote such nonsense? You were all vaccinated and none of you had any trouble.'

'It's the National Anti-Vaccination League. Ever since they've unified, their message has spread and their voice has become stronger.'

'Only someone who doesn't understand the true nature of a disease like smallpox will listen to this rubbish. Mark my words, this will be as far as they get.'

But I wasn't so sure. I was beginning to understand that it wasn't always about the worthiness of a cause that got it discussed by the lawmakers, but the support of powerful men within Parliament itself.

I pulled at the tight bodice of my dress, feeling uncomfortable, suddenly feeling nauseous. All thoughts of policy making disappeared from my mind as a single realisation entered it. I looked at Mama. 'I'm pregnant again.'

Mama smiled. 'I thought as much.' She squeezed my hand. 'Roger will be pleased.'

I nodded, feeling dazed. Children were a blessing but three children under three … It seemed that I was like Sarah, falling pregnant at the drop of a hat. Roger had once told me he wanted a big family. Maybe he'd get his wish.

*

My worry for Esther stayed with me and I decided to call on her at home. Mrs Burrows invited Mama and me in for tea and I was relieved when Esther decided to join us.

'How are you, Esther?' I asked. We were all sitting at a small table in the conservatory overlooking magnificent gardens.

'I'm well.' She was neat and tidy, dressed in a lace-frilled bodice and floral printed skirt with her hair fashioned into a chignon. But there were dark smudges under her eyes, loose strands of frizzy hair and her nails were chewed down to the quick. I glanced at Mrs Burrows.

'We're hosting a small gathering on Sunday afternoon to help raise funds for new school equipment and resources before the children go back to school,' she said. 'I hope you can join us. I know Esther would love to have you here.' She looked at her daughter, who nodded silently, then frowned.

'Thank you, we'd love to come,' I said quickly. I felt any chance to visit Esther would be a good thing.

'Do you feel up to it?' asked Mama softly.

I shook my head imperceptibly but it was already too late.

'Are you ill, dear?' enquired Mrs Burrows.

'Hannah's pregnant again,' said Mama, beaming.

My heart sank. I'd wanted to tell Esther myself. I looked over in time to see her eyes drop to the table.

'Congratulations,' said Mrs Burrows. 'You're going to be busy with three children, all so little. I only ever had two and they were a handful enough.'

I nodded, wishing I could talk to Esther privately.

Mrs Burrows patted Mama's hand. 'Grandchildren must be such a blessing, but I think it's going to be sometime before Mr Burrows and I have that pleasure.' She looked pointedly at Esther.

'Would you excuse me, Mama, Mrs Todd?' blurted Esther. She stood suddenly, before anyone answered, and hobbled out into the garden.

Mrs Burrows raised her eyebrows in surprise and glanced at Mama.

'If you'll excuse me too, Esther and I haven't seen each other for a while. We'll take a turn in the garden,' I said.

Mrs Burrows nodded. 'Of course, dear.'

I followed Esther down the path. 'Esther,' I called.

She continued to limp ahead of me and I had to run to catch up.

'Esther, wait,' I said, breathing heavily. Already this pregnancy was making itself felt.

Esther whirled around, tears streaming down her face. 'I'm sorry,' she stammered. 'Just leave me be.'

'No. I'm your friend,' I said gently. 'Tell me what's wrong.'

She brushed the tears from her cheeks almost savagely. 'Nothing.'

I wasn't going to be pushed away again. 'I'm sorry if my news upset you. I didn't want to say anything to anyone yet. I only just found out.'

Esther nodded, fresh tears welling in her eyes. 'I'm happy for you, really ... it's just ...'

I slipped my arm through hers. 'Come on, let's take a walk through the gardens, if you're up to it?'

She nodded and we walked slowly in silence for a while, the crunch of the gravel under our feet a rhythmic counterpoint to our thoughts. The beautiful gardens, magnificent oak trees and flowers lining the path seemed like dull cut-outs as I waited for her to talk to me.

I felt her arm relax against mine. 'Marjorie has lost her baby because of what Fred did to her. She won't see me,' Esther said, her voice breaking.

'She won't see me either,' I said softly. 'But she has Edward to comfort her and when she's ready, we'll be there for her.'

She nodded. 'She might have become pregnant too, if she wasn't already. I saw what he did to her. And now maybe she hates me.'

'Why would she hate you?'

'Because it was her and not me,' she whispered. My heart broke for her. 'I've often wondered what I would have done if it had been me. I tried to get him off her but it wasn't enough.'

'Oh, Esther, I'm so sorry you feel that way.' I kissed her cold cheek. 'I'm sure you did everything you could.'

'I know, but she lost the baby anyway. I thought perhaps if I pushed that night from my mind, I could pretend it never happened. But when you said you were pregnant it all came rushing back with that crushing feeling of guilt, and now I feel that I'll never have any peace until I tell someone I trust all the terrible details.'

'You're so brave, Esther,' I said.

'No, I'm not. Let's keep walking. The only way I can do this is if I keep moving.' She took a deep breath then continued, 'Fred came out of nowhere that night. He must have been waiting for us and he grabbed Marjorie, tried to drag her away. He punched her when she refused to go with him. Reg went to stop him and I pulled Marjorie away while they scuffled. But Fred knocked Reg out and came for us again.'

'What happened then?'

'He snatched Marjorie from my grasp and hit me when I tried to stop him from dragging her into the graveyard. I was stunned by the shock and pain. When I could see straight again, I heard her screaming and followed them into the graveyard, where he had her on the ground. He punched and kicked her until she stopped. I was terrified he was going to kill her. Then to my horror, he said, "I'll show you your place, you bitch," he lifted her skirts and started to rape her.

'I didn't even think that I'd be no match for him. I jumped on him, hitting, scratching and biting, until he turned to deal with me. I felt him grab me by the hair and fling me against a large gravestone. "Now you know who's in charge," he said to Marjorie as he kicked her in the ribs and belly. "Just so you don't forget it." I feared that he'd already killed her baby and would kill her too. But I wasn't frightened, Hannah – all I felt was rage. I only had one thought, to get him away from her. I ran at him, pushing him aside, trying to get between her and him to somehow protect her, but he'd had enough.'

Now I knew why neither Marjorie nor Esther wanted to see any of us, or talk about it. How either of them would be able to come to terms with what had happened, I didn't know. I felt cold to the bone despite the warm summer sunshine.

'He punched me in the face as he did Reg,' she continued, speaking as though she were in a trance. 'I was shocked by the brutality rather than the pain. I tried to get away from him but he was too strong and I started to scream, hoping someone would hear me. That's when he started kicking me too. I curled into a little ball to protect my face and head and felt the toe of his boot on my ribs, back and legs but I didn't stop screaming. He climbed on top of me then. I used all my strength to push him off but he punched me in the chest and belly, like he had with Marjorie, and finally covering my mouth, taunted me with his ugly words. "I'll teach you, you uppity bitch," he whispered into my ear. "Never disturb a man in his work. You are nothing." I'll never forget his voice as long as I live.'

A red rage rushed through me as she gripped my hand tightly. I could hardly breathe for what I knew was coming next.

'I was truly afraid then. He grabbed me by the throat, pushing down so I couldn't breathe and I clawed at his hands. Then suddenly I could breathe again and he was gone. Not long after, I heard you and Clementine.

'Afterwards, part of me wanted to die and the part of me that wanted to be found was also terrified of being found.' She began to shake, as silent tears slipped down her cheeks. 'I don't know if I'm more afraid of seeing Fred again or of people finding out what happened. He didn't rape me, Hannah, but I feel broken all the same.'

I hugged her tight and this time she didn't flinch from my touch. 'I thank God it was Clementine and me who found you both.'

'So do I,' she whispered. 'Who else could I trust to keep this safe? Nobody will believe I hadn't been violated.'

'But you were still attacked, Esther. You suffered terribly. Clementine and I have been so worried about you.'

'I couldn't cope with everyone's sympathy, not after what Marjorie has been through. I'm still not sure I can.'

'Do you want me to tell Clem?'

'No, I'll do it. I just want to find the right time.'

We walked past the old horse stables, used now as Esther and her father's workshop.

'What will you do?'

She sighed. 'I know I can't hide forever. Thankfully, my work with Papa keeps me close to home, but I'll have to force myself to continue my work on the parish council and I promised Mama I'd try for the district council next year. I can't let what happened define me, but I know in my heart I'll never be the same again.'

38

I've learnt from Dr Jenkins that the National Anti-Vaccination League are lobbying Parliament to change the vaccination laws. As much as I disagree with their opinions, I'd be fascinated to hear how their cause has gained greater traction since becoming a national body.

'Did you hear?' asked Jenny, bursting through the parlour door, her voice urgent. Mama, my sisters and I looked up in confusion. Mama had been unwell and Sarah, Mary and Jane had come to spend a couple of days with us. It was a good opportunity for Sarah to get to know Amelia and Tom Brown, Robert's parents. We were sure that a proposal wasn't far away for Jenny.

'Hear what?' Sarah asked, teacup halfway to her mouth.

'They found Fred Duggan's body.' Jenny sat at the table with us. 'At least, they think it is,' she added, taking a biscuit from the plate on the table. It had been six weeks since Fred had gone missing.

Mama looked at me. I felt sure she was thinking the same thing I was: somebody might have got to him after all. 'Where?' I asked.

'At the bottom of Minerva's Pool,' Jenny said.

I stared at her in shock. It was a wild and beautiful place and the incongruity of a body appearing there ... it seemed a travesty to the ancient site. But it wasn't a place that was frequented often. 'Who found him?'

'Clementine Foster and her group of girls from school, you know, the naturalist club, they found the body on one of their excursions.'

My hand flew to my mouth. 'I can't imagine how horrible that must have been for poor Clem and the girls. What a terrible shock.' Then the breath left my body with the realisation that it could have been me if I was still teaching.

'An accident perhaps?' added Mama, but the grimness of her voice suggested otherwise.

'Hope he rots in hell,' said Jenny.

'Jenny!' Sarah admonished. 'That's a terrible thing to say.'

'It's true, Mama. He was an evil man. Uncle Roger and Mr Brown were worried that Fred might threaten us next, because of Aunt Hannah's suffrage work.'

'Roger would never have let anything happen,' I said. 'At least Dorothy can breathe easy now, knowing that he's never coming back.' But secretly, I hoped he would rot in hell too.

Fred Duggan was the talk of the town for days. Stories about Fred returning to the village and of when and how he'd died were plentiful. He was supposedly first sighted skulking through the village at night and then loitering around the schoolyard to get a glimpse of his children and finally around the tea room and the house where he and Dorothy had lived. But nobody knew how or when he'd died, whether it was accidental or if someone had had enough of him. Nobody wanted to imagine that anyone in the village was capable of murder, even if Fred had driven them to it.

Among the swirling talk and rumours, I received a letter from Mrs Fawcett and I shared its contents at our next society meeting.

'Mr Begg's bill has been withdrawn from Parliament,' I said after we'd taken care of all other business. Murmurs of dismay and looks of shock and disappointment rippled through the pub's upstairs meeting room, an echo of my own. It was a large audience; our supporters had now grown to over a hundred and fifty members and this evening the room held about sixty people.

Mr Jones's nod of satisfaction made me furious, but then again, although he'd been a great supporter of the local improvements, he'd stated his opposition to the fight for the vote from the very beginning.

'How far did it get?' Emily asked.

'It made the public bill committee,' I said. 'A lot further than it got last time.'

'Why was it withdrawn, then?' asked Alice.

'Let me guess – was it a filibuster?' asked James.

I nodded and remembered when Edward had told us about this particular political manoeuvre, where parliamentarians prolonged the debate so no time was left to vote on a bill or make any decision. Despite his often arrogant manner, his assessments of the political process were always insightful and eye-opening. But he hadn't been to a meeting since the attack on Marjorie.

'What's their excuse this time?' asked Mrs Scruton. 'We're half the population, for heaven's sake.'

'There are some technical reasons, which we've heard before, like the fact that women can't bear arms and defend their country, but by and large it's the attitudes of the Members of Parliament,' I said. 'They think there isn't enough support for women's suffrage by women.'

Clementine nodded sharply, her mouth in a thin line. 'That's because they haven't seen a groundswell of mass demonstrations and rallies by ordinary working women. There are thousands of us in suffrage societies but what about the millions of women who are supportive but who just haven't taken a stand? Until MPs can see the kind of overwhelming support that threatens their position in power, we won't be successful.'

'The good news is that Mrs Fawcett insists that the bill can be tabled again with new petitions from supportive Members of Parliament,' I said. 'Women already vote locally, so giving us the national vote is the next logical step. Women in New Zealand and South Australia got the vote a few years ago and haven't sent their parliaments into chaos, so that's more good reasoning for the cause.'

'But it could take years to reach the public bill committee again,' said Mrs Adams, shaking her head.

'That will give us the time we need to grow the support we need among working women,' Esther said firmly. She'd spoken to Clementine about what had happened and with the news of Fred's death and with Clementine's and my support, Esther had felt strong enough to return to our meetings.

'What we've been doing doesn't seem to be working. Perhaps it's time for a different direction,' said Clementine.

'What do you suggest?' I asked. 'We're not like men. We don't promote violence. We have to remain logical, rational and peaceful to ever gain the respect of Parliament and win their support. We're close now. We just have to endure and persevere.'

Esther nodded in agreement, but I could see that the opinions in the room were divided. Nobody knew which action would get us what we wanted, which would alienate the Parliament and the powerful men who ruled even further.

The conversation changed to more local matters after the meeting.

'The coroner says there's enough doubt about Fred's death to open an investigation,' said Mrs Scruton as we took refreshments. 'He was dead before he went in the water.' It was only after the police interviewed everyone who had seen him the night he'd disappeared and Dr Jenkins had performed a post-mortem to establish the cause of death that the coroner had delivered his determination.

'Did he fall while he was drunk and hit his head?' wondered Amelia. 'Or maybe an apoplexy?'

I shook my head, suddenly cold to think of the way Papa had died. 'Dr Jenkins has ruled out natural causes.'

Amelia's eyes widened. 'So you're saying it was an accident or murder.'

Mrs Scruton huffed loudly. 'Who knows what happened to him? All I know is that he's gone and that's a blessin' for Dorothy. He was a mean-spirited man and hardly a soul will miss him.'

'How is Dorothy managing?' I asked. She hadn't come to the meeting but neither had Marjorie since the attack.

'Fred's body's been released and she's preparin' a small funeral. She don't expect many to attend but I think she's wrong.'

'Most of the village will turn out for her,' said Amelia.

'Do you think she'd like to have the wake here?' I asked. 'I'm sure the ladies of our suffrage society would pitch in to help with the preparations and food. We'll supply drinks.'

Mrs Scruton nodded. 'I think that's a fine idea.'

'Let's gather everyone and put a plan together before they head home then,' I said, pleased we could do something tangible to help Dorothy. But my thoughts turned to Marjorie and Esther and the police investigation that would follow. How would they hold up to answering questions about that night again?

I pulled Esther aside.

'I can't talk about it again,' she said, as we walked through the field behind The Ox and Plough. 'I can't shed any more light on what happened to Fred.'

'He's gone now,' I said gently. 'And he can never harm you again.'

'I know, but until this investigation is concluded, I won't be able to rest easy.'

'What about Marjorie? Do you know how she is?'

'I saw her the other day. She's heartbroken. She and Edward are mourning the loss of their child and the last thing they need is to be dragged in to an investigation. They've already reported everything they know about Fred to the police.'

'Has she told anyone that she was raped?'

'No,' Esther said flatly.

'Of course,' I whispered. 'Let's hope the investigation is straightforward and doesn't need your testimony or Marjorie's.'

*

Everyone had their opinion as to whether Fred had died accidentally or had been murdered but it wasn't until Constable Peters came into The Ox and Plough one afternoon in September that we learnt what conclusion the police had reached.

'We've ruled against accidental death,' he told Roger and me at the bar. 'It looks like it's murder.'

'Are you sure?'

'It's been checked and double-checked. There's no doubt.'

'Do you know when it happened?' asked Roger, flicking the hand pump and pouring the constable a beer.

'Most likely the night he was ejected from here and disappeared.'

I noticed that he avoided mentioning the assaults of Marjorie and Esther. Perhaps that meant they would be spared the indignity of having to speak about that night.

'Do you have any suspects?' asked Roger.

Constable Peters shook his head. 'You know I can't tell you that. The investigation is ongoing.'

'It could have been almost anyone,' I said. Fred had upset so many people, not just those at The Ox and Plough that night.

'This will cause an uproar,' said Roger.

'I know,' said the constable. 'That's why I thought I'd come and warn you. You may need extra security until this business is concluded. I'm happy to offer my services, of course.'

'Thank you,' said Roger. 'I think you might be right.' Then he looked at me, his eyebrows raised in worry.

*

Sure enough, The Ox and Plough became a hotbed of speculation. It wasn't long before names of suspects were being thrown around.

'It was his wife, Dorothy,' I heard whispered in conversations in the bar and lounge.

'No, she isn't strong enough. It was one of her sons, fed up with the way his father beat his mother.'

I shivered. It was all gossip but I prayed none of the Duggans had had anything to do with Fred's death. They'd been through enough already.

'Don't be ridiculous,' said someone else. 'It was one of the Thompson boys he had a run-in with at The Rose and Crown that night.'

'It could have been a random act,' said Clementine, when I spoke to her and Laura about what I'd heard one evening. 'Fred was morose at the best of times, and downright belligerent when he was drunk. There were people here from all over the district and beyond for the Diamond Jubilee celebrations. Perhaps he pushed someone too far and they snapped.'

'I can't imagine anyone consciously deciding to kill another person,' said Laura, shaking her head. 'Surely it had to be accidental.'

'It's all too sordid,' agreed Mama.

'Mrs Fawcett has written to me,' announced Clementine suddenly. 'She's been voted president of the National Union now that the local suffrage societies have joined forces.'

'Oh, that's wonderful news. Nobody deserves it more,' said Laura, smiling with delight.

'She's offered me work with the Union,' Clementine continued in a rush. 'She wants me to move to London.' She looked at me, then cast her eyes down. 'But as much as I'm honoured by the offer, I have to think about it.'

Laura and I stared at Clementine in shock, speechless, and my heart squeezed.

'You have to do what's right for you,' said Mama, squeezing Clementine's hand. 'Though London's not that far for your friends to visit you, if you decide to go.'

'I know,' she said, trying to smile. 'I've had my doubts about the direction of the suffrage movement, but with the coming together of so many different women from all the societies maybe we *can* find a way forward.'

I'd always known this day would come. Clementine had worked at the school for ten years now, but London was where she could really throw herself into the suffrage movement. It had been a dream for us both, so I couldn't begrudge her this wonderful opportunity, even if I envied her freedom to choose a new life.

'You have to go, Clem – it's what you've always wanted. You'll be a wonderful asset to the Union,' I said, trying to stay positive for my friend. 'And we'd come and visit you all the time.'

We locked eyes and I saw the conflict in her face. She'd be a woman on her own, and leaving behind her friends and a school she loved teaching at. Difficult choices for anyone but perhaps made even harder when she knew I'd wanted this for myself not so long ago.

'I'd expect nothing less,' she said warmly, grasping my hand, her face flushing with relief.

39

I keep drifting back to Minerva's Pool, a site where I once contemplated the beauty and necessity of evolution with my naturalist club, now tainted with Fred's death. I thought then that we needed to evolve or else be left behind, but I never considered how much growth can also hurt.

It was late at night, and finally Roger and I had made it to bed. Sleep was just tugging me under to the warm and welcoming arms of oblivion when I was brought wide awake by a loud knock at the door.

'Who could that be?' I murmured. The knocking came again. 'I've only just got Tommy off to sleep.'

'I'll get it,' sighed Roger.

I listened to the stairs creak as he made his way down and the click of him unlocking the door.

'Hannah,' I heard him call. 'Come down, quickly.'

All drowsiness left me in an instant. My heart pounding, I jumped out of bed and threw on my dressing gown to run downstairs. I stopped dead at the sight of Esther in the hall.

'We didn't know where else to go,' she whispered desperately, holding up a slight woman, her face hidden in the hood of her cape.

'Of course, Esther, come straight into the parlour,' I said.

She nodded. Then she sagged, as though her strength had deserted her now she was in safe hands. Roger caught the woman she'd been supporting and her hood slipped.

'Marjorie,' I breathed. I looked from Marjorie's almost insensible form to Esther's pale face.

'There's much to tell you,' Esther said, tears welling in her grey eyes.

I nodded and took her arm to guide her to the parlour where Roger carefully lay Marjorie on the lounge. Marjorie moaned but her eyes remained tightly shut.

'It's all right now,' said Esther, taking Marjorie's hand. 'We're at Hannah and Roger's and you're safe.'

'Is she injured, or unwell?' I asked, placing cushions behind Marjorie's head and neck before passing a rug to Roger to place over her legs.

Esther shook her head. 'She's overcome by the effort of getting away.'

'Getting away from what?' Roger asked.

'From Dalleymoor. There's so much you don't know.'

'How about a cup of tea while you tell us, and perhaps smelling salts for Marjorie?' I suggested.

'I'll put the kettle on and bring the salts,' said Roger, sensing that Esther needed a few moments alone with me.

'I'm so sorry, Hannah,' rushed Esther, the minute Roger had closed the door behind him. 'I didn't mean to involve you like this, but Marjorie couldn't take any more and she sent word that she was leaving. I had to help her.' I took her ice-cold hands in mine, hoping to calm her.

'Esther, where's Edward?' I asked gently. 'Is he away again?' I remembered Marjorie telling me how she hated to be alone at the manor house when her husband was away on business.

'Oh, Hannah, it's such a mess ... I've been such a fool.' She stood suddenly and began to pace the room.

I selected small pieces of wood from the basket to build the fire while I waited for her to explain.

'I don't really know where to start,' she began as I stoked the embers until the flames took hold. 'But—'

Roger came into the room and passed the smelling salts to me without a word, his eyes searching mine. I shook my head slightly and stepped towards Marjorie while he took over building the fire.

I waved the smelling salts under Marjorie's nose until she drew in a deep breath and opened her eyes. She looked around in confusion for a moment but when she saw Esther and me hovering over her, she relaxed.

'We did it,' she murmured.

'We did,' said Esther, smiling for the first time.

Marjorie tried to rise.

'No, stay still for a few minutes.' I touched her shoulder gently. 'I hear it's been a difficult night.'

She looked at Esther. 'How much do they know?'

Esther shook her head. 'I haven't—' She pressed her hand to her mouth and squeezed her eyes shut for a moment.

Marjorie shuffled on the lounge until she was upright. 'What we have to say must remain in this room for now, until we work out what to do next. Do we have your promise?'

'Of course,' I said, dread swirling through my belly. From the fireplace Roger nodded silently.

Marjorie sat straight and tall, as if steeling herself. 'I left my husband tonight with Esther's help. I couldn't bear to spend another minute in his uncle's house, or anywhere near him.'

I felt the blood rush out of my face, shocked at what I was hearing. It was inconceivable. Edward and Marjorie were dedicated to each other. 'But ... I thought you were head over heels in love?' I replied, finally.

'We were, at first,' said Marjorie shakily. 'But then he started to get more and more possessive ... jealous if I spoke to people he didn't know, if I spent time with Becky or my friends. I tried to brush it off as a sign of his great love for me, but he became increasingly angry and physical in his reactions.'

'Are you saying he hurt you?' Roger stepped away from the fire, which was roaring now, his face as hard as stone.

'Not at first but ...' She nodded. 'It started with him grasping my wrist or arm too tightly, not letting me go when I pleaded with him, pushing and shoving me ... The hurtful things he'd say to me.'

I felt a flame of anger lighting me up from inside. 'How could he do that to you? You're the most kind and generous person.'

'There's more. I ... I didn't come to London with you, because Edward forbade me. I thought he was joking but he was furious when I told him I was going. He told me that there was no way I was going to be involved in the farce of taking our petitions and the women's suffrage bill to the House of Commons. He didn't want his name connected to its failure. He doesn't like failure. We fought and I pushed him and then he lost control and shoved me down the stairs. I lost the baby I was carrying.'

I sat stunned, thinking of Edward's scathing attack on our trip to London and his lies about Marjorie. She'd been alone at Dalleymoor with that brute.

'Clementine was right about him all along,' said Esther, sitting beside Marjorie and taking her hand. 'He's the epitome of charm, grace and intelligence. Nobody would ever say a bad word about him. But behind closed doors and when he thinks nobody's watching, he's a monster.'

Marjorie squeezed Esther's hand. 'Tell them. You have to tell them what he did.'

Esther shook her head. 'I can't.' She looked up at me

helplessly. 'There's so much you don't know and the worst of it is that I've lied to you.'

I started with surprise, then quickly made my expression neutral. Whatever Esther was going through was upsetting enough.

'I'll go and make the tea,' said Roger, placing a steady hand on my shoulder.

I nodded, smiling gratefully at him.

'Perhaps with a nip of whisky?' Roger asked softly, his eyebrow raised in question.

'Good idea,' I said, pressing his hand.

'I never thought to doubt my childhood friend,' said Esther, once Roger had left the room, 'but Edward's not the man I once knew. He took advantage of me. He violated me.'

'What?' I looked from Esther to Marjorie, who nodded.

'I was at Dalleymoor to visit Marjorie after the attack, but when I arrived, Edward told me she was unwell and couldn't receive visitors. We talked like old times, and he insisted I stay for dinner and that rather than use my sulky, his carriage would take me home. We drank gin before dinner and Edward opened a bottle of wine. He was so charming and witty, and it reminded me of how I'd felt about him when I was younger.' Her cheeks were bright red with shame. 'I've ... always loved him, you see.'

'But I think he knew that and played on your feelings. He used you,' said Marjorie softly.

'I was slow and groggy from all the wine and he kissed me.' She shook her head, mortification etched across her face at the memory. 'He told me he wished he'd married me and before I knew it, he'd pinned me beneath him on the dining table.' Her breath caught. 'I struggled and tried to push him away, but he only laughed and then ...' She looked at me and nodded. 'I was numb with shock and for a moment, part of me went back to that night with Fred when I realised I could do nothing to save myself from being beaten. Never once did I imagine I was in danger of being violated by Edward.' The blood had drained from her face, turning her skin pallid. 'Then I saw Marjorie standing in the doorway watching us. I wanted to die.'

'I can't believe it,' I whispered, looking at Marjorie, who nodded grimly. 'After everything you've both been through.'

Roger entered the room with a tray. I helped him set out the cups and poured tea into each while he added a nip of whisky to Marjorie's and Esther's cups. I took the bottle from his hand and poured a generous amount into my cup, my hand already shaking, and then his too. We'd need it and perhaps much more before this night was over.

There was silence as we all sipped our tea. Then Esther sat up straighter, shaking herself almost imperceptibly. 'Perhaps I'd better start from the beginning.'

She looked at Marjorie, who gave her assent, and then took a deep breath and began. 'What I told you about the night that Fred Duggan attacked us was all true, except that Edward found us first.'

'What?' exclaimed Roger.

'When he saw the state of Marjorie, and me unable to breathe with Fred squeezing my throat, he pulled Fred off me and launched himself at him. I saw it all. Edward was furious and punched Fred to the ground. Fred was out cold and Edward went to Marjorie, cradling her in his arms—'

'I told him that I was worried about the baby and he sobbed like a child,' whispered Marjorie, her blue eyes stark against her pale face.

Esther continued, 'I must have made a noise as Fred came to, because in an instant, Edward had a rock in his hand and struck Fred in the back of the head.' She shivered. 'I'll never forget the sound. It was like cracking open a pumpkin. Fred fell to the ground and didn't move again.'

Roger leant forward in his chair. 'Edward killed Fred Duggan?'

Marjorie and Esther nodded.

'I was horrified but also relieved. Fred Duggan was a brute and a coward, terrorising anyone he thought was unable to stand up to him. I was glad the terror was over.' Esther dropped her head in shame. I blinked away the tears in my eyes. She had carried this awful burden all this time.

'But it wasn't over,' said Marjorie, squeezing Esther's hand.

'What happened to Fred? How did he end up in Minerva's Pool?' asked Roger.

Esther swallowed the last of her tea and took a deep breath. 'Edward helped me from the ground. I was shaking so hard my teeth were clattering and he held me close, whispering that it was over, that all would be fine. I asked Edward what we were going to do. He told me he'd take care of it, and that it had to be our secret for the sake of Marjorie and her honour – and for mine too. I realised he was right. If any of what had happened got out ...' Her eyes locked with Marjorie's. 'Edward promised to make it up to me, that he was grateful I was such a devoted friend to his wife. I stayed with Marjorie while he took Fred's body away.'

'Do you know where he took him?' asked Roger. His face was pinched and drawn as he filled her cup with more tea and added a splash more whisky.

'He didn't say, just that he'd be back as soon as he could. I know I should have said something that night but I couldn't face what had happened and was just relieved that he had made the problem go away.'

I frowned. 'How did you end up down by the fence?'

'Marjorie was bleeding so much, and I was worried. I didn't know how long Edward would be and I wanted to get help ...' She shrugged. 'I turned my ankle in the dark and crawled to the fence but I don't remember anything else until I heard you and Clementine calling my name.'

'It must have been the shock and the pain,' said Marjorie.

Esther took Marjorie's hand. 'I'm sorry I left you alone, after everything you went through that night. You were the one who took the full brunt.'

She shook her head, as if she was trying to dislodge the memory. 'I was terrified Fred had killed you or that you were lying injured somewhere,' said Marjorie. 'When I heard Hannah and Clementine had found you alive, I cried. It was all my fault. If you hadn't come with me, you would have been safe.'

'It could have happened to any one of us,' I said soothingly. 'Fred was angry and would have taken it out on the first person he saw that night.'

'But why have you left your home and husband in the middle of the night?' asked Roger, gently. Marjorie and Esther began to look decidedly uncomfortable.

Marjorie's cup clinked jarringly on its saucer. 'I couldn't stay any longer,' she said, a defiant gleam in her eyes as she straightened and squared her shoulders. 'Edward has always been possessive and jealous, but after Fred's attack, he refused to touch me. To him I was despoiled, and when I lost the baby, he flew into such a rage. He told me I'd ruined everything and that it was all my fault for speaking up to Fred, for defending Dorothy.' She took another sip of tea to fortify herself. 'He saw no use for me then, except to take his frustration, anger and grief out on me. That's when the beatings began.'

'He beat you?' I asked. I was shaking in outrage and gripped the arm of my chair to control my fury. I was reeling. I could never have imagined that abuse was going on in such a genteel home and not only that, happening under my very nose. If it could happen there, then who else was it happening to?

'I wouldn't have believed it either, if I hadn't seen the way he treated her last time I was there and seen the terrible bruises for myself,' said Esther. 'Edward was always so devoted to her, and I never thought him capable of the things he's done. On the outside he seems the same charming, outgoing person but when that mask slips, he's cruel and brutal.'

The back of my neck tingled with recollection. Edward's reaction when the fire had started after he'd attacked Fred – it was mortification and fear. He'd lost control in public – his mask had slipped. 'He's no better than Fred,' I exclaimed. 'Nobody deserves to be treated like that. Not you, not anybody.'

'No, he's worse. Fred never pretended to be something he wasn't,' spat Marjorie with disdain. 'The final straw was the day he invited Esther to see me. He was anxious about the talk around the village that he might become a suspect in Fred's murder. He knew I would never talk, but he was worried Esther would say something. I told him that she wouldn't, but that any attempt to persuade her to remain silent could backfire. I worried he'd try to blackmail her. It was enough to provoke another beating and this time, I passed out.

'When I woke, I was in my bed and it was dark. I could barely move for the pain but I was worried about Esther. Then I made my way slowly out to the drawing room, where I heard noise coming from the dining room. And then I saw them. Esther was terrified, struggling, but I was too weak to do anything.' She hung her head, then looked up, her voice hard. 'Edward saw me in the doorway when he'd finished and he laughed. He told me that he should have married Esther after all because she had a bit of spirit in her.' She choked on her last words.

Esther squeezed Marjorie's hand. 'He thought he could shut me up, and now I have the shame of what he did to live with. When he began working in London, he led me to believe that I could expect a proposal from him, but it never came. And then when he forced himself on me, I was terrified that I'd led him on somehow, made him believe I wanted him in that way. But when I saw him taunting Marjorie with what he'd done, I knew I had him all wrong.'

I locked eyes with Roger who appeared as shocked as I felt. Marjorie and Esther were describing an entirely different man from the one we knew.

'Edward didn't kill Fred to protect me or Esther,' said Marjorie, her face flushed with disgust. 'He did it out of rage for damaging his shining reputation with the scandal that might follow, for daring to touch his wife, for ruining my looks, for putting the life of his heir, and the life he'd worked so hard for, at risk.'

'And what do you want to do now?' I asked Marjorie, still reeling.

'Just to be away from him. I would have left the night Edward violated Esther except that I could barely walk and Esther was in no state to help me. Thankfully, she had her sulky and left as soon as Edward turned his attention on me. I felt better knowing that she was out of harm's way. But Esther and I made a plan – Edward went out for urgent council business and she helped me get away when nobody would see.'

'And the police?' I asked.

They shook their heads. 'We've already lied and the scandal would ruin both of us,' said Marjorie. 'Edward can rot in his uncle's manor house; I won't be part of his manipulative schemes any longer.'

'Of course,' said Roger. 'You can stay here tonight, and tomorrow we'll work out what to do.'

'I can't stay with Becky, he'll find me there.' Marjorie was pale with fright now.

'Stay with us as long as you need,' I said. 'You'll be safe here with Mama, me and the children. And Roger's either here or next door in the pub, along with Reg and Bobby. Edward won't dare touch you here.'

Marjorie nodded nervously and clutched my hand and Roger's. 'I can't tell you how grateful I am to you both. If I'd stayed much longer, I think he would have killed me.'

40

I feel the hard resolve setting within my bones even though my nerves are humming. I am overcome with sadness and anger but determined to protect my friends. I cannot remain silent and yet I must, although the thought of Edward getting away with his crimes unpunished goes against everything I believe.

Marjorie and I were in the parlour the following day when Mama came in, looking worried. All she knew was that Marjorie had left her husband but I was certain the fading bruises on her face and arms told Mama everything she needed to know.

'Your sister's here to see you,' she said.

Marjorie was on her feet in an instant. 'Becky! What are you doing here?' She hugged her sister, who had come in behind Mama, and then drew away. 'You're shaking like a leaf.'

'What's happened, Becky?' I asked more sharply than I intended.

'Come and sit down,' Mama cooed soothingly. 'I'll make a nice pot of tea.'

'I'm so sorry,' Becky said once Mama had left the room. 'I know I wasn't supposed to come here, but I had to warn you.'

'Warn her about what?' I asked.

'Edward came to visit me this morning.' Becky wrung her hands.

Marjorie drew in a sharp breath and my heart began to beat faster.

'He waited until Jack was at work and I'd returned from taking the children to school. He forced his way into the house when I refused to let him in.'

Marjorie squeezed her sister's hand. 'He didn't hurt you, did he?'

Becky shook her head. 'No, no. He scared me more than anything.'

'What did he want, Becky?' I asked softly.

'He wants to know where you are, Marjorie. I told him I didn't know, and that I hadn't heard from you.'

'You did well,' said Marjorie, kissing Becky's cheek tenderly.

'He checked each room of the house, but he didn't believe that I hadn't seen you. Then he told me to give you a message.' She dropped her head in her hands. 'I knew there was something dangerous about him when you were courting,' she whispered. 'But you couldn't see it, you were too much in love. And once you were married, it was too late.'

Marjorie stared at her. 'But I'm free of him now,' she said. 'I'm never going back.'

Becky lifted her head, her eyes glistening with tears. 'I don't know if you'll ever be free of him if you stay here.'

'What are you talking about? What did he want?'

'He wanted me to tell you to go back to him, to return to Dalleymoor.'

'That will never happen,' Marjorie said, shaking with anger.

Becky closed her eyes as a grimace passed over her features.

'He threatened you, too, didn't he?' I asked.

Becky stared at me in surprise. 'How did you know?'

'Because that's what a bully does.'

377

'He wants me to persuade Marjorie to go home to him and he says that everything will be forgiven.'

'Or?' Marjorie straightened up, rigid.

'Otherwise, he'll ruin Jack and make us destitute.'

'No!' Marjorie stood quickly, using the arm of the lounge to support herself.

Becky was beside her in an instant, hugging her tight. 'He can't hurt us, my darling. Jack's job is secure. And I'll never let him hurt you again. Maybe you should leave for a while, go home to Yorkshire or visit Aunt Milly in London.'

Marjorie nodded, tears running down her cheeks now. 'I can't go back to him. I'll write to Aunt Milly and ask her if I can stay,' she said, her voice thick.

'Once people know who Edward really is, maybe he'll have enough sense to leave the district. Then you can come back and live a life free of him.' Becky wiped the tears from Marjorie's cheeks. 'I won't stay any longer. Send me a note when you've arranged to leave. I want to know you're safe.' She glanced at me. 'Please apologise to your mother about the tea.' She hugged Marjorie again and slipped out the front door, blending swiftly with the foot traffic on the street.

'I'll write to my aunt now,' said Marjorie, hobbling towards the table.

'Don't do anything just yet, Marjorie,' I said, my mind ticking over. My first impulse after I'd heard what Edward had done was to confront him. I'd seen many faces of violence in Ebberfield but never imagined finding one lurking behind the closed doors of Dalleymoor. I'd respected him in our business dealings and even called him a friend. He'd tricked us all into believing he was a rational, genteel man of the world who wanted to help make change alongside us. The involvement he'd had in any of our shared projects now felt tainted. It had all been a facade, and I felt deceived and betrayed, even humiliated.

But now that his true nature had been revealed, I realised it was too dangerous, not just for me and my unborn child but for my family and friends – especially Marjorie. Edward was a man of strategy and we had to make a careful plan, rather than react to his moves.

'Edward is only trying to scare you, to get you to panic,' I said, holding her hands. 'He knows where your Aunt Milly lives, yes?'

Marjorie nodded.

'He'll go there then, to find you. But while you're in this house, you're safe with me and Roger. And Roger can warn Jack about Edward's threats too – and you know what a capable man Jack is.'

*

Talk continued to swirl around the murder of Fred Duggan. In The Ox and Plough, in the tea room, the grocers and drapers. I listened but said very little, waiting for Edward's name to be dropped. Besides Becky's encounter with him, Edward hadn't been seen for days, no doubt licking his wounds and considering his options. Maybe he was also waiting to see what would happen, waiting until the police focus shifted to a new person of interest.

Esther remained safely ensconced at home with her parents and servants, announcing she was unwell, and agreeing with Roger and me that it was safer not to set foot outside the house, let alone the estate, especially after Edward had threatened Becky. Marjorie was still with us, but despite her concerns for Becky and us, had agreed not to leave the district until the police investigation was concluded.

'I heard there's a new suspect,' whispered Mrs Scruton to Amelia and me after our next suffrage meeting.

I followed her gaze to where Dorothy was talking to Clementine and Laura. Dorothy was slowly picking up the pieces after Fred's death, but until the investigation had concluded and someone was charged and convicted of Fred's murder, she'd have no rest.

'Just about everyone in town has been named by someone now,' said Amelia. 'The rumour mill is working overtime and next it will be one of us.' She was being flippant, but I rubbed my ever-growing belly as a spike of tension rushed through me.

Mrs Scruton put her hand on Amelia's arm. 'This is serious, pet. It's not gossip or hearsay.'

'What have you heard?' Amelia asked in a low voice.

'That it's Edward Partridge.'

'Really? Who told you that?' I asked, holding my breath.

'You might remember that I'm Constable Peters' godmother. It was his dear departed mother's birthday just the other day. I was placin' flowers on her grave when he arrived with flowers of his own. I ain't seen him properly for months—'

'Did Constable Peters tell you?' I asked, interrupting gently.

'That's right, pet. He's been busy with the investigation, and told me how frustratin' it's been 'cause things just ain't been addin' up. He let slip that they want to talk to Edward again, that maybe someone saw Edward where he shouldn't have been, that maybe he was somehow involved in this terrible matter. I told him it's ridiculous. Edward's a Justice of the Peace and an upstandin' citizen, loved by the community. He agreed but reminded me of the row Edward had with Fred the night he disappeared. The police want to check his whereabouts after.'

'No, he can't be involved,' said Amelia, aghast. 'After what he and Marjorie have been through. They must have it wrong.'

'That's my thinkin' too,' replied Mrs Scruton. 'It's inconceivable. Won't be long before they learn they're wrong about Edward.'

I held my tongue, my promises to Esther and Marjorie anchoring me to the spot. I understood how they felt, the incredulity at the thought that someone as beloved as Edward could be involved, but there was so much more. He was a man living in the darkness and pretending to be the bearer of light.

'Maybe it was one of the strangers who came in for the Diamond Jubilee,' said Amelia.

'Maybe they'll never find who did it.' Mrs Scruton looked across to Dorothy. 'Maybe it's a blessin' in disguise.'

I said nothing still but prayed that the truth would soon come out for the sake of my friends and my family.

I was surprised when Esther made an unexpected trip into the village the following day. We'd promised not to meet but something serious must have happened. She was pale and her eyes darted furtively around the street before she came in the door of the cottage.

'I had to come. I asked Papa to bring me. He's having a pint next door until I'm ready to go home.'

I was glad that Marjorie was upstairs helping Mama get the children down for a nap. She was already worried out of her mind about Edward.

'You have to be careful,' Esther whispered as we sat in the parlour. 'Edward is getting desperate.'

'What's happened, Esther?'

'He came to call on us this morning. Thank goodness Papa was home. Edward couldn't threaten me directly because he and Mama were there. Just looking at him made my skin crawl. I refused to talk to him. He pretended that Marjorie was at Dalleymoor but unwell and since he was in the area, had called in to ask if I would go with him to see her, to brighten her spirits. I mumbled something about being unwell myself and said I'd see her another time. As much as I wanted to place as much distance between him and me as I possibly could, I didn't dare leave the room. He went on to speak about how he appreciated the loyalty of long-standing friends and how those who didn't support his cause and betrayed that friendship would suffer the consequences.'

'Meaning what?'

Esther shrugged. 'I'm sure my parents thought he meant his position on the district council, but I know he was talking about the Duggan case. When he got up to leave, I tried to step away but he took my hands and leaned in to kiss my cheek. I was petrified, I couldn't move. Then he whispered in my ear. I don't know that I'll ever forget his words. "Remember who your friends are. A word from me, and everyone will know you're just a common slut."

'Then he shook Papa's hand and kissed Mama's cheek like we were all still the oldest friends in the world.'

I gathered her into my arms. 'I'm so sorry. He knows the longer Marjorie is gone, the less control he has over the situation. Once he finds out the police want to talk to him again—'

She sat bolt upright. 'What do you mean?'

I told her what Mrs Scruton had said.

'That makes him even more dangerous.' Esther's face was white.

I nodded. The only way forward was for them to take their power back, protect themselves by speaking up. 'Esther, you and Marjorie have to tell the police what happened to Fred Duggan. He can't hurt anyone else once he's arrested and in prison.'

Esther shook her head sharply. 'You don't understand. Edward will come for us if we say anything. I know we might be interviewed again, but our best hope is to say nothing and to stay out of his line of sight until the police have found the evidence they're looking for and charge him. But even then, there's no guarantee he'll go to prison. He has friends everywhere, in London, in high places.' She dropped her head in her hands. 'I don't know how we ever thought we could get away from him. All Marjorie and I want is to be left alone and to forget what happened.'

I sighed, feeling chastened. All anyone wanted was to live a normal life, something most of us took for granted. But life might never be normal again for Marjorie or Esther, especially if Edward remained free.

'I'm sorry, I had no right to tell you what you should do, but I hate to see what he's done to both of you. He's a monster and deserves to pay,' I said fiercely. We all had a responsibility to shine light into the shadows and show that these unspeakable acts were unacceptable.

'Not at the risk of destroying our lives and the ones we love most.' She squeezed my hand. 'We should never have involved you and Roger. I'd never forgive myself if anything happened to you or the children.'

The sound of footsteps on the landing above made her jump to her feet. 'I have to go.' She kissed my cheek. 'Just be careful. I pray that soon this will all be over.'

41

If a woman speaks up about her abuse, not only is she often dismissed or not believed, but she is tarred a loose woman, one who deserves her abuse, a woman who is out of control or has stepped out of line. It is fear that stops women from speaking up, when a man has no such compunction at all.

The news spread through the village like wildfire. Edward was officially a suspect in Fred's murder.

First it was a few murmurs that Roger and I picked up at The Ox and Plough about Edward arriving at the police station to be interviewed and not emerging for hours. But it didn't take long for those murmurs to become full-blown conversations, mostly expressing disbelief that such an upstanding member of the community and a district councillor could be in any way involved with such a crime. It made me furious that Edward had the entire community fooled into thinking he was the perfect gentleman, including me until very recently.

I worried about Marjorie's safety, though she seemed as happy as she could be in our home, keeping to herself and out of sight, refusing to open the door to anyone. I could imagine Edward's rage at not being able to get to her. We kept the children indoors and Roger and I remained vigilant about no visitors to the house. Neither of us trusted what Edward might do next.

Early one morning I stared, bleary eyed, at the papers on the office desk. I yawned, rubbing a hand over my growing belly, wishing I could go back to bed, but the accounts had to be done. My sleepiness was gone in an instant, however, as I realised there was a problem with the beer order. We had a wedding party to cater for as well as our regular customers and not enough beer. Roger was knee deep in cleaning the beer tap lines and I'd left the children asleep in Marjorie's care as Jenny had gone home for Sarah's birthday, taking Mama and Robert Brown with her in the cart. I had no choice but to visit Mr Worthington at the brewery.

'I'm going to the brewery,' I yelled to Roger as I rushed past, who was somewhere behind the bar. 'We don't have enough beer for the wedding.' I didn't wait for his reply.

I was wheeling my bicycle onto the street when a figure stepped out of the shadows, startling me. I only had enough time to register that it was Edward Partridge before he grabbed me, sending the bicycle clattering to the cobblestones, and pulled me into the alleyway.

'Where's my wife?' he demanded in a low voice, his hand across my mouth to muffle my cry of alarm.

I shook my head, trying to remain calm despite the terror flooding my body. I had never been accosted like this before, but I knew what Edward was capable of now.

'I thought you were different, had a bit of sense, but you're just like the rest of them,' he spat in my ear in disgust. He held me tight, pulling me against his body, and ran his hand over my front to rest on my belly. I gasped. 'My wife lost our child at this stage. It would be a terrible shame if the same thing happened to you.'

Panic bloomed in my chest and I began to struggle wildly.

'Now, now,' he whispered. 'Stay still. I'd hate for you to get hurt.'

I shook my head and lashed out with my free hand, clawing at his face. For a moment he let go of me and I screamed and tried to run towards the street, but he was on me again almost immediately, holding my arm in a vice-like grip. I tried to scream again but the sound never left my throat as his hand made contact with my face, hitting me so hard that my head was thrown back. I saw stars.

Somehow, I managed to wrap my arms over my belly and opened my mouth to shout but only a moan come out. Then Edward pushed me hard against the wall with a thud, one hand pressed hard over my mouth and nose, making it hard to breathe. Instinctively, I raised my knee as hard as I could and felt it connect. He doubled over in pain and groaned, releasing his hold on me.

I darted away, still dazed, but felt myself being pulled back by my skirt. 'Roger!' I screamed.

Then Edward had me by the hair, dragging me deeper into the alleyway. 'Quiet, you bitch,' he snarled.

And that was when I felt the cold, sharp edge of a blade at my throat. The faces of my precious children, my beloved Roger, my mother, sisters and friends flashed before my eyes. I thought of the child in my womb, who might never get the chance to experience life. I stopped struggling and looked into his face, a face I'd once thought handsome, now distorted by rage, fear and desperation.

'I want my wife. If she isn't back at Dalleymoor by tonight, I'll come for you or perhaps one of your beautiful little children. You have just as much to lose as I do and if you don't persuade my wife to come home and remember her place, I'll make sure you understand grief and loss, just as much as me.'

A sob broke free as the edge of the knife cut into the skin of my throat then moved over the front of my body to press against my distended belly.

'This would be just the start,' he whispered.

I saw it then – cold, pure evil – and I knew that this man would stop at nothing to get what he wanted.

I screwed my eyes shut, my thoughts chaotic. Then – thank God – I heard footsteps pounding on the flagstones, and I saw Roger rushing up behind Edward. He grabbed Edward by the shoulder, throwing him off balance and I stepped out of reach, sobbing with relief.

'How dare you touch Hannah!' Roger roared. He launched himself at Edward, full of fury and rage, and swung the first punch, delivering a glancing blow as Edward jumped back. Only then did Roger's eyes narrow as he saw the knife in Edward's hand. 'You're a coward, threatening and hurting women. Fight like a real man, with your fists.'

My back was pressed into the bricks of the far wall of the alley and I was rooted to the ground, unable to move. I wanted to see Edward beaten, to see him on the receiving end of Roger's fury, but I was terrified for Roger, too.

Edward lashed out with his blade, but Roger moved deftly away, ready for Edward's move.

'So, you're going to play dirty. You're no gentleman,' Roger spat. 'You're the lily-livered coward you've always been.'

It was enough to make Edward explode with fury and he ran at Roger, who timed his next punch perfectly to smash into Edward's face. Blood gushed from his ruined nose. He delivered a second blow to the gut while Edward was still stunned, but Edward had his knife and while he had Roger close, he slashed at him.

I cried out but it was too late. Blood bloomed on the front of Roger's shirt but he paid it no heed. He hit Edward again and again until Edward struck at him like a snake, holding him at bay with his blade.

He threw a look of pure hatred at me and at Roger. 'You'll both pay,' he hissed. Then he flung the knife at Roger, who ducked, leaving the knife to clatter to the ground, and ran past Roger and into the street.

Roger chased after him.

'Leave him!' I called.

By the time I reached the street, Roger had returned to my side. 'He's gone,' he said grimly.

'He's not worth fighting.' I put a hand on his arm, feeling limp and faint.

'Are you hurt?' Roger held me gently at arm's length, brows knitted and his face white with worry, as his eyes travelled over my body. He touched my throat and I winced.

'He held his knife to my throat,' I whispered.

'It's not deep,' he said, inspecting the wound. He held my face gently, turning it to one side. 'You'll have a bruise on your cheek tomorrow and maybe a black eye. And you have a split lip. Let's get you home to rest. I'll get a steak from Tom's shop to put on your face.'

I touched his shirt, wet with bright red blood. 'You're hurt more than I am.' I lifted his shirt up carefully and breathed out slowly. The cut was long and shallow, but against the ribs. He was going to be sore for a few days.

'Don't worry about me,' he said. 'Are you all right, my love?'

'Thank God you came when you did,' I said shakily. 'I don't know what might have happened otherwise.'

Roger enfolded me in his arms. 'He's a coward, Hannah. He was trying to scare you.'

I shook my head. I had to make him understand. 'No, Roger. He's unpredictable and dangerous. While he's free, Marjorie, Esther, their families and our own aren't safe.'

Roger was quiet for a moment. 'Then we'd better make sure he's safely behind bars, where he belongs,' he said grimly.

*

There was no time to waste. Roger and I sat in our parlour with Marjorie and Esther.

'You have to tell the police what you know,' urged Roger. 'None of you will be safe until he's in prison.'

'I'm so sorry,' said Marjorie, covering my hand with her own. 'I should never have dragged you into this mess.'

'No,' I said. 'No woman should have to go through what you have endured. Roger and I are happy to help in any way we can but it's time for Edward to be held accountable for his actions. The only way we can guarantee that happens now is for you both to tell the police about him killing Fred.'

Esther put her wine down on the side table. 'I agree, it's gone too far now. For Edward to come after us is one thing, but for him to attack you and threaten your family is another.' She took Marjorie's hand. 'We have to go to the police. We have to tell them what happened that night.'

Marjorie began to cry softly. 'I know. But I'm afraid it won't be enough, that he'll weasel his way out of it. And then we'll all be vulnerable again.'

'That won't happen,' said Roger firmly.

I grimaced. It was so like a man to think something wouldn't happen because he said it wouldn't. But there was nothing else we could do, except try.

I put my arm around Marjorie. 'If we don't try, he'll think he's got away with it and can do whatever he likes, treat others however he likes. Men like Edward who believe they have all the power need to understand they're not untouchable.'

'We have to trust in the legal system, like we trust in our council,' said Esther. 'There are processes in place to make sure the law is followed. Edward isn't the only one who has friends in high places. We'll gather all the support we need to ensure justice is served.'

Marjorie nodded slowly, blue eyes bright with tears. 'All right. We tell the police.'

*

He was arrested the following day.

'The police went out to Dalleymoor and, accordin' to Mr Carmichael, the caretaker, arrested Edward for murderin' Fred Duggan,' said Mrs Scruton. 'I can't believe they think Edward did it. It's the most preposterous thing I've heard.' I opened my mouth but she continued to speak. 'I know he had the run-in with Fred that night, the way Fred was talkin' to Marjorie.' She sipped on her tea, and I made some non-committal noise. 'I often wondered what had happened to Marjorie when we found her in the graveyard. Of course, I never said anythin' about that. A woman's virtue and reputation are judged by such things out of her control ... But if Fred was the one who beat her and Edward found out, nobody would blame him.'

'Murder is murder, Mrs Scruton,' I said. 'Whoever killed Fred Duggan should be brought to account.'

She nodded. 'Yes, of course. Dorothy was in tears when I told her. "Fred had it comin'" was all she said to me, but I'm thinkin' she's relieved the mystery of his death is bein' unravelled.' She patted my hand. 'Perhaps you could send young Bobby home to his mother so she can tell him and to make sure she's all right?'

'Of course.' Mrs Scruton was a terrible gossip, but she had a kind heart and knew how to keep a secret when it counted.

I went upstairs and found Marjorie sitting on her bed. I sat beside her and told her what had happened.

She hugged me tight. 'Thank you. I wouldn't have had the courage to do this without you, Roger and Esther.'

'You're one of the bravest women I know.'

She dabbed her cheeks with her handkerchief. 'I'm not brave. I had to do this. Edward has to pay for what he's done.'

'I'm surprised he was still out at Dalleymoor,' I said.

'I'm not. He loves Dalleymoor and everything it represents – all the wealth, power and influence that he wasn't born to … More than he ever loved me,' she said bitterly. 'And he really believes he is untouchable.'

I squeezed her hand. 'Well, he's in police custody now, and can't hurt anyone.' Edward was in Bishopdene, in a cell next to the courthouse, awaiting his indictment at the Court of Petty Sessions. But I worried about the bias of the other magistrates he worked with regularly and whether they would treat the case fairly.

'Before we gave our statement to the police, Esther and I spoke to the solicitor, Robert Sanderson. He advised us against making an accusation of rape or wife beating. Edward will face just the one charge of murder, and no one will know the extent of what he's done to us, but if murder is what sends him to prison, then so be it.'

'I'm sorry it has to be that way,' I said, swallowing the injustice. 'It's not right. The law has to change to support women in these circumstances.' I thought again of Kitty. She'd had no way to fight back but Marjorie and Esther and I did, though it was rare for a woman to succeed in court on an accusation of rape or abuse. The system and the law were weighted heavily against us as credible witnesses. 'But if it makes no difference to the outcome, your testimony of the murder will see him sent to prison for a very long time.'

'I hope so,' said Marjorie grimly. 'But our reputations will be questioned anyway. No matter what we do, neither of us will be seen the same way again.'

'I hope that's not the case. Anyone with half a brain will see you were both victims of a terrible crime that night. You're both strong women who survived and were courageous enough to tell the truth. And then you'll be free of him, free to live your life however you want.'

Marjorie nodded and sighed. 'I don't know what I'll do, but it will be worth it if we're all free of him.'

42

Murder is the worst sin of all.

Edward was charged with murder. James Duffield and Reverend Mason had been discharged from their duties and magistrates from outside the village had heard Edward's indictment.

John Duffield came to give us the news from his father. 'Nobody can believe that Edward was indicted, let alone charged,' he said. 'Papa wasn't privy to the details because he'll likely be called to help set up the Court of Assizes in Durham where the trial will be held.'

'Durham?' I asked, in surprise.

John nodded. 'Murder charges can't be heard by the Quarter Sessions Court. A judge will travel up from London to do the winter sessions and select the jury for the trial.'

'Who's eligible to be a juror? Surely not locals from the parish?'

'Well … it could be,' he said. 'Any male ratepayer. There are property qualifications. But mostly the jury is drawn from around the county, although Justices of the Peace aren't eligible.'

My stomach dropped. So there would be men on that jury who would know Edward. I prayed impartial men would be chosen, those who wanted to see real justice done. And I hoped the weight of evidence and the witness testimonies would be enough to show the truth.

Shock and consternation reverberated around the village and there was indignation from Edward's friends and colleagues on the district and parish councils.

'They've got it all wrong,' said Mr Bilberry in the lounge of The Ox and Plough as he waited with others for the auction of a deceased estate to begin. He was a prominent farmer who was on the council with Edward. 'Partridge is as good a man as you'll ever find.'

'He has a good defence barrister,' said Mr Franks. 'If the judge doesn't throw it out of court, then he'll get him out of it easily. It's preposterous that a man of his standin' can be accused of murdering a common brickmaker.'

My blood boiled. I wanted to tell them that the law applied to all, not just the poor or defenceless, and that even men of standing could be brutes. But I conserved my strength for the fight ahead. Just that morning I'd received a summons myself to appear in court as a character witness in the trial and I was going to do all I could to support my friends in the case against Edward.

*

A couple of days later, Marjorie found Esther and me in the kitchen of The Ox and Plough. Esther had come to visit me, while her father was at the tailor, to discuss the upcoming suffrage society meeting.

'What's wrong, Marjorie? You look very concerned,' I said. I was making Mama's famous pies. She'd been tired the last few weeks and I'd realised with a shock that she was getting old. The years without Papa had been hard on her.

Marjorie shook her head. 'I've just been to see Constable Peters. The police wanted to follow up on some background on Edward's past and his work in London before the trial.'

'Sit down.' I gestured to the table where Esther sat with a cup of tea and wiped my hands on my apron.

'Are you all right?' asked Esther, pouring a cup for Marjorie.

'I don't know. He asked about Edward's financial dealings in London and abroad, but I couldn't tell him anything. Edward was always so secretive about what he does in London or about his life before we married.' She hesitated. 'He also wanted to know about Philip Usher's will and about Dalleymoor.'

'Why do you think they want to know that?'

'I have no idea.'

Esther put her teacup down. 'Funny you should say that. Papa and Edward's uncle were close, as you know. I remember Papa talking to my mother about a letter he received from Philip. Edward was having problems with his business, a deal had gone bad – some kind of miscalculation on the foreign markets – and it had affected not just Edward's clients but some of Philip's too. Edward wanted his uncle to bail him out, and Philip had written to my father to ask his advice.'

Marjorie sat up. 'After Edward and I married, I gave him some of my inheritance to tide him over until a financial deal came through. 'Philip died not long after and Edward inherited Dalleymoor. As far as I knew, his business was doing well.'

'But why do the police want to know about his London dealings? What could it have to do with Fred's murder?' I asked.

They shook their heads, as puzzled as I was.

'Let's ask Papa about it when he comes to collect me,' said Esther.

We were still in the kitchen when Roger came in with Esther's father.

'I've come to take my daughter home,' said Mr Burrows, smiling brightly at Esther.

'Please stay and have a cup of tea and one of Mama's famous pies before you go,' I said, pulling out a chair for him.

'All right. I can't miss the chance to have the best pies in the village.'

'Join us, Roger. It's been too long since we've seen Mr Burrows,' I said with a look that made him agree instantly.

After some small talk, the conversation inevitably moved to Edward's trial.

'Papa, I remember you telling me you received a letter some time ago from Philip Usher about Edward's business being in trouble,' said Esther. 'Whatever happened with that?'

Mr Burrows nodded. 'Philip asked for advice about what to do with young Edward. I thought long and hard about it. Edward was his family after all, but he'd compromised himself and Philip's reputation. Whether he deliberately duped his clients or whether he made a series of poor judgements and decisions, I don't know. But I advised Philip not to give Edward the money or the boy would never learn to take responsibility for his actions or how to manage his business – or the estate, which Philip was leaving to him.'

'And did he listen?' I asked.

'Philip wrote back to tell me he'd had a terrible row with Edward, who'd married instead.' He smiled apologetically at Marjorie. 'He'd threatened to disinherit him if he didn't own up to the mistakes he'd made and recompense his clients. It meant Edward would end up with nothing and his business would be finished but it was the only way to teach him. The boy was furious, said some awful things to his uncle, and stormed out. Philip was heartbroken and wondered if he'd coddled the boy too much over the years ... And that was the last letter I received from him. Philip was dead a week later, found in his bed by his housekeeper. The shock must have been too much for him.'

'Whatever happened to those clients?' asked Marjorie quietly.

'From what I understand, the whole matter went quiet. Any evidence of wrongdoing disappeared, some of the clients lost part of their fortunes, none the wiser that Edward had any involvement in their losses. And then Edward inherited Dalleymoor and his business and filled the position Philip had left on the sanitary board. Poor Kathy, Edward's mother, was left with next to nothing, only a small stipend. I couldn't believe that Philip hadn't left her more or that Edward didn't provide for her more generously.'

'Edward never let me visit his mother. He told me she thought I wasn't good enough for her son,' Marjorie said.

'I don't see why she would,' said Mr Burrows. 'Kathy has never had any airs or graces. Edward grew up here in the village but I know she worried about him when he went to London. He didn't come home to see her for years.'

'Was there anything suspicious about Philip's death?' asked Roger. We all turned to look at him, aghast.

'You think Edward had something to do with his uncle's death?' I asked.

Roger shrugged. 'He was always ambitious, and we know what he's capable of, especially when he's cornered.'

Mr Burrows shook his head sadly. 'I admit there was a time when I wondered, but then I saw him at Philip's funeral in London. He was distraught and I admonished myself for being cruel just because I didn't like the boy.'

'We'll never know,' I said, shifting uncomfortably. I couldn't voice the worry that remained: if Edward Partridge had got away with defrauding people in London and had possibly even played a role in his uncle's death, what were the chances he'd escape justice for Fred's murder?

Later that evening, after Roger had closed the pub and I'd finished up in the kitchen and banked the fire for the night, I put my arms around him and rested my head on his chest.

'Another day,' I said with a sigh.

'You must be tired,' he murmured into my hair. 'You didn't need to stay.'

'How else do I get to see you these days?'

'We're starting to get ahead.' He kissed the top of my head. 'Soon you won't have to work as much.'

'I know, my darling. And I don't mind working hard, I just miss you.' I reached up to kiss him.

He pulled me to him, his hands resting on my lower back, but my belly prevented us from fitting together as we used to. 'Remember the days when we did just this after closing?'

'I remember,' I said softly. 'But these days we have a nice comfortable bed. So, let's continue there, shall we?'

'Where's the romance in that?' he replied with a grin.

Then the baby kicked me hard. I put his hand on my belly and watched his face transform to pure joy and amazement.

'Baby says let's go home.'

He nodded. 'I'll be happy when this business with Edward is over. If anything had happened to you or the children …'

I touched his cheek, rough with stubble. 'But it didn't.' The sense of disquiet I'd experienced with Mr Burrows' visit swirled around me once more. 'But what if he escapes the charge and prison? He has a good barrister and powerful friends. And I'm worried about the jury. It reminds me of Parliament and the House of Commons, powerful men closing ranks, keeping women out. He could make our lives a living hell, make us a laughing stock and nobody would want to come to The Ox and Plough.' I laughed a little bitterly. 'Just what Mr Franks has wanted all these years, for us to lose our reputation. And then there's our suffrage society. Everything we've worked so hard for will come to nothing. Who will want to support us? Who will believe anything we say?'

He took my hand and kissed it gently. 'One day at a time, my love. And he won't get away with it, Hannah, no amount of influence or money can help him with this. The case is iron-clad – there are three witnesses, remember?'

I looked into his face, etched with weariness and something else, perhaps fear. 'I hope you're right.'

*

There was a sense of freedom and joy at the next suffrage meeting a couple of days later. Dorothy and Marjorie had returned and I wondered if Dorothy would bear Marjorie any ill will for the role Edward had played in her husband's death. But I needn't have worried. Dorothy came to Marjorie immediately, hugging her tight.

'I'm sorry for all of it. I don't want what our husbands did to come between us. Anythin' I can do to help you through this trial and after … I know how it is to be alone but I've had the support of the wonderful ladies of this group and no matter what, you will too.'

'Thank you, dear Dorothy. We're both fortunate,' Marjorie said, smiling through the tears.

'We missed you,' said Alice, who was sitting next to Emily Duffield. She came to every meeting with Elizabeth, insisting that her husband look after their sleeping baby while they were away. 'Come and sit next to us. We've just heard about a potential purchase of land within the district by a new coal company and we're going to discuss how that might affect tenants who've farmed here for generations.

Now Clementine is about to tell us about the launch of the National Union.'

Marjorie smiled and nodded, clearly happy to be back among friends. 'I've missed you too.'

Clementine spoke about how the focus of the Union would now move to promoting the suffrage movement in the rural districts and increasing membership there. She kept her job offer quiet, though. She had told me privately that she had accepted the position, but wanted to announce her departure after the trial.

Afterwards, she joined Esther and me as we tidied the room.

'How did you go with the solicitor?' asked Clementine, as Esther helped her move a table.

'The police prosecutor will be taking the murder charge to trial. We discussed adding rape to the charges again but decided it will muddy the waters and we may not get a conviction.' Esther had told Clementine everything. Besides Robert Sanderson, the solicitor, Clem, Marjorie, Roger and I were the only ones who knew her secret.

Clementine dropped the table and shook her head in disbelief. 'It's disgusting that you have to remain silent about what he did to you. Fred was a rapist too and I think he got what he deserved.'

'We have to, Clem,' said Esther. 'If we're going to get him on anything, it's murder. There's clear evidence and motive for Fred's death, especially with Harry Thompson confirming Edward was near the graveyard at the time, but with the rape, it's the word of two women against a respected man – and the jury are all men. We'll claim that Edward beat Marjorie and threatened me with physical violence to keep us silent but even with Hannah's testimony of Edward's attack on her, they still might not understand or be sympathetic, especially if they know Edward. Nobody will believe he'd rape someone ... someone like me. But commit murder after his pregnant wife was beaten, that *is* believable.'

'But my God, Esther! It's so very wrong!' Clementine, slapped the table in frustration. 'We should be shouting about it from the rooftops.'

Esther nodded, her face crumpling, tears slipping down her cheeks. 'It is, but we have to fight with what we have. One day it will be different.

Clementine held her tight. 'One day. I'll be fighting by your side until then.'

'And we're all coming to Durham with you,' I said. 'Clem, Laura, Alice, Mrs Scruton. We've rallied our supporters here in the village and we'll be there every step of the way when you're in court. Just be brave, like I know you are. We won't give up without a fight.'

43

One day we'll have the law behind us to give women
the protection they need. But now we fight to protect
ourselves in the courtroom and we continue our fight
in Parliament to gain the power to protect ourselves.
We need the vote.

The day of the trial had arrived. We'd travelled to Durham
by train and as we made our way on the omnibus to the
Court of Assizes situated at Old Elvet, I was reminded what a
beautiful city it was. The court was impressive, far larger than
our local courthouse, and we were ushered into a courtroom
while Esther and Marjorie waited in the witness room. The
tiered public viewing area was already filling up, locals from
the city and our village looking forward to the drama ahead
and the salacious details that would come out. Dorothy and
Bobby Duggan had decided not to come to the trial, but I
wondered how they were feeling. Constable Peters would give
them the verdict after.

The jury sat to one side, twelve men from the county. As
Clementine, Laura and I sat, I took in their faces. Five of the
men I didn't know, but the rest were men from our district
and parish: Dr Taylor; Mr Jones; Mr Bilberry; John Duffield;
Tom Brown; Mr Yule, the publican of The Hare's Foot ...
and Mr Franks. My blood ran cold.

'We have three definite supporters and at least two who
are most likely not,' I whispered to Clem and Laura. 'Then

two I'm not sure about and five unknowns. I don't know how Esther and Marjorie will tell their stories with that many of the jury being men from the district.' But they had no choice, and if they could do it, then so could I.

'Not only that, many of them know Edward,' said Laura. 'How will they get a fair or reasonable judgement?'

'They have to be strong,' said Clementine. 'I told Esther to look at us when she answers the defence barrister's questions. We'll give her the strength she needs to hold her nerve.'

'Look,' muttered Laura, 'here he comes.'

Edward Partridge entered the dock dressed immaculately as usual, walking with the subtle swagger of a confident man used to being in charge, his head held high. I couldn't help but shudder.

Marjorie was called to the stand, where she recounted the events of that night as she remembered them, answering the prosecutor's questions. The room became silent as she spoke about the attack by Fred Duggan, about her beating and rape in the graveyard.

'Dr Jenkins did all he could for me but even with bedrest, I lost my baby a few weeks later,' said Marjorie, blotting her eyes with her handkerchief.

'And was your husband in the graveyard the night of the attack?' asked the prosecutor.

'He was,' said Marjorie. The murmuring rose in the room: shock, surprise and grim acceptance swirling through the crowd. 'He saw what Fred Duggan had done to me and Edward hit him with a rock to the head and Fred fell and didn't move again.'

The courtroom was abuzz with the implications of Marjorie's testimony before the defence barrister stepped up to cross-examine.

'You say your husband was there that night, Mrs Partridge, but if you were as injured as you say you were, drifting in and out of consciousness, how can you be sure?'

'Because he cradled me in his arms and when I told him that I was worried about the baby, he sobbed like a child. I'd never seen him cry like that, before or since.'

The barrister continued to try to discredit Marjorie and what she had seen, implying she'd put herself in harm's way by being out late at night and at the whim of men, especially Fred, who was under the influence of drink. He posited instead that together with Esther, she had killed Fred in an act of revenge for his drunken attentions, and that it was ludicrous to expect the court to believe her lies that it was her husband who had killed him.

'How ridiculous,' I muttered, outraged. I knew this day would be hard to witness, but the audacity of the barrister's theory was breathtaking.

'All women are whores and liars, remember, ruled solely by our emotions,' whispered Clementine bitterly.

Despite the brutal line of questioning, Marjorie did not break and my heart swelled for her.

Then Esther took the stand. Her testimony as a respected parish councillor and member of an esteemed local family could send Edward to prison, but it could also ruin her reputation. There was so much at stake.

In a clear, unwavering voice, Esther gave her account of what had happened that night. I only hoped I could be as calm and strong as Esther and Marjorie when it was my turn to take the stand.

'So you say that Edward Partridge saved you from being choked by Fred Duggan,' asked the prosecutor.

'Yes,' said Esther. 'Then I watched him beat Fred Duggan until he fell senseless.'

'You saw Edward Partridge hit Fred Duggan with a rock, which killed him.'

'Yes. Fred never moved again after that.'

'What did Mr Partridge do then?'

'He asked me to stay with his wife while he moved Fred's body.'

'He left his beaten and bloodied wife to dispose of Mr Duggan's body. Surely that's an act of a guilty man. Did he tell you where he was going?'

'No. But Marjorie and I were found not long after.'

'So he didn't have much time to hide Fred Duggan's body.'

'No, I don't think so.'

The defence barrister rose to cross-examine Esther. 'Mr Partridge claims that he was visiting his mother at her house at the time of the attack on you and Mrs Partridge. Isn't it true, in fact, that you and Mrs Partridge conspired together to lure Mr Duggan into the graveyard and kill him for his attentions to Mrs Partridge.'

'No. Mr Duggan attacked us. He wanted to prove his power and authority over us. He wanted revenge over our defence of and friendship with his wife, because we're suffragists. I'm thankful that Edward Partridge arrived before Fred Duggan could choke me to death but I have to tell the truth about his murder of Fred Duggan.'

The barrister paused a moment, his eyebrows raised at Esther's firm denial. 'Well then, why did it take you and Mrs Partridge so long to come forward with "the truth", as you say? Surely if it happened as you say it did, you would have told Constable Peters, Dr Jenkins, the magistrate, or any other member of the police, that very night or the next morning.'

Esther glanced at us briefly before answering. 'Because we were afraid.'

'Afraid of what?'

'Edward Partridge threatened both of us. He beat his wife to keep her silent and threatened physical harm to me and said that he'd ruin my life and my family's life if I said anything.'

There was a ripple of noise through the court at this.

But the barrister's face was unreadable. 'I suggest instead that Mr Partridge chastised his wife because he discovered that she was a participant in the murder of Mr Duggan. And as to any threat against you, it was of a devoted husband trying to protect his wife's reputation. There's no crime there. Instead, both you and Mrs Partridge colluded to blame Mr Partridge to hide your own crimes.'

'That's not true,' said Esther evenly.

'I have no further questions,' said the defence barrister.

I clenched my fists to contain my outrage over the defence barrister's circular arguments, designed to complicate and confuse, to conceal the truth. Would the jury be deceived, persuaded by his clever words? Clementine put her trembling hand over my closed fist, clearly containing her fury as well.

Harry Thompson took the stand next, testifying that he spotted Edward outside the graveyard an hour after leaving The Ox and Plough. Next Constable Peters, Dr Jenkins, some of the visitors to our Diamond Jubilee who swore they saw nothing unusual that night, and witnesses who vouched for Edward's upstanding character all took the stand. It was a long and draining day but we were determined to stay until the end, for Esther and Marjorie.

'The defence barrister is good,' said Laura, heaving a sigh, as we left the room. We were meeting Esther and Marjorie outside.

'Money will buy you the best,' said Clementine.

'But did you notice that Edward's mother wasn't there?' I asked. 'I expected her to be a witness for him.'

'Maybe she refused to lie for him,' said Laura.

'More like he threatened her to keep quiet, like he did with you and Esther,' said Clementine.

I nodded with a clenched jaw. 'His barrister might be good, but we have to hold our course. Standing up and speaking the truth in this courtroom is the only way we can protect ourselves and take back our power,' I said, feeling myself rise an inch taller. After watching the courtroom ordeal, I was nervous about delivering my testimony the following day, but I refused to be silenced.

*

As I took the witness stand the next morning, my heart was thumping.

'You attended Mrs Partridge after she was attacked by Mr Duggan?' began the prosecutor.

'Yes,' I said. 'I was searching for Mrs Partridge and Miss Burrows with Constable Peters, Mrs Scruton and Miss Foster. Miss Foster and I found them in the graveyard.' I was facing the jury but didn't dare to look at them. I didn't want to be distracted by the derision that I knew would be on Mr Franks' face or the sympathy on John Duffield's. I had to focus on what I was saying.

'What state were Mrs Partridge and Miss Burrows in when you found them?'

'They were both injured and unable to walk on their own.'

'Were they capable of moving an unconscious or dead man?'

'No. Mrs Partridge had a broken leg and Miss Burrows had a sprained ankle, among other injuries they'd sustained. They needed help to be brought back to The Ox and Plough, where Dr Jenkins tended to Mrs Partridge.'

The prosecutor nodded. 'Did you see Fred Duggan or Edward Partridge in the graveyard?'

'No. Miss Foster and I searched the graveyard but found nobody else there.'

I then told the court how Marjorie had left her husband and come to Roger and me in the middle of the night with Esther. It was then that we learnt that Edward had killed Fred Duggan the night of the attack and had been beating his wife and coercing both Marjorie and Esther to remain silent about what had happened. But it felt wrong to make no mention of how Edward had raped Esther. I *was* under oath and I so wanted the court to know the kind of man he really was, but I understood that speaking up about it wouldn't help the case against him and would only harm Esther.

'How did Mr Partridge threaten you?'

My eyes searched the room for Roger and my heart leapt when my gaze locked on to his, his smile and nod reassuring. 'He said he'd hate to see me end up like his wife and—' I rested my hands over my belly, '—lose this baby I'm carrying.'

A murmur of outrage rose through the crowd.

'In fact, Mr Partridge ambushed you in an alley, assaulted you and attacked you with a knife.'

'Yes. He punched and restrained me, and put a knife to my throat and over my belly.' I pulled down the collar of my blouse to show the just-healed scar of the cut at my throat. 'Then he threatened the lives of my baby and my children if Mrs Partridge didn't return home to him.'

The noise in the room grew louder.

'Could the court please note the injury to Mrs Rainforth and the knife used in the attack?' asked the prosecutor. The judge nodded and I noticed the court clerk writing in his book. 'Now, can you tell the court what happened?'

I nodded and recounted the events of that morning. 'That's when Mrs Partridge and Miss Burrows decided that the risk to their friends and family was too great and they went to the police with the truth of what had happened.'

'In your opinion, is Edward Partridge a dangerous man?'

I took a deep breath to steady my nerves. I was putting everything on the line and if we lost the case, I knew Edward would try to destroy me and my family. But if I didn't, the cost was too great – to Marjorie, to Esther, Dorothy, Kitty, to myself, and to any other woman who had suffered violence ... even to despicable Fred Duggan. I looked around the courtroom and found Roger's and Clem's faces and the women of the suffrage society. I could do this with them behind me. 'After what I've experienced, yes. He killed a man and he'll clearly do anything to hide the truth and his crimes.'

When it came time for the defence barrister to ask his questions, a spike of anxiety shot through my stomach.

'I put it to you,' he said, 'that Miss Burrows has been scheming to take her revenge on Mr Partridge ever since he returned to the district and married Marjorie Partridge, his wife.'

'No, that's not true,' I answered.

'Furthermore,' he continued, 'when Mr Partridge deemed it fit to reprimand his wife for her friendship with inappropriate people and women with dangerous ideas, Miss Burrows brainwashed Mrs Partridge into joining her scheme against her husband, which you were privy to.'

I nearly laughed out loud at his ludicrous suggestion, but Clementine's snort from across the room stopped me. We, the women of the local suffrage society, were dangerous, brainwashing and inappropriate for genteel company? It was disappointing for a man of the law to be pushing such an antiquated view. I glanced up at the jury. Tom Brown, John Duffield and Dr Taylor had expressions of distress and concern on their faces, two of the unknown men seemed sympathetic, three stared stonily ahead. Mr Bilberry was frowning in puzzlement, Mr Yule, the publican of The Hare's Foot appeared deep in thought, but the cold, aloof expression from Mr Jones and the sneer of Mr Franks reminded me that it was exactly this attitude that could influence the outcome of this trial.

'That's ridiculous,' I said. 'Edward Partridge presents himself as a charming, obliging man of the world but in fact he is a controlling, manipulative fraud who expects to get his own way, and when he doesn't, he exploits the vulnerabilities of others or threatens them to get what he wants. He hides behind the veneer of respectability when his behaviour is anything but.' I looked at Edward, who returned my stare with a hard and stony glare. I flinched when I saw his lip curl with a cold smile, wondering what more he would do to me if he was free from the scrutiny of others.

My attention was brought back to the barrister who was red in the face. 'That's enough, Mrs Rainforth,' he said. 'It's "new women" like you and your suffrage society who try to tear men down and diminish their position in their own homes and in society. You may refuse to defer to the superiority of your husbands, fathers, uncles and brothers but you do a great disservice to your own kind and to the many women who do understand the importance of their place within the home.'

'Hear, hear,' said the men across the courtroom, nodding in agreement. I heard the protests of women before the sound of the crowd faded and I stared at the man, dumbfounded. I'd heard all sorts of arguments against our suffrage movement, endured insults and verbal abuse, but never with language or arguments like this that I knew would be wholeheartedly accepted and welcomed by many of the men on the jury. The barrister used persuasion to frighten the men into believing that if they allowed women any agency, men would lose control and their power. If it were me who was on trial – or Marjorie or Esther – we'd be convicted before the actual facts of the case had even been heard.

I realised that this was how powerful men spoke. They used clever rhetoric to get what they needed, here in court and in Parliament. Now I could understand how Mr Begg's bill and our petition never stood a chance. Our efforts had been dashed behind the closed doors of Parliament, where men were fed fear. They were terrified that by sharing the decision-making process, women would take their power away from them. They did not understand us at all. It was all so clear to me now. If we were ever going to get what we wanted in Parliament, we, the suffragists, had to sharpen our arguments like steel to become even more convincing and persuasive, to have an answer for every question and every attitude that might be thrown at us. It was a war of words and we needed to win it.

'Mr Partridge is the one on trial here, not the good women of Ebberfield,' interjected the prosecuting barrister. 'This is a man who threatened a woman, her unborn baby and her children.'

'No further questions,' said the defence barrister with a smirk of satisfaction. My heart dropped. He'd caught me and, with his arguments, swayed the jury.

The rest of the proceedings followed in a blur.

'I don't know how this will go,' whispered Esther nervously, picking at her sleeve.

'They can besmirch us all they like but nobody can prove that Edward wasn't there that night,' I whispered, stilling her hand. 'Harry Thompson testified and Edward's mother isn't here. She's the only one who can say that he was at her house at the time of Fred's death.'

Clementine took Esther's other hand and squeezed it in encouragement. 'The defence is desperate. They have no evidence to blame visitors to the Jubilee celebrations and had to resort to making up stories about you and Marjorie. They have no case.'

'I can accept the slurs to my reputation if he ends up in prison, but if not, it will all be for nothing.' Esther turned her gaunt face to me. 'My life will be ruined.'

Finally, all the evidence had been presented and the witnesses' testimonies examined. The jurors withdrew to the jury room to discuss the verdict. Marjorie and Esther held hands, their knuckles white. I was glad to have the strength and support of Roger beside me.

'You've done all you can,' said Roger, kissing my hand.

'I know. I hope it's enough.'

*

When the jurors returned to their seats sometime later, one remained standing.

Roger took my hand.

'Have the members of the jury reached a verdict?' asked the judge.

'On the charge of murder, we find the accused, Mr Edward Partridge, not guilty,' said the unknown juror.

The courtroom erupted. It was as if my heart had stopped, then ice flooded my veins, and I gripped Roger's hand tight. All around us was the stamping of feet and howls of approval from the men, and cries of protest and horrified gasps from the women.

'No!' Marjorie moaned. I turned to see her huddled on the bench, her hands over her face. Beside her, Esther was deathly still and white, staring at the floor.

In a daze I flicked my gaze to Edward, triumphant and smiling broadly, as if the verdict had come as no surprise to him.

I couldn't believe it. The men of our county had rejected us. Nothing had changed. Edward's lies, deceit and manipulation had conquered over the truth. I felt my chest constrict. We'd lost – lost everything: our safety, our reputations; the suffrage society, The Ox and Plough … Suddenly I couldn't breathe.

But then Roger shook me, and I realised he'd been saying my name. I looked up and he pointed to the judge, who was banging his gavel to bring order to the court, so the juror could be heard.

When all was quiet, the juror continued. '… Instead, we find him guilty of the charge of manslaughter.'

The courtroom erupted again, and I turned to Roger in confusion. 'Manslaughter?'

'Edward killed Fred … but it wasn't premeditated,' said Roger slowly, as much in shock as I was.

I heaved in a deep breath. The jury had given us justice the only way they could. There was support for us after all. Even so, I didn't know how to feel – devastated that the verdict didn't reflect what such a man deserved or grateful that he was convicted at all. Perhaps the killing wasn't premeditated, but the beatings Marjorie endured and the violent rape of Esther were.

'Will he go to prison?' asked Marjorie, her eyes wide with shock.

I looked once more at Edward. The triumph had faded from his face and his mouth was a hard, thin line of fury.

'It's up to the judge now,' said Esther, gripping Marjorie's hands.

'Quiet in the courtroom!' yelled the judge, banging his gavel once again. 'In the sentencing of this man, I must consider all that has been presented in this case.' A hush descended over the room and the minutes seemed to stretch as we waited for him to deliberate.

'It is my decision that Mr Edward Partridge be sentenced to five years imprisonment, to commence immediately at Durham Prison.'

'This is a travesty!' howled Edward, his eyes bulging as he rushed towards the judge. Officers of the court and members of the police grabbed him before he reached the bench, and he struggled against them, yelling, kicking and scratching.

As he was dragged from the room he looked over to where Marjorie and Esther sat, his face contorted with rage. Then his gaze met mine and I shivered as the full force of his hatred hit me like an oncoming train.

*

Finally outside the courtroom, Esther, Marjorie, Clementine and I stood in a huddle at the top of the stone steps, breathing in the fresh air.

'We did it,' said Marjorie. 'I can't believe it, but he's gone.' Her smile was jubilant. 'Esther and I are so grateful, Hannah, for everything you did on the stand.' I was enfolded in a tight embrace.

'Five years,' said Clementine. 'It should be double for what he did, but you can rest easy for a while now, my friends.'

'He's got some of what he deserves, at least,' said Esther, her arms around us all. 'I'm so proud of what we did here.'

'Me too,' I whispered. 'More importantly, you're free,' I whispered. 'We're all free.'

44

My eyes have been opened to how men make decisions
behind the closed doors of Parliament. I see now how
they exert and retain their power over others. We can use
their tools, such persuasive arguments against their own
to further the suffrage cause.

'Edward's asked to see me but I won't go,' said Marjorie one afternoon as she helped me make tea in the kitchen. She'd been staying with Becky since the trial, no longer in fear for her life. 'But I've been to see his mother.'

'How did that go?'

'I was worried she wouldn't want to talk to me but she was glad I came. Edward had been blaming all sorts of things on me: for not visiting her; not helping her with the family ... But when he asked her to lie for him, she refused, and was worried about what other lies he might have told. I told her everything, how I'd adored him in the beginning, how I'd wanted to be part of his family, the controlling and manipulation that got worse over time, then the cruelty and the beatings ...' She blinked tears away. 'She'd always suspected there was a darker side to him but he shut her out of his life before she could recognise what he'd become.'

I squeezed her arm. 'I'm so sorry, Marjorie.'

She smiled sadly. 'It's not the way it was supposed to be. We were so in love ... at least I thought we were.' Placing the teapot on the kitchen table, she shrugged. 'I'm not sure what I'll do now. I've asked Edward's mother to move into Dalleymoor with his younger brother and sisters. She assures me that Edward's brother can help her run the estate.'

'And you? You have the chance to begin a new life.'

'I think I'll spend some time with my Aunt Milly in London. Staying here is no good for me. I need to get away for a while. I'm sorry I won't be here for your Christmas party.'

I hugged her tight. 'We'll miss you.'

'And I'll miss you all. I wouldn't have got through this time without you and Roger and Esther and Clem. How is Esther? I heard from Becky that she's campaigning for the district council this time.'

I sat heavily at the table. Standing for any length of time made my legs ache. I was sure I hadn't been this big with the other two pregnancies and a pang of panic rushed through me. I hoped I wasn't carrying twins.

'Mrs Burrows insisted it was the only way to push through the unkind chatter after the trial.'

'She knows a thing or two, Mrs Burrows,' Marjorie said, pouring the tea. 'I've been called all sorts of nasty names, mainly by men who are friends of Edward's, but by some women too. They should know better, but maybe they can't understand what I've been through, or don't want to call out the violence in their own marriages.'

'I'm so sorry you had to go through this,' I said softly.

'That's why it's easier to go somewhere nobody knows me or knows about the trial,' she said. 'But I admire Esther for dealing with the talk directly.'

'You're both so courageous. I think you'll have inspired many other women to stand up and speak out too, you watch. Though it might not feel like it now,' I said.

'I couldn't stay silent any longer, not when it affected my family and dearest friends. But Esther has such strong connections in this village. It can't be easy for her.'

'That's why it's so important for her to keep campaigning, to keep her busy and to prove that she has nothing to be ashamed of, but even more than that – that she belongs there. And when she's not campaigning, she's focusing on her scientific studies and the engineering projects with her father. Both her parents are so supportive.'

Marjorie toyed with the handle of her teacup. 'I was so lucky. She was the one who fought for me that night. She put herself in danger trying to get Fred away from me. It could have been so much worse – I think I owe her my life. Esther is a true hero and that's how people should see her. She'll fight for the people of this village and for what's right. There's no better person to be a district councillor.'

I nodded. 'Make sure you tell her that. We can all see it, but I don't know that she can.'

*

By nightfall on Christmas Eve, the pub was full to overflowing. Men were cheek to jowl in the main bar, Roger, Reg and Bobby all behind the bar. Both lounges were filled to capacity; downstairs, the sounds of lively fiddle, accordion and flute playing popular and folk tunes kept the audience captivated, while upstairs, the magic show had adults and children riveted. In one meeting room, where an ornate Christmas tree had been erected, Christmas carols were played on the piano for a singalong and in the other, games had been set up. Jenny, Polly and I flitted between the rooms, serving food and drinks, and making sure all was running smoothly.

'Hannah!'

I smiled to see Clementine, Esther, Laura, Emily and Alice together.

'We haven't seen you all night,' said Esther, her cheeks rosy from the heat of the room.

'It's been busy,' I said.

'You look tired,' said Emily, frowning. She'd recently had her second child and knew what I was going through. 'I have to get home soon to the baby, but come and sit with us for a few minutes.'

I wished I could sit with them and enjoy the evening, but I shook my head. 'I can't, too much to do. I still have food to get out, pies in the oven—'

Clementine took my arm. 'We'll come and help you in the kitchen while you take the weight off your feet and have a cup of tea.'

'You don't have to do that,' I said.

'No, come on,' said Laura. 'You're nearly seven months pregnant and you haven't stopped all day.'

I was ushered back to the kitchen, where I directed the action from my comfortable perch at the kitchen table, my feet elevated on a cushion and cup of tea in hand.

'It's going well out there,' said Laura, pulling pies out of the oven. Everything had been done and Emily and Alice had gone home to their small children. 'You and Roger definitely have the best Christmas party in the village. Your father would be proud. William was an extraordinary man, he had a special ability to bring people together, make them feel comfortable and at home, just as you and Roger do now.'

Tears welled in my eyes. 'Do you really think so?'

'You're just like him. I know you always wanted to teach, but I could never imagine anyone but you and Roger running this pub. I see why Will wanted you to take over from him.'

I smiled wistfully. Yes, Papa would be proud. I wondered if he was looking down on us now and smiling. 'Do you know, it's been seven years since the first time I met you and Benjamin,' I said. 'The very first Christmas I was here, after Papa bought The Ox and Plough.'

'I remember that,' she said.

'I'll miss this place when I'm gone,' said Clementine softly. All eyes were on her in an instant.

I reached for her hand. I didn't want her to go, but I understood that the opportunity was too great to pass up. It was my dream too.

'Tell us everything, Clem,' Esther said, a wobble in her voice.

Clementine nodded, her eyes bright with excitement. 'I have a position at a new school and Mrs Fawcett has helped me find a small place of my own. It's everything I want,' she said, sitting forward, 'the chance to get more involved in the work of the National Union, right at the centre of it all. There are so many new voices all coming together and so many news ideas; change is inevitable. But Private Members' bills and petitioning Parliament isn't enough and I'm so excited about finding other ways to be heard.'

I felt the fire grow within me as I heard the passion in Clem's voice. How right she was, I thought. With every new woman was a new idea about how we could promote the vote for women. We were definitely on our way to achieving it.

Esther smiled wistfully. 'If I wasn't committed to running for council, I'd come with you.' If plans for a new coal mine just outside the village were approved, our community was on the precipice of great change, and we'd need someone like Esther more than ever.

'I know,' Clementine said, grasping Esther's hand. 'It's just that it's time for us to make our mark on the world in different ways. I have the opportunity to make a difference on the national stage, just as you have here with the parish council and running for the district council. And you, Hannah – bringing us all together in the first place with our own suffrage society and creating change in Ebberfield for the women and children here, building a safe, warm place in The Ox and Plough. So many of us are making change every day – you too, Laura, with the children at school.'

Clem's words struck a chord. I was doing the work I had dreamed of, albeit differently than I had ever envisioned. Mama had said it months ago, but maybe Papa had really foreseen more than I gave him credit for in handing over The Ox and Plough to me. For so long I'd believed the pub was an albatross around my neck, but I hadn't realised that in fact it was a lighthouse, a beacon of hope. I was my father's daughter, a female publican in a conservative rural village. I had my ear to the ground, I could provide a safe haven, a place of respite and community and a meeting place for suffragists. What I did mattered and I had found fulfilment where I had expected little. I wasn't holding the burning sword, but my role, my place here, was still important.

We were so lucky to have each other, I thought, as we all grinned, proud of our achievements. I remembered Mrs Fawcett's words about how a woman's best protection was the power to protect herself. We had begun that process in court and with our victory, something had shifted. Attitudes were changing. If a prominent man of position, power and influence could be convicted by a jury of his peers, predominantly on the testimonies of three women, then who knew what else was possible? One thing I had learnt was that we had to have the courage to step out of the shadows and into the light, to step up and be heard. If we could all do that, perhaps anything was possible.

I clambered to my feet awkwardly. I loved these women. 'We're joined in our passion and dreams of making a better world and we always will be.'

'The examples we set shine a light on what women can do,' said Laura.

I nodded. 'Change is coming, we can all feel it, and I pray that Annie and all our daughters grow up in a world where their voices matter and are counted, where they can choose the life they want for themselves. I want Annie to have it all, just as I do for Tommy and this little one too,' I said, rubbing my belly.

'Then we have to stay focused and build that world for her and for all little girls,' declared Clementine. 'It's our responsibility.'

I hugged my three friends tightly. Each of us, in our own way, were New Women, determined to be trailblazers for the next generations. But we could only do it together. Wherever we were, we'd always be friends with a singular purpose and passion. I knew there were many more like us with that same dedication and commitment, and because of that, I knew the future was bright – for us, for our children and for our grandchildren. I couldn't wait to see what the future held for us all.

EPILOGUE

THE OX AND PLOUGH
JUNE 1898

'A letter's come for you, Aunt Hannah.' Jenny stopped short inside the office. 'Oh! I'm sorry, I didn't realise you had the baby with you,' she whispered.

'It's all right,' I said quietly, laying my pencil down on the ledger, which held the weekly accounts. I gazed at William in his bassinet, a shock of dark hair standing up on his head, no matter what we did to smooth it down. 'Not much wakes him.' At three months old, he was already sleeping through the night.

Jenny nodded, handing me the letter. 'Annie and Tommy aren't exactly quiet.'

'No, they're not,' I said, smiling. 'But right now, it's blissfully quiet, and I'm taking the opportunity to get some work done.'

'I'll be in the kitchen if he wakes and you want me to take him,' she said.

'Thank you.' But my attention had already shifted to the letter in my hand. From the distinctive looping handwriting on the front, I could see it was from Clementine. I pulled out the sheets of paper, eager for her news from London.

I scanned the contents. She was already settled in her new placement, teaching at a high school for girls and had begun work with Mrs Fawcett.

Hannah, you would love it here. I've met fascinating women from all over Britain, at meetings of the National Union and the Fabian Society too. Hearing their stories and difficulties and their ideas about creating change has been so inspiring. With them and our supporters in the Parliament, our efforts to push Mr Begg's bill through the House of Commons feel more positive than they have ever been. I've been lucky to attend some sessions of Parliament with Mrs Fawcett and seen the energy and enthusiasm from our supporters first-hand. There is no doubt that our cause is gaining momentum! But as you know, the process is slow.

I nodded, deep in thought. It was impossible to predict how long until the balance was tipped in our favour, but I knew we'd be victorious. I returned to the letter.

In the meantime, we continue to build our support and membership with the launch of the local associates scheme, signing up people who have offered any form of sympathy for our cause – we'll contact them when there are meetings of interest with the hope many will become full and active members. But I believe this is only the beginning. Some of my new friends believe that the Parliament will only take our cause seriously with loud mass support across the country. If that's the case, I will do everything I can for as long as needed to rouse our nation.

London is so dynamic and alive and it's exciting to be at the coalface of change. I know this is where I'm meant to be, but I miss you and Esther and wish you were both here with me to herald in the next stage of our fight.

I shivered. Clementine's enthusiasm was infectious. I was excited for the new century ahead – it felt as if we were on the cusp of a new world. I could almost feel the world changing around us, with new ways of thinking fuelled by progress, reform and scientific and technological advances. But where I once thought that idealists like Clementine and me could single-handedly spearhead suffrage, I knew now that everyone had a role to play and I was proud to be involved with this collective, this sisterhood, and more determined than ever to support the suffrage movement with my work here in Ebberfield. Clementine could fight for our rights in the city, and I would do all I could here in the country, to bring about national change.

My gaze fell across my collection of found objects on the windowsill, the afternoon sun glinting off the rough edges of my most prized possession, the fossilised acorn. It had taken thousands of years of gradual change and pressure to create the preserved artifact it had now become: harder, stronger and here to stay. Any worthwhile change took time and I knew equality between men and women would become the cornerstones of our society and democracy one day.

Baby William stirred. I watched as his clear blue eyes opened, filled with the endless possibilities of life, as yet untouched by the world beyond. All my motivation for change was right here, as mother, protector and champion of my children. They were the future: it belonged to them, and it was up to me to ensure the world my children stepped into was better than the one I'd found – safer, fairer and full of love and hope.

I was playing my part, and to me, it was the most important part of all.

AUTHOR'S NOTE

A Woman of Courage is inspired by the Blanchard family that owned and ran a pub in Durham, England, on the cusp of the twentieth century. My father-in-law, Terry Blanchard, heard about the pub from his grandfather who lived there with his parents, Robert and Eleanor, before coming to Australia as a young man in 1914.

I was intrigued by Eleanor, about the kind of life she might have had as a publican's wife. Through census documents I discovered that she was a schoolteacher in 1891, living at the same pub with her parents. I wondered how she went from teaching to running the pub with her husband and had to learn more about her story.

Terry knew little about Eleanor, so my first stop was to talk to his cousin Melvyn, who lives in Durham. Eleanor was Melvyn's grandmother but she had died when he was young and he only had a few stories about her older years. Like many people of her generation, life had been hard, but between the lines, I got the sense of a strong, resilient woman. I wondered what obstacles she had faced and how she'd made her mark on her family and community. I decided I had to write about her life in the late 1800s. What would she have thought about the big movements of the day? Advances in science, health and sanitation, smallpox vaccinations, the reforms to education, including higher education for girls and of course, about the fledgling suffrage movement that gained momentum through the 1890s.

Because I knew virtually nothing about Eleanor's daily life – only the large moments recorded in births, deaths, marriages and census records – it gave me the freedom to imagine Eleanor's life and fashion my heroine, Hannah Todd. The Blanchard strength, determination and spirit lives within Hannah. Through my research I found that many of the early suffrage supporters were teachers (perhaps Eleanor was a suffragist as well) so it felt natural to weave Hannah's story with that of the suffrage movement: a perfect cause to direct all of Hannah's ambition and drive.

Like Hannah, Eleanor had three older sisters and was born and raised in the industrial port city of Hartlepool. She joined her parents after her studies, in the small agricultural village where her father had bought a pub. I could only imagine the culture shock for her, beginning her new life there.

At first, it seemed that Eleanor's father disappeared from the records beyond 1891. After much digging and some luck, I discovered him in the Durham County Asylum. He entered in 1892 and remained there until his death in 1902, almost ten years to the day. There was no information about his cause of death, or why he was there at all, and I couldn't uncover any related familial history. He had been an engine fitter in the shipyards and I began exploring work-related injuries and diseases and learnt that a disease called manganism had been discovered with the advent of steel. Manganese was necessary to make steel, and inhaling it during mining or being exposed to fumes during the welding of steel could cause Parkinson's disease–type symptoms. If manganese poisoning could not be arrested or the long-term build-up in the body was too great, the symptoms led to a slow mental and physical decline until eventually the respiratory muscles were affected and many of its sufferers died of pneumonia. Perhaps one day I may discover his patient records and find more information, but manganism was a likely possibility in his drastic career change and time at the asylum.

William's earlier demise in the story enabled me to saturate Hannah's arc: a dramatic transition from her being a young, idealistic schoolteacher with dreams of activism in London to virtually becoming the head of the household and a woman managing a pub in an agricultural, conservative village. The challenges would have been enormous for a woman at the time, owning and running a public house in a community ruled by the relics of patriarchy. And I loved exploring how those challenges changed from Hannah as a single woman to Hannah married with children. I have no doubt that Eleanor faced those same sorts of challenges in her lifetime, challenges women still face today.

Eleanor's nephew did die at the age of ten in 1896. Childhood deaths were more common at this time, many due to the scourge of infectious diseases that ran rampant not just through villages and cities in England, but across Europe, America, Asia and Africa. Fast global travel helped circulate disease, with the expanding railway networks and new steam-powered steel ships, transporting passengers and goods to and from the colonies and various trading partners. Cholera, smallpox, typhus, diphtheria, scarlet and typhoid fevers were still circulating in waves of epidemic proportions in the late 1800s and the first global pandemic of influenza occurred in 1889, called the Russian flu, where it had originated. Interestingly, some have drawn parallels between that pandemic and Covid-19.

I was fascinated to learn that with the advances in medicine, public health and sanitation, it was vaccination that really gave hope to families across Britain in preventing or mitigating the effects of smallpox, which had decimated communities during the previous century. But there was opposition to the successful national vaccination program and during the 1890s an anti-vaccination group was on the rise, and many, while not outrightly opposed to the program, had become complacent about vaccinating their children. It was interesting to learn that childhood deaths began to rise in unvaccinated children once again. This trend prompted the new vaccination programs that Dr Jenkins rolled out in the book, including the booster given to ten-year-olds, after the discovery that the smallpox vaccine lost efficacy after ten years. Compulsory vaccination for smallpox in Britain ended in 1948 but smallpox wasn't considered eradicated globally until 1978.

The late-Victorian era really was the germination of the modern age, standing on the precipice of the twentieth century and the new world. I really wanted that curiosity and excitement, the urge and desire for progress to be evident in *A Woman of Courage*. It was a time when ways of thinking changed dramatically: positivism debunked the airborne miasma theory of disease due to the scientific process that discovered bacteria and pathogens; the rise of the secular movement with the separation between religion and science emphasised by Darwin's theory of evolution; and egalitarianism with the rise of socialism, evident in the Fabian Society, trade unionism and the co-operative movement. But underlying all these changes was the way that women began to think about themselves.

The beginnings of the suffrage movement can be attributed to the petition that aimed to amend the *Great Reform Act* to include universal suffrage. It was sent to Parliament with 1499 signatures but the amendment giving women the vote was unsuccessful in 1867. From here the first suffrage societies were born and prominent suffragists began to lobby for changes to laws that affected women – including property, marriage and parenting, child welfare, public health and sanitation, education and, of course, the vote for women. A key reform came with the *Married Women's Property Act* of 1882, where the legal identity and rights that women had when they were single were reinstated to married women, making them separate from their husbands. With this act, the vote for women became a real possibility for the first time.

I was intrigued to know why women's enfranchisement took so long to be legislated in Britain when women had achieved the vote in New Zealand in 1893 and South Australia in 1894. It inspired me to explore the path of the fledgling suffrage movement in the lead-up to the twentieth century and the parliamentary process that was necessary to give women the vote.

The Chartist movement of the mid-nineteenth century understood that improving rights for men could only be secured through legislation and the vote for all men. But even with the added pressure of mass protests and strike action, the Chartists were unable to achieve the change they desired. The women in *A Woman of Courage* refer to this movement as inspiration for their own aims in suffrage.

I discovered that Millicent Fawcett was a leading figure in the women's suffrage movement that followed, a suffragist who was highly influential in furthering the cause for women's rights and emancipation. She had to be an integral part of my story, especially as I realised how unknown she still is today – overshadowed by the famous Pankhursts and the suffragettes who rose to prominence in the early-twentieth century. Millicent Fawcett believed in democracy and a reasoned, moderate course of action, using the same peaceful means that the Chartists had initially used to sway parliamentary opinion, such as lobbying MPs to present their petitions and to add women's enfranchisement amendments to their bills going before Parliament. A memorable Private Members' bill was the Begg Bill which failed in 1896 (as illustrated in the novel) and was subsequently withdrawn from parliament. The National Union of Women's Suffrage Societies was formed under Millicent Fawcett to bring all societies together and achieve their aims with a unified vision and voice after this parliamentary failure. These moments in history were stepping-stones to long-lasting change: a journey we are still on today.

There are so many things I learnt along my researching journey – what an incredibly fascinating period it is to write about. I would have loved to include so much more: about the wonderful bathing machines; the changing fashions and the face of retail shopping and department stores; how Victorians were entertained as their leisure time increased, the rise of Gothic novels; Victorian food and the new food products and preserving methods that revolutionised what and how people ate and lived. And I could have waxed lyrical about Victorian traditions around weddings, Christmas and festivals like St Valentine's Day. But of course, this book would have been twice as long! It really was a time of great change and flux. I write about the inspiration and background to my novels in my monthly newsletter, and about all my research too. If you'd like to learn more about the world of *A Woman of Courage*, please head to my website to sign up.

Many of the themes in *A Woman of Courage* are perennial, touching the lives of us in the twenty-first century as they did in the 1890s. With the arrival of Covid-19, fascinating parallels exist between public health issues such as vaccination and the management of contagious disease and the public fears and concerns surrounding such emotionally charged subjects. Today, the fight for women's rights is still very much front and centre. With issues like the gender pay gap, the #MeToo movement, the debate around women's rights to their bodies, particularly in the overturning of Roe v. Wade in the United States in 2022, the degree of agency around decisions involving pregnancy, childbirth and motherhood and the tragedies around homelessness, women are raising their voices: demanding action, demanding to be heard.

As Hannah said, real, lasting change can be slow, but we've also come a long way in over a century. We now take many of our modern privileges for granted – privileges that were fought for by Victorian women and hard won. We have much to thank them for. They really were women of extraordinary courage.

ACKNOWLEDGEMENTS

I first heard the story of the pub that the Blanchards owned and ran in Durham, England, from my father-in-law, Terry Blanchard. He is the keeper of his family stories and I feel honoured that he has shared them with me. My first thank you is to him, for the many hours of conversation over tea brewed in an old tin teapot, served hot, dark and strong – just how we both like it. He's a very special man.

My thanks also to Melvyn Blanchard, who still lives in Durham and was kind enough to provide me with further details about his grandparents who ran the pub at the turn of the twentieth century. Melvyn too is the keeper of his family stories and was very generous with his time, back and forth over email, answering my questions and providing background information.

A Woman of Courage wouldn't have come to life without the wonderful support of the team at HarperCollins Australia. My thanks to the fabulous sales and marketing team, who have helped me birth this precious baby out into the world. I can't thank the incredibly talented Louisa Maggio enough for the absolutely gorgeous cover – it's beyond what I had imagined and embodies our Hannah so perfectly. My deep gratitude goes to the editorial team, especially to Kylie Mason and Rachel Cramp for their invaluable insights, patience and expertise, which elevated this book and allowed it to shine. But most of all, thank you to my publisher, Roberta Ivers, who has guided me through the editing process and supported me in this new chapter of my writing journey. She has always been my champion, mentor and friend, and that means more to me than I can say.

To my fabulous, dedicated and loyal readers. Thank you, thank you, thank you. You make all this possible. It's because of you that my books are out there in the world. There's nothing better than knowing that I can share my stories with you and that I'm part of a community that loves storytelling, especially when I'm deep into writing or editing – a very solitary process. Your messages of support inspire me to keep writing the stories that are meaningful to me. And I love reading about your own family stories as well: it's an honour and a privilege to be privy to them.

My friends and family have been an enormous support while writing *A Woman of Courage*, especially my sister-in-law, Trish Casey. She's encouraged me when I've hit writer's block and sent me motivational cards and inspirational gifts. Her belief in me and what I can achieve has been so unwavering that it had to rub off eventually! Thanks Trish, you're my rock, my mentor and dearest friend.

My mother is my number one fan, there through it all, sharing my exciting milestones, spreading the word about my books and events and replying to all my social-media posts. It warms my heart that she takes an interest in all the stages of my writing journey, and even listens without yawning to my long explanations when I've disappeared down the historical research rabbit hole! Thanks, Mum, for your constant support and love. It means the world to me. I couldn't do this without you.

Finally, thank you to my husband, Chris. It's been so special to share this journey with him by my side as we've learnt about his family history. His insights, always perceptive, pragmatic and useful, have often steered me in new (but inevitably the right) directions. And of course, he's my go-to for help with technical aspects within the story, anything to do with building, farming – all things practical. We make a great team! I'll treasure the detective moments we've had together while I sift through research and look forward to the next family mystery we can solve.

As we all work and study from home so much more these days, I'm lucky that my husband and children have been there at the coalface, supporting me all the way. Their belief in me makes me feel like I can do anything. They give me physical and emotional support from tiptoeing past the office when I'm deep in concentration, cooking when I just can't muster the energy or I'm pushed to reach a deadline, commiserating when things aren't going well and celebrating the small and bigger victories with me. I've loved being able to tell them all about their family history and about the story I've woven around their ancestors. And better still, they've enjoyed hearing about it, amazed at the richness of their family stories. I'm so happy that my children will be able to one day pass these stories on to their children and grandchildren. My family makes it all worthwhile and ultimately I write books for them.

COMING NOVEMBER 2024

AN UNDENIABLE VOICE
The sequel to *A Woman of Courage*

Follow Hannah's passionate journey to help
achieve the vote for women – and as she fiercely
protects those she loves – as she and her friends enter
the twentieth century.

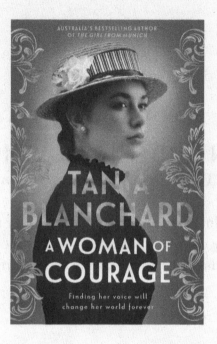